MADISON KELLER

FLOWER'S FANG

Hundeliebe Publishing

Seattle, WA

Flower's Fang
Madison Keller

Hundeliebe Press
Seattle, WA
www.hundeliebepublishing.com

Publisher's Note: This is a work of fiction. Names, characters, places, and incidents are a product of the author's imagination. Locales and public names are sometimes used for atmospheric purposes. Any resemblance to actual people, living or dead, or to businesses, companies, events, institutions, or locales is completely coincidental.

Book Layout © 2014 BookDesignTemplates.com

Cover by Johnny Atomic
Edited by Marlon McAllister and Shelly Jones

Flower's Fang/ Madison Keller
Third Edition

Dedicated to my dog Kerka

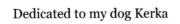

CONTENTS

CHAPTER ONE

A PRINCE ARRIVES

The meadow grass made a soft bed for Arara to watch fluffy white clouds roll across the blue of the sky. The breeze carried a cold biting smell of snow and pine, ruffling her long, white fur and swaying the grass around her. It made her glad she'd worn a vest and thick shorts. Even at the height of summer, snow packed the peaks of the North Wind Mountains nearby.

Arara rolled onto her stomach and plucked a long, thick strand of grass with one paw. She manipulated it between her thumbs, like her father taught her as a child. Then she blew through the loop, producing a shrill blast. Her tail wagged with joy. Another blast and a little, furry raop scrambled from the rocks nearby into the forest at the edge of the meadow. Her father would've chided her for scaring away more prey with her love of music.

The sun's warmth lulled her, and soon she dozed, half asleep.

A low howl sounded from nearby, signifying prey. Arara rolled over and jumped to all fours, preparing to run but it was too late, she could feel the pack's presence all around her.

If she'd been paying attention she would have heard them coming. Ever since she was young she'd been able hear other's thoughts in her head, even from a distance. But the pack had caught her napping and now she paid the price.

A moment later a howling, barking pack of the local bullies had her surrounded. Everywhere she turned, snapping teeth or sharp claws blocked escape.

The Jerlings surrounding her were all her age or younger, but even the youngest stood over two heads taller than her. They all wore the same utilitarian vest and shorts as Arara, and most carried their school panniers slung over their backs and strapped to their sides. Their short fur ranged from brown, gray, to a dark black with thick furry tails and pointed ears, in sharp contrast to Arara's long white fur and curly tail. Her size and coloring set her apart and made her the target of every bully in school. Even her ears refused to stand up straight at the tips like they should.

The pack circled around, keeping her trapped as they lunged at her from staggered directions. She spun around, off balance, and dodged away from the attackers. A black form broke away from the shifting mass of brown and black fur, stood, and held up a paw. The group stopped and sat back, still and silent.

“Well, well, look what we caught," Kerka said, short muzzle gaping open to reveal sharp white teeth.

“What are you doing out here?” Arara snarled, ears flat back against her head. Kerka was the ringleader of the local bullies and her chief tormentor. She should have known he'd organized this. She should have been safe here. He'd never targeted her outside of classes before, which was why she'd felt safe enough to doze.

Kerka chuckled as he strode closer, short black fur gleaming in the sunlight. His furry bulk blocked out the sun as he got closer, and Arara had to lock her legs to keep from bolting. Her tail tried to tuck itself between her legs before she regained control. Long experience with bullies had taught her that the more she showed fear, the worse the torments would be. Kerka glared down at her, and by the time he got close Arara had to crane back to see his face.

“We came out here to find you, for your farewell party. We wanted to have it before you greet the Prince. Consider it a graduation present.” He bared fangs and reached out for her arm.

But Arara'd heard him thinking about the movement and ducked away. No one else in the pack, besides her parents, knew about her special power, so Kerka grasped at air. He stumbled, off-balance for a moment.

"Party? No, thanks. I was actually on my way home. I still need to pack and buy my Poku ticket out of here." She tried to back further away but ran into the circle's edge. She hesitated, unsure of how to escape.

"What, and miss out on this chance to relive all the good times we've had together?" Kerka said, edging closer.

Another day, another beating, Arara reflected with a shudder. She'd been hoping against hope that today would be different. She cracked her mental shields, trying to hear him.

<I'll back her up against the others, make a grab for her.>

Massive fists shot out towards her as Kerka lunged for her, just as she'd known he would. She ducked and weaved forward, but he managed to snag the curl of her tail with one paw. He yanked back hard, jerking her to a stop and into the air. Pain shot up her tail as all her weight hung suspended from it.

"Let go!" Arara howled. She curled up and behind, grabbing her tail and using her arms to try to relieve the pressure.

Kerka laughed and cuffed Arara's head with his free paw, spinning her to the side. Her tail felt it would pull right off, but she wouldn't give Kerka the satisfaction of hearing her scream.

"That's cute. You'd better stop struggling or your tail might come off! Or, if you ask nicely we could have a go at straightening it again."

He lifted her higher, until he looked her in the eyes. "You'd be much prettier if your tail was straight."

Morbid curiosity prompted her to peek at his thoughts. In his head, Kerka imagined a taller Arara, with short fur and a normal Jegeran tail, making out with him. Arara gagged at the vivid picture and slammed mental shields shut, wishing she could scrub her mind out with soap.

"Put me down!" Her voice cracked with fear.

He swung her around a few more times, laughing, and then tossed her into the grass. “Fine. You’re no fun.”

As she scrambled to her feet, he made a public *gefir*-thought sending to the encircled Jerlings. <*Party time!*>

All the Jegera could do this simple trick. It was only Arara who could do more. Since her parents were worried about what their insular pack would think, they’d made Arara keep her abilities a secret. That suited Arara just fine, as it usually gave her an edge in her never-ending quest to escape the bullies. But today they had her surrounded and she was beginning to panic. She had to escape now, no matter the consequences.

“Have you heard that the Prince will be attending the graduation hunt tomorrow?” His tone was conversational, as if they were best friends.

As Kerka talked, the circled Jerlings stripped off their panniers, pulling out scissors and razors. With the pack distracted, Arara saw her chance to escape. She dropped to all fours and dashed towards the smallest Jerling, who struggled to remove a too-large pannier. Arara leapt straight at the girl.

The jump wouldn’t clear the Jerling, but at the leap’s apex Arara reached out and mentally shoved herself. While she'd been telepathic since birth, the ability to manipulate things with her mind had only started a year or so ago.

The extra push launched her completely over the distracted girl, who stared up at Arara in shock. Arara's back legs just brushed the tips of the girl’s pointed ears.

Even as she completed her flight, Arara could feel the headache starting to bloom. While most things were beyond her, pushing was relatively easy, although not without its consequences. The mental effort would leave her head aching for hours, but it freed her from the pack’s clutches.

Arara landed on the other side and bolted as fast as she could away from her tormentors. They howled and chased after her. The dubious safety of home lay behind the pack, but Arara knew a place nearby in the forest where she could lose them.

The pack howled fast on her heels, getting closer and closer with every step. At this pace they would catch up before she could reach the pine trees. She forced herself to run faster, but she couldn't keep up this pace for long. Her breath pounded in her ears.

The plains gave way to the mountain's foothills, and the searing scent of pine filled her nose. The incline slowed her down. Only hot breath on her tail warned her. She dodged to the side. Teeth snapped a paw's breadth from her back legs. The pack leapt over each other trying to get to her.

Arara tripped on a rock, breaking her stride. Kerka tackled her, caught her hind legs, and threw her face first into the dirt. Grit filled her mouth and she coughed.

Kerka sat on her back and pinned her down while the pack surged around them. Arara tried to catch her breath, but Kerka's weight made it difficult to breathe.

"We hadn't... planned...on a run ...during this party." He sounded winded, at least. "Now we've got to get you...*all* the way back to the supplies before the party can go on." Kerka grabbed two cavorting pups by the scruffs of their necks.

<Check and see if anyone still has their pannier.>

Kerka's thoughts echoed like a shout to Arara, despite the fact that he hadn't sent the gefir to her, pounding at her already aching head.

The two ran off, returning a few moments later with a brown female, the too-large pack still tangled around her. It was the same one Arara had leapt over to escape. Kerka remained on her back while the three pups removed the pack and dug through it for the rope.

Arara clawed and kicked at them as they approached, but her position on her stomach limited movement and reach. They bound her arms and legs together, then tied her to Kerka's back. She struggled against the bonds, fighting against the headache threatening to overwhelm her. Out of spite, she twisted her front paws around and dug them into Kerka's vest, trying to reach skin, but the thick leather defeated her.

She wished she could use her mental powers to loosen the rope. The gift was powerful, but she was unpracticed still, and subtle manipulations were beyond her.

The pack headed back to Arara's spot, where most of the supplies had been abandoned during the chase. When they arrived, several of the youngest pulled her down off Kerka's back and dropped her into the dirt. Arara used the opportunity to pull her hands towards her muzzle, and chewed on the bonds.

"As I was saying," Kerka's bulk towered overhead. "The Prince arrived today."

Arara growled around the rope. "I know. It's all anyone has been talking about for the last few moons." Arara closed her eyes, willed her head to stop pounding, and forced herself to keep gnawing.

Kerka grabbed the fur on the back of her head and jerked back. The pain forced her eyes open and she grimaced. With his other paw he grabbed her arms and forced them down.

"Since we're such good friends, we decided we'd all get together and give you a make-over before you meet him tonight." Kerka stroked a clump of her long fur with one claw. "After all, you want to look your best for royalty."

Arara whimpered in pain as her hauled her to her feet, claws digging into the back of her neck.

"Such long, shaggy fur." He tisked. "We can't do anything about your ears." He snorted and yanked on one of her floppy ears, making her clench and tense her whole body. "Or your twisted tail." He glanced down at her tail, which refused to uncurl itself and wagged his own straight tail. "But at least we can shorten that mess down to a respectable Jegeran length."

The pack members all held up scissors, yipping as they snipped them at the air.

Kerka looked up at the sun. "We don't have much time, so we'd better get started."

The pack barked and jumped up and down in excitement. As one, they lunged. Kerka stood back, tongue lolling out in a grin.

Arara snarled, and she clawed and swiped as best she could with her paws bound in front of her. A few of the pack grabbed her bound arms and legs as the rest attacked her fur with the scissors, cutting off her vest in the process. They left her shorts alone. Arara yelped when one enthusiastic pup grazed her skin. A few moments later it happened again and this time she screamed in pain as the pup laughed.

"Hey, now. Fur only, remember?" Kerka growled and stepped forward. "We're done. Cut her loose."

They snipped off the bonds and left her lying in the grass. They grabbed their bags, and Kerka led them back south towards the town, howling victory.

Most of her fur had been hacked off in uneven chunks, which were rapidly being blown away by the late afternoon breeze. A deep cut ran down the side of one of her arms, and Arara could feel several more lighter cuts stinging on her scalp and legs. The setting sun stabbed her eyes, and her head throbbed.

She curled up in a ball, sniffing and hugging herself, trying not to start whimpering and crying like a newborn pup. She would be an adult tomorrow and she needed to be strong. After all, it was just fur. It would grow back, and she'd be gone from this place by this time tomorrow.

When she'd cried herself out she picked up what remained of her favorite vest and left what had been her favorite place.

*****

A blast of cold air greeted Prince Sels as he stepped off the Poku pod train. He shivered and pulled his thin silk robes tighter as his vine-hair whipped around his face.

"I thought North Wind was cold. I swear it's even colder here." Sels shook his head, stamping to keep himself warm. "It's summer, for Brightness and Light!"

Jeron, his Jegera guard since birth, bared his teeth and let out a bark. "Don’t swear. And, yes, the name 'North Wind' is a bit of a misnomer, since Last Home is windier and farther north. Don't worry, the wind isn't as bad once you get into the village."

Sels hoped so. He couldn’t understand why the Jegera race insisted on living in such inhospitable places. Sure, they had fur to keep them warm but Sels still couldn’t wrap his head around why they’d want to. Although he was curious about this strange phenomenon called ‘snow’ that he’d read about so much.

Once inside the waiting carriage he escaped the worst of the wind, but the air still held a cold nip. Sels sank into the soft cushions with a sigh and covered himself with a thick blanket from underneath the seat. His cousin Sesay slid in across from him, followed by her *sedyu*-bonded, Recka, a huge midnight black Jegera.

The *sedyu*-bonding spell was one of the Royal Magic spells known only to a select few in the Royal family. In addition to forming an empathic mental bond between a chosen Jegera and the Kin Prince or Princess, the spell had the benefit of speeding up their reflexes, making them heal faster from injuries, and, most importantly from Sels perspective, increasing the Kin’s power and capacity for casting Sun Magics. It was Sels secret hope that a *sedyu*-bond would solve his little problem with spell-casting, where everything else had failed.

Sesay's pink petal-hair seemed to glow against the dark wood of the carriage. Her tapered, green Kin ears were barely visible through the thick mass of petals framing her heart shaped face. Sesay flashed a tight smile at him, her blue eyes sparkling under her leafy eyelashes, and primly folded her hands in her lap. Sels suppressed a wince, knowing that smile meant a lecture was coming. Even after a full moon-cycle of constant travel, Sesay’s clothes were immaculate. His own robes looked worse for wear, despite Jeron's diligent care.

Where Sesay had a mass of petals flowing down around her face and over her shoulders, Sels had an elegant growth of vines tipped with dark purple flowers. The wind had left Sels vines in a messy tangle, and

Sels made a mental note to have Jeron braid them tomorrow morning before the hunt.

Sesay rapped the roof three times, and the carriage rocked to a start as the vines underneath lifted it up.

Sels kept his eyes on the window, trying to get a glimpse of Last Home. The blue pine trees sped by, faster and faster, as the carriage picked up speed. The vine legs scurried at ground level.

“Good people of Last Home,” Sels said to the window, warming up for his speech. “It is an honor to..um... witness your ... Graduation, crap. Um, your children’s graduation as they become adults and full members of your Clan.”

"You realize this is your last chance to find a *sedyu*-bonded candidate, right?" Sesay's voice startled him, and he sat back to regard her.

"Yes, I know." He frowned and resumed staring out the window while rolling his eyes. Like he didn’t know how important this was. “It is an honor to-”

"Sels, Aunt Seuan isn't just going to laugh off you returning home with no candidates." Recka chuffed and nodded along with Sesay.

"I know." Sels squirmed under Sesay’s gaze, his hand sliding into his sleeve-pocket where he kept the precious candidate tokens. Their magic made his palm tingle even through the silk bag. The tokens were the spell’s catalyst and once given would mark his chosen Jegera. “It’s just-”

Sesay waved a hand, cutting him off. "It’s just that none of them have been 'perfect'. You've been saying the same thing the whole trip, but now you can't afford to be picky. Aunt Seuan sent me along to advise you, and so far you've ignored everything I’ve said. You've spent the whole trip whining and complaining." She sat forward and glared at him across the small space.

“So?” Sels squirmed under her gaze, too embarrassed to admit that he’d lied. He couldn’t feel the magic connection of a *sedyu*-bond to any of them. But then again he didn’t have to explain anything to Sesay.

Just because mother picked his cousin Sesay as the heir to the throne over him, she thought she knew everything.

"So, when we get to Last Home, this is how it is going to happen. Recka and I will pick out two candidates for you. You will present them *both* with tokens."

Sels sat forward. "But, you *know* I can't form a *sedyu*-bond with just anyone, and--"

"I don't *care* what you have to say at this point, Sels. If you choose to present another one of your tokens, that is your own prerogative." Sesay sat back and looked out the window, ending the conversation.

Sels knew he wouldn't be able to get any more from her, but still he tried.

"Sesay, if I don't feel their Potential, I won't be able to complete the bond when we get back home to Sebaine." He crossed his arms and gave her a hard look. As he expected, she didn't respond. "This isn't like a marriage contract that you can arrange to suit your whims."

Jeron shifted towards him, torn ear cocked back. "Perhaps after spending the trip getting to know them better you'll be able to bond with them?"

Across the carriage, Recka responded with a loud voice, deafening in the small space. "No, a *sedyu*-bond is mystical in nature. It is either there or it is not, it cannot be forged or forced."

"Then why force me to pick candidates that I won't be able to bond with?" Sels turned to Recka. As Sesay's *Sedyu*-bonded, he would have an insight into her thought process.

Recka smiled at him, causing Sels to shudder and draw back into the cushions. "Our job is merely to advise you during this trip. We can't be held responsible if you fail to complete your bond. But we cannot allow you to return home with no candidates."

Jeron huffed and glared at Recka. Jeron had been Sels's guard since he had sprouted, and, as a result, tended to be overly protective.

Sels held up a hand, glancing at Jeron. "Calm down. He's just trying to bait you."

An uneasy silence pervaded the remainder of the journey. The tension broke only when the carriage stopped and the door folded open. Sesay gathered up her robes and swept out first, ignoring royal protocol. Sels climbed down after her, still fuming. Despite his anger, diplomacy demanded he plaster on a fake smile, lest the locals think he disapproved of their quaint village that would probably be just as dreary as the other nineteen places they'd visited.

He stopped, stunned. The place was gorgeous. Bright pines towered around him, and suspended walkways hung between them high in the air. Taiga grass and a staggering variety of northern flowers grew from the domes of the mud-brick buildings. Brick lined paths threaded throughout the village.

Jeron elbowed Sels's side and gave him a prompting look. For the first time Sels saw the villagers thronging around the carriage, everyone still and silent, waiting for him to speak. Most were Jegera, but he saw scattered among them the distinctive bright colors of Kin petals.

A large black Jegera with an aged gray muzzle stepped forward, head tilted almost imperceptibly to the side and presented his neck. Sels narrowed his eyes at the arrogant gesture.

This must be Last Home Clan's Chieftain, Grawka. Sels needed to make a speech, but the words floated away, forgotten.

Jeron cleared his throat and poked Sels again.

Sels nodded and smiled at the Chieftain. "Good people of Last Home, it is an honor to be invited here to witness your children's sacred Graduation as they become adults and full members of your Clan. Your village is even more beautiful than it is rumored." He hadn't heard of this place until mother had added it to the schedule, but it sounded better if he told the white lie.

He plowed on, doing his best to remember the speech, which mother had written with similar nice-sounding claims and insincere praise. She made him memorize it before the trip. He could simply recite the same thing, replacing the village name each time.

The speech was supposed to end with the Royal Magic, said to bring good luck to the caster and those around him. The spell filled all who witnessed it with happiness and good cheer. Only the Royal Family could harness its power.

Sels looked over at Sesay, who stood off to the side, and gestured for her to step forward. Sesay narrowed her eyes and made a shooing motion back at him. What did that mean? He gritted his teeth together in frustration. Sesay knew he was going to fail, again. Why wouldn't she just do it for him?

Jeron leaned down to whisper in his ear. "Hurry up."

Resigned, Sels mumbled through the incantation. This time, he told himself, it would work. His hands shook as he tried to weave them into the complex patterns the spell required. He finished, arms flung wide. The air crackled around him for a moment, but nothing else happened.

"Allow me." Sesay led him aside and stepped into his place. The incantation sang out over the crowd, Sesay's voice clear and loud. Her delicate hands danced gracefully through the movements, making Sels look awkward in contrast. A brilliant double rainbow shimmered into life over the awed crowd before dissolving into a fine mist.

The crowd went wild, howling and cheering. Sesay smiled, basking in the attention.

Sels stalked around the carriage and kicked at the cobblestones. Jeron came up behind him.

"Not once have I been able to cast that spell correctly," Sels said, head hanging low. "Nineteen times I've completely botched it, in front of huge crowds of strangers."

Jeron pulled him around. "So you aren't any good at magic. You have other talents."

Sels growled and looked at the ground. "Yeah, very hidden talents."

Jeron put a paw under Sels head, tilting it up. "Not hidden, just ones you don't appreciate. Like storytelling. My kids keep begging to come and visit the palace again, to hear more of your tales."

"Great, I can be the first King to hold story-time in between rounds of petitions." He turned away with a humph.

"Maybe that was a bad example. But right now you need to smile and greet the people of Last Home." He grabbed Sels arm and led him back out to the crowd.

Sels sighed and steeled himself for another day being social with complete strangers.

CHAPTER TWO

PARTY TIME

Evening had fallen by the time Arara arrived home. She avoided the main den entrance. The rustling of the lush plant growth covering it would give away her arrival, and she didn't want her parents to see her in her current state. Instead she circled around the hillside, to where she had dug out a small escape tunnel years ago. She'd kept the tunnel hidden and in good repair.

Arara shoved her vest's remains in first, then wriggled in after them. The tunnel exited into her room, under her sleeping mat.

Arara quietly replaced the mat and tunnel cover, then dug through her room for her clippers. Perhaps she could clean up her butchered fur so no one would notice. She didn't have a mirror, but she didn't dare try to sneak through the den into the living room, where the mirror hung, since she could hear mother humming to herself in the kitchen.

Before long chunks of fur littered the floor, but her coat didn't look any better. She would have to shave herself bald to get it even. A whimper escaped her as she looked down at herself in despair. She couldn't meet the Prince like this.

Mother would be furious. Arara's unusual white fur had always reminded her mother of fallen snow. Her mother loved Arara's fur, despite the fact that it got Arara bullied for being different. The bullying had been going on for years. Arara hid it from her parents as it got worse.

Arara threw down the clippers in disgust and sunk to the floor. She curled up in a ball, paws over her head, unable to stop the cries of distress.

A moment later she heard padding footsteps and smelled her mother, Athura. The aroma of cooking hukra meat wafted in with her. "Arara, what's wrong?"

Soft fur brushed her arm as Athura crouched down beside her. "What in the Moon God's name happened to your poor fur?"

Arara whimpered and made herself smaller, too ashamed to reply.

Her mom snuggled up and pressed her muzzle up against Arara's. They lay there for several long moments until Arara could talk again.

"I..." Arara began, "I was trying to trim my fur before I met the Prince tonight, so I'd look more like a proper Jegera, but I messed up. Now I look awful!" She started howling.

"Shhhh...calm down." Athura sat up and gathered Arara in a hug, licking her face. "We still have a little time. I'll help you fix it. But, you know you look lovely with long fur, no matter what anyone else says."

Arara cleared her throat. "I know," she responded softly. She felt bad for lying to her mother.

"Now, let's try to get this looking a little better." Athura grabbed the clippers and got to work.

A claw-mark later her fur looked a bit more presentable but still marred by random bald patches. Blue silk ribbons that matched her formal silks covered the worst of the cuts. Her mother complimented the ribbons, saying they brought out the blue in Arara's eyes. When they finished, her mother turned her around in a circle.

"We have faith that we've raised you well, and trust that the Sun and Moon gods will watch over and protect you. Your father and I know that you'll make us proud tomorrow." Athura's ears and tail stood high. She smiled at Arara, love filling her eyes.

Arara's emotions overwhelmed her. "Thanks Mom," was all she could manage.

*****

The sun had fully set, and the moon already risen by the time Arara arrived at the ceremony grounds. Soft light filtered down from Kin-made lanterns strung in the trees. The drums pounded in time to her fading headache. Dancers swirled around a bonfire in the center.

Athura leaned over Arara's shoulder and rubbed her daughter's head. Arara looked up at her mother with fondness. For the party tonight her mother wore a pretty yellow and orange silk outfit that matched her golden brown fur.

A tug on her ear pulled her from further contemplation.

“Arara," Athura said. "Stop day-dreaming. I found your father, he’s over by the buffet line.”

Scents poured over her as they entered the crowd. The musky smell of the Jegera, the tangy bite of fresh blood coming from the hukra meat butchered for the feast, and underneath it all lingered the Kin’s flowery perfume. Arara trailed along behind her mother as they made their way through the crowd.

A large sandy brown Jegera wearing red leathers waved as they neared the buffet tables.

<There you are! What kept you?>

The wave of affection that followed the gefir made Arara smile. <*Hi dad!*> Arara threw her arms around Eraka's middle and squeezed.

Eraka held Arara at arm’s length and looked her over. <*Did you cut your fur in the dark?*>

"No, I just did it on a whim. Luckily Mom was there to help me when I messed up.” She had to yell to be heard over the crowd and the music. Answering in gefir would have been better. However, it was impossible to lie in mind-speak unless one truly believed.

He shook his head and pulled his ears down. "Lucky you. But you took too long! All the best bits are gone; all that's left is the scraps."

Athura looked down, her ears and tail drooping. <*I've been looking forward to this all week, too.*> Her jaw trembled.

Eraka chuckled, pulling out two seared chunks of meat from behind him. “Well, luckily I saved you some.”

As Athura reached out for hers, Eraka pulled her close, nuzzling her neck.

“It's getting late," he reached down to rub Arara's head between her ears. "You'd better go present yourself to the Prince. It's already dark, he won't stay out too much longer."

He gestured towards the stage. Through gaps in the crowd, Arara caught flashes of Jegera on the raised platform, but she couldn't make out any details in the dim light.

"Don't worry about your mom and me.” He winked at Arara and leaned over Athura, licking up the some of the juice that ran down her muzzle from the hukra meat. "We can handle ourselves."

Arara wrinkled her muzzle and pulled her ears back. Parental affection should be kept in the den.

She turned away from the mouth-watering scents of the feast and made her way towards the stage. She skirted the edges of the crowd to avoid being stepped on. Her tail drooped, and she just wanted to be done with the whole ordeal.

<... runt Arara dying before the end of the hunt?>

She'd had her defenses up, trying to tune out the crowd, but her name had drawn her attention. She stopped, and her ears pricked as she focused on the conversation.

<I doubt you'll find another taker for that bet, everyone else already had the same idea.> The Jegera sent with a chuckle.

Arara snarled and swiveled her head around, trying to locate the speakers.

The first Jegera bark-laughed. <Figures. How bout on the method of her death then?>

She bounded through the crowd, angry responses buzzing through her head, but she couldn't find the speakers. Arara gritted her teeth and continued on her way. Her paws wrung together. Her mom had assured her the hunt was safe, but Arara began to have doubts. However, she couldn't quit now, no matter the consequences. Defiance filled her steps as she ascended the stairs onto the platform.

Black and silver uniformed Alpha-Guards ringed the booth, blocking her view. Then someone shifted, and she got her first good look at the Prince.

She'd never seen a Vine Kin before. He had the long, pointed, leaf-like ears and light green skin she was familiar with in the flower Kin. But instead of petals, he had a multitude of twisting vines. Each ended in a small violet bud. Matching purple silk robes covered brown tunic and pants.

The Prince conversed with one of his guards. This guard's uniform was trimmed in gold and featured a stylized golden flower on the collar. Arara hung back, daunted. A grimace marred the Prince's delicate features as he gestured to the guard. Curious, she opened her mind so she could hear what they discussed.

A wave of sound nearly knocked her off her feet before she pulled her shields closed. Shaking, this time she cracked her shields, but only just, and was rewarded with only a few faint voices.

Arara turned towards the Prince and hesitated, uncomfortable with the thought of eavesdropping on royalty. She shifted her attention to the guard he spoke with. Perfect. Her eyes drifted shut as she moved into his head to catch the end of their conversation.

"No, Recka, I won't leave, not yet," Prince Sels said. "This is the last stop before we head home. I will retire for the night only after I have met *everyone* that will be participating tomorrow."

<*Why won't the Prince listen to reason!*> Recka thought. Then he glanced down at the memory-board in his hand. "Just one left, someone named Arara."

<Although why he insists on meeting her, I'm not sure. From what this Clan's Alpha told Sels she's not worth the time.>

Not worth the time?

Her fury at the day’s humiliations boiled over. She had lots to offer. No one else in the clan could do the things she could. How could he just dismiss her based on a rumor? She’d show him.

She sauntered over to them. The guard holding the memory board glanced in her direction and snorted before crouching down to her.

“Hey there little puppy, did you lose your mommy and daddy?" He might have been trying to smile, Arara wasn’t sure.

“I'm an ADULT as of tomorrow, you hukra-dung!” she snarled. With a growl, she shoved him, augmenting her strength with her mind just enough to knock him over onto his rump. Even that small effort caused her headache to flare up full force.

The Prince gawked at her from a few tails away, mouth hung open in surprise. Arara forced her ears up and composed her expression, then raised her head and presented her neck to him in polite gesture.

"My name is Arara," she said. "I'm sorry you have such a rude guard." Before he could respond she fell to all four legs and launched herself off the stage into the closest group of dancers.

There. The meeting didn't go as well her parents would have liked, but she got the distasteful, pointless task over with. Her head pounded in time to the drumming. Pushing things around with her mind tired her out, and with her exertions earlier she had reached her limit. Her limbs shook, and her vision blurred. But it'd been worth it just to see the expression on that arrogant guard's face.

Arara only hoped she hadn't upset the Prince too badly with her actions.

*****

Prince Sels burst out laughing. “I like her! She certainly has attitude to spare.”

The other guards barked in laughter and hurled good natured insults towards Recka as he picked himself up off the ground.

"What was that for?" Recka growled.

Sels jumped. Without realizing it he'd turned to scan the crowd for a glimpse of white fur and Recka's growl in his ear had startled him. "Recka, you scared her off before I even got a chance to talk to her."

"I don't know why she was so mad. I even smiled at that awful fur-cut of hers." Recka twitched the last button into place and smoothed his vest.

"I've seen you smile, Recka," Jeron barked from nearby, laughter crinkling his eyes up. "I'm surprised she didn't hit you harder."

"I've never met an adult Jegera shorter than me before." Sels said. "Is she really in the hunt tomorrow?" Sels caught himself turning towards the crowd again. But between the dim lighting and the crowd he'd never find her again tonight.

Recka flipped the memory board around to show Sels. The picture attached to the graduation application showed an undersized white Jegera with startlingly blue eyes. His eye brows rose in surprise at the long fur in the picture, and how soft it looked. He'd never seen fur so long before and wondered why she'd cut it all off.

"She'll never survive a hukra hunt, even with all that spunk." Recka spat, shaking his head.

"Let me see." Jeron pulled the board up and away. He studied it for a moment before handing it back. "Looks in order to me. She got excellent marks in communications and gefir. She'll do fine, as long as she's smart enough to play to her strengths."

"A little Jerling like that?" Recka said. "She'll trip over her tail and chip her fang before they even reach the hukra."

"Oh, yeah?" Jeron snarled up at Recka, puffing out his chest. "Wanna bet on that?"

They made quite a sight, Jeron growling up at the larger Recka. Sels stepped back. He didn't want to get caught in the middle.

Recka stared down at Jeron for a long moment, one ear cocked back. "If you want to give me your money that badly, sure."

Jeron grinned. "A hundred chips then. On whether or not the little pup finishes the hunt."

Recka laughed. "Done. Easy money."

They shook paws, big grins plastered both their faces. Sels let out a breath and relaxed. For a moment he'd almost been afraid of Jeron, which was crazy. Jeron had practically raised him up from a little seedling.

A howl drew his attention back to the party. Even more Jegera had packed into the space, and a few gestured up at the stage, arguing with the Alpha-Guard on the stairs. He stifled a yawn, hoping Jeron didn't notice.

"Who do you think will win tomorrow?" Sels said, jaw cracking as he stifled another yawn with a hand.

"My bet is on that big one, Kerka," Recka said. "Although I can hardly call him a Jerling, his muscles are almost as big as mine." He flexed his bulky arm in Sels's face and growled.

Sels pushed Recka's arm away. "Muscles aren't everything. Some of the best fighters in the Guard are female."

Recka snorted and stepped back. "They cheat."

"No," Jeron said. "They're smart enough that they don't have to, unlike you."

Sels rocked forward and smirked. Jeron always managed to get the last word in.

"What about you, Jer-." A huge yawn cracked Sels's face. He turned away and covered his mouth, trying to hide it.

"I saw that." Jeron's paw came down on his shoulder. "It's way past your bedtime, Prince Sels."

"But, the party's just getting started!" Sels waved towards the crowd, who obliged him by howling greetings.

"Not for you." Jeron's grip tightened and he guided Sels off the stage. The rest of the guards fell in around them.

The music roared behind them, louder than ever, and Sels jumped, tripping into Jeron.

"What happened? It's so loud." He shouted to be heard over the din. He pressed his hands over his ears to keep out some of the noise.

"They were keeping it down," Jeron yelled back, "Out of respect to you. Now that you're gone, anything goes."

"Can't believe Sesay is making me miss this in order to sprout-sit." Recka turned away with a sigh. "That looked to be the best party yet. Did you see some of those 'tails, Jeron?"

"Hey, Recka, there are kids here." Jeron glanced down at Sels.

Sels rolled his eyes. As if he didn't know what they were talking about.

They bantered back and forth as they walked. The darkness pressed in on them from the sides, making the lit path seem to float about on nothingness. Sels fell back, behind Jeron and Recka's arguing.

Bored by the long walk, Sels dug in his pocket. He pulled out a tiny figure of a raop, carved out of living wood. A magical toy, given to him by his mother when he'd bloomed for the first time.

A word whispered in its ear set off the magical enchantment bound to the wood, and the carving sprang to life on Sels's palm. Sels smiled as he watched the raop dance across his hand and up his arm. A moment later the magic died, and the figure fell lifeless, tumbling off its perch towards the ground. Sels bent over, managing to catch it just before it hit.

As he straightened, the Alpha-Guard walking next to him reached over, wrapping Sels entire hand in his massive paw. After a squeeze, he settled back into place, leaving Sels empty handed. The sleight of hand took only an instant.

Sels jerked back and spun, fist clenched and eyes narrowed at the offending guard. "Give that back!"

The guard smirked down at him. "I'm sorry, Your Highness. I saw a cive bug about to bite you and I just reacted."

"Thank the light you killed it before it did," Recka had turned to see the commotion. "Nasty things."

"It wasn't a bug!" Sels turned to Jeron. "He-"

Jeron put a hand over Sels mouth, leading him away from the guard. "Now Prince Sels, you're lucky Sesay wasn't here to see you acting like a sproutling. You need to apologize." Jeron dropped his palm.

"He is a thief-" Sels sputtered, outraged. He couldn't believe the audacity of this new guard, first stealing from him and then lying. And now to top it off Jeron obviously didn't believe him.

"Prince Sels," Jeron cut him off. "Royalty should always behave like royalty while in the public eye. Do not cause a scene. Now apologize."

Sels faced the offending guard. "Yes, thank the light you killed it in time." He repeated dully, at Jeron's prodding.

He sulked next to Jeron for the rest of the walk, refusing to speak to anyone. This trip was a disaster. Not a single candidate, his clothing stained and grubby from a month of travel, and now the guards were stealing. His guards had never treated him so badly in the city. He'd speak to Sesay tomorrow about their lack of discipline.

Thinking of that made him remember Sesay's threat. Would she really choose a candidate for him if he failed to make a decision? He wouldn't put it past Sesay to pick someone she knew he disliked, just to spite him.

And now, he finally felt the tug of a *sedyu*-bond, and it was to a mangy runt. He almost dismissed her completely, despite the connection, except for what she'd done.

She'd knocked over Recka almost casually, as if he'd been off balance. An Alpha-Guard would never be caught off guard, let alone a *sedyu*-bonded like Recka. Their magically heightened reflexes and senses made that impossible.

As soon as they reached the Guest House, Sels waved off Jeron and headed to his truck. He pretended to root through the tangled mess as he watched the guard who had stolen his toy. The thief glanced back at Sels and narrowed his eyes for a moment before turning away and disappearing through the curtain to the guard's quarters.

Sels stood, intending to follow, when Jeron growled behind him.

“Whoa there, what do you think you’re doing?” Jeron flipped the lid of the trunk closed. “You've already stayed up too late as it is, Prince! Now go to the rooting area!”

“But, I need to write in my diary." Sels put his hands together and raised them to Jeron, pleading. "It will only take a couple of scratch-marks, at most a claw-mark!” While mother had said he was to document his trip, he really wanted to follow that suspicious guard to see what he was up to. Maybe he should just come clean with Jeron. After all, Sels had known Jeron for his entire life.

“That guard, something is strange about him. Now that I think about it, I’ve never seen him before tonight.”

Recka drifted over, one ear cocked back. "Now this I've got to hear."

Jeron threw up his paws. “Sels, that guard has worked at the palace for the last decade. You look right through the servants. You only noticed him tonight because he jostled you a little bit, killing that cive fly. Maybe if you bothered to get to know them, you’d know he was helping you.”

“He still stole from me.” Sels crossed his arms. “I was playing with my raop figure and I dropped it. I managed to catch it, but that guard wrapped his paw around my hand and took my figure.”

“He probably thought it was a cive bug.” Recka shrugged.

“Bet he crushed it in his paw and threw it away without looking.” Jeron nodded.

Sels sighed. Jeron was right. He’d probably over-reacted. The guard had probably only seen something on Sels and thought it was a bug. But still, something about the whole thing smelled bad to Sels.

“Obviously something else is bothering you.” Jeron bent over to look Sels in the eye. “You’ve been acting funny ever since we left the party.”

"I felt a *sedyu*-bond connection to that white Jerling." Sels wrung his hands together, feeling self-conscious under their twin stares.

Jeron's pointed ears pricked up so high it almost surprised Sels they didn't fall off. "Really?"

Recka crossed his arms and snorted. "Very funny. Would have been funnier if you'd waited until Sesay was here."

Sels stiffened and clenched his fists.

"I believe you." Jeron smiled down at Sels.

"You do?" Recka's reaction hadn't been a surprise, but Jeron was usually his silent shadow, never offering his opinion. Why now?

Recka just snorted and left, ducking into the guard's quarters.

"You've let Sesay get to you too much, Sels." Jeron's firm paw on his back pushed him towards the rooting area. "You need to trust your instincts."

"So? She would get to anyone, sooner or later. I still think that-" He pushed back and twisted, trying to get free but Jeron held him fast. "I need to write in my diary. Mother said I should document everything that was going on when I felt a *sedyu*-bond Potential."

"You have some spare time in the morning, as long as you get up early."

Jeron dragged him into the back, where the other Kin slept, their feet rooted in the sleeping soil. They swayed in their sleep, dreaming. Sels changed into pajamas under Jeron's watchful eye.

The soft soil slid around Sels feet, warm and comfortably moist, as Jeron pushed him down. Sels complied with a grumble, digging his feet into the soil as Jeron watched. He closed his eyes and feigned sleep, struggling to stay awake with the soothing soil on his feet, until he heard padded footsteps receding down the hall. Sels peeked out of the bottom of his eye lids. Clear. Sels pulled himself out of the dirt and crept down the hall towards the guard's quarters. Something odd was going on, and Sels was determined to find out what.

Only a few moonbeams came into the room through the open windows, making it difficult for him to see. He reached for a candle when a strong paw wrapped around his wrist.

Moonlight glinted off sharp teeth as Jeron smiled down at him. "Sels, I said no." Caught again. How did Jeron always know?

"Jeron, wait." Sels said as Jeron dragged him across the room.

"You can write in your diary in the morning. Now sleep."

Jeron shoved Sels's feet into the soil and pushed him down, holding him until Sels shut his eyes. He'd just have to wait longer this time. A bit later, the room was silent. Sels peeked open one eye to see Jeron sitting in a chair, watching him. His eyes drifted shut again. He struggled to stay awake, to outlast Jeron, but he was tired, and the soil called to him.

CHAPTER THREE

OPENING CEREMONIES

Arara woke up in a bad mood. Her limbs felt heavy and her head leaden, as if she hadn't slept at all. The remaining fuzz on her arm did little to stop the cold morning air and she shivered: a reminder of yesterday's humiliations.

She couldn't get away from Last Home quickly enough.

Her half-empty pannier lay discarded on the floor, next to a pile of clothing. The clothing was old and falling apart, fit only for rags, but it was all she had, so she carefully folded and packed it into the bag. Her special box went next, carefully wrapped in a blanket to keep it safe.

With a sigh she fingered her almost-empty money pouch. Why had her parents wasted money on *that* when they knew she needed money for her travels? She barely had enough coin for the Poku ticket to North Wind, but she desperately needed new clothing. The box was useless; she didn't need a portrait of her parents weighing her down. Plus she'd need to take special precautions to make sure it didn't get broken during transport.

The travel pack was stuffed to overflowing, and she still needed to pack her music flower. She tore apart her room looking for her spare hunting panniers, but was unable to find them. Frustrated, she pulled out half the clothing, tossing the lot back onto the floor. Her mother could use them for rags.

In their place she carefully nestled her precious music flower. The flower held recordings of all the songs she had written, and was vital to her success in North Wind. Before she tied the pack closed, she reached in and touched the flower. A sweet melody filled the room. Any band in North Wind would love this song.

Arara dragged her overstuffed bag towards the door, then looked back at the clothing piled on the floor. Perhaps her parents would be willing to loan her some money. Then she could replace them at her leisure once she got to North Wind. After all, who'd want to buy a song, no matter how pretty, from a badly shaved pup wearing rags?

She found her parents in the larder. Her mother hummed to herself as she cut a chunk off an aged hukra haunch they'd been saving for a special occasion. Her father set out platters on the low table in the dining room. Arara licked her chops at the sight, her favorite.

Athura looked up when Arara walked in. "Good morning honey. We heard your music and were just about to get you for breakfast." Her mother's ears and tail drooped. "Are you still planning on leaving tonight after the Ceremony ends?"

Arara nodded.

Athura gave her a bittersweet smile and finished setting out the meat, dishing big globs of gravy over each piece. She set the gravy boat down, then pulled Arara into a tight hug.

Arara hugged her back, fiercely. "If you could bring my pack with you when you come back for the awards ceremony, I'll head out to the Poku station straight after."

Arara let go and plopped down into her spot at the table, next to her father. He gave her a quick hug and licked her face affectionately before settling back in his spot. She grinned as her mother sat down but her face fell as it hit home. This would be her last meal at home for a long while.

Conversation stopped as they all dug into the delicious food. Her mother's savory giblet gravy tasted amazing, and the home-made taproot beer was bitter with just the right amount of sweet. Arara finished too soon and licked the plate clean, trying to get every perfect drop. When they had finished her father gathered up the dirty dishes and placed them outside the door to wash later in the brook.

"Mom, about my trip." Arara fiddled with the straps of her vest. "Can you loan me some money for a new outfit? I won't make much of an impression dressed like this." She stood and held up her arms, showing the cracked and stained leather.

"Arara," Athura said, "why don't you reconsider leaving?"

"This is my dream, mom, how could you say that?" Arara sunk back down into her seat, her paws curled into fists.

"Snow flower, look at your fur." Her mother reached across the table and grabbed Arara's paw. "At least wait until it grows back."

"I can get you a job with me at the tannery." Her father grinned. "You can wait, save up a bit more for your trip, and head out fully prepared next summer."

"I can't stay here." Arara wanted to curl up into a ball. Her parents had always supported her decisions before and she thought they'd understood why she needed to leave.

"Of course you can," Athura scooted around the table and wrapped her arms around Arara.

"No!" Arara shoved her mom away and jumped up. Someday soon, she knew, Kerka and his bullies would go too far. The thought of staying here in the village with him nearby made her stomach twist into knots, and her breakfast threatened to come up.

"Arara," Her father pulled his ears back and gave Arara a hard look. "Be reasonable. You aren't ready."

"I am ready and I am leaving." Arara slammed her paws down onto the table and her claws popped out, leaving long gouges in the wood.

Eraka clenched his fists and jumped to his feet. "Young lady!"

"Snow flower, calm down. This is why we're worried." Her mother looked stung and disappointed. "You can't control your temper. Not to mention what you did to your fur, just to try to fit in. I know you have dreams, but the big city won't be any better than here. At least in Last Home you have friends and people who love you."

"I thought you understood." Arara snarled, scrambling to her feet. The vines at the entrance caught on her claws as she swiped them aside. Cheerful birdsong and warm morning sunshine greeted her outside. Broken vines fell to her feet as she ran down the path, away from her childhood home as fast as she could.

*****

Sels dug frantically through his trunk looking for his diary. Around him, his Kin entourage belted on their robes and elaborate jewelry, each wearing their house colors. He could hear the Jegera bodyguards in the next room, Recka barking orders, as usual.

The house emptied around him, and he still hadn't located it. Finally, he tilted the trunk onto its side, dumping the entire contents out onto the floor. The diary slid out last, tangled in his traveling silks. Perhaps Sesay had a point about packing things carefully rather than just throwing everything in.

Sels picked up the book and noticed Jeron, watching him and tapping his back leg impatiently. Jeron turned and looked at the sundial in the center of the room, then back to Sels. So he was running a little late. Sels turned around and settled into a seat with his back to Jeron and flipped the book open.

Sels carefully jotted down everything that had been happening around him when he felt the tug of the *sedyu*-bond.

Jeron was right, he needed to trust himself more. That petite white Jerling from the night before was almost certainly his first true candidate. And she was a terrible choice. He sighed and wondered who Sesay and Recka would choose for him if he didn't make a decision.

Maybe he would get lucky and feel the bond with one of them, or one of the other Jerlings on the hunt. He tried to remember who else he had met yesterday, but the only other he could remember was a giant black monster named Kerka. The bully blatantly tried to intimidate Sels, to the point where Jeron'd had to intervene. Patchy snow-white fur and a curly tail overshadowed the rest of the night, almost as though the evening before he met her was a dream.

A sleeve brushed over his arm. Sels looked up to see Lilsa bent over him, smiling.

"Coming, Prince Sels?" Her pale blue petals cascaded over her shoulders and brushed his face, while her canary robes gaped open slightly at his eye level.

Lilsa was Sesay's friend, so he'd always avoided her on principle. Maybe that was why he'd never noticed how beautiful she was before now. He could feel his face heating up, and knew his cheeks flushed bright emerald. His could only stare at her, his mouth gaping open.

Behind Lilsa someone giggled.

Lilsa stood up, her smile faded. "I'd hoped you would walk with us."

"Oh," Sels stammered, "I'd love to but I'm not ready yet."

Lilsa stepped back, her mouth quirked up on one side as she slowly looked him over. "I can see that."

Sels flushed again when he looked down and realized he still wore his favorite pair of old pajamas, ragged from constant use. He pulled himself to his feet, dropping the book into the chair with a thump.

"Let me at least walk you to the door." He offered Lilsa his arm.

She took it with an eyelash flutter. "How sweet," she cooed into his ear as he led her away.

"May I have a dance?" Sels turned his head to see her reaction and promptly walked into Lilsa's friend ahead of them.

Lilsa pulled him back with a giggle. "Now?"

Sels cursed his brain. Nothing was coming out the way he meant. "I mean, tonight, at the dance."

"Not yet."

Lilsa turned and leaned her head down to Sels. Was she going to kiss him? Sels panicked, glad to see they'd reached the door.

He stopped. "Well, here we are."

"Yes." Her breath tickled his ear and he let go of her arm, stepping back.

His face felt flushed, and he knew he was blushing again. "Well, have a nice walk."

"Aren't you going to ask me?" She clasped his hand and pulled him back to her.

He stared into her smile, startled to realize they were the same height. She was so pretty, his heart skipped a beat and he lost track of what they'd been talking about. "Ask you what?"

"To dance."

Sels blinked in confusion.

"Tonight." She squeezed his hands. "Honestly, Prince Sels. May I have a dance with you tonight?"

His brain stuttered and it took him a moment to realize she waited for his response. "Yes."

"So eloquent. That's what I love about you." She stepped away and blew him a kiss. His eyes followed her back as she turned and swept aside the vines, the bright light stabbed his eyes.

"Bye."

He continued to stare after her, watching her walk away through the vines as they stirred in the breeze until a hand waved in front of his face. He slapped it away and turned, intending to yell at whoever dared, only to find Sesay giving him a stony look.

Sels stepped back. Perhaps he could feign conversation with someone until she went away. He looked around the room, surprised to see it empty.

"Sels," she huffed, drawing back his attention. "It's past time to leave and I find you flirting with my best friend, and still in your pajamas."

"What's the hurry?" His stomach rumbled and he swept around Sesay towards the breakfast buffet. "They can't start without me."

Slowly, he picked up a plate and loaded it with roast vegetables in root gravy, spiced nuts, and other delicacies. He licked his lips and turned, looking for a seat. Sesay came up behind him, and when he turned, grabbed the other side of the plate.

"Just because you have power doesn't give you the right to abuse it."

"I'm not abusing it, I can't get ready to leave until I've eaten." He pulled back.

Sesay fought him for a moment, then let go. The plate flipped back towards him, dumping food all down the front of his pajamas. Sauce and vegetables dripped from him onto the carpet grasses as he lifted his arms in disbelief.

"You don't have time to eat. Go get dressed. Now."

Sels felt like crying. "How could you? These were my favorites and now they're ruined."

Sesay folded her arms. "Recka and I have talked. We think the reason you can't find any candidates is because you're not mature enough to handle the responsibility of a *sedyu*-bond. It's not too late to call it off. You can try again next year." She looked at him with pity. "I'll even tell the Queen for you."

He'd always disliked Sesay and knew the feeling was mutual, but he never thought she'd betray him like this. His arms came down to his sides and he curled his hands into fists. He glared back at her. "I won't give up. In fact, I did find a candidate yesterday. I plan to give her a token today, after the hunt."

"Really?" Sesay smiled. "Why didn't you say anything to me yesterday?"

"I didn't meet her until after you left for the night."

Sesay burst out laughing, which wasn't quite the reaction he'd been expecting.

"Recka," she wheezed in between peals of laughter, "told me about your little joke, but you still caught me off guard."

Sels stiffened. "What's so funny?"

Sesay wiped tears from her eyes, still giggling. "I can picture it now. You presenting that tiny, mangy freak of a Jegera to the Queen. The look on her face would be priceless." Another round of laughter had her doubled over.

He'd forgotten the *sedyu*-bond let Sesay and Recka share memories with each other. Sesay continued to laugh.

Tears streamed down his cheeks. Unwilling to let Sesay see him cry, he turned and fled from the front room. He peeled the wet silk top off and used the back to wipe his face before wadding it up and tossing it in the corner.

Jeron would know what to do. Growing up, Jeron had always been there.

He found Jeron in the back by his trunk, laying out his ceremonial dress silks over a chair. He turned as Sels entered, grinning until he saw Sels face. His mouth snapped closed and he growled.

"What's wrong?"

"Sesay" was all he could get out before bursting into fresh tears.

Jeron wrapped him in a hug. His fur scratched Sels face and arms, but Sels didn't care. A moment later Jeron released him and dabbed at Sels face with a cloth.

"Is that girl from last night really such a bad candidate?" Sels looked up into Jeron's face as he towered over him.

"Let me guess. Recka told her about what you said last night." Jeron sighed.

Jeron's breath as it wafted over Sels smelled like blood, and Sels covered his nose and nodded.

"So, I'll repeat what I told you last night. She's a fine choice because she's your choice." He held Sels out at arm's length. "In fact, I liked her more than anyone else we met on this trip so far. She didn't try to flatter, intimidate, manipulate, or curry favors from you. In fact, she was nice and polite."

Sels grinned. "You only say that because she doesn't like Recka."

Jeron just laughed and held up Sels's dress silks.

*****

Arara arrived at the Ceremony Grounds. Colorful banners swung from the trees on a light breeze. A large group of Jegera had gathered around the long tables, already preparing for the feast later tonight. Brightly dressed Kin socialized in a patch of sun. Jegera bustled around them, hanging decorations and cleaning up the remnants of the party.

Her age mates had already gathered on the stage. Kerka, flanked by his litter-mate Koe, held court in the middle with several Jegera in the black and silver Alpha-Guard uniforms. A quick look around confirmed the guard with the gold trimmed uniform she'd humiliated last night wasn't anywhere in sight. She breathed a sigh of relief. One less thing she'd have to deal with this morning.

Something moved in Koe's shadow. Arara jumped before she recognized Indy's mottled, dark gray coloring, then she pulled her ears back. All three had been there yesterday. And today she'd have to play nice with them so she could graduate. The good luck charm was a reassuring weight on her arm as she climbed the steps up to the stage.

She stepped up onto the stage, and ran right into Grawka. Grawka, the clan chief, Kerka and Koe's father, and the one person she'd been hoping to avoid this morning.

“I had fifty chips riding on you not even showing up." Grawka said. "Didn't think you had the guts. Literally.” He howled with laughter at his own joke.

Arara cocked one ear back and shrugged. She'd heard much worse.

“Like the trim. Very refined, *little flower*.” Then he winked at her and laughed again.

Arara didn't respond, just started at him icily as he loomed over her. She walked around him, trying to keep her face and ears neutral, although she could feel her tail drooping, threatening to tuck itself between her legs.

Normally she had to concentrate to pick up thoughts, but sometimes they came to her whether she wanted to hear them or not. Especially when someone thought very intensely about something.

<So, Kerka took my suggestion about the fur-trim. Wish I could have come along to watch.>

Arara seethed inside. Not only did he know what Kerka and the others had done to her, but even worse, it was the clan-chiefs idea. A nasty headache was the only thing keeping her from force-shoving him from behind as he walked away.

“We about ready to get started?” Grawka's voice floated up from behind her.

“As soon as the Prince arrives.” An Alpha-Guard's voice responded.

Arara ducked around the guards, putting them between her and Kerka. Hopefully he hadn't seen her yet.

"Everyone," Grawka roared from somewhere near the front of the stage, "line up!"

Arara jumped in surprise. A paw hit her back, and she fell to her knees as Koe shoved past her. Jerlings streamed by her, and gefir flew about as they tried to get in a semblance of order. Grawka stood with his hands clasped behind his back, nodding at the chaos. Arara was thrown aside several more times before she limped to the very last place in line.

With everyone in place, Grawka dropped to all fours and stalked back and forth along the line of Jerlings. “While we wait, let's review the rules of today's hunt. First, in order to finish you need to kill a hukra as a team and then bring at least part of the meat back to the ceremony grounds.

"Second, since this hunt is monitored from afar, all gefir should be public. If you get into trouble we will come to the rescue, but sometimes we can't get there in time. Jerlings have died on the hunt, and will again.” He sat back on his haunches, his expression grim.

After a moment he stood up and grinned at them. “Now the fun part. The points system. Points are awarded for merits – speed, agility, tracking, teamwork, tactics, leadership, and strength. Each judge has a certain number of points to award, and no more. The points are awarded at the end of the hunt before the feast.

"Although you are trying to earn points as an individual, a hunt is a teamwork exercise at its core. It is possible for the entire team to earn points for working well as a group."

While the group nodded along with Grawka's words, Arara sighed and looked up at the clouds, bored. The points system really was only used for gambling since every Jerling that finished the hunt graduated.

Grawka's grin got wider. "In addition, this year the Prince will be handing out tokens to his favorites."

Kerka puffed out his chest. "I think we all know who's going to get one of those."

Grawka snarled and leapt at Kerka, pinning him to the ground. Kerka growled but didn't try to fight back. Arara rolled her eyes sunward at this, not surprised Kerka would say something so stupid in front of his own father, the Clan Alpha.

Grawka stood on Kerka's chest and continued. "A token from the Prince means you'll get to travel with him to Sebaine. Once there, you'll compete in the Trials for a chance to become the Prince's *sedyu*-bonded."

Grawka stood back up on two legs, freeing Kerka, who stood back up and tried to look meek.

"Now, the Prince isn't here yet, so take advantage of this time to sort out your group roles for the coming hunt, since a few of the Jerlings here are strangers to you. Good Luck."

Grawka stalked away, leaving the Jerlings staring at each other. Chaos broke out as the group scrambled together, teeth and claws flashing. Arara jumped back, hands in the air and head up, glad she'd lined up at the back. Gror crawled out of the mess first, blood dripping from his nose, to huddle next to Arara.

A chunk of bloody black fur flew by and she looked up to see Kerka, Koe, and Indy had teamed up together. They made quick work of Yegra and the three strangers with well-coordinated moves. When Yegra at last rolled over, indicating defeat, Koe and Indy joined her in acknowledging Kerka as the leader.

Kerka puffed up, towering over the small pack now huddled below him on the planks. "I'm Kerka and I'll be leading this hunt." His gaze swept over the group and each Jerling presented their necks to him. Arara did the same, averting her eyes. Today, as much as it galled her, she needed to get along with Kerka.

Kerka rubbed his paws together. "Good. Now, let's go around and introduce ourselves."

One of the newcomers, a smallish gray Jerling with a black muzzle spoke first. “My name's Roan. I'm the best tracker in our little village. I can track a snow raop through the middle of a blizzard.” He gestured to his side at two more gray and black pups Arara didn't recognize. “These two lovely ladies are my litter-mates.”

Kerka grinned. “Nice to meet you Roan. I'm glad you're here.” Kerka cocked his head down at the girls Roan stood between. “You two, Roan's sisters. Names and skills.”

As all attention focused on the girls their eyes went wide and the both tried to hide behind Roan. Roan turned and said something to them. The girls growled and turned away from the group.

Kerka clapped his paws together. “Skip them for now.” He slapped Koe's shoulder. "This is my brother, Koe.”

Koe winced in pain from the blow then straightened and spoke in a deep growl. “Yes. I'm Koe. I'm strong.” He finished by thumping his chest.

Kerka spoke up. “He's a good hunter, as long as he is given orders. Gror, you're next.” He looked straight across the circle to where Gror stood next to Arara.

Gror flinched and slunk forward with his tail pulled between his legs. He spoke so soft that Arara, standing right next to him, had to strain to hear. "My name is Gror. I'm really good at sneaking up on things, being quiet, and staying unseen." He slunk back to his spot.

He looked terrified, so Arara gefired to him, trying to cheer him up.

<Gror, my parents gave me a luck charm. I'll wish for luck for us both.>

Gror looked down at Arara and his expression remained pained, so Arara reached up and squeezed his hand. <*We'll look out for each other today.*> She quickly let go so Kerka wouldn't see her.

Indy stepped forwarded from his spot next to Kerka, his tail wagging. "I'll go next. Everyone here already knows me, but I'll introduce myself to the lovely ladies who are gracing our presence today." He turned and dipped his head toward the two sisters, who growled back at him. "My name is Indy. I'm not too good at hunting, but I love telling stories and entertaining pretty tails." He winked and his tongue flopped out in a huge grin.

At this Kerka broke in, pushing Indy back. "Enough. Just ignore him girls. Yegra, you go next."

Yegra's amber eyes glittered coldly as she surveyed the newcomers. "Yegra," she barked, and stepped back.

Kerka let out a woofing sigh and shook his head. "Thanks for the eloquent introduction. Yegra made the killing strike during our successful training hunt a few weeks ago. And last, and certainly least, we have our useless runt, Arara."

With a sigh, she stepped forward and did a public gefir to the group. Some of the recruiters were still close enough to hear it, but Arara didn't worry about that.

<Hi, I'm Arara, I'm good at gefir. Kerka won't admit it, but I have the farthest range of anyone in the entire village.> She included a detailed image of their successful practice Hunt showing her role in the pack. <I can mind-link the pack as we're hunting.> That should get their attention, since mind-linking was a rare skill that allowed the pack to act as a single unit for a short time.

The three strangers all stared at her.

"Is this a joke?" Roan growled. "It's not funny. You are NOT old enough to be participating this year. I thought you were just Gror's hanger-on younger sibling! And what happened to your fur?"

The two girls just looked at her, their eyes wide.

"I'm the same age as all of you," Arara said, flattening her ears back. "I know my limitations, and I won't get in the way."

"Yeah, right." Roan stalked forward, dropping to all fours to growl in her face. "Do you realize how much you'll slow down the rest of us, trying to wait for you and your short legs?"

He had a point. Arara thought fast. "One of you can carry me until we get close!"

"No," Roan said. "If you can't keep up you'll be left behind." He snorted into Arara's face, stood back up and stalked back over to his sisters. "How did you not get culled when you were born anyway?"

Arara ignored him. "I can help, you know."

A roar of laughter drowned her out and Arara cut herself off.

"Moving on...girls." Kerka said with a chuckle. "That's everyone but you."

The girls looked at each other. The one with the gray muzzle stepped forward.

"My name is Janrey, this is my litter-sister Jenra." She gestured to her sister, identical to her except for Jenra's black muzzle. "I guess our talent is that we're fast and nimble."

Kerka nodded, and reached into his vest pocket. "Catch."

He flipped two coins out of his pocket and threw them in quick succession at the girl's heads. Their paws blurred, and each of them caught the coin a claws length from their muzzles.

"Great." Kerka grinned. "Keep them."

He turned to address the group. "Here's the plan. Roan and Indy will be our advance scouts, Roan tracking and Indy gefiring directions to the rest of us. Jenra, Janrey and Gror will separate our target from the rest of the herd. Yegra will lead the ambush team of Indy and

Roan, while Koe and I will coordinate a pincer move to keep the target from escaping. Everyone got it?”

Kerka's gaze swept around the group and over Arara's head.

"What's my-" Arara tried to ask, but horns blared out, drowning her next words.

Arara turned with the group toward the path leading up from the village. A group of Alpha-Guards came into sight first. The silver piping of their decorations gleamed in the morning sunlight, contrasting with the black of the Alpha-Guard uniform.

The Prince stood in the middle of the group, boxed in by a pink Petal Kin and the gold uniformed guard from the night before. Sels wore ornate blue and purple silks, as brightly colored as flower petals.

Everyone tilted their heads to the side and back in gestures of respect while he made his way towards the stage.

CHAPTER FOUR

SURPRISE

Sels watched the pack run to the north while the gathered crowd howled and cheered. By the time the candidates disappeared from view, the white Jerling was already at the rear.

The judges congregated at the base of the platform. Sels joined them, along with Jeron and Recka. They would be his bodyguards while they conducted their own observation for the Alpha-Clan recruitment. Sels would be the only Kin with the group, since Sesay elected to stay behind.

Recka dropped to all fours and Sels climbed up onto his back. The pack would be moving fast, and Sels couldn't keep up on his own. Sels settled down, gripping Recka's vest back tightly so he wouldn't fall. He would have preferred to ride Jeron, but Recka's *sedyu*-bond enhanced strength made him better suited. Sels signaled to Jeron and the group took off after the pack.

"That white pup... you were watching, she ...broke off alone." Jeron huffed out, tasked with keeping Sels apprised of the conversation since Kin couldn't hear gefir. "She asked permission....North-East, said ...smelled something."

"That's odd!" Sels yelled over the pounding paws and the rushing wind. Even he knew pack members should travel in pairs. "Why didn't they send anyone with her?"

"Don't...know."

They reached the pine forest's edge, and the roar of the wind died down, softened by the trees. The canopy overhead blocked out most of the sun's light and cast the ground into deep shadows. Despite the darkness, Sels was glad for the respite. His throat was getting sore from yelling.

"Why aren't any of the judges going with her?" Sels frowned and tightened his grip on Recka's jacket.

Under him Recka shrugged.

"Like I... said." Jeron barked.

"We're following Arara." Sels was lost in the woods, so he pointed in a random direction, hoping it was the correct way.

Recka stopped so suddenly Sels almost fell. The judges slowed and turned around. Grawka said something Sels couldn't hear, and the group wheeled around and ran off.

Grawka stalked over. "You want to do what?" He growled and stood up so he towered over Sels. "Arara's just trying to hide the fact that she was left behind."

Sels sat up straight and composed his expression in an attempt to look commanding. "It is my choice who I observe during this hunt." Sels kept his back straight and looked down his nose at Grawka from his perch. He was done with being pushed around. "It is not your place to give me orders."

Recka growled underneath him. "Jeron and I need to observe the rest of the Jerlings for Alpha-Guard recruitment."

"Fine, I'll go on my own." Sels slid off Recka's back and looked around, trying to orient himself. He gave up and walked away in a random direction, knowing the guards wouldn't let him get too far away.

"Where do you think you're going?" Recka snarled.

"I am going after Arara." Sels turned around stared up into Recka's snarling maw. "You can come with me or not, but I *am* going to follow her."

"I'll take you, Prince Sels, as long as Recka agrees." Jeron winked at Sels.

"No," Recka growled. "I don't dare take my eyes off you after what happened in Blue Cove. I'll take you."

"That is acceptable." Sels nodded and climbed back onto Recka's back.

*****

Sels was bored. At all the other village ceremonies the prey had been scouted and marked beforehand. The actual hunt had taken barely a claw-mark. One village had even corralled the animals into a pen beforehand.

Last Home was traditional, forcing the pups to find their own prey, but Sels could see why the rest of the Empire had made the change.

Watching Arara scout for hukra was dull. He hadn't realized it would take this long. She stopped, sniffed around, ran again, then repeated the process. It was over a claw-mark later, with the sun high in the sky, before Recka declared Arara had found the herd.

"She stopped," Recka said. He halted and allowed Sels to get down.

Sels hobbled around for a few moments before his circulation came back.

Recka crept closer to Arara. A moment later he returned, holding his head like it pained him. "Wow, that was a loud gefir. My head is still ringing. Why did she make it so strong?"

"What did she say?" Sels asked.

"That she found the herd." Recka cocked his head to the side and closed his eyes for a moment. "It's strange. Jeron is too far away for me to contact. That must be why she made it so loud. It's a common mistake among young pups, thinking a loud gefir can be heard farther away than a quiet one, but it's not true. Arara is old enough she should know better." He put his hand on Sels's shoulder and started to push him away. "We should go. It's obvious this pup doesn't know what she's doing."

Sels ducked out from under Recka's hand. "No, I think she does. I'm going to go ask her." He pushed through the bushes and started moving through the trees.

"We can't interfere." Recka whispered as he ran after Sels.

Sels stopped and turned. He spoke normally; royalty didn't whisper or hide. "I just want to talk to her."

Recka stumbled to halt in front of him, panting. "You can chat with her when she returns from the hunt."

"But -" Before Sels could get any more out, Recka yelped, his eyes rolled back in his head, and he crumpled to the ground. A large gash on the back of Recka's head spurted blood, matting the dark fur and dripping to the forest floor.

A large beak, blood dripping off the end, poked through the foliage behind Recka for a moment before snapping back behind the large leaves.

"Recka?" Sels stepped forward in shock, staring down at him. A loud squawk drew his attention back to the trees.

Beady black eyes stared at him through a hole in the foliage. Bushes rustled as a massive bird stepped forward and cocked its blue-skinned head towards Sels. Black feathers glinted in the mottled sunlight making its way through the trees. The bird's crest brushed low-hanging branches on the trees. Sels estimated the bird stood eight tails high, from its clawed feet to the crest.

Sels backed away slowly, leaving Recka lying between him and the bird. The bird stepped towards him, cocking its head to the side. In a rush, Sels remembered where he'd seen this bird before. In a tapestry hung in the Throne room back home, depicting the legendary final battle in the Northern Mountain Wars. This had to be a kwaso, the mounts of the mythical Yaka, capable of cracking a skull in two with a single blow of its beak.

The bird looked down at Recka, then pecked at his back. The beak came back bloody, holding a small strip of meat. The beak snapped, and the meat was gone.

Sels crouched down and without taking his eyes off the bird, felt around in the dirt. A sharp seed pod sliced his hand as he grabbed it. He stood and threw the pod at the bird as its head cocked back for another blow.

The pod bounced off the bird's wing. Its head turned, and one beady eye focused on Sels. The bird squawked and started towards him. Sels turned and ran, ducking and weaving through the unfamiliar bushes and pine trees.

Terror lent his legs strength as he ran. He could hear the bird crashing through the bushes behind him. Alright, now he'd saved Recka, but who'd save him?

The thick foliage above him cast the forest floor into perpetual shadow, and Sels continued to trip over unseen obstacles.

Before long he was sticky with pine sap from stumbling into the trees. He panted with exhaustion. The kwaso hadn't caught up to him so far. The bird's powerful legs were built for running on the flat, open plains of Sebaine, and weaving around the trees seemed to slow it down.

Just when Sels thought maybe he would get away, the bird let out a tremendous shriek, piercing his ears and causing him to stumble. The sound grew stronger, pulsing in his ears and rattling his brain until he was face down on the dirt screaming in pain.

He rolled over to see the kwaso leaping through the shadows towards him with its sharp talons pointed right at his face. Mid-leap, the bird was thrown to the side, straight into the pine tree next to him.

Sels tried to get up, but his head felt like someone was tearing it apart from the inside. The kwaso pulled itself to its feet, then Arara leapt out of the trees and landed on its back. The creature squawked and started pecking at her with its sharp beak.

From his position on the ground he could only see the blue of the bird's bald head and a few white tufts of Arara's fur, which stood out against the midnight black of the feathers. He heard her cry out in pain, and blood flew through the air, splattering on the dirt in front of him. He had to do something.

Maybe he could distract it long enough to allow Arara to act. The shadows were thick around him, with barely enough sunlight peeking through to power a light breeze, but he had to try.

He concentrated on pulling in a ball of air between his hands. The energy twisted away from him and he lost control. Blue light streamed out, and the ball exploded with a boom. The force shredded the front of his robe and rocked him back to the dirt.

By the time he sat up the bird lay in the dirt, kicking up pine needles in its death throes. Arara clenched her jaw around its upper throat and clawed at its face and body. Bloody feathers blanketed the dirt.

Sels's eyes widened at the gory sight. He clamped his hands over his mouth and turned away, hyperventilating and feeling nauseated. He waited until it was quiet, then turned around to see Arara tottering away from the bird's still form before collapsing into the dirt.

"Bright light, are you all right?" Sels scrabbled towards her, using a small tree to pull himself to his feet.

Bloody feathers and gore coated the ground around Arara, forcing Sels to watch his step, lest he get blood on his shoes. He rushed over and knelt down next to her. He exhaled in relief when he saw the blood came from a gash on her shoulder, and not anywhere vital.

Sels pointed to the dead bird, hand trembling. "You killed a kwaso! Those birds are legendary, I mean, I thought they were a myth. A story used to scare little sproutlings." She was amazing. No matter how she looked, she deserved a token.

Arara groaned and turned her head to look up at him. "Shut up and help me."

"Really, your shoulder doesn't look that bad." Sels leaned over for a better look. It still didn't look bad enough for her to be in that much pain. The only other injuries he could see where long scratches crisscrossing her arms, leg, and head, but they looked to be at least a day older.

"My head... really hurts." Arara placed a paw over her eyes and whimpered.

"Did you get hit on the head?" Sels didn't want to aggravate a concussion by moving her.

"No, just my shoulder."

“I could try healing it, but I’m not very good.” He stopped, unable to admit multiple magic tutors had quit, claiming he was ‘hopeless.’

She moaned again. “You can’t make it any worse, can you?”

“Well...” He trailed off, looking down at her with wide eyes. Actually, he probably could. He remembered that when his magic tutor had covered healing he had managed to kill the poor snow raop suffering from only a minor head cold.

Arara cried out in pain then vomited her breakfast up next to Sels knees. Sels wrinkled his nose and pushed himself back. The smell was appalling.

"Alright." Sels gulped and forced himself to scoot back up next to her. He brought up his hands and held them over her wound. “This may sting a little bit as everything knits back together.” If it worked.

The healing chant rolled flawlessly off his tongue. A trickle of energy flowed into his palms. According to his tutors he should be getting a flood, but this was the best he'd ever been able to do. Dim blue light flared for a moment, then the energy he had gathered faded away and the spell fizzled. He grimaced and clenched his hands.

Sels closed his eyes and ran through a quick meditation exercise. His tutors had all assured him his problem was a lack of concentration. So he dutifully did his meditations, although they never seemed to help. The more he concentrated on holding the magic in place the faster it seemed to fade.

Then he moved back into position, his outstretched hands shaking like leaves. Before he could begin his spell, Arara spasmed under his outstretched hands, and her injured shoulder hit his palms. As soon as she touched him, a peaceful expression washed across her face. He jumped back and stared at his bloody palms. What happened? He hadn't even started yet.

He shuddered and wiped his hands in the dirt. This wasn't going to work. He'd just have to bandage her up until a real healer could help her, except... he didn't have any supplies. Well, his robes were already ruined. The sash had fallen off at some point, so he shrugged the rest of the way out of the robe. When the cold mountain air hit his bare arms, he couldn't suppress a shiver. At least he still had his pants and sleeveless tunic to keep him from freezing.

The robe's fabric was too thick for him to tear, so he wadded up a corner and pressed it down against Arara's shoulder with one hand. Arara scrunched her eyes closed and pulled back her lips as he pushed down on her wound.

With the other he stroked Arara's head between her ears, trying to reassure her. Her face relaxed, causing Sels to grin in relief.

Arara's eyes popped open. "Thanks for the healing, Prince Sels. I feel a lot better."

Healing? But his spell had failed. Sels relaxed the pressure on her shoulder. "Are you sure? Your shoulder..."

"Well, that still hurts, but my headache is gone." Arara's tail wagged, hitting him in the side as she sat up.

Sels peeled his robe off her shoulder, happy to see the bleeding had slowed to a trickle.

"Arara, can you shred some long strips off the bottom of this? Then, take off your vest so I can bind up your shoulder." Sels pushed his robe into her lap.

Arara nodded and in a few moments she passed him back a few long strips of purple fabric. He waited while she slowly pulled her vest off, wincing in sympathy as it pulled away from her injured shoulder. The movement had caused it to start bleeding again, but Sels tied a compress in place. Those healing classes came in handy after all.

When he was done, he helped Arara slip her vest back on. She stood and rotated her arm with a wince. Standing, he was surprised to see the top of her head barely came up to his shoulder. He hadn't been this close to her last night and hadn't noticed quite how small she was. Most Jegera were at least a head taller than him. Now he was even more impressed she'd been able to kill such a massive bird by herself.

Sels turned to stop himself from staring and crouched down. "Get that looked at by a healer as soon as possible." He said over his shoulder as he used some leaves to clean the blood off his hands. When he finished he stood up and brushed pine needles from his legs.

Birdsong resumed in the trees above them. Sunlight filtered through the leaves and danced around the ground as the wind rustled the branches. The scene would almost be peaceful except for the smell of vomit... and the dead kwaso a few tails away.

That, and Sels felt like he'd forgotten something. Recka! He spun around to face Arara. "Did you see Recka on your way here? Is he hurt?"

Arara shook her head. "I don't know. I didn't see him."

A cold gust of wind hit and Sels wrapped his arms around himself, shivering uncontrollably. "We need to find him," he chattered, almost unable to talk.

Arara wrapped the remains of his robes back around him. The bottom was shredded, but the sleeves were intact. He hugged the warm fabric close, trying not to think about the blood smeared all over it.

Arara stepped back and gestured to the kwaso, her face looking pensive. "What should we do with this?"

He held up his palms. "I guess, leave it here and hope the scavengers don't get to it before I can send someone for the remains." Sels really wanted to show it to the zoologists in Sebaine. A living legend, he got excited just thinking about it.

Before Sels finished talking, Arara ran around the clearing, rubbing herself on the trees.

She must have seen his puzzled expression, because when she finished she waved towards the carcass. “The Jegeran scent nearby will warn off any scavengers."

Sels nodded, satisfied. "Good, let's go." Sels walked away. Arara tapped his arm and pointed away from where Sels had been headed.

"We came from this way."

Oh. He'd been sure they'd come from the other direction, but Arara knew these woods. He followed her, trying to keep his robes closed with his free hand. The woods all looked the same to him. Even if he'd managed to evade the kwaso on his own, he would have been hopelessly lost.

Before, back at the palace, he'd prided himself on his ability to navigate the hedge maze and exotic gardens with ease, but in the wilds nothing grew were it should. Roots came up from nowhere to trip him, and soon mud covered his robes. Panic must have fueled his steps during his wild run, because he couldn't seem to go five tail lengths now without falling into something. The sun had barely moved since the last time he'd checked, but it felt like they'd been walking forever.

Arara walked along, silent, looking like she was deep in thought. Sels decided to talk to her anyway, to try to pass the time.

“Arara," Sels said, "how did you stop the kwaso from jumping on me? My memory’s fuzzy right after it screamed, but something happened to throw it off course.”

Arara was silent for so long Sels started to think she wasn’t going to answer. “I...caught him off guard.”

He frowned down at her while ducking under a low-hanging branch. “Off guard? With what?”

Instead of answering his question, she pointed ahead of them. “Look, we’re getting close. I smell Recka.” She dropped his hand, fell to all fours and bounded away.

“Arara, wait up.” Sels said to her retreating form.

She stopped and waited until he caught up, then stood back up and walked next to him. Sels tried to take her paw again, but she pulled her arm out of reach with a huff.

Sels did his best to mimic a Jegeran growl under his breath, unconsciously imitating Jeron. "What did I say?"

Arara lifted her head and stalked in front of him. Sels sighed and turned his attention to his feet, watching the ground for pitfalls. However, his thoughts kept circling back to the attack. An extinct bird, attacking in the middle of nowhere? The only logical explanation was that it had to have been an assassination attempt.

Or, it could be a set up by one of the political groups, trying to get him to pick their candidate. The perfect setup - the hero Jerling, saving the Prince from certain death. Except, for such a plot to work, their hero would have to be someone more traditional looking, like the muscled oaf Kerka he'd met the night before. Or perhaps that was the point, they thought this would interest him in their candidate.

He groaned, causing Arara to look over at him with concern. "Am I going too fast, Your Highness?"

Or maybe growing up in the palace had left him seeing plots behind every shadow. "No, I'm just thinking. How did you know to come save me?"

"I heard you scream." Arara turned her head away so Sels couldn't see her expression, but her ears were pulled back. She was a lousy liar.

"Ah." Sels knew he hadn't made any sound or cried out for help. Why would she lie unless it was a plot? His mind circled again, and again he rejected the idea. Too many things didn't add up. Arara was a bad candidate all around, plus, how would they have known he'd come this way at all? No, this had to be just a horrible coincidence.

His thoughts were interrupted when he tripped over another root, and he forced himself to concentrate on the path for the rest of the trip.

When they found Recka, Sels stumbled and sank to his knees in the dirt. Arara shook Recka awake.

Recka sat up, groaning and holding his head. "What happened?"

"I don't know." Sels wrung his hands together. "A kwaso knocked you out and then Arara saved me from it."

"Sels, those are just stories." One of Recka's ears pulled back, but he didn't pull his face out of his paws. Dried blood matted the fur on the back of Recka's head, but even from here Sels could see the wound had already stopped bleeding and scabbed over. Fast healing was a benefit of the *sedyu*-bond.

"I know," Sels said. "I want to bring it home with me, to show it to the professors at the University."

"Sels," Recka groaned, "whatever it was tried to kill you, and you're excited because it's a mythical animal?"

Sels blinked. "Well, yes." Now that he'd gotten over the shakes.

Recka's head lifted. "I'm taking you back to the village before you get hurt."

"No. I need to observe the Hunt." Sels looked to Arara for help, but she just shrugged and looked away.

"Don't make me repeat myself." Recka snarled at him.

"I'll be safe here with you, Jeron and the rest of the Jegera judges. I'm not missing this."

"Quiet, I heard something." Recka huffed and stood, his nostrils flaring. He dropped to all fours and sniffed around the clearing in a circle. "They're gone. But I smell puo berries."

"What?"

"They're smelly, good at covering up other scents. This wasn't a coincidence Sels, someone set this up." Recka finished his circuit of the clearing and stopped in front of Sels, who was still crouched on the ground. "I need to take you back to town."

"Sels is safer here." Arara jumped between them. "What if they attack again on the way back? With how easily they took you out before... The judges will be here in a few scratch-marks, and then you'll have a whole group to protect him."

Sels grinned. "She has a point."

Recka growled at them for a moment before throwing up his paws. “Fine, I'm obviously outnumbered. We stay. But, you will follow all my orders without question. Understand?”

"Yes.” Sels nodded vigorously, not really listening as Recka rattled off a list of orders. His mind was whirling, debating possible suspects for who would want him dead. Arara flashed her teeth at him and vanished back into the woods.

*****

Arara made her way back to where she’d spotted the hukra herd, moving carefully to avoid aggravating her shoulder. In her head, she could feel the pack approaching. They would be here soon, but not as soon as she'd told Recka and Sels. Sels had looked so upset at the prospect at leaving that she'd had to help him out.

She’d begun building a pine branch blind before hearing the Prince's mental cry for help, but in all the excitement she couldn’t remember where she’d left it. Her nose dropped to the ground, and she limped around sniffing for her own scent. The wind howled through the trees, blowing leaves into her face. She sneezed before recognizing her own smell. Hers, but oddly faded, as if it were older. She shrugged and followed it.

The scent-trail led to an old raop burrow. The scent was strong here, as if she'd spent time in the area, then it continued on, headed back towards the village. She started to turn away before she noticed a leather strap sticking out of the hole. A quick tug revealed it was attached to something heavy.

She dug around at the burrow’s opening until she could pull the bulk of the bag free. Dirt trickled off the leather to reveal her old hunting pack. She fell back on her haunches and stared at it. Her missing bag, the one she'd been searching for just this morning. She couldn’t remember when it might have gotten out here. She sat up and sniffed the bag. Her scent was all over it, less than a day old. No other smells lingered on it. So how had it gotten here?

What had she done yesterday? Her mother had helped her patch her formal blue silks for the party, and then she'd gone out to enjoy the afternoon sun in the meadow. There she'd run into Kerka, and then attended the party. She'd gone to bed as soon as she got home, and then slept. She had been tired when she woke up this morning. Perhaps she'd gone out in her sleep, and brought the pack out with her?

Well, let's see what her dream self had packed. She pulled the pack open. Nestled at the very top were two long black feathers. With a trembling paw, she picked one up and sniffed it. Kwaso feathers. Underneath the feathers was a folded map. The side facing her showed the woods north-east of town. A small red x marked her current position.

Further in, she spotted a coil of rope. Something metallic glinted underneath it, and Arara dropped the bag with a start. Possessing metal was forbidden. The punishment for being caught with it was worse than for murder.

<*Arara, where are you?*> Kerka said. The gefir scratched her mind with irritation.

Her head shot up. She hadn't been paying attention, and now she could feel the pack's presence in her mind. They were close.

<I'm a bit south of the river ford meadow.>

She shoved the feather back in, tied the flap shut, then stuffed the pack back down into the burrow and limped away. The implications of her find terrified her, but she couldn't do anything about it now.

She trotted away and almost immediately stumbled over her half completed blind. Her sensitive nose picked up hukra from the other side of the hill. The breeze was with her, blowing her scent away from the herd. She crouched on all fours and inched her way up, wriggling through the grass like a snake. She peaked down to see the herd below munching on the blue meadow grasses.

The hukra were each an impressive sight. Arara shifted in the grass to get a better look at a big male drinking from the ford below her position. The male stood around twenty-five tails tall and had three sharp horns in a triangle shape on his head. The sun glinted off the hard armored plates ridged along his back. His tail thumped into the ground, and a small puff of dirt obscured the razor sharp spikes around the clubbed end.

Another hukra lumbered up as the male pulled his head out of the water. This one, a female, came up to the male's shoulder, and lacked horns and tail spikes. She pressed up against the male, their ridged side plates clacking together as she lowered her head for a drink.

The river ran along the edge of the meadow and made a lazy turn before flowing back into the trees. In the distance she could make out the blue outline of the Northern Wind mountain range. A flat expanse of grassy plains rolled up the foothills.

Arara studied the field until she found one with a lighter colored muzzle than the rest. The old hukra bull looked injured, favoring one side as he walked. Even better, he stood a bit away from the rest. Perfect.

Carefully, she backed down the hill and sat next to her blind to wait. The pack materialized out of the woods shortly afterwords. They were in a wedge with Kerka at the head. Most of the pups wrinkled their snouts and pulled their paws over their noses in reaction to her gory appearance.

Kerka stood up and put one paw over his nose. <What did you do, roll through an offal pit on your way here?>

Arara looked down. Blood and gore already smeared her outfit from the fight with the kwaso. *<It's nothing. I got attacked, but I took care of it.>*

He shook his head, but let the matter drop. "So where are the hukra? And how did you find them so fast?" He growled down as he approached at her.

Typical Kerka, trying to intimidate her with his larger size. Arara narrowed her eyes and pulled back her ears. *<Quiet, you don't want to scare them off!>*

Kerka glared down at her but at least his growling stopped.

<The hukra,> Arara said, <always summer to the north-east of the village, which you'd have known if you'd listened to me.> She grinned smugly up at Kerka. <Didn't I tell you this morning that I had the farthest range of anyone in the clan?>

<She is correct.> Yegra stepped forward and turned to face the group. <I recall now that my father has mentioned that before.>

Arara inclined her head back to Yegra in a gesture of respect.

The rest of the pups gave Arara a variety of strange looks – Jenra and Janrey looked at her wide eyed, while Indy grinned with his tongue hanging out. Gror stared at her with narrowed eyes, Roan gave her a once-over appraisal, and Koe outright glared at her.

Kerka snarled silently. <Fine, you were great. Now clean yourself up before the herd gets a whiff of you. The rest of us need to get started.>

<I picked out a likely target.> Arara jumped in front of Kerka, her tail wagging. <I found one with a white muzzle and lots of broken tail spikes, sleeping away from the rest of the herd.>

<We don't have to listen to you.> Koe's gefir dripped with contempt. It felt so much like an oily film in her head that she grimaced.

Kerka nodded his head in her direction with a glare. <We can pick out our own target. We need to impress the judges. Taking down an old slow Hukra that's wandered away from the herd is too easy.>

Kerka paced around the group, stopping in front of each pup. <Gror, you and Yegra go scout the herd for a more impressive target. Once you find one, gefir it to Jenra and Janrey. Same plan as we discussed before, they will draw it away from the herd to where the rest of us will be waiting. Roan, you, Koe and I will go scout the area around the herd and meet back here.>

The pack scattered, leaving Arara standing alone in the clearing.

CHAPTER FIVE

THE HUNT

Arara huffed and crossed her arms. <*I'll coordinate from the ridge.*> She made her gefir louder than it needed to be. She sighed and sat down to complete her blind. When it was done she carefully pushed up the hill to the place she'd found earlier with the great view of the meadow.

The grass was soft and warm under her and Arara struggled to keep from dozing off. Her eyes kept sliding closed and she was continually shaking herself awake.

A soft giggle floated up from nearby. Arara snapped her head up, startled to feel Janrey and Jenra right behind her. Snuck up on again. The fight with the kwaso must have worn her out more than she realized. A huge yawn cracked her mouth open and next thing she knew, both girls wriggled into the tight space with her.

<*Hi, Arara.*> Janrey gently head-butted Arara's side as she wriggled farther in.

<*Why do your Clan mates give you such a hard time?*> Jenra's mind-voice felt hesitant. Ah, she was afraid of risking Kerka's wrath.

<And why doesn't the Clan Alpha stop them?>

<*Grawka, Kerka's father, ordered me culled when I was little.*> Arara ducked her head and scratched at the dirt with her claws.

<Wow, what happened?> Janrey's fascination was almost palatable in her mind-voice. <I've never heard of anyone surviving the culling.>

<My mother stood up for me, and refused to take me to the woods.> Arara smiled, flashing her teeth at Janrey. Arara knew the story by heart, as she'd heard it at bedtime almost every night growing up. *<Then Grawka said he would do it for her, and tried to take me away. My mother went berserk and tore into Grawka. That's how he lost most of his left ear. It took four males to pull her off of him.>*

Jenra's eyes widened, glowing brightly in the dim light. *<But, that was ages ago.>*

<Grawka's not used to people standing up to him.> Arara shrugged. <He still considers me useless and the rest of the clan follows his lead.>

Silence for a bit. Then Jenra spoke again. *<Both of us and Roan think you're useful.>*

<You should talk to the Alpha-Guards tonight, about Grawka's treatment of you.> Janrey's anger stabbed at Arara's mind, hot and sharp. Her wards trembled, close to shattering. Arara flattened her ears and reinforced her mental wards. Now would be a bad time to lose control.

<No,> Arara clenched her fists. <I'm leaving anyway. And I don't want Grawka to retaliate against my parents.> The curl of her tail tapped both girls as it wagged. <But thank you for the offer. It means a lot to me.>

The girls both nodded at this. Jenra wriggled back out of the blind.

Janrey grinned at her. <Want to meet up after the hunt and go to the party together?>

Arara grinned back and nodded. This was worth staying in Last Home for another half-day. She could always catch the first Poku tomorrow morning if she missed the last run today.

Janrey clasped her paw and squeezed gently before following her sister. Their presence faded away, leaving Arara suddenly lonely. No matter how much fun she had with the girls tonight, tomorrow they would all scatter. The girls to their town, Arara to North Wind.

<Targets?> Kerka's harsh growl pulled her moping.

<*We should go after the biggest one.*> Indy's enthusiasm made his mind-voice sparkle.

<No, the one with the biggest horns,> Koe said by gefir. <That male over there, his front ones are really impressive.>

Males, always focused on size. Arara rolled her eyes.

<Yeah, those horns look impressively sharp.> Yegra, the voice of reason. <Too dangerous.>

Arara nodded, hoping that Kerka would pay attention, but that was probably a futile hope.

<Yegra has a point.> Roan said. <How about that male with the broken left horn and chipped tail spikes?>

<A broken horn?> Koe's mind-voice dripped with contempt. <Everyone would laugh if they saw that above the entrance to my den.>

An intense shudder rolled down Arara's back to the tip of her tail as she tried to keep Koe's anger from burrowing deeper into her psyche. Strong emotions in a gefir had never bothered her before today. Perhaps it was the mind-link? She'd never linked so many at once.

<What about,> Even Gror's mind-voice was quiet enough that Arara had to strain to hear it, <that full grown male drinking at the ford? He is at least twenty-five tails and has all his horns and spikes.>

Arara rolled her eyes, Gror was probably trying to impress Kerka. What a back-rolling submissive move. Of course, Gror wasn't planning on leaving Last Home, so she could understand that he wanted to get on Kerka's good side.

<Yes, perfect!> Kerka said. <Suitably impressive and he's at the edge of the main group. Janrey and Jenra, work with Gror to drive him across the ford, away from the rest of the herd. The river narrows a bit to the west, so the rest of us can easily cross there and then ambush him on the other side. Arara, set up that mind-link you bragged about - if you can.

Everyone got it?>

A chorus of <*Yes*> echoed through Arara's head and she winced.

Arara closed her eyes, willing herself to stay awake while she brought herself into a light trance. The universe expanded as her mind probed out, looking for the silver-bright pin-points of intelligence that stood out in the mental din like stars against the night sky. Lightly, she brushed her mind against two at once, leaving a line of light between them. Soon a web of light linked everyone together.

A cluster of lights at the south edge of the field marked the group of judges. She tied one of the lights in at random, feeling Jeron's surprise as she touched him. As she finished up, a glint caught her attention. A thin string of light branched out from the group, leading back to town. Curious. She reached out, but stopped herself. She had a job to do, and she didn't have time to indulge her curiosity.

The sensation of wind ruffling her fur greeted her as she opened her eyes, the trance broken. Her body felt sore and stiff, although from the position of the sun it had only taken her a few scratch marks to set up the mind-link.

Bleary eyed, she peered out through the criss-crossing branches of the blind as she stretched and shifted. Her eyes finally cooperated, and she focused on their intended target.

The mind-link glowed, a silver spider web in the back of her mind, as she shared her vision with the group. Those tail-spikes looked nasty, and the animal had fully grown horns that could easily kill an adult Jegera. He bore numerous scars from fighting over females. Even relaxing in the river, his tail swished back and forth angrily, disturbing the water around him. Luckily, mating season, when the males would be highly aggressive, wasn't until later in the summer.

<It is more likely he will do anything to stay close to body of the herd, and crossing the ford means heading directly away from the group. What if they fail?> Yegra said. The mind-link showed the group Yegra's entire thought process, branching out to show other possible outcomes of their current course of action. Of the ten or so scenarios she had thought up, the pack succeeded in only one of them.

<Yegra, we can't plan for every possible course of action.> Kerka snarled, his mental-voice booming. <We do it my way.>

Arara grit her teeth and reinforced her wards again.

<Who made you the boss?> Janrey snarled back. <She has a point. We should at least make one backup plan.>

<Yeah,> Roan said, backing up his sister. <A full-grown male, at the peak of his strength? Something is bound to go wrong. Arara's target was better.>

<I don't remember any of you challenging me back on the stage for the position as leader.> Kerka said.

<Only because if I had,> Roan snarled, <you and your posse would have ganged up on me..>

<Exactly.> Kerka mind-voice was smug. <Now, with the whole group of us working together, we can easily take down that male. He's our best chance if we want to feed the whole Clan.>

Arara pulled her ears back. She didn't recall anything in the rules about the kill needing to be a certain size. Kerka probably just wanted to impress the judges.

<Now, let's get going. We need to hurry before he moves away from the water.> Kerka growled.

<Yes, sir.> Gror and Koe replied in unison.

The others grumbled a bit, but soon each of them had replied except for Arara.

<Well, Arara? Do you acknowledge my leadership?>

<Yes, I won't challenge you.> She may not like Kerka, but there wasn't much she could do about it.

A moment later Janrey and Jenra appeared in the grass underneath her position. They were on all fours, crouched low in the tall grass. Even in that position they were able to move quickly heading towards the target.

Gror came in from the other direction. He was very impressive, so much so that if Arara hadn't had the mind-link to guide her she might not have even seen him. The grass was hardly even swaying as he moved in towards the target. The girls caused more disturbance in the grass as they crept forward, but they also moved at a much quicker pace. Arara marveled at their speed.

As the girls passed the main herd, one of hukra on the edge of the group snorted and lifted his massive head. He stomped, drawing the attention of several of the nearby females, who stopped grazing and swung their heads back and forth. They probably noticed the disturbances in the grass.

<Everyone, hold and lay low. They're getting nervous. I think they smelled the girls going by.>

<I concur. Hold.> Kerka replied. <This will also give Koe and I time to get into position.

The twins and Gror stopped, holding perfectly still. The first hukra grumbled, still a bit out of sorts. Most of the rest of them lowered their heads after a moment and went back to grazing.

The lone male at the river splashed out of the water and started heading back to the main part of the herd. His current path would take him directly between Gror and the girls. If they didn't move now, the target would rejoin the herd. But without Kerka and Koe, they stood little chance of success.

<Problem.> Arara panted, close to panicking. She needed this hunt to succeed. <The target is on the move. Yegra, take your team and circle around to the other side of the herd. We are switching targets.>

<Arara, I'm in charge here, not you. And I say proceed,> Kerka roared into the mind-link. An image of him and his bullies shaving Arara's fur quickly followed, showing exactly why he was in charge and not her. She knew she'd overstepped her bounds, but it frustrated her all the same. He refused to admit that he was wrong.

<You're still at the far end of the meadow. The only way you'll get there on time is to cut straight through the hukra herd!> Arara shot back angrily. She couldn't believe how arrogant Kerka was being. He was putting the whole group at risk just to satisfy his own ego.

<It doesn't matter. I say we'll be there on time, we'll be there!>

The entire exchange had taken only moments, the mind-link allowing near instant communication, and the target was still lumbering his way towards the herd. Arara brushed her mind against the web, linking herself into the mind-link as she watched the hukra brush through the grass.

The hukra turned a bit, and his new path took him only a few tail lengths from Gror. When the hukra's shadow fell over him, Gror lunged, seemingly appearing out of nowhere and slashing with his razor sharp claws. The claws swiped empty air as the target reared back, bellowing. The sound echoing as hukra throughout the herd took up the cry.

When the hukra stomped back down to all fours the ground trembled. The impact knocked Gror off his feet, and the hukra trumpeted as he stomped around. Gror's panic as he dodged stomping feet flooded the mind-link.

The rest of the herd stomped, and a stream of hukra started running away from the attacking Jegera. The pounding grew louder, and Arara could feel the ground vibrate under her, all the way at the edge of the meadow. One of the larger males wheeled and broke off from the group. He charged back, towards the attack.

Jenra and Janrey abandoned all attempt at stealth, dashing on all fours towards the new threat. They howled in unison, crying for blood as they intercepted the charging males.

The male startled, rearing up. He turned and slashed his spiked tail towards Jenra. She quickly dodged, and swiped at the tail as it passed. Four crimson lines blossomed on the upper part of the tail. Janrey used the distraction to slash at his lower leg. Her claws bounced off the thick skin, but their combined attack did its job. The male bellowed and wheeled, stomping in a circle and charging away.

The target finished stomping and followed, leaving Gror spitting out dust in his wake. The girls ran as fast as they could, but Arara could tell they wouldn't get there in time.

As the hukra ran past Gror it swung its tail. Gror ducked, dropping flat on his belly. The spikes passed a hair's length over his back, ruffling his fur.

<*Too close.*> Gror whimpered, the mind-link showing how close the attack had come. <*He's going the wrong way and I can't stop him. Help!*>

<New plan,> Kerka snarled. <Forget the ambush. Just kill it. Yegra, take your group in.>

<*Coming.*> Arara saw Yegra's group stream out of the trees and start splashing their way across the river.

The target bellowed and picked up speed as it lumbered away. The girls charged, but Janrey got there first. She leapt, snarling and slashing, trying to keep him off guard. He veered to the side and kept running, ignoring her claws as they bounced off his armored sides. Jenra leapt but fell short, smashing hard into the grass and throwing up a cloud of dirt.

<*It's not working.*> Arara said. Agreement echoed around her, the whole group was frustrated. This time she didn't give any orders. She figured that Kerka would be able to see what was happening and would abort.

She was shocked a moment later when he responded. <*Slow the target down as much as you can. Koe and I will be there soon.*> The mind-link showed them running as fast as they could along the river, towards the second crossing where the river narrowed enough to jump over.

Why couldn't he see that they needed to abort? They could find another herd, or take down one of the stragglers of this stampede. There had to be something she could do to help. She didn't want to see anyone get hurt.

Gror, Janrey and Jenra ran after the target, taking turns slashing and harrying him. Blood dripped from several shallow gashes, but they were barely slowing him down. Yegra and her group were falling farther and farther behind.

Meanwhile, the steady stream of charging hukra were throwing up a cloud of dirt and grass behind them. From her vantage point, Arara could barely make out the shapes of her pack-mates in the gloom. She stood, throwing off the useless blind so she could see better.

A black shape dashed in from the far side of the meadow, howling a cry of assistance. Arara recognized Koe's voice. The howl was low and deep, and hukra dodged out of his way rather than trying to trample him. Kerka plowed after him.

The dust in the air caused Jenra to start coughing violently and she doubled over, helpless. Gror grabbed her, pulling her away seconds before the target's foot came down right where she had been.

While Jenra recovered, Janrey and Gror started alternating lunges from opposite sides of the beast. The tactic worked. The target stomped in a circle, disoriented. Jenra staggered to her feet and joined them, keeping him off balance.

Yegra and her group were almost there, and the brothers were making good time. Gror and the girls just had to hold him a little longer, but they were getting tired.

Janrey almost got hit by a slow, lazy swish of his tail. A move like that she should have easily been able to dodge. The smoke made it hard to tell, but Arara thought that Gror wasn't using his left arm, and it looked like Jenra was bleeding from her side.

The hukra was also showing signs of tiring. His strikes were slower, his stomps not as hard. He also bled from dozens of slashes along his tail and lower legs.

<Kerka, they're too tired, they can't dodge his attacks anymore.> Arara pleaded with him, hoping he would listen to reason. <Call it off.>

<No,> Kerka growled back. <They can rest when we're done. The rest of the pack will be there in a moment, they can hold him that much longer. We need to take this one down, the rest of the herd is gone.>

Kerka and Yegra's group were both close, but both still had almost a tree length to go. Arara looked up and around, and realized he was right. The meadow was now almost completely empty, except for a few stragglers pounding away into the trees as she watched.

An unfamiliar voice flooded the mind-link. Arara started before recognizing the voice as belonging to Jeron, Sels body-guard and one of the judges. *<Be careful. You are all getting tired, and the beast is getting desperate. Tell us if you need help and we will intervene. It is not a sign of weakness to recognize when you are defeated.>*

<Understood, sir, but we can do it.> Kerka said. <Janrey, you're the fastest. Go for the throat and eyes. That'll hold him. Gror, Jenra, distract him so she can strike.>

<Yes, sir.> They chorused.

The hukra, apparently realizing the danger was getting desperate. It lowered its head, sharp horns parallel with the ground, and charged straight at Janrey, attempting to break free of the circle. At the same time, he whipped his tail around at Gror and Jenra, who'd been about to lunge at his sides. They leapt away, but Gror wasn't quite fast enough. The tail caught his side, throwing him away into the dirt.

Janrey rolled under his head, giving her access to the soft skin of its throat. Her mouth caught a fold of skin and she hung tight. The hukra continued its charge while Janrey hung on, slashing and kicking with all twelve of her claws.

The hukra bellowed in pain and collapsed on his side. A wave of dirt washed away as he slid to a stop. Janrey snarled and ripped at his throat with her sharp teeth. Kerka and Koe closed the distance and started tearing as his exposed belly. A few tail lengths back, Jenra pulled Gror to his feel and they both staggered forward.

Yegra and her group were only a tail length away when the beast pulled to his feet. The movement knocked off Kerka and Koe, but Janrey managed to hang on. Arara could see her hanging off his throat, looking like a fuzzy red beard from this distance. The beast violently shook his head from side to side as it bellowed. A small shape dislodged, flying through the air. The shape hit the ground and lay motionless.

In her mind, a small silver light winked out. Arara closed her eyes and reached out, searching. The remaining web faded away, the mind-link dissolving as all her concentration went to the search. Nothing, in her mind, the shape on the ground was dark and gray. Janrey was gone. A howl escaped her, building and building, drowning out all other sound. Jeron said something she didn't catch by gefir.

She opened her eyes, her grief building even as her howl faded away. The hukra recovered, pounding away towards the trees. Their target dripped blood from several nasty wounds, but his long strides ate up the distance. The pack chased after it but fell further and further behind.

No, they'd worked too hard for this. Janrey had given her life for this. Without thinking, Arara reached out with her mind, easily finding the dim pin-prick light from the target in the nearly empty meadow. Like before, she reached out and touched the light, but this time she wasn't gentle. She wrapped herself around it and squeezed. Pain flared out from her temple, but she kept going until she'd smothered the light completely.

A massive vibration almost knocked her off her feet. Her eyes focused on the meadow below her to see that the hukra had collapsed into the dirt and now lay still. The pursing pack fell on the prone form in a frenzy, howling victory.

After a moment, Kerka stepped back, stood up on two legs, and surveyed the dead hukra. <*Great job, everyone!*>

Kerka's gefir stabbed into her head like a thunderclap, and she sank down into a crouch, whimpering, her paws cradling her head. Headaches, she was familiar with, but this was something else entirely. Her vision swam. The buzz of an insect sounded nearby, and the noise burrowed into her ears until she couldn't hear anything else. The sunlight, when she cracked her eyes open, sawed her mind in half.

<*Where is Janrey?*> Jenra sounded puzzled.

<Ask Arara,> Yegra said. <She was supposed to be keeping track of everyone.>

<Yeah, except her mind-link failed at a critical moment!> Kerka snarled into her head.

She needed to tell everyone what happened. Normally she could do a gefir almost without thinking, but the haze of pain made it so hard to think. Carefully, she crafted a gefir and sent it on its way. It curled around lazily and vanished.

<Janrey dead.>

The small effort cost her. She whimpered in pain and lay down, curling into a fetal position.

<*What?*> Jenra's response was layered with so much grief that Arara howled again in sympathy.

<*Janrey!*> Roan cried in her head.

Arara imagined the pair running back through the meadow, finding Janrey. She had to be there for them. Arara staggered to her feet, her eyes barely slitted open against the blinding glare of the noon sun. She missed her footing and fell, sliding to the bottom of the hill. She landed in a heap at the bottom. A tree helped her to her feet, and she shambled her way across the tall grass.

By the time Arara got there, Roan and Jenra stood over Janrey's body. Janrey lay on her back, her head lolling to the side. Blood matted the side of her head and stained her fur, slowly trickling down the side of the large rock that had broken her fall.

"No, Janrey! No." Jenra fell forward, gathering her sister up in her arms.

Roan bent over and gathered both Jenra and Janrey's limp form into his arms. A low howl rose up from his muzzle that was reaching towards the sky. Jenra followed suit, her howl low and soft. Arara joined in as best she could, her voice still hoarse for earlier.

Kerka swaggered up behind them, followed closely by the rest of the group. He folded his arms and looked over the scene. His lips curled up and his large ears pricked back, as if he'd bitten into a bad piece meat.

"Lovely." He snarled. "What a mess."

Roan snarled, dropped the girls and leapt for Kerka in one smooth motion. They rolled away, and the long grass blocked them from Arara's view. The sound of snarling rose above Jenra's howling, and someone cried out in pain.

The grass parted in front of her, revealing Kerka and Koe pinning Roan to the dirt. Roan went berserk and thrashed and clawed in a frenzy. Even though together the brothers outweighed Roan by three stone, they couldn't hold him. Both of them soon had large gashes on their stomachs, arms and legs.

The group fell apart. Indy wrung his paws together, dashing back and forth. His eyes darted around between the three combatants, reluctant to get involved. Gror fell back, his eyes wide. Yegra watched for a moment, expressionless, before she turned and walked away.

*****

Sels leaned forward against a tree, trembling. He'd been watching the hunt from the crook of a tree, surrounded by Recka, Jeron, and the judges. His perch had allowed him to see almost the whole meadow, including a perfect view of Janrey's death.

This was the twentieth hunt he'd watched, but this group still managed to impress him. He knew they were lurking in the grass, but he couldn't see them until right before they struck. They'd worked in perfect harmony, silent and deadly. Right up until one of them was killed.

The girl, limbs flailing, flying through the air. She'd landed with a crack, audible even to him, and lay still. The sight haunted him, replaying in his vision again and again.

He'd stayed in the tree, watching the hunt finish, only out of duty. The rest of the hunt, it seemed to him, was a mess. No teamwork at all. In fact, he saw one of the group snap and bite at one of the others.

The killing of the hukra was sloppy, too. He'd been sure it was going to get away, until it had collapsed for no reason that Sels could see. He'd looked away at the end, turned and stared at the limp form of the girl lying alone in the grass, until Jeron tugged on his robe.

"Put me down," Sels said, barely able to talk around the lump in his throat.

Jeron pulled him down just in time for Sels to lose his breakfast all over the grass. He stood there, shivering against the tree, as panic broke out around him.

The dead body lying here now could have been his, if Arara had not been there to save him. It could have been Arara's, too. That quieter thought somehow scared him more than the first one.

Sels pushed away from Jeron and ran through the crowd towards the meadow. Now that it was over, he needed to make sure Arara was safe.

Recka caught up to him and grabbed his arm, pulling him to a stop. "Sels. You don't need to see this. We can leave now."

Sels turned, and met Recka's eyes. His eyes briefly flickered over to Jeron, who stood behind Recka with a worried look on his face. "Yes, I need to see this."

Recka nodded, understanding in his eyes. "Stay with the group, then."

Sels moved to the tree line, his bodyguards close behind him. Most of the judges were gathered in a knot here. Sels followed their gaze to see Roan fighting with Kerka and Koe. The rest of the group ran the gamut from panicked to upset. Arara stood away from the rest. She was swaying on her feet, her muzzle turned to the sky howling a sad melody.

Grawka and one of the Alpha-Guard ran towards the scene. They yelled something unintelligible, and the Jerlings scrambled to attention, except for Roan. He bounded after Kerka snarling, until a couple of the Alpha-Guard pinned him to the ground. The guards held

Roan in a headlock until he fell limp in his arms, then carried him over to the rest of the judges.

More orders followed and the group surrounded the body in a loose circle. All the Jegera raised their muzzles to the sky and started howling, low and quiet. The howls rose in harmony, intensifying until it felt like the ground around him was rumbling in tune. Gradually the noise lowered until it was gone altogether. Tears stung Sels eyes, and he wiped them away with his sleeve.

Grawka barked again, but Jeron pulled Sels away before he could see what happened.

"Time to go," Jeron said.

"But, what about Janrey?" Sels pulled back. "Aren't they going to make her a pyre?"

"They'll leave her there." Jeron took Sels hand as he walked him away. "In the wilds, we leave the body for the scavengers. In Sebaine, that isn't possible, so we do the pyre. Either way, the body goes back to the earth while the spirit rises on, lifted on its journey by the howling of her kindred."

Sels thought about it as they walked back towards Last Home. In a way, the practice was poetic, leaving the body to complete the circle of life naturally. She would become part of the soil, which nourished the hukra that fed the Clan.

*****

A good portion of the judges traveled with Sels. They moved at a walking pace, not in any hurry. The Jerlings still needed to butcher their kill and return with it before the ceremony could be finished. Sels rode atop Recka, though not by choice. At first he'd walked, but after the fourth time Sels tripped and fell, everyone had insisted.

Sels was still conflicted about what to do. On one hand Arara saved his life while showing abilities far beyond her tender years. On the other, Kerka, powerful and charismatic, was the perfect example of Jegeran strength and leadership. Perhaps a Jegeran point of view would help order his muddled thoughts. He listened carefully as the judges and guards reviewed the hunt play by play, dissecting performances.

"Kerka," a guard said. "A strong leader, to get them to follow his orders so well."

Jeron snorted. "But bull-headed. A good leader listens to his team, and doesn't just throw out orders."

Underneath him, Recka huffed. "But willing to take risks, and prudence can be taught."

"So then," Sels mused out loud, interrupting a guard, "Kerka isn't to blame for the death of his team-mate?"

A snort came from one of the locals Sels didn't recognize. "Of course he is."

Around him, heads nodded in agreement.

"Then Kerka," Sels smiled, "would be a poor choice as one of my candidates." He tried to catch Recka's eye, which proved difficult to do from Recka's back.

"What?" a guard growled. "No, he's an excellent choice."

"But you all said-- "

"As a Guard, you can't be scared to tackle things head on." The Alpha-Guards and Recka all nodded at this statement.

"Or back down just because you or someone else might get someone hurt."

More nods.

"The life of your charge is more important than the life of your pack," Recka growled, and the group barked in agreement. Jeron, walking next to Recka, was silent, his head still.

Sels twisted to see him better. "Jeron, what do you think?"

"I think they are correct, as far as being an Alpha-Guard. But we are talking about a *sedyu*-bonded. They are more than a guard. They will serve alongside you as your right hand in all matters. They need to have more than brute strength and intimidation. When they are with you on a diplomatic mission, or judging Trials, they need to be able to listen and have compassion."

Sels nodded. Jeron's words paralleled his own thinking.

"Enough of Kerka," Sels said. "What of the rest?"

Recka shrugged so hard, Sels had to hold on to the scruff of his neck to stay on. "Nothing to speak of."

Jeron grinned. "Arara, she was impressive. Being able to set up a mind-link at her age, untrained."

Sels smiled back at him. "I agree. I'm thinking of giving her a token." He wished he could mention how she saved his life, but Jeron had explained to him at length before they left on this journey that any contact with the Jerlings during the hunt would be considered grounds for disqualification.

The local Jegera all exchanged glances and growled, until one finally said, "Bad idea. She's too small."

"And twisted. That tail is proof of it."

"Ghost-touched, too, with that white fur."

"That doesn't mean anything," Sels said, balling his hands in Recka's mane. "The Captain of the Alpha-Guard has a twisted - I mean - curly tail, too. Tell them, Recka."

"It's true," Recka said.

A snort, from another of the locals. "Maybe so. But she's still a white runt."

Sels sighed.

Conversation started up around him. The judges debated points and dissected the hunt. The rest of the trip passed quickly, and Sels had yet to make up his mind.

*****

Back at the Guest House, Sels stripped off his shredded pants and robe and cleaned up as best he could in the short time. He emerged feeling much better, at least until he spotted Sesay standing in the doorway, her legs planted wide and her arms crossed. Her pink petals were opened so wide they formed a pink haze around her face. He groaned internally and steeled himself to endure her latest lecture.

She walked forward until she was directly in front on him, her face an angry mask. “Are you trying to humiliate me?" She pushed her finger in his face. "I thought I made this clear this morning. I forbid you to give that runt Arara a token.”

“You can’t do that,” he responded as calmly as he could, while inside he was shaking. Sels looked around for Jeron, but the room beyond Sesay was empty.

“Don’t think you can get out of this conversation, Sels. I sent Jeron away on an errand, so we could talk.” She stepped back and took a seat in one of the stuffed chairs placed around the edges of the room. Her face and petals smoothed out and she smiled, but Sels knew that smile was a trap.

“Come, sit with me.” She patted the chair next to her.

Sels eyed her warily and stayed where he was. Recka ducked through the vines at the entranceway and growled at him until he made his way over to the chair and sat down.

“Now Sels,” Sesay began with a smile. “Let's be reasonable here. What would your mother and the Council say if you came home dragging that mangy runt with you?”

“Mother would be glad I followed my instincts.” He folded his arms and glared at his cousin. "And the Council, they don't have any say in the matter.

Sesay shook her head. “Sit down and think Sels. This is an important choice. The Jegera you pick as your *sedyu*-bonded reflects on you and has repercussions for your entire political career. Anything they say or do will be your responsibility. What will you do if she loses her temper in Council, like she did last night? What if she pushes over the Council's Speaker?"

The Speaker was so old he required a wooden staff to walk. The thought made Sels laugh —the Speaker on his back, flailing his arms and complaining with a stunned expression on his face, while the rest of the stodgy old Council gawked and mumbled about the 'manners of today's youth.' Sels snickered. He clapped his hands over his mouth, but it was too late.

Sesay narrowed her eyes. "It's not funny, Sels. What if she hurt someone?" Sesay sat forward until her knees touched his. "I still think you should try again next year. Who knows? Perhaps with another year of training you may even master the Greeting Magic."

"Look, Sesay, we already went over that this morning." Sesay thought she could run right over him in everything, just because his mother had picked her as the heir. Ever since, Sesay had held it over his head. Sels couldn't understand why it was so important for the heir to be able to cast one stupid spell. The Greeting Magic was just a pretty light show to please the crowds.

He heard Sesay sigh. "Still being stubborn. Well, I planned on that. Recka and I picked out a few candidates for you. All you have to do is present them with tokens."

"No." He turned back and met Sesay's gaze. "Arara is qualified. She saved my life earlier. Ask Recka."

"Recka didn't see anything. He was knocked out and woke up to the sight of you - covered with blood - with Arara."

"But, the dead bird -" Sels sat forward and clutched the arms of the chair.

"There was no bird Sels." Sesay sat back and gave him a hard look. "Recka sent a few of the judges to pick up the corpse on the way back. They didn't find anything."

"What? That's impossible."

"I don't know what she convinced you of, but it's a very obvious set up." Sesay smiled at him, a smug turn to her lips. Sels recognized the look. It was the same one she wore whenever she managed to back him into a corner.

Well, not this time. "I won't let you push me around on this." Sels crossed his arms and glared at Sesay. Somehow, the perpetrators had disposed of the evidence. But he clearly remembered being chased through the woods by that terrifying creature and healing Arara's headache. The sharp smell of blood and gore that still assaulted his nose from his ruined robe testified to the truth of his memory. One thing he was certain of, Arara had saved his life earlier.

"I can and I will." She stood. "I've already sent one of your tokens off to Hidden Cove for you."

"Hidden Cove?" He struggled to pull himself up off the too-plush chair after her.

"Yes, to Nathira. I'm sure you remember her. Her parents are both members of the Council and major political players." Sesay smiled.

Sels ground his teeth in frustration. He did remember Nathira, a shy thing too scared to even introduce herself to him before the hunt. Her father had to come up and talk for her. The only reason Sesay was sending her a token was because of her father's position as head of the Jegeran trade council.

Sesay waited a moment, frowning when Sels didn't respond. "The other you will give to Kerka."

Sels mouth fell open. He didn't deserve a token after what happened today.

"No, I refuse!" He yelled at Sesay's back as she headed toward the exit. His hands flew over his mouth. He'd never had the courage to directly refuse his cousin before.

Sesay stopped, halfway out of the door. She turned to face him, her mouth forming an 'Oh' of surprise.

A frown pulled down the corners of her mouth. "Well, then, what do I care. I'm just trying to save you from major embarrassment." Her eyes grew moist and a few tears trailed down her cheeks. Her petals pulled back tightly against her head. "All I'm trying to do is look out for your well-being, Sels."

Sels swallowed, suddenly ashamed of himself. Sesay was just trying to look out for him after all. Perhaps he was just being silly? Or was he being strong?

At that moment, he couldn't tell.

CHAPTER SIX

UNEXPECTED GIFTS

Arara's head pounded. It felt squeezed and tight. At times the pain was so strong her vision blacked out. She wasn't sure how she managed to stumble back to the Ceremony grounds, especially loaded down with meat like she was. At least she was able to keep up now since everyone else was sore and loaded down.

As soon as they broke through the trees into the clearing, Jegera rushed up and unloaded them. Arara collapsed. She could have slept for a week, if not for the drums in her head.

Kerka pawed at her. "We're not done yet. Get up on stage." He hesitated for moment, and then added. "You did better than I expected."

She pried her eyes open and turned her head to look up at him. Through sheer force of will she crawled to all four paws, and dragged herself over to the steps. Grawka ushered her to the far end of the line, next to Yegra.

Grawka placed Kerka in the spot of honor at the other end of the line from her, closest to where the Prince stood with his entourage. The Prince stood next the same pink Petal Kin Arara had seen that morning. Recka and Jeron stood on either side of the two Kin. Recka stood tall, beaming across the stage towards the line of Jerling. Jeron slouched low, his head turned, whispering something in the Prince's ear. The distance made it hard to tell, but the Prince looked upset.

Jenra and Roan mounted the stage together, their heads down. Grawka placed them on the other side of Yegra, as far from Kerka as they could get. Indy, Koe, and Gror arrived as group. They took their places in the center of the line.

As soon as they were in place, Grawka stepped to the edge of the platform and raised his arms. “Pack-Members! I’d like to announce that the hunt was successful!”

Loud cheering and howling drowned out his voice. He paused, lowering his arms and waiting until the sound died down. “However, I am sad to say that Janrey did not survive the hunt."

Some in the crowd gasped, while others glanced about or bowed their heads. A few mumbled darkly about the loss, about how it only happened this year because of the unlucky presence of the Ghost-touched Jerling. Arara searched the crowd for Janrey's parents, and spotted them at the edge of the crowd being led away by the stooped old priest.

“Let us give her a moment of silence before the awards are presented.” Grawka dropped down and bowed his head. The crowd followed suit. For a few moments the only things that could be heard where the wind blowing through the trees and the tinkling of the paper lanterns as they bobbed in the wind.

A short time later Grawka raised his head. “Thank you.” He stood back up and raised his arms out. "With Janrey’s loss hanging heavy on our hearts, I would like to take the time to remind you of why we have this tradition.

“This story takes place before the dawn of the Empire as we know it today. We Jegera were just venturing out of our forest home, in a quest for food to feed our growing civilization.

“During this time, a male Jerling named Isok, hunting alone in the woods for the first time, ran across a young female named Henra from a nearby competing tribe. They fell in love, but they knew they could not ever become mates while the clans fought over hunting grounds.

"Isok came up with a plan to find the fabled northern hunting grounds in order to reunite the tribes. He and Henra secretly gathered together a pack of young Jerlings and headed to the north.

"After a moon of travel, Isok, Henra, and their pack first saw the signs of destruction. Whole swaths of the forests around them were smashed. The remains were covered in prey-sign, and the pack's mouths watered at the delicious smell. That night, the mists came. The night was dark, the twin moons and stars hidden behind dark, low clouds that spoke of coming rain. They'd just set up camp for the night when the mist rose, seemingly billowing out of the ground itself to envelop the forest in a shroud of white. A low howl rolled out of the forest, telling the young hunters that they were now the prey.

"The Jerlings huddled together in their tents, remembering the scary stories told in the dark over the coals of the fires. Only Isok was brave enough to leave the tents and howl defiance. A few of the braver Jerlings watched between the folds of the tent as the mist swirled, coalescing in front of Isok into the form of a huge Jegera. The tips of its pointed ears brushed the tops of the trees that surrounded the camp. Glowing red eyes opened, glaring malevolently down at the Jerlings.

"The beast's oversize jaws opened, revealing fangs larger than Isok's head. Curls of mist dripped from its muzzle as it spoke. 'Puny pup. You dare to steal prey from the mighty Yaka?'

"'We seek not a challenge,' Isok bravely stared up, meeting the gaze of the red-eyed monster, 'but an alliance.'

"Mist swirled off the monster, now its ears only brushed the lowest branches of the trees. 'What could you possibly have to offer the mighty Yaka?'

"A gout of mist shot from its mouth, blowing down on Isok's head, yet Isok refused to back down. 'We will stop whatever it is that destroys your land.'

"'What makes you think the mighty Yaka need help?' The mist swirled off again, now the beast was only a head taller than the largest

Jegera. Fangs of mist snapped closed a hair's breadth from brave Isok's muzzle.

"'We Jegera can hunt and kill these invaders before the destruction gets any worse.' Isok managed to wag his tail even as he stared up into the monster's glowing red eyes.

"'Show me.' The monster drooled. 'Tomorrow, kill a hukra for us. You will know them by their size and their armor.' The mist-Yaka leaked away bit by bit, but the voice continued. 'And if you don't succeed, you'll never see another sunrise.'

"The mist curled away, back into the ground, as if it had never been. The terrified Jerlings tumbled out of their tents and surrounded brave Isok.

"'What will we do?' They pleaded.

"Isok calmed the Jerlings, and together they came up with a plan on how to take down an armored giant. The next morning, Henra's tracking found the first hukra. Fast Corop led the beast on a chase, driving it into a trap set by wily Muika. Strong Onba lifted the hukra, exposing the belly for the brave Isok to attack the soft flesh found there.

"And thus, with teamwork, this small pack defeated the mighty foe.

"That night the mist Yaka returned. It thanked them for their help and gave them leave to hunt in the north, so long as the Jegera killed only hukra. The discovery of the hukra by brave Isok and his band saved the Jegera from starvation.

Grawka fell silent for a moment as the crowd reflected on the story. "That is why, to this day, the young ones hunt the hukra, to honor Isok and Henra's pack and the bravery they showed in providing food for their clans."

A drum beat split the air and Grawka's fists hit the air above him. "Now, the time you've all been waiting for!" Grawka yelled. "I will be awarding the points to each new Clans-man!"

The crowd howled, different voices cheering for their favorites.

Grawka stalked down the line of pups. "Kerka, you showed good leadership, assigning each an appropriate role for their abilities."

"*However*," Grawka said, his voice lowering, "you lost a pack member due to your pride. Your insistence on picking a bigger target than one within the abilities of your pack directly led to the loss of a team-mate. Furthermore, you declined assistance from the judges when it was offered."

The crowd hissed and booed. That woke Arara up. It wasn't often that Kerka got called out on his mistakes. She tried to peer around Jenra. Unfortunately, every other Jerling in the line was doing the same and she couldn't see anything. Her legs wobbled and she slumped back into place.

"This is a mistake of inexperience," Grawka said when the roar died down, "so the judges went light on you. We were impressed that your small pack was able to take down such a large male by yourselves. Overall you ended up with a total of twelve points."

The crowd went wild, screaming and howling. Arara's jaw dropped. Twelve points was a lot. Most only ended up with five or six, and in the years Arara had attended no one had ever ended up with more than fifteen.

Arara watched as money changed hands, the winners of bets waving their newfound wealth in the air. She bared her teeth. That kill was rightfully hers. The hukra would have escaped if she hadn't acted.

If they just knew what she'd done... she followed the thought. If they knew, they'd be terrified of her. No way would she tell them she'd killed that hukra with nothing but her mind. She knew pack logic. If she could do that to a hukra, she could do that to them. They'd never stand for her to live.

Never mind that the effort had almost killed her. And the hukra's life-force was dim. The effort that would be required to smother the bright spark of a Jegera life would kill her for sure.

When the noise level dropped to a low roar, Grawka moved on to Koe. "Koe, you did a good job following orders. I'm also impressed with the strength and agility you showed while dodging charging hukra. You earn seven points and my hearty praise." He clapped Koe on the back, then moved down the line.

Arara's tired mind couldn't process the words any longer. Her eyes drooped close.

A loud bark startled her awake; she was so tired she'd fallen asleep standing up. Grawka stood in front of her, his muzzle curled up in contempt. Arara pulled herself to attention, swaying only slightly.

"Last - and certainly least," Grawka barely glanced at her as he read off his memory board. "Arara. Your skill at mind-linking is impressive. However, you endangered yourself and your pack by going off on your own. Plus, your mind-link failed at a critical time in the hunt, endangering your fellow pack members. Therefore, you are awarded one point, the minimum required to graduate."

Arara's ears pulled back. That wasn't fair. Kerka's actions killed someone, yet he wasn't docked any points. In the long run, she supposed it didn't matter. With Janrey gone, there was no reason at all to stay here any longer than she had to. She intended to catch the last Poku out of town tonight. The long light slanting through the trees told her dusk was almost here. She would need to leave straight after the ceremony in order to make it on time.

"Next, the Alpha-Clan will offer qualified pups a place in the Guard. Indra, would you do the honors?"

"Thank you, Grawka." Indra's furry brown tail wagged as she stepped forward. She wore black and gold, the colors of an elected Council member. The Council voted on the laws and rules of the land.

Indra walked along the line of Jerlings. She stopped first in front of Kerka and presented him with a wooden shield token. He puffed up and accepted it, tilting his head back respectfully.

Indra presented another token to Yegra. When the cheers had died down, Indra nodded to Grawka to continue.

Now, I would like to announce Prince Sels, who will be choosing *sedyu*-bond candidates. Prince Sels, please approach if there are any you would like to so honor."

The entire crowd held their breath.

Sels nodded and stepped forward, turning to address the crowd. "Yes, there is." He reached into his robes and pulled out a small, flat wooden flower token.

His footsteps echoed loudly in the silence as he made his way down the stage. Arara craned her head around to watch. Sels passed Kerka and stopped in front of Koe. Sels looked in her direction, and Arara would have sworn he was looking straight at her. Then the moment passed, and Sels shook his head and turned around.

Sels faced the crowd and held the token up. The crowd roared. If possible, even louder than they had earlier when Grawka awarded Kerka his points.

Sels flipped the token over in his hand then turned around and held it out towards Kerka. Kerka swiped it so fast that Sels jerked his hand back in surprise.

Kerka raised it over his head triumphantly and howled victory. The noise increased until Arara cringed back and placed her paws over her ears.

The howling went on for quite a while. Arara watched the Prince. He stood in front of Koe, looking deep in thought. Every few moments, his head turned and his gaze met hers. Arara's ears perked. On the way back, carrying the heavy load of meat, she'd been daydreaming of the Prince presenting her with a token. After all, she'd saved his life. Perhaps he might favor her.

The cheering eventually tapered off, and the silence was deafening. Kerka stepped back in place. The Prince still stood in place, looking deep in thought. Arara held her breath, willing the Prince to come her way. As if he'd heard her, he turned, head bowed, and walked down the line of pups toward her. He got closer and lifted his head. His gaze met hers and his eyes lit up. A smile tugged the corners of his mouth up for a moment before his expression smoothed out.

Arara perked up, wagging her tail in anticipation. The Prince passed Yegra. Arara risked a glance away from him, looking down the line of Jerlings. A line of wide eyes and shocked expressions greeted her.

The Prince stopped directly in front of her and faced her, his arms folded up in his sleeves. Sels sighed, opened his mouth, then closed it again, as if debating something. Finally, he spoke. “Arara, I'd like to thank you for your assistance earlier. As a symbol of my gratitude, I'd like to present you with a gift.”

“What?” Was all she managed to get out.

"What would you like? While I cannot present you with a token at this time, I'd like to do something to thank you." One arm withdrew from his sleeve, holding a clinking bag.

Her tired mind wasn’t working; she couldn’t get her mouth to do what she wanted. Her jaw worked up and down a few times before she could speak. She didn't know why she'd been expecting him to be holding a token. "Thank you, Your Highness, but I cannot accept that." As soon as it left her mouth she mentally hit herself. Just this morning she'd been wishing for more money.

He frowned down at her. "Please, I'd like to do something for you."

"The only thing I need right now is to get to North Wind." She growled, unable to look at him, inexplicably disappointed.

"Then, how about a ride there with me? Tomorrow morning. You can ride with me in my private pod. I will pick you up at your den at dawn for the trip."

A grin spread across his face as she lifted her head to meet his gaze. "That would be...would be great. Thank you."

The bag disappeared back into his sleeve and he held out his hands to her.

Arara tried to get up and fell. Yegra shot her a look, snorted, grabbed her arm and hauled her to her feet. She reached out and Sels clasped Arara's paw between his hands.

At his touch the pounding in her head tapered off, then stopped all together. New strength ran down her arms and radiated out. She felt refreshed, as if she'd just rested. Arara stared up into Sels eyes in shock. His expression mirrored her own surprise.

Sels eyes widened, his thoughts coming to her in a rush. *<I feel amazing. Was that what a sedyu-bond feels like?>*

A growl from her right broke the spell. Sels bobbed his head and blinked, then took her paw with his other hand and pulled her forward and faced the crowd.

"I'd like to personally thank Arara for her assistance with a personal matter of mine earlier today. I'm sure she will be a valuable asset to the Last Home Clan in the years to come."

Arara stared up at him. "Thank you."

Whispers and surprised barks followed the Prince up the stage as he rejoined his guards.

"What just happened?"

She hadn't realized she'd spoken out loud until Yegra answered her. "You got the Prince's personal thank you and a ride in the Prince's personal pod to North Wind." Her voice sounded bored, like it was the most natural thing in the world to have happened.

Arara's gaze shifted to Yegra. "Yeah, but...even I can afford a Poku ticket. It sounded like there was a fortune in there! I could have had anything, and I ask for a ride. Why didn't I take the money?!"

*****

Sels crossed the stage in a daze, certain he'd just made the biggest mistake of his life. Like a fool, he'd let Sesay manipulate him again. He'd thought his plan perfect, slip Arara a token inside the pouch with the money, leaving Sesay none the wiser. Arara was poor and the fact that she would turn down money never even crossed his mind.

And then magical energy had welled up from inside of him the moment he'd touched her paw. The magic sung as it poured into him, the most beautiful melody Sels had ever heard. It felt amazing, like he was flying, like he could reach out and touch the sun.

The feeling, it had to be the mystical connection spoken of in his book. Why hadn't he just given her a token outright, instead of trying to be clever?

Sels couldn't remember saying his thank you to Arara, or how he'd gotten back down the stage. The magic still sang inside of him, although the music had started to fade the moment he'd released Arara's paw.

"I'm proud of you, Sels." Sesay smiled at him, a genuine smile this time that crinkled her cheeks and lit up her eyes. "Although you scared me for a moment. Warn me next time you pull something like that."

Sels opened his mouth to reply but was cut off by Grawka announcing the start of the feast.

The crowd roared, and the noise drowned out any chance he had of responding. The scent of roasting hukra filled the air as cooks threw the fresh meat onto the grill. The Jegera began to file towards the edge of the stage.

Ahead of the crowd, Sesay took his arm, and they stood at the bottom of the stairs. Recka and Jeron stood behind them, looking menacing.

The newly minted Clan members came down first, Kerka strutting in the lead.

Sels felt nothing as he shook Kerka's massive paw. "Congratulations," he mumbled to the dirt.

"Thank you for the honor, Prince Sels."

Sels expected him to move on, but Kerka remained in front of him.

Next in line, Sesay elbowed him lightly in the ribs.

"He's your *sedyu*-bond candidate," she whispered to him. "Try to act at least a little bit excited."

The way he felt now, a pained grimace would be about all he could manage. So he settled for a blank, haughty stare as he craned his neck up. "I'm pleased you decided to accept my offer."

Kerka inclined his head and grinned down at him before moving to shake Sesay's hand.

As he shook Koe's paw, next to him he heard Sesay say to Kerka, "Prince Sels would be delighted to offer you a ride to the Poku station. He'll pick you up tomorrow at dawn."

His eyes widened as he realized the implications of what Sesay had said. He couldn't pick up both Arara and Kerka. He turned, but Kerka was already a dozen steps away, melting into the crowd. Sels was powerless to follow, stuck where he was, shaking paws for who knew how long.

Jeron grabbed his arm and gently turned him back around. Without looking at who it was, he reached out and shook. "Congratulations."

The line moved past, tortuously slow as Sesay smiled and chatted with each and every one. Sels struggled for anything to say, so he let the excited villagers do most of the talking. Mostly, he was preoccupied with what he was going to say to Arara when her turn in the receiving line came.

Sels should just tell her he made a mistake, and hand her a token. But, he still struggled with the consequences of Sesay seeing him give it to her.

When he stepped back, he could see Sesay's point about Arara. Who you chose for your *sedyu*-bonded reflected highly on your political career. Sesay's choice of Nathira, daughter of highly influential Council members, made sense in this light.

Her choice of Kerka also made sense because of his physical prowess and size. Arara boasted neither advantage. In fact, her small size and mangy fur marked her as weak and powerless. And a member of the Royal Family could not afford to look weak.

Sels offered another congratulations, and shook another paw absentmindedly.

Arara was strong, and Sels knew it, but he also knew that convincing anyone else of this fact would be difficult. Giving her a token would only end in humiliation, for both of them. At least, this is what Sesay had convinced him of only a few claw-marks ago. Yet, now he wasn't so sure.

He was so deep in thought that when Janrey's brother and sister got to him, he barely stopped himself from saying congratulations, turning it into condolences at the last instant. They stared at each awkwardly until the line moved forward again.

Yegra moved to stand in front of him, and she inclined her head farther back than was necessary. "Prince Sels." Her muzzle snapped closed on the last syllable, and her eyes raked over him.

"Congratulations," he smiled. Seeing Yegra meant Arara was next. He reached in his sleeve, into the pocket sown into the lining, and fingered one of his tokens, his mind made up. He could deal with Sesay for the week it took to get back to Sebaine. He looked past Yegra down the line. Where he'd expected to find Arara, instead a row of strange faces greeted him. "Where's Arara? I thought she was next to you."

A shrug from Yegra. "Still where I left her, I think." She narrowed her eyes as she looked down at him. "Why do you care, Your Highness?"

Sels grimaced, looked away. "I have something of hers," he mumbled, putting both his arms up his sleeves, suddenly embarrassed.

“Of hers?” Yegra shook her head in disbelief. "What did she do to help you? And if she was such a big help, why didn’t you honor her with a token?”

Sels glanced over at Sesay, who was still offering condolences to Roan and Jenra. Their parents had joined them, and Sesay's eyes were moist as she held the paws of a Jegera Sels guessed to be the sibling's mother.

"I didn't trust my own judgment about the matter," he admitted, clenching his hands into fists inside his sleeves.

"After that personal favor, that left her covered in gore, *Your Highness*?" Yegra huffed, her breath hot on his face as she leaned towards him.

Sels went cold. Sesay hadn't believed him about the attack, yet Yegra had smelled the evidence on Arara. Why hadn't Recka? "Did she tell you what happened?"

Yegra straightened and huffed again. "No. Not a word."

Sels frowned, wanting to ask more, but the line moved on, taking Yegra with it. "Well," he sighed as Sesay beckoned Yegra forward, "it was nice to meet one of Arara's friends."

"What gave you that impression?" She cocked one ear back as she turned away.

Sels shook paws for what seemed like an eternity. He hadn't seen Arara again, although it felt like he must have personally greeted the entire village by now. He'd lost Sesay at some point, and he now stood alone in a sea of black and gray fur. His stomach growled in protest as he greeted yet another grateful villager. Sesay certainly wouldn't fault him a break, he'd more than fulfilled his Royal Duties. He signaled to Jeron that he needed a break before the next person could approach him.

"Of course." Jeron turned to the gathered crowd of Jegera still lined up to speak to the Prince. "I'm sorry to disappoint all of you, but His Highness needs a break."

There were a few disappointed growls, but most of the crowd took it in stride as Jeron led him away.

The setting sun cast long shadows across the clearing as they made their way toward the buffet line. Sels was hungry, but he stopped walking as soon as they were out of sight of the crowd that had been waiting for him.

“What’s wrong?” Jeron drew even with Sels and stopped.

“I need to find Arara.” Sels folded his arms into his sleeves, frustrated. His short stature meant he couldn’t see much through the crowd except furry backsides.

Jeron’s ears perked up and he grinned. “I heard what you said to Yegra. Change your mind?”

Sels frowned, his eyes searching the crowd. "Actually, I had a token in the bag of money I tried to give her, but she refused it." He sighed.

"I wish you'd shared this with me. I could have told you that would happen. She's too proud to accept money." Jeron shook his head. "Besides, you have to give her the token in public, where there are plenty of witnesses."

"What? Why?"

"Try to think like Lady Sesay, Your Highness."

Sels crossed his arms and lowered his head, thinking hard. "I suppose...if I were Sesay, I could think 'Sels's lost a token, and Arara found it. Or perhaps stole it, right from my pocket."

“Exactly. She would have the grounds to disqualify Arara. But if there are lots of witnesses..."

Sels head snapped up and he grinned. "She can't deny it later."

Jeron’s wagging tail slapped Sels legs as Jeron patted Sels back. “We’ll make a politician out of you yet.”

CHAPTER SEVEN

THE JOURNEY BEGINS

Before dawn the next morning Arara was trying to figure out an appropriate outfit for a trip with a prince. Her only nice outfit was the blue one she'd worn for the party the night before last, and he'd already seen her in that. Since Kerka's pack of bullies had ruined her favorite vest, all she had left were her leather school outfits, which were stained and dirty from constant abuse.

With a sigh she donned the blue dress silks, picturing the fabulous wardrobe she could have had if only she'd swallowed her pride and taken the money.

The reflection in the mirror revealed a short-furred stranger. In their hurry to leave the day before, Arara hadn't had a chance to see her new look. Bald patches marred her head and arms, and without her fluffy fur, the blue outfit hung strangely. Her ears flattened to her head and she growled, furious at Kerka. She looked hideous, but her mother had done her best to fix it. There was nothing else to do but wait for her fur to grow back out.

Arara picked up her bag, staggering under its weight before collapsing in the hall. She gave up and dragged it through the front entrance. Frost coated the trees and crunched under her feet as she dropped the strap with relief.

The stars above her faded as she watched the sun rise through the trees. Normally she loved the morning, but today she shivered as the brisk breeze hit her exposed skin. Of course, her warm winter jacket lay packed at the very bottom of her bag, underneath the heavy pots and pans, her portable piano, and the potting soil.

By this time tomorrow she would be in the big city. Alone, with no friends, no family, no money. No real skills except her music – and her untrained mind-powers, which she feared to reveal. For the first time, it occurred to her that her parents might be right about waiting.

Birdsong cut through the morning, interrupting her thoughts before they became too dark. The high notes of the bird's melody reminded her of a singing Kin. Her thoughts turned to Sels. Last Home was too cold for Kin, so she'd never spent much time with one before. The few times she had, their strange fur-less skin and perfumed scent had set her on edge, but Sels seemed different somehow.

She wasn't sure why, but she liked him. The thought of spending the day with him caused her tail to wag with excitement. Her tail stiffened as she mentally heard her parents start to move around the den, and she wasn't surprised when her mother called out something to her a moment later.

Arara ducked her head through the vines. "I'm outside," she barked.

A creaking sound caused her ears to swivel around, and she spun back, eyes searching the trees. Something moved between the densely packed pines, something large with too many legs. As it scuttled into view, Arara's mouth gaped open. A tangle of vines grew out of its bottom, weaving a complex pattern along the underside, propelling along a large wooden oval. The large green leaves on top swayed and bounced as it moved. The Royal seal on the side grew in a brilliant green against the dark grain of the wood.

The carriage crawled up the path, slowing as it neared. She sensed four Jegera and one Kin inside. Stopping about ten tails away, the carriage lowered to the ground, the vines folding underneath it. The door rolled down to the ground like a tongue. Arara closed her mouth with a snap, already feeling out of her element.

Jeron strolled down the ramp into the road and waved at Arara before turning around to help Prince Sels step out. She was amused to see Sels wrapped in a large fluffy blanket, until a freezing blast of wind hit her bare patches and she wished she'd thought to do the same thing.

Sels eyed her and pulled his blanket tighter. “I thought you'd be used to the cold by now.”

Arara inclined her head back, although not as far as she had the day before, due to their growing familiarity. "I cut it short for summer. I didn't realize how cold I would get without it.” She lowered her head and scuffed at the ground with one claw.

Out of the corner of her eye, she saw Athura and Eraka come outside. Arara ran over to them, wrapping her arms around her mother's middle.

“Good luck, Arara.” Her mother ran her paw over the charm bracelet before letting go and stepping back.

“Write us often.” Her father ruffled her ears, then scooped her in a massive hug, crushing her ribs.

“I love you both!” she yelped, almost unable to speak. Eraka chuckled and lowered her to the ground.

Wheezing, Arara stumbled over to her overstuffed pack and grabbed a strap.

Sels, who'd been watching the whole exchange with a puzzled expression, arched one eyebrow. “You can lift that?”

“Well enough,” she said, hoisting it up onto her back and immediately toppling over backwards. Arara sprawled on her back on top of the pack, her legs kicking at the air.

High pitched giggles filled the air for a moment before something muffled them. She lifted her head to see Sels laughing with the blanket pressed over his mouth. Jeron stood next to him, his face buried in his paws and his shoulders quaking.

Before Arara could wriggle out of the straps, Eraka grabbed the bag with one arm, lifting it and Arara off the ground. She slid free, landing on the grass with a thump, tail between her legs.

Eraka curled the pack higher off the ground and gestured with his other paw towards the carriage. "Where to?"

Jeron, still huffing with suppressed laughter, stumbled over and rapped on the wood. A panel swung open at the bottom, revealing a hidden compartment. A large wooden trunk took up most of the space inside. Arara's father stuffed in her bag to one side of it and the panel swung closed, melding seamlessly back into place.

"Ready?" she turned to see Sels gesturing towards the carriage with one blanket covered arm, all traces of laughter gone from his face.

She nodded and followed him to the door. Jeron met them there and helped Sels climb in. Warm air wafted out as Arara followed him inside. She turned and waved to her parents, who now stood arm-in-arm in front of the den.

"Bye, snow flower!" her mother yelled right before the door clicked shut. Arara's ears flicked back in distaste at the use of her childhood nickname in front of the Prince.

As alien as the outside appeared, she'd was afraid of what she might find inside. She steeled her nerves, turned, and gasped in wonder. Morning sunlight streamed in through the translucent roof, revealing a small egg shaped room paneled in dark colored living wood. Bright fabric covered plush benches around the edges of the room.

Sels already sat at one end, still in his blanket cocoon. The corner of the blanket shifted, freeing one of his green-skinned hands. He grinned and patted the seat next to him.

The floor felt oddly warm on the pads of her feet as she shuffled forward and took the proffered seat. Sels waited until she'd settled into place, then reached up and rapped on the roof three times.

Her view of the trees outside the window tilted this way and that as the floor moved under her. Arara yelped and gripped the fabric of the bench, glad she hadn't yet eaten today as her stomach rolled.

"There are more blankets under the seats. Help yourself." Sels snuggled back under his own blanket, looking entirely unaffected by the movement of the carriage.

After a moment, the ride smoothed out, but the trees flying by outside the window disconcerted her. They rode in silence for a moment before' Sels voice startled her.

"I'm sorry."

"What?" That was about the last thing Arara expected to hear.

Sels eyebrows pulled down and he frowned. "For not giving you a token when I had the chance. You deserved one."

That was news to her. Arara twisted and stared at him, unable to form a response. "I did?"

"Yes," Sels sighed. "I still want to give you one, but I can't do it now. I need an audience to witness the act, otherwise the Council can have you disqualified."

Arara cocked her head. "But then, why didn't you just give me one yesterday during the ceremony?"

Sels fidgeted under the blanket, and looked away. He spoke so softly Arara strained to hear him, even with her Jegeran hearing. "Sesay was watching, and I was afraid she would intervene. I had a token hidden in the money pouch. I honestly never thought you'd turn it down."

Arara winced. "I'm sorry." Grawka probably had told Sels and Sesay all sorts of lies about her. At least Sels had apparently been able to look past to the truth. Arara shifted, uncomfortable, half afraid Sels might change his mind about her. Time to change the subject.

"Are we picking up Kerka next?" she asked softly, looking away and cringing at the thought of being stuck in such tight quarters with him.

"Since he lives on the other side of the village, we'll be meeting him, along with Sesay and Recka, at the Poku station." She felt Sels shift towards her.

She sighed in relief and flopped back against the plush cushions. Another thought struck her. “He won’t be riding in your pod as well, will he?” Despite her best efforts at control her voice quavered.

Out of the corner of her eye she caught Sels frown.

“What’s wrong?” His concern penetrated her mental defenses.

She wondered why he cared, and she was tempted to drop her mental shields to find out. But he was royalty and it felt somehow wrong to dig through his private thoughts. She squirmed, uncomfortable with admitting to him how much Kerka bothered her, when she hadn’t even told her parents most of what had been going on. She could feel his eyes on her, but she refused to turn her head to meet his gaze.

The silence dragged on.

Sels shifted next to her. “There is something I’ve been wanting to ask you.”

Arara pulled her legs up underneath of her and shifted to face him.

He grinned at her. “How did you knock over Recka the first night we met? Was it the same way you hit the kwaso?”

Of course, another subject she wanted to stay away from. Her powers made her feel like a freak, almost more so than her mangled fur and tail. “I don’t want to talk about it,” she growled.

Sels eyebrows pulled down and his grin faded. “I can order you to tell me.”

Arara whimpered and pulled her knees up to her chin.

“I’ll let it drop, as long as you answer my next question.”

She bobbed her head in agreement.

“Why do you flinch whenever you bring up Kerka? Is it because of what happened to your fur?”

“That’s two questions.” She pointed out, to stall him. Of course he picked another subject she didn’t want to bring up.

“Well, answer the first one then.”

“He’s a bully. He’s been tormenting me for years. And I shouldn’t have nitpicked, because really your two questions are the same. Kerka and his pack of thugs did this to my fur.

“I try to fight him, but then it just makes it worse." She glared at Sels, daring him to say anything.

Fury filled Sels eyes. “Why hasn’t Grawka put a stop to it?”

"Grawka is Kerka's father,” Arara pulled her ears back. “He encourages it."

Sels's eyes opened wide in shock and he fell back against the plush seat. "But it’s the Clan Chief's duty to protect his Clan members!"

“I was culled, so I’m not considered a Clan member anymore.”

Sels narrowed his eyes. "Culled? That hasn’t been practiced in centuries.”

Arara shook her head in disbelief. He really was naive. "Maybe in the Empire’s interior, but out in the wilds...”

Silence filled the pod. Sels looked deep in thought. Outside the window the trees flew by in a blue-green blur. They were moving so fast, it wouldn’t be long before they reached the station.

“I understand a bit how you feel.” Sels melodic voice broke the silence, a dark green flush spread up from his neck. “My magic is broken. I can’t complete even the simplest spells. Around the court, people are polite to my face, but I’ve overheard some of what is said behind my back.” He wound one of his vines around his fingers. “I feel like no one takes me seriously because of it.”

Arara sat forward, staring at Sels. “But, what about the spell you did to distract the kwaso? I would have been done for if not for your help.”

“I don’t know. I was desperate, and terrified. I thought at most the spell would just poof away like normal, but this time...” He shook his hands free of the blanket and cupped them as if he held a ball, then spread them wide. “The poof was more like a boom.”

Arara barked happily. “Sounds like your spell worked.”

This perked Sels up a bit and he gave Arara a lopsided smile. "I guess so."

"Where did the giant bird come from? I've lived here my whole life, and I've never seen anything like it." She hadn't thought about it at the time, but the entire encounter now seemed odd and out of place in the normally familiar woods.

"I don't know. The Alpha-Guard I sent to retrieve the corpse said they couldn't find anything. No blood, no evidence of a fight."

The carriage tilted, and Arara grabbed at the seat. There were so many questions she wanted to ask. The floor rocked again, then settled to a stop.

The morning sun back lit Jeron's profile as he opened the door. "Your Highness, we've arrived at the Poku Station."

*****

Sels shivered as the cold wind cut his skin, already missing the warmth of the carriage. Jeron had offered the advice that Royalty shouldn't be seen in public wrapped in a fluffy blanket. Normally Sels would have ignored him, except that he'd been thinking over what Sesay had told him the day before, about not being mature enough for a *sedyu*-bond. She was wrong, and he wanted to prove it to her.

A squad of Alpha-Guard jumped off the carriage roof and assembled in a perimeter around him before he'd taken two steps. Another shiver wracked him as he joined Arara for the short walk to the platform.

The platform was crowded. Sels guessed that almost half the village milled around, hoping for another view of the Prince.

Arara cocked one ear back and regarded the guards for a moment. "I felt them, but couldn't see them. Where did they all ride at?"

"I asked for privacy, so they rode in the upper compartment."

They reached the steps and Arara froze, her ears flattened against her head and her nose wrinkled. Sels stopped and followed her eyes to

Sesay. She was flanked by Kerka and Recka, waiting to greet them at the top of the stairs.

"About your earlier question. It's traditional for the candidates to ride in my private pod during the journey." After Arara's revelation in the carriage he didn't want Kerka in his Poku pod. But as his candidate, there would be questions if he denied him entrance.

"Oh." Arara's tail tucked between her legs and she cringed. "I think I'll just catch the next Poku then."

Sels put a hand on her shoulder and smiled at her. "No, please stay. I'll think of something." The weight of the token he'd hidden in his sash reminded him of their connection and how much he wanted her to stay. He dropped his hand to her back and led her up the stairs.

Sesay smiled broadly as they reached the platform. "Sels, right on time. Arara, if you'll follow Recka I've arranged a space for you."

"What?" Sels composed his expression, trying to look serious and not mad. "No, she'll be riding in my pod."

Sesay stepped back, her face surprised for an instant before her expression flattened out. "Alright then." She flipped her petals over her shoulder and turned, moving through the crowd with an easy grace.

Recka was close behind her. Sels took Arara's arm and followed behind. Kerka strutted over and walked on Sels other side.

While he'd bantered with Sesay, the squad of Alpha-Guards spread out and kept out the gawkers. They trailed after Sesay, cries of 'Prince Sels's and 'Lady Sesay' sounding in their wake.

In the sea of black fur, Sels spotted a pale blue head bobbing towards them. A moment later Lilsa stepped out of the crowd in front of the lead guard. She glared at Sels with narrowed eyes over the guard's outstretched arm, her blue petals pulled tight against her head.

"Let her through." Sesay waved airily with one hand.

The guard lowered his arm, and Lilsa sashayed past him. Sels flinched and stepped back, putting Kerka and Arara between them.

With all the excitement yesterday, Sels had completely forgotten about the dance he'd promised her.

Lilsa glared at him for a moment more, then turned and linked arms with Sesay as they walked.

"Your cousin," Lilsa said. She pretended to fluff her petals up in order to give Sels a dirty look before turning back to Sesay. "Stood me up last night."

"What? No!" Sesay and Lilsa turned in unison to look over Arara's head at him for a moment.

Sels fell back further and stared at the boards under his feet as he walked, his face feeling flush with embarrassment.

"And this is after he drooled all over me yesterday morning, like a sproutling who'd never seen a pretty bloom before." Lilsa spoke in an exaggerated stage whisper, her voice carrying back to Sels even through the noise of the crowd around them.

"I know. He inherited my aunt's good looks, but none of her brains."

Sels groaned, struggling to keep his expression composed and wishing he was anywhere else but here. Then he felt a furry paw touch his arm.

"Ignore them." Arara's tail thumped into his leg as she walked next to him. "She's just upset and she's trying to get a rise out of you."

"Well, it's working."

"Why did you ask her out, Prince Sels?"

"It seemed like a good idea at the time." Visions of Lilsa, robes gaping open enticingly in front of his nose, ran through his head. Yes, it had seemed like a very good idea. He ran a hand through his vines, then fiddled with one of his flowers.

Arara yipped, amusement quivering her voice. "Looks more like she was fishing for a Royal wedding to me."

"Fishing? What do you mean?"

"Yeah, do you really think she normally goes around with her robes half undone, leaning over young men's shoulders?"

Sels stopped short, barely noticing the contortions the rear guard went through not to run into him. Arara turned around, slowly walking backwards so she could watch him. How could Arara have known that?

Sesay kept walking, seeming not have noticed Sels absence. The guard's breath was hot on his neck, and the other guards struggled to keep onlookers from walking into the stretched perimeter.

"Your Highness," she said, sounding harried, "if you could keep moving, please. We're on a tight schedule."

"Of course." He resumed walking, quickening his steps until he paced next to Arara. "How--"

A shrill howl cut through the din, cutting him off. That was the signal to board. The guards pushed a path clear to the ramp leading up to the pods while everyone waited. The pods swung from the trees above them by thick vines. Kin mages kept them from swaying in the strong winds.

As heir, Sesay boarded first, Recka and Lilsa at her side. Sesay turned and waved, eliciting a deafening howl from the crowd.

Sels boarded next, Kerka and Arara behind him. He, too, turned at the railing and waved to cheers and well wishes. Kerka pushed up next to him and leaned over the railing, his paws clasped above his head, and Sels got a mouthful of fur as Kerka pushed him back away from the edge. The villagers went wild, the noise surpassing even Sesay's cheers.

Kerka's shadow blocked out what little warmth the sun provided. The cold cut right through his silks, and Sels shivered. He reached up and tugged on Kerka's arm, ready to go to his warm and silent private pod, but Kerka continued to pose for the crowd.

Some bolder villagers pushed across the platform carrying a long, cloth wrapped bundle. They pulled away the cloth and tossed the contents up the ramp. Something gleamed bone white in the sun as it flew through the air. Kerka grabbed the end of it and raised it above his head, to the delight of the crowd. Sels backed up and turned his head, trying to figure out what the thing was.

Arara pushed around behind Kerka to join Sels. She turned to look up, following Sels gaze.

"It's a hukra horn. Probably from the one we killed yesterday."

Sels shook his head, disgusted, and walked away, leaving Kerka basking in the crowd's attention. He felt the brush of Arara's soft fur as she followed him. The green pods towered overhead, the morning sun throwing long shadows over the walkway.

Jeron lurked in the gloom ahead of them, meaning the rest of his crew had probably flanked Sels. Nice of them to be discrete about it, at least. At times like this he almost envied the easy privacy commoners enjoyed.

The cheering faded away behind them as Sels led Arara down the living wood walkways, which ran midway along the outer edges of each pod. Arara pestered him with questions the entire walk, as if she'd never ridden a pod before. At one point she hung off the side of the railing to look down to the ground beneath the swinging pod. Sels grabbed her tail, terrified that she was going to fall.

She pointed to the underside of the pod. "What are those?"

"Those link the pods together. See how the vines from above wrap around through those? Then the mages move the vines to pull the linked pods along. Now get down before you fall." Sels tugged her tail until she slipped back down onto the platform.

Jeron waited in plain sight at the door of Sels's pod, grinning as they approached.

"I see you shook off Kerka." His tongue lolled as his grin widened.

"For the moment." Sels hand raised and twisted through his vines as he pondered.

Jeron nodded to the door. "It's clean, go on in."

Arara tugged her paw out of his hand and ducked through the vines before he could move. He followed after her and found her stopped right inside the entrance.

"All this space just for you? You could fit my whole den in one corner." She spread her arms as if trying to grab the whole room. "And it's so extravagant."

Sels looked around his private chambers, trying to see it as she did. Compared to his rooms at the palace, he'd thought the travel quarters were rather plain and cramped.

Soft grass coated the floor, springy and soothing to the feet. A grouping of plush chairs sat to the left of the entrance. Directly across from those was a low table, stacked with games and books. The back wall of the pod contained Sels's sleeping soil and his wardrobe, currently hidden from view behind a curtain of interlaced vines. Elaborate carvings covered the living wood walls, each side of the pod with a different theme. Higher up, the walls curved together and turned translucent, letting in the natural sunlight while keeping out the rain.

Four small oblong plants were spaced around the interior, regulating the temperature to a perfect ninety degrees. Still a little cool for his tastes, but more palatable to the Jegera candidates that should have shared the space with him, if he'd had any before now. Near the sleeping soil at the back a ramp curved down into darkness. It led to the Jegera dens where his candidates, and Arara, would stay during the journey.

While he looked around, Arara ran around the room, stopping at the low table. She moved everything off and dumped open one of the wooden boxes. Game pieces scattered across the table, some of them sliding off into the grass.

Sels walked over and sat on one of the pillows next to her. Arara scrambled around on all fours, scooping pieces back into the box, her tail wagging furiously. His mouth curled up at the corners as he watched her. She was so funny. And she would be leaving in just a few short hours. When would he find a chance to give it to her? If only he had the full week trip to Sebaine...

He cleared his throat. "Arara, what are your plans once you reach North Wind?"

She cocked her head, arranging pieces across the table. "I'm going to audition for a band."

His heart fell. That sounded time sensitive. "Oh, that sounds like quite an opportunity. What band? When is the audition?" He tried to keep his voice upbeat.

"Um, well," her ears pulled back and she lowered head, "I don't know yet."

His ears perked out and he straightened. "In that case, would you--"

The rattle of vines at the door interrupted him. He turned his head to see who would dare enter his private pod unannounced. As if on cue, Sesay came pushing through the doorway. She stopped after only a few steps into the room. Recka and Kerka followed through the vines after her and took up positions at her side.

"Sesay!" He squeaked and jumped to his feet.

"Sels, you left Kerka behind." She crossed her arms and glared at him.

He shot a look down at Arara, but she had turned her back to them and had her head down. Her ears were forward and she looked relaxed until he noticed her paws were tightly clutching the edge of the game box. He looked back up at Sesay's stern expression and Recka's look of boredom. Then he turned his attention to Kerka, who was grinning, his attention fixed on Arara.

Sels swallowed hard. "No, I didn't forget. I don't want him here." His voice quavered, but he forced his eyes to lock with Sesay's.

Kerka's mouth closed with a snap and his ears flattened against his skull.

“Sels, he is your candidate.” Sesay's voice rose an octave.

He balled his fists behind his back to keep his hands from trembling. “No, he is *your* candidate. Not mine.”

Her mouth opened and closed a few times but nothing came out. Next to her, Recka snarled silently.

"What?" Kerka barked out, the sound echoed through the silent pod.

Ah, of course, he didn't know. He turned slightly to address Kerka directly. "I wanted to pick Arara. Sesay manipulated me into picking you instead, but I realize now I made a mistake." He raised a trembling hand and pointed to the door. "Now, all of you get out."

Kerka's jaw fell open and he took a step back.

"Where will Kerka go?" Sesay had found her voice again.

"I don't care. That's your problem. I don't want to see him again until we reach Sebaine." He crossed his arms and glared at his cousin, hoping she wouldn't notice the way he trembled.

"Fine, Kerka, you can travel in my pod." Sesay pointed at Sels and narrowed her eyes. "I'll be talking to you later."

She turned and marched out, followed closely by Recka. Kerka stood gaping at him until Recka came back and dragged him out. Sels fell back into the pillow with a thump, still shaking.

*****

Arara remained on edge until Kerka's mind signature was well and truly gone. She wondered why her paws ached for a moment before realizing her claws were gouging furrows into a wooden box. The box fell to the table with a thud as she blew out the breath she hadn't realized she'd been holding.

Kerka, gone from her life for good. North Wind, next stop. This day just kept getting better.

"Thank you." Arara's tongue lolled out in a huge grin.

Sels still sat where he'd fallen, slumped over with his back to her. His face, when he pulled himself around, looked stricken. "Of course." He whispered.

<Poor Arara. I never should have let Sesay bully me into choosing Kerka. But she gave up way too easily. What is she planning?>

Without meaning to she'd picked up his mind-talk again. She checked her shields, and they were all tight as she could make them. It was almost as if he was gefiring his thoughts to her, except that was impossible. She cocked one ear back and regarded Sels. He sat staring at the table. It looked like he was deep in thought.

"Why did she force you to pick Kerka?" Arara blurted out.

Sels's head jerked up, as if he'd forgotten she was there. "I'm sorry you had to see that." He shook his head, his mouth pulling down in a frown.

Arara cocked one ear back and scratched at the wooden table with one claw, waiting.

With a groan, Sels head hit the table with a light thump. He reached up and pushed game pieces away from his head before wrapping his head in his arms. "My mother sent Sesay along with me as an adviser." His voice came out muffled. "Sesay wants to impress my mother and thinks that if I return with no candidates, it will reflect badly on her." Sels hands curled into fists. "After next week I'll be an adult and old enough to be named heir. Sesay doesn't want that to happen, so she needs to stay in my mother's good graces."

Arara wrinkled her nose in disgust. "But why Kerka? Why not Yegra, or Jenra, or well, anyone else?" Or her.

"Like you?" Sels lifted his head and propped his fists under his chin.

Arara bared her teeth. "That's not what I meant."

Sels shoulders lifted and fell. "I think, Sesay is obsessed with power and in her mind size is everything. You've seen Recka."

Of course she had, he was a bit hard to miss, towering over everyone like a menacing shadow. Arara thought hard, crossing her arms, furrowing her brow and lowering her head. Politics wasn't her arena, but something Sels said bothered her. "So, then, if she wants to stay heir, wouldn't she be trying to undermine you, not help you pick a good candidate?"

Moisture filmed Sels's eyes for a moment, and he blinked rapidly to clear them. "That's the beauty of it. She doesn't need to. I told you my magic doesn't work right. No matter who she picks, I won't be able to form a *sedyu*-bond with them since I can't sense Potential."

Oh, that was it then. He still just wanted to reward her for helping him. Her lower jaw trembled, her ears flattened and she forced down a whine.

He sat up straight, his expression horrified. "I'm sorry Arara. I misspoke. I can sense your Potential, but no one else's."

Arara cocked her head to the side and raised one ear. "Just me? No one else?"

Sels nodded. "Sesay says Kerka has lots of Potential, but I feel nothing from him."

She ruminated on it for a moment. "Maybe it's not because your magic doesn't work. Maybe you just don't like plumberries."

"Huh?"

"Most Jegera love plumberries, but I can't stand them. Maybe your magic doesn't like the plumberry-Potentials that everyone else's magic loves." She wagged her tail and opened her mouth wide in a big grin.

"That's an interesting way of putting it." He grinned back at her. "I never thought of it like that."

The grass shivered. Sels and Arara both paused. A moment later the pod lurched and swayed. Game pieces toppled and rolled off the table onto the grass. Arara grabbed the table with a yelp, feeling like the pillow she sat on would slide away. Sels somehow managed to stay completely still, although his expression turned thoughtful. The pod continued to sway gently as it moved, making Arara slightly sick to her stomach.

Arara held up her paw, and a familiar pressure in her mind spoke of Jeron's approach. A moment later he pushed through the vines. Sels heard the noise and turned.

"Your Highness," Jeron bared his neck to Sels. "May I do anything for you?"

Sels glared at Jeron, mouth turning down into a frown. He looked furious. "Why did you not warn me that Sesay was on her way in?"

"Sorry, Highness, I was on an errand." His ears pulled back and his tail tucked under. He looked very contrite to Arara, but Sels's glower deepened.

"Who guarded my pod in your absence?"

"My team." He ducked his head. "I'll discipline them for that oversight."

"Do not leave again without my permission. You left your team without an alpha, leaving me vulnerable." Sels turned his back to Jeron and pointed to the empty pillow-seat next to Arara. "Sit."

"Sire, my duties," Jeron began, but Sels waved his hand, cutting him off.

Sels pointed at the pillow again without looking at Jeron. "I said sit. You asked, this is my order. This game requires three."

"Kerka..."

"Is not welcome in my pod." He turned and craned his neck back to look Jeron in the eyes. "I will not repeat myself again."

Jeron let out a long sigh and padded across the grass. He settled in next to Arara and picked up the fang and bone turn markers.

Sels turned to Arara. “As I was about to ask before Sesay interrupted us, would you be willing to accompany me to Sebaine, as my guest?”

Arara looked surprised at first, but then she smiled. “Of course. Will I get to compete at the Trials, then?”

“That’s my plan.” Or, it would be as soon as he figured out how to get Arara a token.

CHAPTER EIGHT

ARARA THE HERO

For the first time in a long while, Sels just enjoyed himself. Now that he had an entire week to figure out how to give Arara a token, he could relax. Sels laughed in delight as he completed a complicated move that stole Jeron's best piece. He'd just finished up his turn when Arara's ears pricked up.

"Jeron, did you send away your team?"

"Of course not," He huffed. "After what happened during the hunt, I would never leave his Highness undefended."

“Jeron’s the best.” Sels smirked at Arara's puzzled expression. “The Alpha-Clan’s Master of Lessons, Darach, personally assigned him to guard me. If he’d been with me instead of Recka, the whole affair would have been avoided.”

"Well, Jeron might be good, but his team is gone.”

"What?" Jeron's left ear twitched back for a moment and his eyes widened. "They aren't responding to any of my gefir."

Jeron jumped to his feet and bolted to the door, his claws sending tufts of grass flying up behind him. Sels frowned at the divots now marring his perfect carpet-grass.

At the door, Jeron whirled. “Prince Sels, please stay here until I get back.” He ducked out the door before Sels could respond.

Sels turned to Arara, his eyes wide. “He left me.”

Arara’s ears perked forward. “Don’t worry. I’m sure it’s nothing.”

A flash of white teeth betrayed her nervousness and Sels shifted, glad it was her here with him instead of Kerka. "Then where did all the guards go? And how did you know they were gone?"

Arara wagged her tail and sat up straighter. "I can feel the presence of nearby Kin and Jegera. At least, when I pay attention." She looked at the game board and her ears drooped. "I don't know how long they were gone before I noticed."

"I'm just glad you did."

Jeron still hadn't returned, and Sels grew more concerned. He reached around the table and grasped Arara's paw, smiling at the feeling of safety and serenity he felt when he did so.

They heard a rough scraping noise from above that marred the tranquil silence in the pod. Sels and Arara both looked up, and the translucent wood at the apex of the dome shattered, showering them both with slivers of wood. Sels squeezed his eyes closed, ducking and covering his head with his hands.

Arara barked something that sounded like his name, but Sels couldn't hear her over the sudden roar of sound. Wind howled through the opening, whipping Sels's vines and robes around. Something thumped into the grass next to him, and rough voices shouted, adding to the din. Rough hands grabbed his shoulders and pulled him to his feet.

Sharp claws dug into his lower arms and Sels screamed. His hands were wrenched down and behind his back. Thick leather wound around his wrists, tying them behind his back.

"Target secure." The Jegera holding him growled above his head.

An arm wrapped around his neck, the rough fur scrapping his skin. The Jegera dragged him backwards, choking him. His sandals slid when he tried to dig his heels in, unable to find purchase on the soft grass. The harsh restraints dug into his wrists.

"Prince Sels!" Jeron's familiar voice sounded from somewhere in front of him.

Sels tried to reply but he couldn't get enough air to do more than let out a strangled gasp. The pressure let up and Sels coughed, panting.

Three Jegera stood with their backs to Sels. In the middle of the room, Sels spotted Arara and Jeron standing between the intruders and the door. All five Jegera crouched in combat stances, balanced on the tips of their toes, ready to spring in an instant.

Sels cried out in alarm, and the arm holding his neck tightened, silencing him. He struggled, but the pressure didn't let up, and spots danced before his eyes as he struggled for breath. The rough material rasped against his fragile skin. Wetness slicked his hands, still bound behind his back. Dimly he registered the pain, but terror kept him struggling.

<I'm coming, Sels!> A voice echoed in his head, shocking him so much he stopped fighting against his captor. He must be hallucinating from lack of carbon dioxide. Except that something about the voice sounded familiar and safe.

<Go limp and pretend to pass out, so they'll focus on Jeron and me.>

His memory clicked, and he recognized the voice as Arara's. He collapsed back against the villain's chest and fluttered his eyes shut. The howls and growls of fighting Jegera almost jarred his eyes open, but he resolutely kept them closed. A moment later the arm pulled away from his throat, Sels stayed limp and fell into the grass, landing painfully on his side.

Pollen puffed around his head. Sels blushed when he realized he'd crushed several of the blooms at the end of his vines with his fall. At least there weren't any female Kin around to yell at him over his faux pas.

A paw brushed his face as his captor stepped over him. Sels waited a few heartbeats before slitting his eyes open. His vantage point made it hard to make sense of things. He lay on his side near the sleeping soil at the back of the pod. The low-table he'd been sitting at was some distance in front of him to his left.

The intruders stood in the grass a few tails in front of him. The four each wore authentic looking Alpha-Guard uniforms, perhaps stolen from Jeron's missing team. Except the uniforms looked tailor fitted, not saggy or tight like he would have expected.

A light flashed in his eyes, and Sels squinted up. Each of the kidnappers wore unfamiliar silver circlets around their heads, not part of the standard guard uniform.

Forbidden metal! Perhaps these kept Arara from feeling their presence like she had with the missing guards.

The kidnappers split up, circling around either side of Jeron and Arara, obviously trying to flank them. Sels twisted his arms, wanting to signal their intentions to Arara. The leather dug painfully into his wrists. His teeth ground together, muffling his cry of pain.

A yip drew his attention back to the middle of the room. Arara rubbed her wrists, a look of puzzlement on her face. One of the intruders, taking advantage of Arara's distraction, picked up a small table and hurled it at Arara's side. The table seemed to change direction mid-air, veering away from Arara at an angle.

Sels couldn't see the intruders faces to read their expressions. He did note that they all paused, their ears and tails twitching. The intruder on Sels's left-side crouched on the abandoned game table, looking out of place among the brightly colored game pieces. One of his ears was missing, only a small torn stump left in its place.

Another intruder, this one a brindle color black and brown, stood at the far right of Sels's sight, crouched low behind one of the heating pods. A third, a female, paced warily towards Jeron, obviously seeing him as more of a threat. The last one, the leader of the gang by Sels's estimation, still stood close to Sels.

No-ear leapt off the game table, aiming at Jeron in front of him. The force of the jump split the table with a crack, spilling game pieces and cards across the grass. Jeron met the left intruder head-on in a flurry of teeth and claws.

The brindle jumped at Arara at almost the same time. The female charged forward, moving in to help the left Jegera, who was being overpowered by Jeron. Sels marveled at how in sync the three intruders moved. It was almost like watching a perfectly choreographed Kin dance, only much more deadly. Watching the hunts Sels had thought the Jerlings seemed to move as a unit, but this team put the youngsters to shame. The left intruder baited Jeron into moving just so, and two Jegera's hind legs pounded in rhythm as they charged him from behind.

Arara howled, throwing her arms out wide. The female intruder fell backwards as if she'd hit an invisible wall. She landed on her back with a gasp and curled onto her side, struggling to breathe. The brindle lifted off his feet, flying backwards to crash into the heating pod. The pod deflated underneath his weight, sending up a billow of steam as it was crushed flat. He howled in agony and jumped up. The peculiar smell of burned flesh and hair made Sels wrinkle his nose.

In front of Sels the leader dropped to all fours. He crab-walked off to the right, putting one of the large plush chairs between him and Arara. Sels used the opportunity to roll onto his stomach. Sensation rushed back into the arm he'd been laying on. A few quick tugs, and his hands slid free of the leather bonds, helped by the slippery sap still oozing from his bleeding wrists. Then he rolled back into place, keeping his now free hands behind his back.

The wind roared down from the top of the broken pod, almost drowning out the sound of Jeron still fighting with no-ear. Sels prayed to the Sun Gods for Jeron's safety. He'd noticed all the intruders looked like powerful warriors. Scars marred their fur and sleek muscles showed as they'd run. Jeron was well trained but out of practice, since his duties mainly consisted of following Sels around all day.

Sels craned his neck, trying to see Jeron. He spotted Arara bounding on four legs towards him. She leapt the fallen warrior still struggling to breathe, landing with a thud in the grass only a tail away from Sels. A blur of black and silver struck her from the side, flipping her over on her back and pinning her arms to the ground. The leader snapped his jaws down, aiming for Arara's throat. Arara snarled and lunged up as much as she could, causing the leader to flinch back.

Enough pretending. Arara needed his help. Sels pushed himself to his feet and lunged towards the black Jegera form holding Arara.

"Get off of her!" Sels screamed, punching the leader in the nose as hard as he could, then crouched protectively over her head.

The leader just huffed, not even reacting to the blow. "Pathetic."

He lowered his head and butted Sels in the chest with the top of his skull while keeping Arara pinned beneath him. Sels stumbled back. Arms flailing, he grabbed the metal circlet around the leader's head to try to remain upright. However, just as he snagged it with his fingers he tripped over Arara's face.

He heard Arara whimper and felt himself kick her in the muzzle. One of his sandals flew off, and he landed on his butt behind Arara's head. The circlet flipped off the leader's head to land in Sels lap. Sels shuddered and pushed the evil thing off of him with one finger.

The leader screamed and lifted one paw to claw at his head between his ears. Arara squirmed under his legs and laughed.

Sels stared, unable to react. Arara slashed at his muzzle with her now free paw, leaving four red gashes. The black Jegera screamed again, arching his back. Suddenly his whole body flipped towards Sels. Sels ducked as the leader flew, upside down, over his head, to hit the wall of the pod behind the sleeping soil with a loud thud.

Sels winced and turned his head away. Arara lay unmoving in front of him.

"Arara?" He crawled forward and leaned over her, shaking her shoulder.

Her eyes opened with a snap and she sat up so suddenly she knocked Sels back to his heels.

<*Sels, is there another exit out of here?*> the voice, Arara's voice, sounded in his head again.

"There is," Sels pointed to the ramp behind and to their right. "But, we already won."

<*No, we didn't.*>

Sels followed Arara's gaze to see Jeron lying trussed up in the middle of the room. The three warriors paced slowly towards them, the female in the lead. She looked in the best condition. The two males looked badly hurt. No-ear had burns all down his back. Blood dripped from the brindle's side, running down his fur and onto the floor.

Even without their leader and hurt as they were, Sels didn't think Arara could beat them. He hung his head, wishing he wasn't so useless.

His cousin would have been able to cast a spell to fly the two of them up and out of the ceiling. Or a spell to moving through the living wood walls, out of the pod to safety. No, actually, wait. With that metal nearby, blocking all magic, she would have been as useless as him. The thought made Sels feel at least a little better.

<*Can you use your magic to make a 'boom,' like you did with the bird?*> Arara said in his head.

Sels shook his head. "No, it's hopeless."

<*Please, try! I know you can do it.*> Arara believed in him, he could feel it in her words.

The three intruders were getting bolder now, moving into a slow trot.

Well, he supposed it couldn't hurt. Maybe the intruders would be fooled by him chanting a spell, slow down a little. "I'll try."

Sels held up his hands and concentrated, mouthing the first words of a light spell. A red pin-prick of light materialized in front of Sels's face before he'd even completed the first word of the spell. The prick spun, growing in size. Magic sang through his blood as he chanted,

He'd never felt the elemental energies this easily before. He almost felt like the words held him back. He stopped chanting and just moved his hands into the ritual positions. Except, those felt subtly wrong. He allowed instinct to guide him, changing the hand movements. The red ball of light grew bigger, and now pulsed with Sels's heart-beat. Magic's song grew louder, and Sels closed his eyes, savoring the feeling.

"Sels, now!"

Arara's voice shattered the song in his head. Sels staggered back and gasped. It felt like he'd been holding his breath. The glowing ball of light spun forward and hit the female Jegera square in the chest. She screamed, high and tight. The air in the room all seemed to rush toward her before exploding out in a wave of flames.

Sels could only stare as a wave of fire raced towards them. He raised his hands and cried out, turning his head away. Arara hit his chest, knocking him onto his back. Tongues of flame licked the air above them for a moment before vanishing. The walls of the pod were scorched but intact thanks to the magic that infused the wood.

Sels coughed, acrid smoke burned his eyes and lungs. Arara already stood at his feet, growling at the doorway. His stomach ached where she'd tackled him, but his scorched forehead and eyebrows told him she'd saved him from worse. Almost fried by his own misfired spell. Yet, he still felt pride that it had worked at all.

*****

Arara lay on top of Sels, smoke stinging her nose. On top of that, her head pounded intermittently, but not as bad as it should have considering how much she'd used her powers. She pushed off of Sels and took a look around at the remains of the pod. Smoke wafted through the space, obscuring the door, although the wind still whipping through the hole in the roof was quickly clearing the air.

Arara could feel more Jegera moving towards the door.

<*They failed. We need to get Sels out of there.*> One of the Jegera gefired to the other.

<What about the Prince's guest?>

<I'll take care of her.>

Smoke drifted through the air, and charred grass crunched under Arara's paws. The smoke clogged her nostrils. She helped Sels stand. His legs shook under his robes, but he managed to stay on his feet.

"I'm going to help Jeron." His voice cracked. Sels headed to where Jeron still lay bound in vines, passed out. He walked in a wide circle around the three dead Jegera attackers. He stopped for a moment, putting his hand over his mouth and bending over. Arara thought for a moment he was going to throw up, but he impressed Arara by straightening up and continuing on.

With Sels safely away from the door, Arara dashed across the pod. The grass burned the pads of her feet. Two Jegera pushed through the slightly burned door vines into the room. They wore the black and silver of the Alpha-Guards, but Arara had overhead their discussion.

"Thank the light you're here--" Sels called from behind her.

Arara growled, using her mind to force push the two fake guards. They tumbled backwards out the doorway with a satisfying wail. Their presence fell away quickly. Arara realized she'd pushed them clear off the walkway and entirely off the Poku. She wagged her tail with delight.

"No!" Sels screamed behind her.

Arara cocked her head. The intruders were gone. Satisfied no else was around, she went over to Sels. He lay over Jeron, his face in his hands. Sels looked up at her approach, his eyes full of tears and his face covered in sap from his hands and wrists.

Arara wrapped him in a hug. "Sels, you're safe. I got rid of them."

"Got rid of them? You did that?"

"Yes." Arara let go of him and sawed at the vines holding Jeron with her claws.

"You weren't anywhere close to the door."

"I can push things with my mind." Arara kept her gaze on the vines. She'd never told anyone her secret before.

"Well, those two you shoved out of the door? They were Epoka and Keora! Real Alpha-Guards!" He shoved her away and swiped at his face with his hands.

Arara sat back on her heels, her ears drooping. "I didn't know that. I heard them gefiring about detaining me and how best to get you out of the room, and I thought they were with the bad guys." She hung her head and wrung her front paws together. "I can't sense them anymore, I think they fell off the Poku."

Sels pulled himself up straight and regarded Arara. "You, you talked in my head earlier. And that's how you knew about Lilsa earlier on the platform. You can somehow hear my thoughts."

Sels raised his hand and started ticking off fingers. "You killed a legendary kwaso," one finger down. "And the first day we met, you knocked over a fully trained *sedyu*-bonded like he was a puppy." A second finger. "Then Lilsa and talking in my head." A third finger down. Sels narrowed his eyes. "I'd like to know exactly what it is that you can do. What else aren't you telling me?"

Arara looked down at the grass and then away. "Not just thoughts, I can pick up memories and emotions as well, if I'm not careful. I wasn't trying to eavesdrop, but I don't really have control of it."

Next to them, Jeron woke up with a muffled bark and Arara went back to sawing at the vines engulfing him.

She heard Sels sigh. "I wish you'd confided in me earlier," he said softly.

Arara winced. She really hadn't totally trusted Sels. She opened her mouth to apologize when an Alpha-Guard burst through the remnants of the door vines in a spray of plant matter. Another Jegera followed close behind him. Sels jumped to his feet.

"Your Highness! Jeron! We're so sorry! I don't know what happened! I blacked out, and when I woke up, I, all of us were in the guards' quarters!"

The two guards rushed across the pod towards them.

"Prince Sels, you're hurt." The guard's nose widened as he reached them and leaned down to sniff at Sels face.

"It's nothing. Just my hands." He stepped to the side and waved down at Jeron with his free hand. "Jeron's trapped by these things, but they just get tighter when I try to get them off."

The second Alpha-Guard brushed past them and started sawing at the vines with his claws where Arara had left off. "Choke vine. The more you struggle the tighter it gets. Cutting's the only way to get it off."

Arara leaned down over the guard's shoulder as he worked, fascinated. The vines shifted and moved, trying to escape.

"Prince Sels, let's get you somewhere safe."

More Alpha-Guards arrived. Arara recognized one of Jeron's guards standing at the doorway directing each new arrival. They bustled about, placing the leader in a muzzle and shackles. He'd been knocked out by Arara's throw, and since he'd been on the ground he'd survived the flames.

As Sels tugged Arara along with him, her paw clung tightly to his hand. The feel of it comforted her. She allowed herself to relax. No one would hurt him now, not with so many real Alpha-Guards around.

Suddenly, Sels's hand pulled away from hers. He turned to face her, putting one hand into his sleeve.

"I want you to have this. You deserve it." Sels pulled his hand out, and presented it to her, palm up. Something in his palm glinted in the unfiltered sunlight.

All activity in the room stopped. Conversation hushed as all eyes turned in their direction. The only sound was the roar of the wind howling through the hole above them.

Arara reached out and picked it up. A cheer rose up from the crowd, Sels recognized Jeron's hoarse voice. More followed until the walls seemed to shake. Sels smiled hesitantly down at her. Arara looked at the token in her hand in amazement.

"Arrest her!" Recka stood in the doorway. His growl carried over the din.

A hush fell, and the guards looked at each other in confusion. Jegera fell back, clearing a path between him and Recka.

Sels clenched his hands and spun to face Recka. "What? Why?

Jeron lurched into his path, arms held wide. "You'll do no such thing without the order of your Prince."

"The white one." Keora entered the doorway with two guards. Blood matted her fur, and her lower jaw trembled as she lifted her paw to point accusingly at Arara. "She's the one that killed Epoka. She pushed us both off the side of the pod. I managed to grab the railing, but Epoka...he's gone."

"What?" Jeron whispered, staggering back and turning to Sels. "Is that true?"

Sels looked down at Arara. Arara stared up at him, whimpering. That poor girl was hurt because of her. Sels looked away from Arara, then down at the floor, tears pooling in his eyes.

"I didn't mean to." Arara whimpered, her ears pulling back flat to her head. She, pressed up against Sels and squeezed his hand. "I was trying to protect Sels."

Arara didn't struggle as they clipped ironwood shackles onto her aching wrists. They slipped a leather muzzle over her face. Both were too large to fit her properly. The shackles kept sliding down over her paws, and the muzzle hung off the end of her nose until they punched a new hole through the leather strap to cinch it tighter.

"Hey, let her go! That's an order!" Sels yelled.

"Yes, Prince Sels," One of the guards said, dropping Arara's arm and stepping back with a snap of his tail.

"Princess Sesay ordered the arrest. As heir, she outranks you. Take it up with her." Recka growled, and turned to the guards who had dropped Arara. "Take her away."

Another guard stepped up and snapped the muzzle shut. Arara whimpered as the guards dragged her away. She craned her head around and gave Sels a wide eyed look, pleading with him to help her as the guards pulled her out the door.

CHAPTER NINE

HOMECOMING

Sels sat cross-legged on a plush pillow, glowering at the platter of food in front of him. He was alone in one of the first-class pod's cabins. The paying passengers had been moved elsewhere until Sels's pod was repaired and cleaned.

Earlier, a healer dressed in holy emerald robes had tended to his wounds with her magic despite his protests that he wasn't feeling any pain. When she was done she'd advised his guards that he needed food and rest, to replenish the resources his body had used during the healing. The spell left Sels feeling drained and tired, but his stomach roiled, and the thought of eating made him gag.

He worried about Arara and couldn't help but feel her situation was partially his fault. He wondered where she was and hoped she was being well taken care of. Keora and Gouk guarded his cabin, and they refused to answer any of his questions and gently rebuffed his every attempt to leave.

Mentally, he reviewed the fight. He saw Epoka fly back into Keora, saw both of them fall out of the doorway.

The sound of Jegera voices drifted in from the doorway and he lift his head. They sounded familiar, but he couldn't immediately place it. The vines fell back to reveal black fur and a sneer. Sels groaned internally when he recognized Kerka, doing his best to plaster a smile on his face as he stood up to greet him.

Kerka's tongue lolled out of his mouth as Sels approached him. "Your Majesty." He bared his neck slightly before continuing. "I'm excited about becoming your *sedyu*-bonded."

Sels raised a brow, folded his arms, and regarded Kerka with a flat stare. "You seem very certain of yourself."

Kerka wagged his tail and looked very self-satisfied. "Well, yeah, I mean, I heard you gave Arara a token and then she immediately got disqualified. And you didn't choose any others before you go to Last Home."

"Arara is still on board," he said through gritted teeth.

Kerka bark-laughed. "Sure, she is. I saw her getting thrown off in chains when we stopped at North Wind."

Sels frowned, wondering if perhaps Kerka might be right. Except, even Sesay wouldn't dare to mess with one of his chosen candidates.

"Wow, this is plush." Kerka gazed over Sels head at the cabin.

A quick step to the side around Sels, then Kerka wandered around the room, rubbing his paws over the walls.

"Hey!" Sels followed, his fists clenched. "I didn't invite you in."

Kerka picked up a game box from the shelf at the back of the room and flipped it open. "This looks fun. We're playing this first."

Sels grabbed it out of Kerka's hand and slammed it down. Pieces bounced out with a clatter. "No, we are doing nothing. I..."

<Sels, where are you? I need help.>

Sels jumped, knocking the box off the shelf. Arara's voice echoed in his head.

<Sesay had me confined. Are you well? Do you know why Keora says you killed Epoka? Are you being disqualified from the Trials?> He only hoped she could hear him.

<I'm with Sesay and Recka right now, I think in the guard's pod. They mentioned taking me to the eld-->

Sels staggered and almost fell when her mind-voice cut out. How did Jegera manage to gefir while doing other things? He opened his eyes to see Kerka's paw waving in his face.

"Sels? Sels?" Kerka bent over, showing his worry.

"Stop that." Sels slapped Kerka's paw away, certain Kerka's only real concern was with his future position as *sedyu*-bonded.

Kerka stepped back and held up his paws defensively. "Alright. Fine."

"I told you she's still on board." Smug satisfaction fueled the smirk he threw at Kerka.

"Huh?" One of Kerka's ears fell back in puzzlement.

Oh, that was right - some gefir could only be heard by the intended recipient. "Um, nothing." Sels sighed, then had a thought. While he could only hear Arara's gefir, Kerka could hear anyone's. "You can stay for now. But on one condition. You have to tell me anything you happen to overhear - gefir or conversations."

Kerka wagged his tail. "Sure, I can do that."

"But we aren't playing that." Sels swept the game box off the shelf, scattering pieces everywhere.

Sels chose a different game, one he hadn't been playing with Arara and Jeron. The one he choose was a Kin game, one he was sure would bore Kerka to tears. Unfortunately, this plan backfired. Out of the twenty rounds they'd played so far, Kerka had won nineteen of them. Sels was fairly sure he was cheating but hadn't been able to catch him in the act yet.

His turn done, Sels discarded. "Your move."

Kerka wagged his tail and, for his turn, snatched up Sels's discard. "Hah, I win." He yipped and threw his collection of cards on the table, revealing a full Winter Pack.

Sels looked at the cards in disbelief. How had Kerka gotten them all so fast?

"Oh, and I just overheard the guards-," Kerka said, offhand, as he shuffled the deck together. "Sesay is on her way to see you."

After three claw-marks spent with Kerka, Sels actually looked forward to her visit. He stood, gesturing that Kerka should do the same.

“Put those away, then stand one step behind and to the left of me.”

Recka pushed through the vines right after they'd gotten into position, Sesay following behind. Her face lit up when she saw Sels.

“I'm glad to see you spending quality time with Kerka.” Sesay said.

Sels scowled and crossed his arms. “What's happening with Arara?”

“After speaking extensively with Jeron, I'm impressed.” Her mouth twisted. “Arara's abilities are amazing. We talked to her and Keora. She was trying to protect you--”

“Great!” Sels cheered at the thought of kicking Kerka out and spending more time with Arara.

“The charge of murder will most likely be waived. However,” Sesay continued like she hadn't heard him, “after what happened to Epoka she'll be confined for the rest of the journey.”

Sels eyes went wide. "But, that's five days!"

"Yes, it is.”

“Can she still, um, I mean the Trials and my token. Is she still a candidate?” Sels reached for his vines, twisted them nervously between his fingers.

“With the circumstances the way they are, I don't know.” Sesay must have seen Sels expression fall, because she took pity on him. “She will be taken to see the Elders when we reach Sebaine. They will determine if she can still participate.”

“Oh.” Sels twisted his vines painfully tight around his fingers.

“You seem to be enjoying Kerka's company. He can stay here for the rest of the journey." She turned in a swirl of pink petals and robes.

Sels head shot up. “What?”

He tried to follow her but the unfamiliar Jegera grabbed him and pushed him back into the pod. On his fifth try, Kerka intervened.

"Sels, come on. Sit down." He steered Sels towards the chairs at the side of the room. "Hey, what was your sister talking about?"

"She is my cousin, not my sister.”

“Whatever.”

“Which part?" He kept his gaze on the doorway as they took turns, hoping the guards would all suddenly take a break at the same time.

"About the Elders?" He leaned forward in his chair. "We learned about them in school, but," he snorted, “the Alpha-Clan chief always has the final say.”

Sels shook his head. “You must not have paid attention. Most of the time that is true, but if the Elders speak even the Alpha-Clan chief listens.”

*****

Arara had been locked in this den for what felt like an eternity, although she knew the journey had only taken five days. She could feel the Poku slowing down by the time Gouk showed up. Maybe she'd get this annoying muzzle off, too. It was very disconcerting not to be able to talk to people.

Gouk didn't say anything as he unlocked and removed the collar, the shackles, and the muzzle. Arara massaged her sore wrists. Gouk grabbed her arm and pulled her to the upper level, which was filled to the brim with young Jegera.

"What’s going on?" Arara twisted against Gouk's arm, trying to get free.

"These are the Jegera who accepted invitations to join the Alpha-Guard." He gripped her arm tightly and led her around to the front of the crowd. He threw a gefir to her privately.

<Stop twisting about. You are still under arrest.>

Arara spotted Kerka towering over the milling crowd and shrank back against Gouk.

A gray furred paw waved from the group, and Yegra's mind-voice sounded in her head. *<Arara! I'm surprised to see you here! I thought you were headed to North Wind.>*

<No, Sels gave me a token...>

<*Really? You don't sound too happy about it.*> Yegra's mindvoice felt hesitant. <*Good luck against Kerka. He fights dirty, so be careful.*>

<*Oh, I know, although I doubt I'll even get to compete.*> Arara shifted, trying to see Yegra in the milling crowd, but Gouk held her fast. <*Do you know what's going on?*>

<*We're forming the procession to make way to the amphitheater where Sels will introduce his candidates and the new Alpha-Guard.*>

Yegra materialized out of the crowd in front of her, her expression pensive. <*What's wrong? Getting a token is a huge deal, but you sound upset.*>

<*I, something bad happened...*> Arara hung her head, her tailing curling between her legs. <*I don't really want to talk about it.*>

Yegra cocked her head, but before she could say anything someone yelled "...observe the Trials. Now, line up!"

The room went nuts. Everyone raced towards the door of the pod in an attempt to be first in line. Chunks of fur flew through the air and Kerka rolled by, grappling with two other Jegera.

Arara backed up, intending to take the last place in line but Gouk still had her arm pinned in his paw. "Um, Gouk, you still have my arm. I can't line up."

He grinned down at her. "That's because you aren't lining up. You get the special transport. We can't have you getting hurt on the way there."

She narrowed her eyes at him and loosened her mental shields. Nothing. It was like he wasn't even there, just like the kidnappers in Sels pod.

"Heh, can't hear me, can you? Sesay gave me a little toy."

Of course. She tucked her tail under and widened her eyes as she gazed up at him with her paws tucked under her chin. "Can Yegra ride with me?"

Gouk glared down at her. "No," he growled and dug his claws deeper into Arara's arm.

She wondered how the other girls did it. They seemed to always be able to get the boys to do whatever they wanted.

Gouk dragged Arara out of the way, and another group of fighting Jegera flew through the space they'd just been in.

After a bit, the losers had limped to the back of the group, and it was down to just the few strongest Jegera, Kerka and two others that Arara didn't recognize. One of them was the biggest Jegera she'd ever seen – even bigger than Grawka. She couldn't really make out much about the third fighter, except for a quick moving gray blur. She concentrated her mind-scan on the fighters and was surprised to recognize Yegra as the third fighter.

Finally, Kerka got knocked on his back. He crawled to his feet and limped over to the front of the line. Now it was just the huge brown Jegera and Yegra. Yegra danced out of the way of the giant's wide swings, then darting in to score wide scratches on his legs and torso before nimbly evading another blow. Finally she ducked between his legs, tripping him. He fell heavily, and Yegra snarled and jumped for his throat. She stopped with her mouth around the brown Jegera's throat.

<*Give up?*> Yegra did a public gefir, unable to talk with her jaw wrapped around the losers throat. Yegra had clearly won, but the big Jegera kept struggling and growling.

<*Never!*>

At this point Gouk stepped in. "The gray Jegera is the winner. She gets to lead the group to the Garden. Lead the way." He gestured to Yegra and she grinned, then jumped up wagging her tail and sauntered to the front of the pack.

She turned to face the gathered pups and pumped her paw up. "Everyone, follow me."

A loud cheer sounded from outside as Yegra parted the vines. Behind her the rest of the Jegera filed out, one by one. Once the pod was clear, Gouk dragged Arara after them.

A wall of heat hit her as Gouk dragged her outside. The sun blinded her after so long indoors. Arara staggered back, whining. Gouk chuckled and grabbed one of her feet. Arara's head knocked on the platform as he pulled, lifted her up and dangled her in the air. Arara squinted, catching a glimpse of the crowd where the sky should be. She panicked, swinging around wildly as she clawed at Gouk. Laughter floated up from the crowd as Gouk shook her.

Arara grabbed her muzzle, trying to keep from throwing up. A few moments later Gouk's grip loosened at the top of one of his swings. She screamed as she somersaulted through the air. Air whooshed out of her as she hit something soft. Behind her, a door clicked shut and the ground lurched.

Arara rolled over and sat up, blinking around her. The room was dark, the gloom impenetrable to her sun dazzled eyes. Outside, the sound of cheering could still be heard, slightly muffled by the walls around her. Arara raised her head and sniffed around her. The damp smell of living wood hit her nose, as well as the scents of several Jegera.

<Ah, right on time.>

Arara spun at the voice. Four Jegera sat on the benches around her. Their muzzles were gray with age, and their fur hung in patches off their spindly limbs. Loose flesh hung off their bones, bouncing and swaying with the movement of the carriage. Arara recoiled, bumping into the doorway behind her. She had never seen Jegera so old.

"Oh, hello." Arara hoped her voice didn't quaver too much.

"Have a seat," warbled the smallest in a soft voice.

Arara swallowed, sliding onto the forward bench next to the speaker. Sitting next to her, Arara realized the speaker was so bent with age they were almost the same size. A third Jegera shared the bench with them. He looked to be the youngest of the group. His muzzle was darker than the other three, his light fur less patchy. The gloom inside made it hard to tell, but Arara thought his fur looked almost white.

Two more Jegera sat on the back bench. The first was a giant male Jegera, now bent and twisted with age. His paws curled back in on themselves like the feet of a bird. The second male met her gaze with his one good eye. A scar ran down his face where the second eye would have been, twisting one side of his muzzle up into a permanent leer.

Arara shifted in her seat, the silence weighing heavily on her. Where were they taking her? What did they want from her?

<Don't worry. We mean you no harm. We are here to determine your guilt or innocence in the matter of Epoka's death.> The gefir came from the youngest. He opened his mouth in a toothless smile when Arara looked in his direction.

Arara twisted her paws together, wondering what to do. True, she'd pushed Epoka and Keora out the door of the carriage, thinking they were more kidnappers. But she'd done it to protect Sels. The thought reminded her of the token, still nestled snuggly in her vest pocket. She reached up and tapped with a claw through the thin silk to reassure herself it was still there.

<You have been Chosen. None can take that from you. Not even Queen Seuan would dare risk the consequences of breaking that tradition.>

<But, she's Queen! She can do whatever she wants.>

<Even Royalty must bow to the will of the gods.> The youngest's gefir was tinged with conviction and righteous fury.

The scarred Jegera nodded and held up his front paws, palm up. "My name is Johka. We," he nodded around the carriage at the others, "are the Jegeran Elders."

Arara straightened, sucking in a startled breath. The Elders had ruled the Jegeran tribes in the time before the Empire. Now they served as advisers to the Royal Family. She stared at Johka, her jaw working up and down, before remembering to present her neck to him.

Johka continued to speak, ignoring Arara's reaction. "I was *sedyu*-bonded to Queen Seuan's mother, Se'lvn, before she passed. Next to me," he gestured at the massive black Jegera with the twisted front paw, "is Lolop. Lolop was the Alpha-Guard's Clan Leader until he injured his paw."

Lolop lowered his head to Arara and spoke. His deep voice boomed too loud in the small space. "I've heard much about you."

Arara gulped and nodded, still not trusting herself to speak. She politely offered her neck to him before he nodded at her. She wondered how he'd heard any information about her, since Sels had gifted her with the token mid-journey.

"Sitting next to you is Pira," Johka said. "She served as the Jegeran Speaker in Council until her appointment to the position of Elder."

Pira's eyes twinkled up at Arara and she whispered more than spoke. "Such pretty white fur. Why ever did you hack it off like that?"

"An accident." Arara mumbled as she paid her respects.

"Hmm..." Johka voice rumbled. "Last, our youngest and newest Elder, Darach."

"Before we go any further," Darach said, turning his gaze to her. His eyes seemed to bore into her, and Arara squirmed. "We must know. Have you been present when the Greeting Magic has been cast?"

"No, sir." Arara whispered, shrinking back in her seat. "I, um, had an accident and didn't make it in time to see the Prince and Princess as they greeted the city."

"Good, good." Johka mumbled, and all the Elder's stances relaxed as if they'd all been holding their breath.

Darach sat up and placed his hand on the wall of the carriage. The room brightened as light flooded in from above. Arara looked up to see the ceiling glow as it turned translucent. Soon she could see the blue, cloudless sky above them, slightly hazy and distorted from the carriage top.

She lowered her head and looked around, blinking when her gaze met Darach's. In the light, his short fur shimmered, almost pure white except for a black patch around one eye. His eyes crinkled up, and he shifted on the bench to show her his tail. It curled back over on itself, just like hers.

"Couldn't see me in the gloom, could you?" Darach settled back into place, one long fang showing as he smirked at her.

"No," Arara shook her head and looked at her paws, her voice dropping. "I've never been able to see well at night, not like the other pups."

Johka snorted, causing Arara to raise her head. "Don't go feeling sorry for yourself. Please relax. Have something to refresh yourself after your long journey." A wooden panel slid up the curve of the carriage wall next to her, revealing a small alcove. Inside were a gilded glass decanter filled with red liquid and five small lapping bowls.

Arara picked up the decanter and took off the top. The unmistakable tart smell of plumberries floated out. She wrinkled her nose and started to put the container down before remembering her company. Turning down the drink would be incredibly rude. She poured only a few mouthfuls into one of the bowls and replaced the decanter in the alcove.

"Thank you, Elders." She intoned, picking up the bowl with both paws and bringing it up to her face. Her tongue lapped up a bit of the juice, and she struggled not to gag as she swallowed.

Down the bench, Darach sniffed and scowled at her. "You don't like it?"

Arara lowered her arms and stared at him. "I was trying to be polite. Honestly, I've never liked plumberries."

Johka snorted. "A common trait for a Yaka."

The bowl tumbled from her paws, splashing red across the carriage floor as Arara gaped at him.

CHAPTER TEN

THE SECRET

A wave of heat hit Sels as he stepped out of his pod. He smiled at the sun, realizing how homesick he'd been during the trip. He'd missed the warm weather, his mother, and most of all the privacy of his own quarters at the palace. Between all the traveling, the parties, and Sesay forcing him to mingle, he hadn't had a moment to himself.

The sooner he got this over with the sooner his life would go back to normal. He stepped up to the edge of the railing of the Poku platform and waved. Normally, his candidates would be greeting the crowd along with him, but Sesay had decreed they would meet him at the park along with the new Alpha-Guard recruits.

Sels descended the platform, still waving. Sesay, Lilsa and Indra joined him at the bottom. Recka and his team formed a wedge around them, pushing easily through the crowd, which was mostly Kin. The odd Jegera towered over them.

Behind them, Sels heard another large cheer. He turned, trying to see what caused it, but wasn't able to see past his bodyguards. In his mind, he heard Arara trying to tell him something, but Sesay grabbed his arm and pulled him forward. His concentration was broken and he missed what she'd been saying.

*****

By the time they reached the garden amphitheater several claws-marks later, Sels's arms trembled from exhaustion. If he had to wave at one more person he thought his arms would fall off. They crested the rise and followed the path that wound down to the stage.

The new Jegeran Alpha-Guard were already lined up except for a gap in the center where the Queen's throne sat. They came to attention as the Royal party neared the midway mark to the stage. Yegra, Arara's friend from Last Home, stood first in line. Kerka stood next to her. Sels eyes eagerly swept down the line as they approached, looking for Arara's distinctive white fur. He'd missed her company during the trip and was excited to be able to see her again. Once, twice, three times he scanned the stage, but there was no sign of her.

Sels was so busy looking for Arara that when Recka stopped in front of him, Sels ran right into his broad back. Sels staggered but managed to stay on his feet when Sesay reached out to steady him.

"Sels, pay attention." Sesay said, and she linked her arm with his.

With a sigh he let Sesay lead him up the stairs onto the stage. When they reached the top, they separated and sat in the chairs on either side of his mother's elaborately carved wooden throne. As Sels settled onto the padded seat, the first notes reached his ears over the roar of the crowd. More Kin stopped cheering and started singing. By the time his mother appeared at the edge of the basin, the entire crowd sang along with the music, lifting their arms and faces towards the Queen.

The Queen sat high in the air upon a litter that rested on the shoulders of four muscled Jegera. The bearers stopped, and the Queen stood, spreading her arms wide to greet the crowd. She wore pink robes set with small chips of rose quartz which sparkled in the sun. Her green skin glowed, as if lit from within. The vines on her head had been piled into an elaborate twist. The pink flowers on her vines burst into bloom, their spray encircling her head like a crown.

The song faltered for a moment as the crowd sighed in appreciation, and then it swelled back even louder. The Queen sat, signaling to her bearers, and they started off again. The Queen paraded down the hillside, her arms still spread. The long sleeves and the train of her dress swept behind her, shimmering like water. A crowd of musicians and couriers paraded behind the bearers.

A few scratch-marks later, the bearers reached the stage and knelt, lowering the litter. A waiting courier rushed forward and steadied the Queen as she stepped down.

Sels and Sesay moved in unison, sliding to their feet in one smooth motion. They struck the traditional sun worship pose, their heads and arms thrown back before joining the Queen at the edge of the stage.

The bearers moved off with the litter while the parade flowed around the stage. The musicians slowed their playing before stopping entirely. The singing faded away, then all the Kin brought their palms together and lowered their heads.

A large group of Kin with instruments took their places around the stage, as well as several Jegera Alpha-Guards. Tukura, Seuan's *sedyu*-bonded, a medium sized brown female Jegera, took her place next to Queen Seuan.

The Queen lifted her palms towards the sun, reciting the Greeting spell. Rainbows cascaded out of her fingers, blanketing the entire amphitheater.

She lowered her arms, twisting her fingers together in a blur of patterns. Sels recognized the movement as an amplification spell, cast at dizzying speed.

“Welcome,” the Queen’s melodic voice trilled across the air, beautiful even at high volume. “On the twentieth anniversary of my son's first touch of the glorious sun, we are here to honor him and celebrate his last week as a child!”

The Queen turned around and held out her hand to him. “Sels, please step forward.” She took his hand and lifted his arm. “I officially present my son, Prince Sels!” The Queen said.

Seuan allowed the crowd to cheer for a moment, then raised her palm for silence.

"Kerka, Nathira, Step forward." Seuan said. The two Jegera stepped forward, but maintained their places in line.

"These candidates are competing in the Trials tomorrow for the honor of becoming my son's *sedyu*-bonded. I present to you Kerka of Last Home." The Queen paused while the few Jegera in the crowd howled their approval. The Kin whistled their appreciation. Kerka raised his arms, clearly basking the attention.

"And Nathira of Blue Cove." Nathira cringed back, flattening her pointed ears to her head with her paws as the piercing whistles of the Kin completely drowned out all other noise. Clearly the Kin in the crowd favored Nathira.

Sels waited expectantly to hear Arara's name announced. His hands clenched in worry for her. Sesay had assured him that Arara would still be able to participate in the Trials, but now he wondered if she had told him the truth.

The silence lengthened, and Sels glanced at his mother. The Queen stood at ease next to him, her hands clasped in front of her. Sels eyes widened as he realized she did not intend to announce Arara.

Arara, the only one of his three candidates he felt a connection to, the only one he had a chance of *sedyu*-bonding with.

Of course, these plans all hinged on him being able to perform the binding magic when the time came. After his dismal performance with the Greeting magic during his tour, he began to doubt he'd ever be able to form a *sedyu*-bond. Without a *sedyu*-bonded, he couldn't become the heir, couldn't become the King. Already he felt like the laughing stock of the kingdom, unable to perform any but the most basic of magics.

Sels had to remind himself that no, that wasn't true. His magic saved Arara from the kwaso and from the fake guards. He came to a decision and straightened, swallowing his unease. He could do this. His hands wove slowly through the patterns of the voice amplification spell. Finished, he spread his hands palm up and stepped forward. The crowd fell silent as they noticed his movement.

"My third candidate." His voice boomed across the bowl of the theatre. A hand, most likely his mother's, gripped his right shoulder from behind. He ignored it and kept talking. "Arara, of Last Home. She could not join us here this afternoon, but look forward to her performance in the Trials tomorrow."

Fabric rustled and stones clinked as the Queen moved up next to him, her hand still gripping his shoulder painfully tight. Sels turned his head and smiled at her. The Queen's mouth turned up to match him, but her eyebrows pinched together, and her eyes bored into him. Sels flinched, expecting a dressing down in front of everyone. The Queen's hand dropped to her side and her expression smoothed out, then she looked up, addressing the crowd.

"Thank you, Prince Sels. Candidates, attend to your duties."

Sels stepped back. His heart pounded and his legs trembled at the thought of what awaited him. He'd rather face a hundred kwasos than his mother's ire. He barely noticed when Kerka and Nathira flanked him, standing a few paces behind. After an announcement like that, what would he do if Arara failed to show up by tomorrow?

"Now, a greeting to our new Alpha-Guards." Queen Seuan turned and swept out her arms.

On the stage, the young Jegera wagged their tails and yipped, unable to contain their excitement. The crowd cheered again. Their whistles and howls merged into a background roar.

Sels eyes swept the crowd in desperation, looking for white fur. His gaze caught on Yegra, Arara's friend. She had to be as worried as he was.

Another thought hit him. Where was Jeron? Sels frowned, turning to look behind him. Right then, Queen Seuan flung her arms wide. Wind sprung out of nowhere to whip Sels robes and vines around, into his face.

Sels faced forward to see a whirlwind of colored petals surround the Queen as she lifted off the stage. Her reaching arms perfectly framed the sun, as if she were embracing it.

Every Kin in the audience turned as one towards the southern horizon. They raised their arms and faces, basking in the heat as they chanted a prayer to the Sun Father. Sels joined them, closing his eyes and enjoying the smooth taste of the high summer sun on his skin. He raised his arms higher, his robes sliding back and exposing his arms. The sun beat down, tasting of home.

The wind died as the Queen returned to the stage. Sels held his position as he whispered a private prayer to the Sun Father for Arara to show up before it was too late.

"Let the feast begin!" His mother's melodic voice sang out, breaking Sels's concentration.

Sels lowered his arms and opened his eyes as Kin bearing platters of vegetables started streaming down the sides of the crater. A smaller line of Jegera holding platters of meat followed. The music of his mother's couriers started up again from the front of the stage.

The newly initiated Alpha-Guard filed away, Yegra among them. With Jeron gone, he'd have to catch her himself before she disappeared into the crowd. Sels hurried away, ignoring his mother's disapproving glare of protest, trying not to lose sight of Yegra's dark gray fur. The hot breath on his head told him Kerka followed close behind.

Sels ducked between a pair of Jegera, giving them a mumbled apology and glanced back. Kerka hadn't been so sly and jostled the two of them. Now they stood between Sels and Kerka, growling for an apology from the impudent pup. Sels suppressed a smile and hurried on.

"Yegra!" Sels called, unable to see her anymore through the press of the Jegera around him. "Yegra, wait!" He stood on his toes trying to see over the Jegera. He dropped down, frustrated that he'd lost her, when a soft paw brushed his arm. It was Yegra standing beside him. Her mouth gaped open, pointed ears pricked towards him. Her tail wagged lazily behind her.

Clasping her paws in his, Sels leaned forward, whispering low. "I need help finding Arara."

Yegra looked down at him in surprise. "She isn't here?"

"No." Sels shook his head. "I haven't seen her since she was arrested."

"That's odd." Her head cocked to the side. "I just saw her..."

Yegra trailed off and Sels felt a hot breath on his neck. He let go of Yegra's paw and stepped back to see Kerka standing next to him. Kerka grinned and rested his paw on Sels shoulder.

"You don't need *her,*" Kerka's grip tightened and his eyes narrowed. "We all know she'd never make it anyway."

Sels flinched, and he reached up to pry Kerka's paw off. "You saw her? When?" His shoulder was still sore from his mother's grip earlier. Claws caught in the delicate fabric and Sels heard something rip. "Was she well?" Sels was finally able to work the last claw free and shove Kerka's heavy paw off.

"Your Highness," Yegra said, nodding. "She was in good spirits despite the chains binding her. I'll find her for you." She tilted her head back, farther than even was required, and bared her throat to him.

Sels nodded, feeling relief. Yegra was obviously worried as well, and with her nose she had a better chance of finding Arara than he did. "Yes, thank you. Bring her to the southern servant's entrance. I'll have Jeron alert the guards to expect you." Well, he would as soon as he found Jeron.

Yegra nodded again, and started to turn away before Sels thought of something else. "If you don't find her by tomorrow morning," Sels said. "Please come back and report in anyway."

Yegra waved in acknowledgment and bounded away.

Kerka looked after her. Sels thought his face looked wistful or perhaps worried.

"Did you want to help hunt for Arara as well?" Sels said.

"Huh?" Kerka started, turning his head back to Sels. "Yegra can take care of herself, but Arara's so small and helpless. She was in the pod with us, right before the procession left the Poku platform. What could have happened to her between there and here?"

"Did you see her after that?"

"No." Kerka frowned, snorting with what Sels now suspected was worry. "I'll ask around, see if anyone saw anything."

Sels glanced at Kerka, trying to figure out his angle. Kerka sniffed around, his eyes darting this way and that. Sels clicked his mouth shut, biting off his sarcastic retort.

"Thank you." Sels said instead with sincerity. "Please let me know if you find anything."

Kerka nodded and walked away, still sniffing the air.

"Sels," His mother clipped his name off in crisp syllables, and Sels turned, cringing at the tone. "Your behavior today has been unacceptable."

Queen Seuan stood several paces behind him, her hands clasped in front of her as she dressed him down with her eyes alone. Her mouth pulled into in a severe frown, and her eyebrows jutted in displeasure. Sels had never seen her look so angry.

Sels clenched his jaw, bracing for the worst.

*****

Arara snarled, leaping off the bench to land on her hind feet with all her claws extended. *<My parents are Jegera! I'm a Jegera!>* She threw the full force of herself behind the gefir, showing them the memory of her mother and father and that of her own birth, which she'd once plucked from her mother's head accidentally.

Johka opened his mouth, probably trying to reassure her, but the scars on his face twisted it into a grotesque parody of a smile. "Despite your parent's claims on your heritage, you are almost certainly half, perhaps even full-blooded Yaka."

The carriage lurched, throwing Arara to the floor. "That's impossible." Her growl reverberated through the small space. "The Yaka were annihilated during the War of the Snowy Wastes, almost five hundred years ago."

"Yes, that is the common perception," a small voice warbled from behind her. "But, as we've discovered recently, it's untrue."

Arara turned her head to eye Pira warily. Pira patted the spot Arara had recently vacated. Arara reluctantly sheathed her claws and returned to her spot with a huff. "So what does that have to do with me?"

"Many years ago, even before the war with the Yaka, a Kin Oracle spoke a Prophecy."

A Prophecy. Kin nonsense. Arara rolled her eyes to the side and picked at sheathing that had begun peeling off one of her claws, tuning out Pira's words. A moment later, Pira batted Arara's paws down with surprising strength then grabbed Arara's muzzle and lifted her nose up until their eyes met.

<Little one, pay attention. The Prophecy speaks of you. It foretold you meeting with us today.>

Arara jerked her head back. The gefir carried the weight of truth and conviction. Pira believed. She scraped her lips and chin, scooting down the bench to press herself against the side of the carriage, putting just a tail's-length of space between the two of them. Her eyes flicked up to Darach on the other side of Pira.

Darach noticed her gaze and nodded to her. Arara sneered and turned away. Both looked raptly at her, as if waiting for something.

Arara heard a growl and realized that it came from herself. With effort, she gulped, swallowing the noise. She watched her own paws clench together as she struggled to keep calm, not trusting herself enough to look up at them. "What does this prophecy say? What makes you think it concerns me?"

"We don't have the full text with us." Johka spoke now, his timbre low enough that Arara strained to hear him over the muffled noise of the crowd outside. "We only speak from memory. You have to understand, we, too, were skeptical of relying on Kin Prophecy. Especially one that pre-dates the Northern Mountain Wars."

"But here you are," Darach interjected. "Just as it said you would be. The favored candidate of the Deficient Prince, unjustly accused, sent to the Elders for punishment."

"Just so." Johka glanced at Darach. "As foretold, this is the final sign before the Fall."

"The Fall?" Her interest piqued, Arara couldn't help but lean forward. Her ears perked up.

"The Prophecy speaks of the Fall of the Kin-Jegera Empire." Johka leaned towards her, balancing his weight on a carved stick.

Arara frowned, pulling on one ear as she thought. "Why are there no Kin here? Surely they want to stop this as much as you."

"They think this Prophecy invalid now." Johka hit the wall with one curled paw. "Because it will only happen when the Yaka return. And since they think the Yaka destroyed--"

Arara sat back with a snort. "I think the Kin are right. I'm not a Yaka."

Johka's ears drooped and he frowned, as he too settled back into place. He propped the stick against his legs. "No?" He placed one paw against the wall and the light dimmed as the skylight darkened, until the only light came from the small windows set into the doors. A wooden shutter snapped closed, throwing the room into utter darkness. Four pairs of eyes encircled her, glowing gold as if lit within by the sun.

"Catch." Johka's voice sounded from his spot across the carriage.

Something bounced off Arara's sensitive nose with a snap. She clapped a paw over the tender spot with a yip, and rolled off the bench onto the floor. She could sense the four Elders all still sitting where she'd last seen them.

"I said, 'Catch'" Johka's voice was tinged with amusement. "Be ready this time. Again."

The carriage was pitch black. She could hear shuffling from in front of her, probably from Johka as he readied another missile. Arara oriented herself to him. Concentrating, she tried to hear Johka's mind-speak so she'd know when he threw it. She could feel him erecting mental barriers around his thoughts. She easily flattened them to peer into his head. He held nothing in his paws.

Another missile hit her forehead. She cried out, scrambling away. Fur brushed her face as she hit legs. By the smell they were Pira's.

"Having some trouble?" Johka cackled. She mentally felt him pick up his wooden walking stick and raise it up.

"Stop!" Arara cried. She could feel blood trickling out of her nose to land with a wet plop on the floor of the carriage. "Of course I'm having trouble. I can't see to catch whatever you are throwing at me. It's pitch black in here."

The room brightened, and the light stung Arara's eyes.

"Darkness isn't an obstacle to a Jegera." Darach leaned over and held one paw out to her.

Arara pushed Pira's legs away, ignoring Darach's paw as she stood and moved back against the door, her arms pulled tight across her chest. Two wooden cups rolled back and forth with the sway of the carriage.

"So I can't see in the dark. That doesn't prove anything."

"It proves you aren't the Jegera you claim." Johka smirked at her.

"Does the Prophecy say how to stop the destruction?" Arara hugged herself tighter as she stared at the rolling cups, trying not to think about the logical conclusion to Johka's claim. What it meant about her parents.

The background noise of the crowd fell away as the carriage turned onto a side street.

"Yes," Darach's voice sounded loud in the sudden silence. He grinned at her, his curly tail thumping into the seat behind him.

"You."

The warm wood of the door pressed into Arara's back as she stumbled back, overwhelmed. How had her simple journey to North Wind transformed into this? The fate of the entire Empire couldn't rest on her. It just couldn't. Her chest heaved and her vision spun. She turned around, clawing at the door, trying to figure out how to open it.

"Calm down." Darach said behind her, his voice low and soothing as she felt him moving towards her.

Curls of wood shavings floated to the floor as Arara clawed at the carriage door. The carriage screamed, its high pitched wail emanating out of the walls. The carriage stopped moving and rocked violently back and forth. The door popped open, and Arara tumbled out onto the deserted street.

Arara managed to get her paws out in front of her face before she plowed headfirst into the packed dirt. A cloud of dust irritated her nose and eyes as she pushed herself up to all fours. She dashed down the street, away from the carriage.

"Arara, wait!" Darach yelled after her.

CHAPTER ELEVEN

PAYBACK

Arara could feel Darach's presence behind her, although the street dust obscured her sight. He must have jumped out of the carriage to follow her. The mental-presence of the other Elders fell away as she ran. Wooden buildings grew out of the ground to her side, topped by leafy boughs of unfamiliar trees. The sides of the living buildings were carved with elaborate murals.

The street was mostly deserted, although a few Petal Kin walking the streets turned to stare at Arara as she ran by. The hot summer sun beat down on Arara, and even with her fur shaved short, she was panting within a few minutes. Waves of heat shimmered in the air around her, and the dirt burned the pads of her paws. She'd heard the heart of the Empire was hotter than Last Home, but this was beyond hot. It was stifling.

Only the fact that Darach chased her kept her going. She still felt his presence behind her, in fact, he slowly gained on her. His age slowed him, so that he hadn't caught her right away, but his long legs meant that one of his strides equaled four or five of hers. He would catch her eventually unless she came up with a plan.

"Stop! I...stop, Arara!" Darach sounded winded.

An alley appeared on her left and she ducked down it. The tree-tops of the buildings curved overhead, dappling the alley ground with shade. Piles of rotting leaves dotted the sides of the buildings. The smell made Arara gag. Darach followed close behind her, gaining ground with every step.

The alley ended and the full power of the sun beat down on Arara from overhead. Family groups of Vine and Petal Kin walked near the buildings. A few carriages crawled down the center of the lane. All the traffic moved in the same direction. Arara joined them, ducking and weaving through and around everything in her path. Her small size gave her an advantage, and she could feel Darach's presence falling behind.

The crowd got larger as the side street joined a main thoroughfare. The buzz of voices increased into a roar. As she ran, she couldn't help but overhear that much of the conversation around her centered on the Prince and the upcoming Trials.

The crowd around her started to overpower her senses. Arara could barely feel Darach behind her, so she dropped into a slow trot while she rebuilt her shields.

Arara continued to move with the crowd, taking time to listen to what the Kin around her were saying. Her tail wagged when she found out that they were all going to the amphitheater where Prince Sels had announced the candidates for the Trials. Everyone was mentioning her name, Sels's mysterious candidate from Last Home.

Arara only hoped Sels was still at the feast. Although, she wasn't sure she would be able to make it. She panted heavily as she walked, and her tongue felt like sandpaper. She staggered to the side and fell into the legs of a Kin walking next to her. They fell in a tangle.

"Watch where you're walking!" the Kin sneered at Arara as her blue-petaled companion helped her to her feet.

Arara was too busy heaving up the contents of her stomach onto the side of the thoroughfare to respond. When she was spent, she collapsed to her side, dizzy with exhaustion. Her eyes drifted closed. She lay there, burning up in the hot sun. Conversations sang out around her, and she felt her consciousness drift away.

A wet tongue licked the side of Arara's face. "Arara, get up."

A presence loomed over her, reassuringly familiar.

"Arara," Yegra said, so close her hot breath tickled Arara's ear. "Sels is looking for you. He's really worried. If we hurry, we can catch him before he goes back to the palace."

Arara tried to respond, but her mouth was so dry all she could get out was a low moan.

Water dripped onto the side of Arara's muzzle, and she licked her lips, catching it as it rolled down. More followed, and Arara soon found herself sitting up, lapping water out of a wide bowl. Yegra stood over her along with a few concerned looking Kin.

"Your friend looks fine now, but you need to get her to some shade." The tallest of the Kin spoke to Yegra. "She's overheated."

"Thank you." Yegra inclined her head, handing the now empty bowl to the concerned Kin.

The Kin took the bowl and moved off with her companions.

"Better?" Yegra looked back down at Arara.

Arara nodded and allowed Yegra to pull her to her feet. She swayed and started to fall, but Yegra grabbed her. Yegra supported Arara, and they merged into the crowd that still flowed towards the amphitheater.

Yegra leaned down and butted the side of Arara's head with her own. <*You'll never believe it, but Prince Sels stood up for you.*>

<*What?*> The relentless heat pounded into Arara's head, making it hard for her to follow Yegra's words.

<*The Queen only announced two candidates, Kerka and Nathira.*> Yegra's wagging tail bumped into Arara's legs and Yegra's paw tightened around Arara's arm as she spoke. Her eyes gleamed. <*And then, Sels stepped forward and said you were the third candidate. The audience probably couldn't tell, but from the stage, I saw the Queen's expression for a moment as he made the announcement. She didn't look happy.*>

<*He did that, for me?*> Arara stumbled forward; only Yegra's paw on her arm kept her upright.

"Yeah." Yegra pulled her out of the crowd, into the shade of a building along the side of the thoroughfare. "Wait here. I'll be right back."

Arara could hear someone yelling something up ahead, but the pounding in her head drowned out the words. She put her head down, panting heavily, and closed her eyes. The cool wood of the house-tree against her back felt so good. She felt herself sliding down its smooth bark. The combination of shade and rest was too much for Arara, and she drifted off to sleep.

Sometime later, Yegra shook her awake. A quick peek at the sun told her she'd only slept for a few minutes, but it was an effort to get her eyes the rest of the way open. Yegra held a large paper umbrella in her paws. She opened it, and the sun no longer stung Arara's eyes. The umbrella kept the worst of the sun's rays at bay.

"Heard a vendor hawking them up ahead." Yegra crouched down, once more helping Arara up.

Yegra crooked her arm, supporting Arara on one side and the umbrella in the other. The umbrella cast the two of them in shade as they walked. Waves of heat shimmered off the hard packed dirt, burning the pads of her feet.

"Almost there." Yegra said when Arara stumbled again.

With an effort, Arara lifted her eyes to see the low grassy hill in front of them. A neat line of trees ran along the top of it. The rows of house-trees ended where the hill began, although the path continued up the side. A trail of Kin flowed along the path in both directions. The crowd pressed around them, growing denser by the step. Before Arara and Yegra had passed the last of the house-trees, a low murmur swept along the line of Kin towards them.

In front of them, the nearest Kin turned and said in a low voice, "The Queen approaches."

The Kin behind them repeated the phrase to their neighbors, and the news spread down the line. A group of Jegera in Alpha-Guard uniforms started shoving the crowd up against the houses on the side, clearing a path in the middle of the street. Arara and Yegra ended up right against the wood of the house, the crowd five or six deep in front of them. Yegra shut the umbrella after accidentally hitting several Kin in the head.

Arara stood on the tips of her hind legs, trying to see over the heads of the taller Kin in front of her without success. Yegra put her paw on Arara's shoulder after Arara started jumping up and down in her attempt to see.

"I'll tell you if I see Sels." Yegra assured her.

Arara nodded in agreement, although she huffed in annoyance at not being able to see. What if Sels was leaving with his mother? They were so close, and Arara didn't want to lose Sels again. Although, now that they were closer perhaps Arara could communicate with Sels on her own, like she had on the train. Gefir with a Kin was harder than with a Jegera, and she had to know his location before she could send it.

With bodies of Kin pressing around her from all sides, she didn't know if she would be able to distinguish his presence from the rest, or if the crush of the crowd would overwhelm her mental senses.

A deep breath, and then Arara slowly lowered her mental shields. The thoughts of the crowd screamed inside her head. She did her best to ignore them, dropping her shields further as she searched for voices that were familiar to her. Closest to her, she found Yegra right away. Encouraged, she pushed out farther into the crowd. The roar of mental voices increased, but Arara tried to focus on the ones she knew.

There, she knew that voice. Darach. He was almost on top of them. They had to get out of here. Arara slammed her shields back up and grabbed Yegra's arm. She tugged on Yegra, but the crowd of Kin hemmed them in on all sides.

<Arara,> Yegra gefired. *<We're stuck, you'll just have to wait until the Queen's retinue finishes passing by.>*

<Darach, he's here.> Arara sent back. *<The one that kidnapped me.>*

<*A Jegera?*> Yegra stood on the tips of her toes and peered over the heads of the Kin around them. <*Big, male, white fur with a black patch over one eye?*>

<*Yes.*> Arara's stomach dropped. He was big enough to push his way through, but they were stuck.

A moment later Arara saw two familiar faces appear over the heads of the crowd. A few muted cries of protest preceded Darach and Jeron pushing through the crowd in front of them. Arara shrank back, trying to hide behind Yegra. Darach growled, grabbing Arara and pulling her out from behind her friend.

"We're sorry we scared you, Arara." Darach crouched down so he looked her in the eye. "If you'll just come back with us to the library, we can assuage all your fears."

"But, what about Sels?" Arara snarled back at him. "He's worried sick about me. I need to go see him and make sure he's safe. Jeron, how could you leave him alone after all the attacks?"

"He is with his mother, the Queen," Jeron said calmly. "Surrounded by almost the entire Guard."

A trumpet blast drowned out the last of Jeron's words. The Queen's retinue slowly wound its way up the street. The Queen waved at the cheering crowd from atop her litter.

<*Safe with the Queen,*> Arara gefired to Jeron. <*That's what you said, but I don't see him with her. I won't come with you until I make sure he's safe.*>

Jeron's ears went back and he snarled. <*And half the guards are leaving with her. I need to get back to my post, sir.*>

Darach stood back up, throwing his paws in the air. <*The other Elders are on their way here. Jeron, thank you. I'd wanted your help to inform Arara of the prophecy, but this nonsense has thrown off our schedule.*> He looked back down at Arara. <*Once we see Sels, promise me that you'll stop running.*>

Arara nodded, when Yegra tugged on her ear. <*I'm coming too.*>

*****

"Sels," The Queen gestured, walking down the stairs. Her *sedyu*-bonded, Tukura, paced alongside her. Sels followed dutifully. "I wish you would think before acting," she said. "Do you know why I failed to acknowledge Arara?"

"Because of the murder charge." Sels raised his voice. "But I was there, she was just trying to protect me!"

"No." The Queen turned, heading to a secluded spot behind the stage. "If that was all there was, I would have announced her." She stopped and faced Sels. "I had planned to tell you tonight, in private. We found evidence that she is part of a conspiracy."

"What?" Sels couldn't have been more shocked if his mother had said Arara breathed fire. "What conspiracy?"

"Part of the Jegeran Resistance." The Queen took Sels's hands in hers. "The attacks were a setup in order to get one of their one chosen as a candidate."

Sels pulled his hands away. He'd considered that after the first attack, but he'd thrown the idea out as being ridiculous.

"The murder charge was just a convenient way to get her disqualified. But your announcement now makes her an official candidate and forces us to let her participate in the Trials."

"You mentioned evidence." Sels twirled one of his vines over his shoulder, watching the bloom spin as he thought out loud. "What is it?"

"I'd rather not say right now," she said, looking over Sels shoulder at the surrounding crowd. "Someone might overhear and I don't know yet who I can trust."

Before she could say more, Tukura leaned over her, her ears twitching. The Queen frowned, and Tukura straightened with a snap.

"Mother, please," Sels said, wringing his hands together. "I need to know." Arara had saved his life twice now. What evidence could his mother possibly have that would implicate Arara in the attacks?

The Queen reached out and clasped her hands around his fists. "Sels, don't make a scene." She squeezed his hands reassuringly and let go. “Now, I have some business to take care of. Stay here with Sesay and finish greeting your guests.”

Sels watched his mother’s procession as it wound its way up and out of the amphitheater. The unbroken blue of the sky allowed the full blessing of the Sun Gods to shine down on the gathering. His mother was easy to spot in the middle of the winding column, her dress flashing and sparkling in the sunlight as it rippled in the light breeze.

The first of his mother’s couriers disappeared into the trees ringing the top of the amphitheater. Sels shifted from foot to foot, wishing he could leave. All he could think of was sinking his aching feet down into the familiar rooting soil in his suite at the palace. He closed his eyes, humming along with the music.

The feel of claws on one of his blooms startled him, and he jerked his head around to see Kerka guiltily lowering his paw. Kerka’s ears pricked forward and his eyes lit up when he met Sels gaze.

“Why didn’t we go with the Queen?” Kerka yelled over the music.

Sels just shook his head and cupped the point of his left ear, pretending to not be able to hear. Kerka seemed to get the message, because his ears drooped down and he didn’t bother repeating himself. Kerka stepped back, his long shadow fell directly over Sels. Sels quelled his rising irritation and made a shooing motion with his hand until Kerka moved back in line with Nathira and Alpha-Guards.

“Don’t be so hard on him.” Sesay whispered into his ear. She stood on Sels's right, her arm linked with his.

Assigned a sitter again, until he could ‘control his behavior.’ Sesay’s angry glare told him she wasn’t any happier about the situation than he was. Sels ignored her, resolutely staring forward and watching the leaves of the trees ripple in the wind.

<Sels, I’m here! Don’t leave!>

“Arara?” Sels looked down, but the stage in front of him lay empty. In fact, so did the grass in front of the stage. All the Kin and Jegera that had previously filled the space now trailed away following his mother's procession. His mother's music still filled the air, but it was fading as musicians headed away.

"Did you say something?" Sesay squeezed his arm and leaned towards him.

"No." Sels frowned. He'd heard Arara in his head, he was sure of it. Just like he had in the pod. But how could he answer her?

<I'm not leaving.> Sels thought hard. <I'm on the stage. Arara, my mother said you're part of the group trying to kill me! Is that true?>

<No, Sels.> Arara wailed in his head. <I saved you! I wouldn't ever hurt you.>

Sels smiled in relief. Of course Arara would never hurt him. *<Where are you?>*

<Right outside the park, with Jeron and the Jegeran Elders.> Sels got an image of Arara and Yegra, unable to make any headway against the crowd streaming out from the amphitheater.

Sels wondered where Jeron had been all day, but was glad to hear Arara had been with him. "I'm stuck, too." Sels said out loud and then winced. He'd meant to think that to Arara. By now the last of the musicians entered the trees and his voice echoed over the stage. This gefir talking would take some getting used to.

"Yes." Sesay sighed. "Honestly, Sels, today is your debut. As host, you need to stay until dark, to give everyone a chance to see your candidates."

"Not all my candidates are here." Sels grumbled. He risked a sidelong look at Sesay. Her pink petals, pulled up into an elaborate swirl on the back of her head, seemed to glow in the twilight. Recka stood on her other side, his black fur a striking contrast to the swirl of pink.

"That's for the best. You heard the Queen." Sesay didn't even glance at him as she continued to wave greetings to the crowd passing below the stage.

Sels bit his lip in thought. They had to let Arara participate in the Trials, but that didn't mean they had to let her see him. If Arara showed up while Sesay was still around... Careful this time to not speak aloud, Sels responded to Arara. <*Wait until the crowd dies down. Hopefully by then I can find a way to get away from Sesay and Recka.*>

Sels head nodded down as he thought, and his eyes drifted closed. The taste of the fading light of the sun on his face and arms called to him to put down roots for the night.

"Sels, you look tired." Sesay said, causing Sels to open his eyes. "I'll have Recka bring the carriage around." Recka flicked his ears at this, probably sending a message ahead to the driver.

"No, you go ahead." Sels straightened. "I haven't greeted the Jegeran Elders yet. Look, is that them coming in now?" He pointed to the western entrance behind them, lost in deep shadows from the setting sun. The shadows bobbed and moved.

"They can wait," Sesay sighed. "They'll be at the Council session tomorrow, Sels."

"You leave if you want." Sels crossed his arms. "I need to stay until dark, remember? It's my duty as host."

"Very true." Sesay said. "I'm glad to see you taking your duties seriously."

"Thank you," Sels nodded, trying to look innocent. "But if you're tired, why don't you go ahead and take off. I'll be alright here alone."

"Alone? After all that happened, I don't think so. I'm not leaving without you."

There went that plan, and any chance for him to talk to Arara without Sesay reporting back everything to his mother.

"Who are they?" Kerka said from behind him.

"Who?" He turned to see Kerka pointing to the western end of the field. A group of seven Jegera were slowly limping towards the stage. The leader of the group leaned heavily on a cane. A tiny female and a medium sized elder walked to either side of a clump of three. A giant of a Jegera brought up the rear. The Elders.

Sels grinned. He moved across the stage to the back so he could get a better look. Jeron walked next to Johka. A small figure in the middle of the group barked. Arara. Sels jumped off the back of the stage, landing hard in the soft grass. He ran to the group, determined to see Arara before the guards with him hauled her away again.

Behind Kerka yelled “Hey, wait for me!” At the same time Sesay shouted “Sels, no!”

“Sels.” Johka held out his cane as Sels ran toward them. “We need to talk.”

Sels ran by him without stopping and scooped Arara into his arms, giving her a big hug. “You need to get out of here.” He huffed, out of breath from the run. “I’m so glad to see you, but you need to get out of here now, before my guards arrest you!”

Although he could feel Arara’s wagging tail hitting the side of his leg, her ears were pulled back, and she wouldn’t meet his gaze. *<Sels, I’m an evil Yaka.>*

<Arara, you aren’t evil. I can’t believe that.> And how could she be a Yaka? They’d been extinct since the Northern Mountain Wars. Sels had even met her parents, a very nice, obviously Jegera couple.

<Mom, how could she have done this to me?> Arara’s arms tightened around him.

“Your parents are good people and you are too, Arara. Remember that.” Sels realized too late he’d said this out loud.

“Yeah Arara, your mom’s good and useless.” Kerka said with a chuckle from directly behind Sels. “Just like you.”

In his arms, Arara shook, a low growl rising from her throat sounding directly in Sels ear.

“Sels, step back.” Recka growled as he ran up. Sesay trailed behind him along with a whole group of guards.

“Just ignore him.” Sels stroked Arara’s head, ignoring Recka.

“Listen to the Prince.” Kerka sneered. “Run away, like you always do.”

"No!" Arara shoved Sels as she freed herself from his arms, knocking him back a step. Her eyes narrowed and she was growling so loud Sels could barely understand her next words. "Never again!"

Sels stepped in front of Kerka with his arms thrown wide. "Arara, calm down."

Her answer was a howl of rage. Although nothing was there, Sels felt something hit his left side and he flew away to the right. He hit Yegra and they fell to the ground tangled together. Arara pounced forward and hit Kerka right in the midsection. Kerka folded in half, a shocked expression on his face.

Jeron's familiar form moved to help Sels up, blocking his view of the fight. Sels could still hear Arara's high pitched growling, now joined by a low deep growl that could only be coming from Kerka.

"We have to stop them!" Sels yelled, pushing himself to his feet. Yegra already stood behind him, crouched on all fours. She'd recovered from their fall almost instantly but now stood as if frozen in place.

"No, Sels." Jeron swept his arm out, blocking Sels from moving. "The Elders want to see how Arara handles herself."

Sesay grabbed Sels's arm and dragged him back while the guards rushed around them to form a perimeter.

"But they're going to hurt each other." Sels clenched his fists and glared at Jeron and Recka.

"The Elders will keep an eye on them and stop it before anyone gets hurt." Jeron moved next to Sels, placing his arm across his shoulders.

Sels huffed but didn't move away. "At least let me watch."

"Reasonable." Recka nodded, gesturing for a few of the guards to drop down into a crouch and give Sels a clear view. Arara and Kerka both stood on two legs, several tail lengths between them. Kerka dropped to all fours and rushed at Arara, growling. Arara stood her ground and lifted her paw, palm facing Kerka.

Kerka smirked at the gesture, grass and dirt flying from behind him as he ran towards her. Suddenly, he ran into an invisible wall, then slumped to the ground, looking befuddled.

In the background, Sels could see a few of the remaining Kin and Jegera staring and pointing. However, the presence of the guard apparently discouraged any of them from moving closer.

In a fit of frustration, Kerka starting throwing clods of dirt and rocks at Arara. Arara batted them to either side with force-pushes. Sels and Jeron ducked, debris flying over their heads. Dirt trickled down the collar of Sels's robe. He glanced over his shoulder to watch the clod roll away over the grass, then turned back and was struck in the forehead by a flying rock.

An explosion covered his vision, and it felt like his head cracked open. The soft grass cushioned him as he fell backwards, clutching his face. The world seemed to shift and distort around him, and riots of flowers danced around the edges of everything. He moaned.

"Someone call a healer!" Jeron barked.

Sels heard shuffling and more barked orders. Paws pulled his hands away from his face. A wet tongue rasped across his face and forehead, then a soft cloth pressed against the wound.

"Hold that." Jeron ordered, pressing Sels's hands back into place. Warm furry arms lifted him up and carried him away. The movement bounced his head, sending off a fresh wave of agony.

"It hurts." Sels moaned.

"I know. Just hold on. I sent Kerka and Nathira ahead to find a healer."

"What about Arara?"

"The Elders took Arara back into custody." Jeron said, hugging Sels closer. "Don't worry, they'll bring her to the palace in time for the Council meeting tomorrow morning."

Sels sighed in relief. Now that she was with the Elders nothing would go wrong tomorrow.

CHAPTER TWELVE

QUEEN AND COUNCIL

Arara howled, staggering back a step. Her forehead throbbed in sympathy, the pain so real she reached up and held her paws over the growing knot. A moment later the pain faded. Arara lowered her paws to see Sels, moaning in pain in the grass. Dark green sap ran down his face from under his hands.

The Alpha-Guard rushed forward, forming a perimeter around Sels. Arara spotted Jeron scooping Sels up into his arms before the Guard's movements blocked her view.

"Guards, take her into custody." Sesay ordered, pointing at Arara.

Darach grabbed Arara's arm and dragged her back. Lolop grabbed her other arm, pinning her between them. Lolop's grip was weak, and his deformed hands made Arara's fur stand on end.

"We can handle her, Sesay." Johka stepped between her and Sesay. He leaned heavily on his cane, and held up one paw in supplication before placing it on top of the other on the cane.

"Like you handled this?" Sesay waved behind her. Arara could see Jeron's back as he rushed away, Sels's vines and purple blooms bounced over Jeron's shoulder. Sels's cries of pain died away as Jeron rushed off, but Arara could still feel Sels crying in her head.

"This," Johka growled, and Arara could see his paws tighten around his cane. "Shouldn't have happened."

"No, it shouldn't have." Sesay sighed and crossed her arms. "And if Sels hadn't impulsively announced Arara as a candidate I could have been done with her for good."

"What?" Arara cocked her head to the side, and her ears perked as she struggled against Lolop and Darach's grip. "What do you mean?"

"I mean," Sesay sneered at Arara. "Accidentally killing an Alpha-Guard in the haze of battle is one thing, but harming the Prince... Sels's little announcement is the only thing standing between you a death sentence." Sesay's sneer twisted up into a parody of a smile. "Fail to complete any of the Trials, and the Alpha-Guards will be waiting for you with a noose."

The world swam around Arara in a blur of blues and greens as the force of Sesay's words took hold. She felt the Elders grip her arms tightly as she sagged.

*****

The plush ground bumped and swayed underneath her. She opened her eyes to find herself back in the Elders' carriage, laying on her back on the padded bench. Her head rested on Yegra's lap. Darach sat next to her, and he leaned over Arara, his face a mask of concern.

"Good, you're awake." Darach said, sliding off the bench. Arara turned her head to watch as he crouched on the floor of the carriage, his back to her. He leaned over something in front of him, and his curly tail stuck up in the air like a raop's.

The other Elders regarded her from the other bench. Johka looked angry, his lips pulled back to show his teeth at her. The other two shared a look of concern, but none of them said anything as Yegra stroked her head.

On the floor, Darach tossed aside a faded pair of leather shorts. A vest followed it, so stained and patched that the original color of the leather was hard to determine.

"Hey, those are mine!" Arara yipped in surprise as Darach continued to toss her clothing into a pile on the floor. She wriggled out of Yegra's lap, landing next to Darach with a thump. "I thought I'd lost my pack when I got arrested!" Arara yipped, wagging her tail.

"You have an audience with the Queen tonight, regarding the incident at the park," Johka sneered down at her, wrinkling his nose at Arara's outfit - now torn and stained from a week's worth of use. The movement tugged on the scar across his ruined eye, and the sight made Arara's stomach flip-flop. "Pick out an acceptable outfit."

Arara nodded, pushing Darach away. She tipped the pack over on its side, then dived in. After a bit of rooting around she found a leather jerkin and short set that she'd made herself the year before.

"These aren't too bad." Her voice muffled by the clothing piled around her head. She wriggled out backwards and held the clothing up with a grin. "It's just a bit faded, but no tears at all."

"You really think *this,*" Darach grabbed the clothing out of her paws and shook it in her face, "Is appropriate attire to greet the Queen and Council in?" Claws slid from Darach's fingers and shredded her clothing.

"But that's the best I have... or had." Arara said, looking mournfully at the remains of her second-best outfit.

Darach growled as the movement of the carriage rocked him back onto his heels as he tried to take a seat. "Where are we going to get you an outfit at this time of night?" He gestured to the moonlight streaming in the window from the nearly full moon. "We could send for an outfit, but you aren't exactly a regular size."

Arara pulled her ears back. "Er, well, actually, I am. I can fit in pup sizes." Growing up she'd been too small even for pup sizes. Her mom had been forced to custom make all Arara's clothing. Arara was rather proud of the fact that she now was big enough to fit any size in a Jegeran store.

"Still, the trial is tonight." Darach scrubbed his face with his paws, thinking.

"No help for it." Johka said, thumping his cane down hard enough to make the carriage twitch. "We'll have to make a detour and get her something suitable to wear."

"Trial? Tonight?" Arara protested, sitting down between Darach and Yegra on the bench. "But, who cares what I'm wearing. I need to know what to say..."

"Not for the Kin." Darach said. "Appearance and presentation mean everything to them. What you look like is almost more important than what you say to them."

Johka snorted. "Preening narcissistic flowers, the lot of them."

"But then, shouldn't we do something about her fur, too?" Yegra spoke up, ruffling the uneven fur on Arara's arm. Arara squirmed as everyone in the carriage studied her. Uncomfortable with the unexpected attention, Arara looked down at her own arm. Her fur had grown out a bit during the week-long trip to Sebaine, and while patchy, at least the bald spots were gone.

"I thought of that already." Darach nodded to the smallest Elder, who smiled and pulled a set of clippers from her bag. "Pira can groom you while I give you some training."

"Strip." Pira ordered as she stood and approached Arara. The paw holding the clippers shook like a leaf in a windstorm.

"Not her!" Arara cringed back.

"I can do it," Yegra said, taking the clippers from Pira. Pira looked disappointed, but returned to her seat without a word. "My mom had another litter a few years ago, and I had to help groom them. I've gotten pretty good."

The carriage bumped along as Arara wriggled out of her blue shorts while trying to ignore the fact that the Elders were all in the carriage with her. Yegra laid her out on the floor. The trimmers tickled as Yegra ran them over her fur, the sensation familiar and comforting. Her eyes drifted closed and she drifted off to sleep. A sharp jerk and the creak of the door opening woke her with a start.

A harried looking young Jegera shoved a pile of clothing in the open door, half burying Arara and Yegra under a pile of silks. The carriage rocked up and lumbered away before the door was even halfway closed.

"Um, I only need one outfit." Arara said, a rainbow of shirts and pants cascading off of her as she stood.

"Yes," Darach growled crawling down and sorting through the pile, "but we don't know which will look and fit the best."

He threw a blue-green outfit at her. "Try it on."

She shrugged into the top and slipped the shorts on, sliding her tail though the slit. Darach gestured, and Arara held up her arms and turned in circle. Johka shook his head no.

They repeated the process several times, with various colors and styles. The Elders finally settled on a formal outfit in purple silk, embroidered along the edges with a yellow flower pattern. The shorts were longer than she was used to, hitting below her knees, more like capris. The matching top was a small double breasted sleeveless vest the same color of the shorts over a pale yellow short-sleeved top. The wooden buttons on the vest matched the buckles on the pants. Overall it fit pretty well, although since it has been made for a puppy it was baggy around the middle. She'd had to belt the pants to the smallest they'd go, and they still kept trying to slide off of her.

"Perfect." Johka grinned, gripping his cane. "The purple will match Sels's robes."

"It's a bit loose," Darach said, pinching the sides of the vest tight and pulling out the flaps of extra fabric.

"Because puppies are so round." Arara said with a shrug. "I'm used to it. Did you see my sewing kit when you were going through my bag?"

"Right here." Darach passed her a little packet of bone needles and thread. "But do you know what you're doing?"

"Where do you think all my clothing came from?" Arara snapped, pulling the vest off. "No one in Last Home was willing to help us with anything. My parents make or alter all my clothing, and they taught me."

Arara dug out a needle and handed it to Darach. "Alright pinch it again and then mark it. But not quite so tight this time."

After Darach had marked the vest and pants, Arara changed back into her old blue outfit. She grabbed the shorts first, flipping them inside out and moving the marker to the inside, careful to hold the place. Thankfully, she'd had practice on silk making her blue outfit. In some ways it was easier than leather, since she didn't have to use tools to make each hole with a punch, but the silk slid oddly underneath her fingers. Several times she'd had to unpick when the light fabric had slid without her realizing it.

Finally she was done and held the shorts up for inspection. She winced. At least the seam was on the inside. She changed quickly, buttoning the pants up and testing the fit. They fit much better and didn't slide off anymore when she moved.

"Out of time, we're there." Johka growled. "And you haven't even touched the vest."

"I have an idea," Yegra giggled and grabbed a set of yellow pants with the same buttons. She used her claws to cut off a strip. "Sew this on the back to gather up the extra fabric."

Arara wagged her tail and folded over the fabric to hide the tears. Each side only needed a few stitches to hold it in place. The strap gathered up all the extra fabric and pulled the vest into a perfect fit. Before she could double check her work, Darach grabbed her paw and dragged her out of the carriage. Time to meet the Queen.

*****

Arara stared up at the gates leading into the palace. The group walked through the opening, flanked by two grim looking Alpha-Guards. The Elders formed a ring around her and Yegra.

The ironwood bars on each side of the opening twisted in her mind's eye into Kerka's face, snarling down at her. His ears twisted back, and he snorted in contempt. Arara rubbed her tired eyes and looked again to see the bars returned to normal. She held her head, hoping she didn't see any hallucinations while in front of the Queen and Council. But she was too tired to really care. Her tail drooped so low she could feel it dragging on the ground behind her.

Carvings of historical scenes covered the wooden walls of the hallway. After a short walk they left the main corridor, turning down a little-used side passage. Johka limped slowly, leading them through so many turns that Arara got dizzy just trying to keep track. At least the Elders plodding speed meant that Arara's exhausted legs could keep up.

Eventually Johka came to a stop in front of an unremarkable section of wall. Darach stepped forward and tapped on the hand of one Kin in the scene carved on that section of the wall. A panel slid open. The lines hidden within the carving made it nearly invisible when closed. Inside, a short hallway led them outside into a walled flower garden, lit only by the stars and the moon. A few days away from being full, the moon provided enough light to read by. A rainbow of flowers filled the planting areas throughout the small space, their colors muted in the gloom. Plush chairs lined two of the walls.

An archway curved over a passage that exited out the other side, and a faint light glowed within. The light bobbed, and a moment later a young petal-sprout with blue petals appeared from the archway. The girl held a sun-flower lantern in one delicate hand. She wore a pink long coat trimmed in silver over a crisp white shirt and short cuffed pants. She stopped and presented her throat, then turned and gestured for the Elders to follow her.

<Silver and pink are the colors of the administrative pages.> Darach gefired to her and Yegra as the page led them along a passageway bordered in tall formed hedges.

The hedge walk branched out in a fork, and the page turned down the left. Another fork, this time a right. The moonlight glinted off something buried deep in the hedge to Arara's right. Arara stopped and leaned into the hedge trying to see what it was.

"Don't touch it!" Darach snarled, grabbing her arm and jerking her back from the hedge so hard that Arara bit down on her tongue in surprise.

Arara massaged her arm, the taste of blood filling her mouth. Yegra stared at Darach in shock. The page stopped and turned back, holding her lantern high. The five needle-sharp points of the hedge's leaves glistened in the light.

"The hedges are poisonous." The page said, frowning as she regarded Arara. "I would have warned you, but I thought..." The sproutling shook her head. "There are many protections in the palace, traps for the uninvited. Do not touch anything unless you see me or one of the Elders touch it first."

Darach ushered her and Yegra up the path after the page. *<I should have warned you, I'm sorry.>*

For the rest of the walk, Arara stayed in the center of the path, although she stared curiously through the archways that led off the main path they followed. Many of them led into small gardens indistinguishable from the first one they'd entered, but several contained elaborate fountains. They passed a marble statue of the first *sedyu*-bonded Kin/Jegera pair. They'd gone on to found the Kin-Jegera Empire. Legends said the Empire would fall if the King or Queen ascended the throne without a *sedyu*-bond.

As if trying to make for his earlier outburst, Darach gefired Arara tips for her hearing with the Council. But Arara was too dazed to take much of it in. In fact, she was so tired that several times she dozed off, only jerking awake as she stumbled and fell.

Finally, the page stopped in front of one of the vined archways. This one was wider than the others, and flowered vines twined around the wooden trels.

"Please wait here." The page blocked the doorway and turned to face them, holding up her hand. "The Queen and Council will see you momentarily."

<Arara,> Darach's voice echoed in her head. <Don't be alarmed by what happens during the hearing.>

<Wait, do I have reason to be alarmed?> Arara started, staring up at Darach.

Darach ignored her, staring into middle distance while his ears swiveled back in forth seemingly at random. Johka had his hands planted on his cane, which thumped the brick walkway rhythmically. The other two Elders stood with their eyes closed, Lolop's ruined paws spasming and Pira's tail twitching.

Yegra looked as puzzled as Arara felt.

<*What's going on?*> Yegra gefired Arara privately.

Arara shrugged and skewed her ears quizzically, one in each direction. Before she could respond, another Petal Kin in silver and blue came up behind the page and blew a silver horn. The page turned and followed the horn blower through the archway, her lantern held high.

The Elders all shook themselves out, a shiver running from ears to tail, then shuffled after the page. Yegra tagged along after them. Arara whimpered and stepped back, glancing over her shoulder. Yegra, bringing up the rear, looked back at Arara, her tail wagging. A picture of Sels, waiting excitedly for her arrival, popped into her head. With a reluctant sigh, Arara padded down the path behind them.

They entered into the top of an amphitheater. The page's lantern bobbed down the path ahead of them. Tiers of plush benches lined the way. A massive sun-flower lantern illuminated the curved stage at the bottom. A line of Kin stood across the stage, each wearing a brightly colored robes. Individually, each robe was strikingly beautiful. Together, the riot of clashing colors hurt Arara's eyes.

<Blech,> Arara gefired to Yegra. <I'm glad I don't have to wear one of those.>

<The colors signify the wearer's basic magics and house alliance.> Darach, who'd obviously been eavesdropping, gefired to her and Yegra. <Now, be polite, respectful, and above all, truthful.>

<*Yes, Sir.*> They chorused.

The page led them down and stopped in an area clear of chairs at the front of the stage. She tilted her head back and exposed her neck while gesturing with her hand, then stood to the side. Darach and the other elders lined up, with Arara and Yegra pushed in front of them. Arara noticed that although the Elders all tilted their heads back in respect, the gesture was so slight as to be imperceptible. The Council members on stage did the same.

Arara stood, feeling like every Councilor stared right at her. She wrung her paws, nervous under the gaze of so many Kin, until Darach prodded her back with one claw. She jumped, then exposed her neck to the Councilors. One of the Kin nodded, and another page entered the stage from the left. This one held a trumpet, which she blasted once. The shrill noise hurt Arara's ears, but she managed to keep herself from wincing.

A few moments later the Queen and her *Sedyu*-bonded, Tukura, swept in from the back of the terrace. Queen Seuan wore a deep red frilled robe that perfectly matched the shade of her blooms. Her vines swept up over her head, braided in the shape of a crown with her red flowers artfully arranged around it.

The Council members all shifted slightly to the left and right, revealing a flowered wooden throne set into the stage behind them. The Queen settled into the chair with a sweep of her gowns, and Tukura took up position at her side. Tukura's crisp black uniform seemed to soak up the light of the sun-flower, creating a spot of shadow on the otherwise bright stage.

Sesay entered from the other side, the soft pink of her petals merged with that of her gown, making her look as though she wore nothing but petals. Recka stalked at her side, and his black uniform matched Tukura's. Sesay and Recka stopped at the line of Councilors, taking position at the end.

The sound of a scuffle from the edge of the stage caused Arara's ears to twitch. Out of the corner of her eye she saw Sels being led onto the stage by Jeron and an Alpha-Guard. His purple garment matched the Queen's, and his vines had been braided atop his head.

Sels was so unpretentious that Arara clasped her paws over her muzzle, trying to keep from giggling at the sight of him decked out in so much finery.

His robe smoothed back into place, Sels walked across the stage with his head held high and his hands clasped in front of him. He stood next to the throne, opposite Tukura, then turned to face Arara and the Elders.

Arara couldn't resist giving him a little wave. Sels's mouth twitched up on one side, and he wriggled one hand in her direction.

"Welcome, Elders," The Queen intoned, her voice loud and commanding, even in the large space. "We called this tribunal in order to hear evidence of the crimes of Arara of Last Home. Speaker, read the list of charges."

The Kin Council member closest to the Queen stepped forward. He wore canary yellow robes trimmed in blue, and was one of the few males among the assembled Council. "Attempted murder of an Alpha-Guard. Assault on a member of the Royal Family. Conspiracy to harm a member of the Royal Family," Arara's mouth dropped open. "Collusion with rebel forces to bring down the government."

"What?" Arara barked.

The speaker continued, although he shot her a withering glare as he finished. "The punishment for such crimes is death."

Arara knew about the murder charge of course, but the Elders had agreed with her that it was clearly an accident. And assault? Could they mean the incident in the park, with the rock? But then, where did the other charges come from? *<Sels, what is he talking about? Conspiracy and collusion to bring down the government?>*

<I just learned about this a few hours ago. I'm as baffled as you.> Sels responded.

"First, let us review the evidence." The Speaker pointed to something offstage. "Guards, bring in the prisoner."

Two Alpha-Guards came on-stage dragging between them a Jegera chained in ironwood bonds. An average sized male, the prisoner was dark brown with a white streak down his face. Arara breathed deep, taking in his scent, and scoured her memory, but she couldn't place his face or smell. The guards stopped in front of the Queen, holding the hapless Jegera up.

"Now, Epoka, tell us what you confessed to the guards." The Speaker ordered.

Epoka... that name sounded familiar, but where had she heard it? She focused on Epoka and cracked her shields, just a little bit, to listen into his thoughts as he spoke.

"Um, Arara," he gestured with a paw off the stage, causing his chains to rattle together. "That little white one contacted me a few weeks before the Prince left Sebaine. She wanted to become the *sedyu*-bonded, but, well, for obvious reasons, needed to do something to impress the Prince." *<What else was I supposed to say? I have to remember my lines if I want to get out of this alive.>* "Before the Hunt, I scouted out where the herd was and hid a pack for her with a gefir booster. That was how she contacted the rest of the pack from so far away." Arara cringed, remembering how she'd found her pack in the woods during the hunt.

"We'd arranged for her to pay me during the trip to Sebaine." Epoka nodded. "That's why she tried to kill me by pushing me off the Poku."

<Arara, please tell me he is lying.> Sels's mind voice pleaded.

<He's lying, Sels. Someone threatened him, forced him to do this.> She replayed what she'd learned from listening in. Sels didn't respond, but she could feel his relief.

As Epoka finished, Johka stepped forward. “Seuan, stop this farce. This Jegera has never even met Arara.”

“Silence.” Queen Seuan’s voice boomed over the proceedings. “You may present your defense only after all evidence has been reviewed.”

“Of course, Your Majesty.” Johka bared his neck and stepped back with the rest of the Elders.

“Speaker, continue.” The Queen commanded.

The Speaker gestured, and a third guard appeared, carrying Arara’s old hunting bag by the handle.

“Is this the pack to which you are referring to?” The Speaker said, his expression blank at Epoka’s nod.

“The guards found this hidden near where the Last Home hunt found the herd of hukra.” The Speaker said. “The contents included, two *metal* knives.” His nose wrinkled. “A rope, map, a strange black feather, and, as Epoka mentioned, a gefir booster.”

As he talked, the guard pulled items out of the bag, and arranged them in a line at the front of the stage. When he got to the black kwaso feather he laid it down with a puzzled expression, his ears cocked, probably having trouble identifying the scent. The knives he handled only with the tips of his claws, dropping them with a snort of disgust. The sharp edges glinted in the light. Last, he placed a small brown nut on the stage, the gefir booster.

Arara hissed in surprise and looked up at Sels, who was staring down at the pile of tools with wide eyes. “Metal knives? Who would make such a thing?” He said under his breath.

The Queen didn’t say anything, but Arara noticed that her gaze, too, focused on the metal knives.

<How did those horrible things,> Arara gefired privately to Sels, sending a mental image of the knives with her gefir, *<get in my pack?>*

<Metalworking has been illegal for so long, those have to be very old.> Sels sounded puzzled. <But from what I’ve read, metal rusts as it

ages so they should be brown and brittle, yet the edges of those glint in the light like the descriptions in the old texts...>

<*Why is it illegal?*> If anyone would know, Sels would. Arara had asked that same question of her teachers when they'd covered the history of the Northern Mountain Wars in school, but her teacher had just rambled on about some nonsense to fight with honor.

<Don't ever ask that out loud,> Sels winced, and glanced around. <Or repeat what I'm about to tell you. Metal...has a strange effect on magic. I really can't say more than that.>

But he didn't have to. When he mentioned the strange effect he had been thinking back to the time his magic teacher demonstrated what happened to spells with metal around. She just got a flash of the memory, the teacher pulling a small lump of metal from the mouth of a wicked looking plant shaped like two paddles with razor sharp teeth. The teach placed the lump on her palm, and tried to cast a simple light spell. The light materialized in the air above her palm, then splintered and shattered a split second later.

<*Is that why no one has cast any spells tonight?*> On the way here Yegra had told her all about the spectacular magic the Queen had done at the park, yet Arara had yet to see her do a single spell.

<*What? No.*> Sels glanced up and Arara followed his gaze to the sun-flower suspended over the stage and the black curtain of sky beyond. It was so bright she couldn't even see the pinpricks of the stars in the sky. <*Without the blessing of the Sun Father, no magic will work. But yes, if it were day the knives would be disrupting mother's spells.*>

<Oh, that's not going to help my case then.> Arara winced.

Arara focused on the Queen and tried to listen to thoughts about the evidence presented so far. All she got was a faint buzzing, but she wasn't able to make out any words. She narrowed her eyes and concentrated on nothing but Seuan. The buzzing got louder, but no more meaningful. Strange. She'd have to ask Darach about it later.

"Your Majesty," Darach said. "May I take a closer look?"

The Queen nodded, and Darach hobbled around to the stairs and up onto the stage. He sniffed each piece, but spent more time examining the knives and feather.

"Please continue." Darach said, limping back down off the stage.

"Take him away." The Speaker said. The two guards dragged Epoka away. The Speaker waited until he was gone, and then continued. "Next, we have testimony from Prince Sels that he was attacked by a strange black bird while in Last Home. And, a black feather was found in Arara's pack.

"Finally, we have the fact that earlier today Arara assaulted Prince Sels with a rock, giving him a concussion."

Arara hung her head, ashamed that she'd hurt Sels at all. But it was an accident. They had to understand.

The Queen held out her hand. "Thank you, Speaker."

"Of course, Your Majesty." The Speaker stepped back to the line of Councilors.

"Now, Elders," Wood creaked as the Queen shifted in her seat. "Your defense to these charges?"

"Your Majesty." Darach growled, and stepped forward next to Arara. "Epoka's testimony is coerced."

"The evidence presented so far is damning." Queen Seuan sat forward, giving Darach a hard look. "Are you saying the evidence is false?"

"Yes, Your Majesty." Darach said. "But I don't have any proof. But I've spent the day with Arara, and even that small exposure has given me an insight into her character. This is not something she would do."

"Is that all?"

"No, Your Majesty." Darach growled. "Your own son would also testify to this, I'm sure of it."

"Yes, I've already heard as much from him." She said with a frown. "But that does not excuse her putting my son into danger, nor the assault upon his person."

"Of course not, Your Majesty." Darach spread his arms wide, throwing his head back in a Kin gesture of respect. "But they are children, and prone to the accidents and mistakes of youth."

"That excuses much," The Queen stood, putting an arm around Sels shoulder. "But it does not excuse harming my only child. Nor does it excuse conspiring against the throne." The Queen gave Sels a slight squeeze and let go, walking forward to the edge of the stage.

"Council, what say you?" The Queen turned her back on the Elders and looked up and down the line of Councilors.

Each Councilor raised their right hand, some palm up but most had their palm down. Arara noticed that Sesay, at the end, held her palm down.

"Thank you for your verdict." The Queen turned and looked down at the Elders assembled below the stage. "And you, Jegera Elders. I'm sure I know what your vote is."

"Yes, Your Majesty." Johka hobbled forward, cane clicking on the stones. "We vote not guilty."

The Queen nodded. "As arbiter and judge, I've made my decision.

"Arara of Last Home," Queen Seuan raised her arms and tilted her face up towards the sun-flower suspended overhead. "I find you guilty of all charges. The sentence is death."

"No!" Sels yelled, lunging forward. Tukura jumped and wrapped her arms around him, holding him tight.

Arara whimpered and clasped her paws together. There was so much she'd never gotten to do. Yegra touched her arm, then took her paw and squeezed it.

"However," The Queen spread her arms. "Since my son publicly acknowledged you as his candidate, you are under his protection. Delivery of the punishment is suspended, until such time as protection is withdrawn."

Arara widened her eyes. He'd done that for her. Yegra yipped in excitement.

"Listen well, Arara of Last Home." The Queen spoke again. "If you fail any of the Trials or fail to become my son's *Sedyu*-bonded, your sentence will be swift and final."

"Yes, thank you, Your Majesty." Arara said.

CHAPTER THIRTEEN

TRAINING AND LIES

"A death sentence? But it was an accident!" Arara's cries echoed off the walls of the carriage. Yegra winced and covered her ears. The Elders flattened their ears to their heads.

"It's not an accident if it's preventable." Darach looked disgusted. "At your age you should be in total control of your abilities."

"I am in control. None of those things hit me." Arara barked back before falling into the seat next to Darach with a huff.

"Very true. Instead they hit Prince Sels." Darach flicked Arara's nose. "Why didn't you drop them to the ground? Or fling them back at Kerka?"

Arara rubbed her nose and scooted away. "Stopping things is hard. Deflecting them is easier."

"Alright, then why not fling them back at Kerka?"

Arara cringed at the thought of saying that she didn't know how. Instead she stared at the claws on her feet as they swung with the motion of the carriage. Darach snorted. The end of Johka's cane tapped the floor.

"This is bad. The Prophecy...you must become the *sedyu*-bonded." Johka trailed off, glancing at Yegra next to him.

"Don't." Arara curled up into a ball, ears pressed to her head. Bad enough to let Sels down. She didn't want to hear how she'd failed everyone in the Empire. At least she wouldn't live to see the awful results of her failure.

"What's this Prophecy you mentioned?" Yegra took Arara's paws, holding them in her lap. Arara's tail wagged and she squeezed Yegra back.

Johka glanced at the other Elders before looking away. "Nothing for your ears, girl. The matter is sensitive and we must be careful. The Queen's spies are everywhere. For all we know you're one."

Yegra's jaw clenched, but she relaxed when she noticed Arara's gaze.

<They said the Empire is on the verge of destruction and that only I can stop it.> Arara sent to Yegra.

<Destruction? From what?>

<I, uh, didn't stick around to find out.>

<So that's why you were running like your tail was on fire when I found you.> Yegra yipped and Arara giggled along with her.

Darach's head snapped around and his eyes narrowed. <Arara, she cannot be trusted. Do not discuss the Prophecy with anyone.>

<What? I've known Yegra since we were both tiny puppies. Of course we can trust her.>

<No, we do not know where she was or what she was doing today. Say nothing until she has been cleared.>

"I know Yegra has nothing to hide. We can clear her right now." Arara snapped outloud, giving Yegra's paws a reassuring squeeze.

"Now is not a good time-" Johka began.

"Actually," Darach cut him off and nodded at Arara. "This is the perfect opportunity to begin her training."

"It is?" Yegra blinked and looked back and forth between Arara and Darach. "What does deflecting rocks with her mind have to do with proving I'm not a spy?"

"Deflecting rocks?" Darach snorted. "There is more to the Yaka's fearsome reputation than just the ability to force-push objects with the mind."

"Yaka?" Yegra's eyes widened and she stared at Darach, pupils gleaming in the deepening twilight. "What does that have to do with Arara?"

"Now, to prepare yourself, it is best to be touching the subject." Darach instructed. He faced Arara, but focused on Yegra. "First, close your eyes and lower your mental shield. Concentrate on the subject, imagine yourself occupying the same space as them."

Yegra pushed Arara away and scrambled back on the seat until she hit Johka next to her. Her eyes grew huge and round. "Subject? Yaka? Just what are you going to do with me?"

"Relax." Johka's cane prodded Yegra back towards Arara. "Darach, finish your instructions via private gefir and stop baiting the girl."

"Yes, sir." Darach leered at Yegra. In the dim light the black fur on his face melded with dark eyes into a black mask.

Yegra whimpered. Arara leaned over and gave her a reassuring lick on the nose before closing her eyes.

Mental shields encircled her mind in a solid field, blocking unwanted thoughts. She concentrated, and the shield faded to nothing. Thoughts from everyone in the carriage and the passersby on the street assaulted her mind.

The din drowned out everything else. Her paws clawed at her ears, trying to shut out the noise. With a painful howl she flung her shields back into place.

<I said to concentrate fully the subject when you dropped your shields.> Darach's teeth snapped a hair's breadth from her nose. <If you'd followed my instructions, you wouldn't be in pain.>

Arara yelped and wrapped her arms around Yegra. *<It would help if you told me what I was trying to accomplish.>* The carriage rocked underneath her, and she squeezed her eyes shut. The movement combined with the pain in her head made her nauseated.

<Just do what I tell you.> Darach growled in her head.

Hot breath hit her face, and she cringed back, burrowing her head into Yegra's side. Yegra's scent filled her nostrils and wiry fur poked her through Yegra's new black cotton uniform. The familiar smell filled her nostrils. Only when Yegra filled all her thoughts did she drop her shields again. This time a surge of memories swept her away.

Arara found herself immersed in the familiar sights, sounds, and smells of Last Home. Yegra's litter-mate Gror stood conversing with her about the start of hunting lessons. Their eyes met, and with a shock Arara realized they stood eye-to-eye. Unfamiliar gray fur covered her paws. Yegra's paws.

Yegra and Gror turned to leave when Arara saw herself burst from the trees ahead at a dead run, Kerka on her heels. Of course. This memory. The day she discovered her ability to push things with her mind. The day Kerka came close to killing her. Yegra'd seen the whole thing. No wonder she hadn't seemed surprised when Arara used her abilities in the park earlier.

Arara watched, helpless to influence the event or look away, as Kerka tackled herself from behind.

<Gror, let's get out of here before he senses us.> Yegra gefired, while ducking behind a nearby bush.

Gror nodded to her and together they slunk back the way they'd come. Behind her, flesh hit flesh and Arara cried out in pain. Yegra turned her head and stopped to watch, although Gror continued on. Through a gap in the leaves, she could see Kerka holding herself, Arara, down with one paw and punching her in the stomach with the other.

Without warning, Kerka's head flew back, as if punched upside the jaw with an uppercut from an invisible fist. Arara wriggled free from Kerka's grip, fleeing down the path on two legs and holding her stomach with her front paws.

Kerka staggered forward, and with his long strides he caught up to Arara in only a moment. He caught Arara's tail in a fist, and used their combined momentum to slam her sideways into the dirt.

"What did you do to me?" Kerka snarled through a clenched jaw, a massive bruise already visible through his dark fur.

The bushes rustled around her as Yegra stifled a laugh. The deep satisfaction Yegra felt on seeing Kerka injured surprised Arara. Why hadn't Yegra ever come to her aid growing up, if she hated Kerka that much?

<Tell me about why you were out searching for Arara today.> Darach's mind voice echoed through their shared mind.

The world dissolved away into the mist, and a new memory swam into focus. Sels requested Yegra to find Arara for him. From Arara's point of view she looked down to meet Sels's eyes. The height advantage was a strange sensation. While Arara relived the memory with Yegra, she could also hear Yegra answering Darach's questions about that very meeting.

<Who do you report back to?> Darach asked next.

Sels's face came back for a moment. However, it wavered, then faded out, to be replaced with Sesay's. Yegra stood in a submissive pose in front of Sesay. The rocking sensation told Arara that this memory happened during the pod ride south, although she couldn't tell if it happened before or after she'd been arrested.

"But does she trust you?" Sesay asked, staring Yegra in the eyes.

"No." Yegra answered, eyes down, her paws clasped behind her. "She has no reason to. We were never friends growing up."

"No matter." Sesay turned and paced as she talked. "Gain her trust. Report back to me or Recka if you discover anything. This is your first duty as a new Alpha-Guard, do you understand?"

The memory faded, and Arara understood why Darach was doing this. You couldn't lie in a gefir, but sometimes there was more to the truth. Yegra reported to Sels, she hadn't lied, but she also reported to Sesay.

Darach continued to ask Yegra questions while Arara monitored Yegra's memories. When he finished, Arara pulled out. Her heart ached. She'd thought Yegra was her friend, but everything was a lie.

<Once you are practiced, you may not even need to touch the subject in order to sink into their memories like that.> Darach sent as Arara blinked her eyes open.

Her head pounded, and she knew she'd overextended herself. Yegra helped her to her feet, and together they stumbled from the carriage onto a hard-packed dirt path. Even this late at night, the hot air burned her throat.

"I don't know what the big deal was." Yegra said to her as they followed the Elders down a moonlit walk. Massive trees lined the path, their leaves dark blots against the stars.

"What do you mean?" Arara stifled a yawn.

"I mean, that big deal about training you, only for you to fall asleep on my lap for the rest of the ride."

"Asleep?" Arara put a paw to her pounding head, trying to think. Not to give away she knew the truth. "I, uh, suppose Darach realized how tired I was."

"This way girls." Darach pointed to a shadowy shape, only visible as a darker blot in the gloom to Arara's eyes.

"A den. Finally." Yegra yawned wide and dropped to all fours. Vines rustled as she nosed her way inside.

Arara stepped from the path, but Darach grabbed her arm. <*Well?*>

<*Couldn't you see what I was seeing?*> Arara asked. She didn't want to say it, didn't want to make it real.

<No,> Darach snapped. Impatience pricked Arara's mental shields. <Diving that deep takes intense concentration. I can tell you are hiding something, out with it.>

<*She's reporting back to Sesay.*> Arara sniffed, staring at Darach's face as her heart broke in half. The admission hurt even more than Arara had suspected it would. For the first time in her life, she thought she'd found a friend.

Darach grinned down at Arara, teeth sparkling bright in the moonlight. <*Keep an eye on her for now. Don't let on that you know.*> He nodded, and turned away.

<Wait,> Arara stared after him, puzzled. <I thought you were going to train me for the first Trial.>

<Tomorrow morning.> Darach waved as he limped away. <You had to learn today's lesson first.>

Far too early in the morning, Arara awoke to a loud knocking. She burrowed her face farther down into her tail and flattened her ears, snuggling up to Yegra behind her. A second later, the knocking stopped, only for the sun-flower above the bed to bloom open, flooding the room with light. Arara squeezed her eyes shut and growled. Yesterday's headache still pulsed in her head, diminished but not yet gone.

"Blooming time!" Darach yelled. "It's a gorgeous day out there. Time to get up!" He grabbed Arara's tail and pulled it from her face.

Arara growled again and tried to pull her tail back, but Darach held it fast. She pried open her eyes and looked up. The sun-flower's light outlined Darach's patchy white fur from behind, making it look gray and indistinct. Darach dropped Arara's tail and stepped back.

Yegra stirred, and a moment later she crawled over Arara, stretching and yawning. Yegra stood, wrinkling her nose as she stretched towards the ceiling. "What is that smell? I didn't notice it last night."

Darach sniffed at the air, then his paws and snorted. "Arara, when was the last time you bathed?"

"I don't know." Arara yawned and stood, rubbing her bleary eyes with her paws. "Sometime before I left Last Home."

Yegra snorted and padded back farther into the den.

Darach growled and pointed towards the hallway Yegra had disappeared down. "Go wash up."

Water splashed farther down the hallway. Intrigued, Arara padded along the dirt. She found Yegra in a small room carved from rock.

Water ran down the wall into a shallow pool. A small stream trickled out of the pool and along the floor before disappearing into the wall. Yegra splashed around in the pool, scrubbing her fur.

Arara's stomach twisted, but she had to act natural. She stripped off her new outfit and jumped into the pool. Water cascaded out, swamping the floor and soaking their clothes. Yegra giggled and splashed her. Arara retaliated, and soon they laughed together as they splashed water at each other.

"Hurry up!" Darach yelled from the front room. "We're already running late."

Yegra and Arara looked at each other and laughed. They splashed each other a few more times before climbing out and shaking themselves dry. Arara's paw shook as she wrung out her outfit, repeating 'Yegra's a spy' to herself in her head, but it wasn't helping the ache in her heart.

Darach waited for them in the bedroom when they emerged from the back. He turned without a word and limped out, and the girls followed after him.

Daylight showed Arara the den nestled inside a massive tree, which explained the wooden walls. The sun peaked above the horizon, burning away the last remnants of dew from the grass. In fact, every tree on the path had an entrance at ground level. A ramp circled up each, allowing access to more vine covered holes spaced up the massive trunks. Thick wide leaves topped each tree. They fanned out like an umbrella, dappling the ground with shade.

"Are those all dens?" Arara stared up as they walked. "Just how many Jegera live here?"

"No," Darach said without looking up. "These are the dorms for Kin attending Sunspire University. Each tree has a Jegeran servant living at the ground level. That particular tree is empty for the moment while the gardeners clear out a leaf aphid infestation. The aphids are harmless to Jegera, so the University lent a dorm to us for your use while you are here."

Darach limped faster. They approached a wider path, crawling with carriages. Pedestrians walked along the sides. The Kin students strolled along in groups, followed by Jegeran servants loaded down with books, scrolls, and bags. Darach ushered them into a waiting carriage stamped with the seal of the Moon. Johka and the other Elders waited for them inside.

Johka rapped on the door, and the carriage lurched up and away, swaying as it picked up speed.

“How are you feeling, Arara?” Johka asked.

“Nervous.” Arara slid onto the bench next to Yegra. “I wish there’d been time for some training.”

“There is.” Darach said. <Remember what I taught you yesterday?>

Arara nodded, remembering being inside Yegra’s head. It had felt different compared to gefired memories, like the difference between watching something happen and experiencing it firsthand. <*Yes, but what does that have to do with training?*>

Darach grinned. <*Concentrate on me and drop your shields.*> He grabbed her paw and held it.

<What?>

<Just do it.>

Arara closed her eyes and followed Darach’s instructions. Just like before, she opened her eyes to find herself somewhere else.

In the memory a younger Darach stood in the snow talking to... herself, still with her longer fur, curled tail wagging behind her. Wait, when would this would have taken place? Darach spoke in some strange language, but in the memory Arara spoke the language. After listening to their conversation a moment, the truth came out. That wasn’t her, but another Yaka. The curled tail. Mostly white fur. Darach must be part Yaka. Why hadn’t he told her before?

The conversation stopped, and the Yaka gave Darach some instructions. Darach listened and then watched as the instructor levitated some snow from the ground. The snow hovered in the air for a moment, then formed itself into a dense ball. The snowball flew towards a target tacked high in the tree, zooming around obstacles to smack the center bullseye.

Darach attempted the same thing, clumsily forming a misshapen snowball. It hit the first branch and exploded. The instructor watched, giving tips, as Darach tried again and again, for hours, getting closer with each try. Since she shared Darach's head, she knew what he knew, learned what he knew. When the sun set behind them, the instructor allowed Darach to stop. Although he still hadn't been able to hit the target, he'd gotten much better at controlling and directing the projectiles. Darach followed the instructor from the clearing, head pounding from the day's efforts.

Claws dug into her arm, ejecting her from the dream. She blinked her eyes and pushed up. Her head didn't hurt any more than before, so she couldn't have been out for long.

"Sorry to wake you up. You fell asleep again." Yegra chided, poking Arara in the arm with a smile. "We're here."

No wonder Darach said she'd had to master memory diving first. She'd gotten an entire day's practice done during the trip to the palace.

*****

The guards pushed their way through the massive crowd gathered outside the palace entrance. Arara, Yegra, and the Elders followed close behind them. It seemed to Arara that the entire city had shown up to watch the Trials.

Inside, Yegra left to get a seat in the arena. As she left, she gave Arara a hug and wished her good luck. Arara just nodded in response, not trusting herself to speak without growling.

Arara followed the Elders. A guard led them through the garden maze. During the day the bright colors and variety of flowers in the gardens amazed her.

This time they were taken to a small garden surrounded by hedges. Exotic flowers, trees and bushes landscaped the small area. A brick path wound through the flowers to a small patio with a white painted gazebo and round carved wooden table. Four matching chairs ringed the table.

A smiling Sels sat in a chair talking to Kerka. Sels wore formal robes dripping with jewels, and his vines were braided around in a crown, just like last night. Opposite Sels sat a small brown female Jegera. Jeron stood at attention a few tail lengths away.

"Arara!" Sels stood to greet her. When Arara reached him, he leaned over and gave her a quick hug. "I'm glad to see you." His distinctive smell, familiar and comforting, enveloped her as much as his arms.

Sels pushed back and held her at arm's length. "You look great! And I'm sure you'll do amazing in the Trial today."

"I... sure hope so." Arara looked down and scuffed the patio with her back claws.

"Hah, I doubt it." Kerka yipped, sauntering up behind Sels. "That failure can't do anything right."

"Shut up, Kerka," Arara sneered at him. "You're nothing without your cronies!"

Kerka growled at her, but stopped when Arara gave him a toothy smile in response.

"I bet you'll both be fine." A soft voice said. "It's me I'm worried about." Nathira stood behind Kerka, wringing her paws.

Sels grinned at her. "I wouldn't have picked you if I wasn't confident in your abilities, Nathira." He tickled her ears. "Just follow your instincts." Nathira ducked out from under the touch, but gave him a grateful smile.

Arara had to swallow to keep herself from growling at Nathira for getting too close to her Sels. Instead, Arara looked away, paws behind her back.

"Your Highness," Johka said. "A pleasure as always. But we must go. We have much to discuss."

"Of course, Elders." Sels said, face smoothed to a blank mask and hands spread wide. "This way." He gestured to the garden's exit.

Jeron marched past, giving Arara a discreet wave. The Elders filed out behind him. Arara moved to follow them. Sels's raised hand stopped her.

"Arara," Sels stooped down to look her in the eye. "I can't see you again until after you've beaten the first Trial. You'll be waiting here, with the rest of the candidates, until your turn."

Arara's ears went back. "Alone? With Kerka? Do I have to?" She looked back at Kerka, who, noticing her attentions, leered back at her.

"No, Nathira will be here, too." Sels stood back up. "I'll send down some food and beverages for you while you wait. Use this time to work things out with Kerka. You'll have to be in close quarters with him for the rest of the Trials."

Sels turned and left, leaving Arara alone with Nathira and Kerka. Kerka came up behind her, huffing under his breath. Arara spun, glaring up at him.

"I know you're planning something." Arara focused on him and cracked her shields. An image of her on all fours with Kerka on top of her came through. She slammed her shields shut with a snarl.

"Gross," Arara pushed past him to sit at the table.

"Now, that's not nice." Kerka dragged a chair around and plopped down next to her.

"You're just jealous that Sels likes me more." Arara flicked the outside fingers of her paw at him with teeth bared.

"Not hardly." Kerka leaned over to huff in her face. Arara again cursed her small size. "I've spent the entire last week with Sels. You have no chance." A smug smile twitched up his lips as he sat back, putting an arm around Arara's shoulder. "Yep, I have him wrapped around my middle claw."

"What about his magic problem?" Arara extended her own claws and turned around, slashing. Kerka's arm snapped up and away, elbowing the back of a chair with a crack. A line of red blood sparkled against the matte black fur. "Doesn't that bother you?"

"Naw," Kerka grabbed a napkin off the table and dabbed at the blood. "Sels will never be King, so who cares if he's a screw up. I just want the perks." The blood kept oozing, so he tied the napkin around the arm, using teeth to pull the makeshift bandage closed. "Think of it, a cushy job following a noble around all day. All you can eat, any girl you want..." Kerka gave Arara a sideways glance.

"Never be King?" Nathira said, causing Arara and Kerka to both turn and stare across the table at her. Nathira'd been so quiet until now, Arara had forgotten about her. "Why do you say that?"

"Well, you know." Kerka grinned when both girls turned their attention towards him. "In order to even be considered heir to the throne, a member of the Royal Family has to meet several requirements." He leaned back, paws laced behind his head. "First, upon turning eighteen, they need to successfully form a *sedyu*-bond. That's where I come in." The chair creaked under Kerka's bulk as he leaned farther back. "Second, they have to be able to cast the Royal Magic."

"How do you know this?" Arara stared at Kerka.

"Like I said, I spent the last week with Sels."

Silence fell over the group. The clink of glassware drew everyone's attention to the archway. Two Petal Kin pages walked up the path, balancing platters of sweat-meats, carafes of juice, and wide-lipped drinking bowls. China clinked as they slid the trays onto the table. Each page presented their throat to the group, then glided away.

"What's the Royal Magic?" Arara plucked up a sweet-meat and popped it in her mouth. The tang of smoked raop meat perfectly offset the sweetness of the candied jelly shell.

"Seriously?" Nathira stared at Arara. "Did you grow up under a rock?"

"No," Arara bristled, and couldn't stop herself from growling as she talked. "I ditched school a lot." She looked at Kerka and narrowed her eyes. "For some reason."

"You know," Kerka sat up and poured them each a drink. "That rainbow spell that Princess Sesay cast when Sels first got to town." He distributed the full glasses around the table when he finished.

"I wouldn't know." Arara flattened her ears and wrinkled her nose as she gagged on the strong stink of the spiced plumberry wine. "A *previous engagement* kept me from attending." Bright red liquid splashed the polished wood of the table as she shoved the glass away from her with a huff.

"I..." Kerka's ears twitched down and he looked at her with sad eyes. "I'm really very sorry about that." He slid the goblet back to her, mopping up spilled wine with a napkin. "How about we drink to a truce?"

Again Kerka thwarted her attempts to listen in - this time showing her a memory of Jegera pups frolicking in the grass.

Arara wrinkled her nose at the smell but lifted her goblet. The sour odor of the wine filled her nose, and she set her still full cup back down with a shudder.

"What's wrong?" Kerka sounded hurt. "What about the truce?"

"It's not that." A dislike of plumberries gave away her Yaka heritage, she remembered. "I, uh, don't want to drink right now. The first Trial is in a few claws and I don't want to have a muddled head."

"It's one goblet. You'll be fine." He picked up the glass and thrust it back at her.

"This will go straight to my head."

Kerka cocked his head. "This drink represents our truce. Finishing the wine seals it. Sels told us we need to get along for this trial, and I agree. We can't compete at our best if we're so focused on watching each other for treachery."

Arara sighed and tried to keep from wrinkling her nose as she held up the goblet. She did manage a grimace-like grin before she took a big gulp. She gagged and almost spit it out. If possible it tasted even worse than it smelled. She couldn't finish it. The next time Kerka took a drink she turned to the side. She pretended to take a drink while tipping it off into the bushes behind her. Now her goblet had only a few swallows in the bottom.

Kerka drained the last of his drink with a loud slurp. No choice. Arara took one last big gulp, shuddering as she licked the last few drops from the bottom.

Glass crunched as Kerka and Arara slammed their empty goblets onto the tray at the same time.

"There, done." Arara snarled and withdrew her paw, flicking away pieces of broken glass.

"Let me help." Kerka reached over.

The chair crashed to the patio with a clatter as Arara jumped to her feet and backed away. She stumbled backwards and would have fallen into the hedge if Kerka hadn't grabbed her paw. He jerked her forward, and she fell into him. Strong arms caught her, lifting her upright.

"Whoa there. You alright?"

She was emphatically not alright. The ground spun out from under her and she staggered. Kerka's arms pulled her close and kept her upright. His heart beat fast against her cheek.

"Wow, that was some str.. strong stuff." Strength drained from her limbs even as she talked. Her mouth felt stuffed with cotton. Arara sagged in Kerka's arms, boneless. At least the room stopped spinning.

"Arara? Are you alright?" Kerka's nose pressed against Arara's forehead. He whined and licked her cheek.

"What's wrong with her?" Nathira whispered from across the table, her eyes wide.

Arara tried to respond, but her mouth refused to obey her at all. She squeaked and coughed as her eyes drifted closed.

"Answer me!" Kerka gathered her up and ran down the path, howling for help. Nathira chased after him.

Arara felt weightless and relaxed as she bounced along in Kerka's arms. She'd always had to be so on edge, watching for trouble from all sides. This forced relaxation felt almost good.

<Oh, no. Not good. Not good.> Kerka's thoughts flew into Arara's mind unbidden. <He said that stuff was just supposed to relax her and make her more open to suggestions, not make her pass out! Maybe it shouldn't have been mixed with wine? But how else was I supposed to get her to drink it?>

Kerka, you no good little bastard! All that talk of a truce, just to poison her the first chance he got! She tried to hear more, but now even her mind betrayed her, floating away on the clouds, unable to focus. The clouds pulled her away and she knew no more.

CHAPTER FOURTEEN

THE FIRST TRIAL

Sels doubled over in pain, gasping and clutching his stomach. The garden swam around him.

"Sels, what's wrong?" Jeron grabbed his shoulders.

Sels pulled his arms tighter around him and slid down to his knees. "I don't know. I just suddenly started to feel sick."

Ahead, Queen Seuan and Tukura stopped and turned.

"Son?" The Queen stepped towards them, worry in her eyes. "Are you well?"

"Your Majesty," Jeron presented his neck to the Queen. "I should take him to the infirmary."

"No. I will heal him." The Queen snapped her fingers. Tukura stripped off her jacket and laid it on the cobblestones beside Sels.

The Queen lifted her robes and then knelt down on the jacket with Tukura's help. She placed a hand on Sels forehead while she began to chant. Red light flared from her fingers before fading away.

"I sense nothing wrong." The Queen sat back, brows furrowed. Her flowers contracted, closing up into tight buds.

"It hurts." Sels said, hugging himself tighter. The pain radiated out from his stomach, more intense each second. "And I feel light-headed."

"Your Majesty, it could be a new type of poison." Jeron scooped Sels up and cradled him close. "Perhaps one you are not familiar with."

Sels focused on Jeron's warmth, trying to ignore the pain. It didn't help much. His stomach cramped up tighter, and he cried out.

"Take him to the healers. I will catch up." The Queen said. Tukura reached down a paw and helped the Queen stand, then dusted off the Queen's robes.

Jeron nodded and jogged away. Sels bounced around clenched in a ball. Running for the healers, again. Then, just as suddenly as it started, the pain vanished. Sels waited a few moments to see if it would come back, but when it didn't he struggled against Jeron's arms.

"It's gone. I feel fine now. Put me down."

"What?" Jeron stopped, still gripping Sels tightly. "Gone? Just like that?"

"Yes. Now put me down."

Jeron lowered Sels to his feet, but kept a tight paw on his arm. Only when Sels stood without wobbling did he let go.

Sels looked down at himself in dismay. Dirt streaked his robes where he had fallen. The back hem was torn and stained, dragged when Jeron had carried him. He could feel where his elaborate braid crown had come undone in several places. Jeron helped Sels straighten everything up as best they could, but Sels knew mother wouldn't be pleased.

"I've informed Tukura of your recovery." Jeron said. "Your mother is relieved, but still insists you see a healer after the Trials."

Sels nodded. He'd expected as much.

"Are you sure you're alright to walk to the arena?"

Sels took a few tentative steps, then bobbed his head again.

They made their way along the path towards the stadium. As they got closer, Sels could hear the roaring crowd. They exited the Royal

Family's private gardens. Rather than enter the public way, they ascended a spiraling walkway up into the trees.

From there they crossed suspended bridges to the still empty Royal Box. Mother had probably been pulled aside on some administrative duty, as usual. Sels and Jeron took their seats and watched the crowd.

The box-trees around them soon filled up with nobles. Some Sels recognized from Council sessions or court. Many had brought their children, including several pretty ladies his own age. One caught his eye and smiled. Her orange flowers bloomed at the ends of her vines, framing her face like a sun-halo. Sels blushed and waved before turning back around, his own flowers blooming in response.

From this vantage point, Sels could see the entire arena. Tiered seating surrounded the hard-packed dirt stadium. Three layers of trees provided seats for the nobles, where the Kin could watch from a safe distance. Jegera filled the ground level seats, so they could be closer to the action.

"Will they each be fighting the same creature?" Sels asked Jeron. He had already guessed the answer, but he wanted to confirm his hunch.

"No. The Menagerie Master was given a profile of each candidate. He picked out a creature that he feels will challenge their weaknesses." Jeron turned towards him. "I will warn you, the guards have been instructed to not interfere unless they absolutely have to."

"But what if they get hurt?" Sels clenched his hands together to keep them from shaking, but he couldn't stop his flowers curling closed. No wonder mother had not allowed him to attend Sesay's candidate's trials. At the time he'd been out of the nursery only a few weeks, having barely pulled his roots out of the ground. He remembered at the time that he'd been bitterly disappointed at being left behind.

"The guards will help if the candidate requests it. A true warrior knows when a battle cannot be won alone."

"If they don't?"

"They will most likely get hurt." Jeron snorted. "But they knew the risks when they accepted your token."

Sels supposed it made sense. If they thought the fight a test of their prowess, a lot of them would be too proud to ask for help.

Soon enough his mother and Tukura joined them in the box. Tukura settled in next to Jeron, while Queen Seuan went to the railing. Mother motioned to him, and Sels took his place beside her.

Her eyes narrowed, but she couldn't say anything about his appearance to him now. Seuan slipped her hand into his, and then raised their arms. The crowd cheered and howled.

"It is my great pleasure to welcome you all here today to usher in my son's twentieth birthday." The Queen's amplified voice filled the arena, drowning out the crowd. "Today marks the first Trial the candidates must overcome before they can be judged worthy of the honor of becoming a *Sedyu*-bonded."

With a flourish she released a small raincloud, which circled the stadium. The droplets it released formed a sparkling rainbow for a moment before vanishing.

Below them, Kerka entered the arena, waving and grinning at the roaring crowd as he made his way to the arena's center. His black fur shone under the bright sun. He wore a thin, black leather fighting outfit.

"Our first candidate, Kerka of Last Home." The Queen announced before they settled back into their thrones.

Movement at the far end of the arena drew Sels attention. Three creatures darted out onto the dirt, too far away to get a good look at. Several members of the crowd howled and cried out for Kerka to be careful.

A tingle ran over him as Kin mages erected a barrier to protect the audience, locking Kerka in with the creatures. Sels turned his attention back to the center, but now Kerka appeared to be alone in the dirt.

"Where did they go?"

"Those are chameleons." Tukura leaned forward, tail wagging. "You aren't going to see them again until they strike. We profiled him as relying too much on his size and strength."

Kerka prowled around the edge on all fours, trying to pick up their scents. A flash of movement to Kerka's left, and the chameleons attacked. Two from the rear and one from the front.

Kerka flattened and swiped at the first one. It fell to the ground and Kerka pounced, tearing out its throat. The ones at the rear latched onto him with their sharp claws.

The chameleons were Jegera-sized lizards with bulging eyes and warm gray scales. Their large claws dug into Kerka. Long snouts filled with sharp, tiny teeth pulled chunks from Kerka's back.

The Kin in the crowd gasped, and many averted their eyes. The Jegera howled encouragement. Kerka growled in frustration, twisting and clawing at his back. He dropped and bucked. A chameleon flew away, ripping a chunk of Kerka's fur out.

The chameleon hit the ground, scrambled back to his feet and vanished. Kerka pounced, managing to catch its tail in his mouth. A mound of dirt faded away to reveal gray scales. Kerka swung it back and forth, whipping the chameleon around by the tail. He spun the chameleon around, cracking its head into the ground until it stopped moving.

Meanwhile, the last chameleon continued to tear at Kerka's unprotected back. The ground around them had turned to a red muddy soup. More blood dripped down Kerka's back and sides. The Jegera in the crowd continued to roar their approval, but now the Kin's musical voices joined them.

Dropping the now dead chameleon, Kerka twisted and attempted to claw the last one from his back. The final chameleon hung on tenaciously, refusing to be dislodged. Kerka slowed, staggering, sides heaving. Blood coursed freely down his fur.

"Mother, he needs help!" Sels gasped and covered his eyes, feeling sick. He didn't like Kerka, but he didn't want to see this.

"Sels, put your hands down. You need to pay attention." Mother scolded.

He lowered his hands, clasping them in his lap to keep them from shaking. By the time he focused on the action again, Kerka looked even worse. Kerka signaled to the Guards, and the magic shimmered, allowing several Alpha-Guards access. They bounded forward and slashed at the remaining chameleon. They pried the dead body off Kerka's back, and green-robed Kin healers assisted him out of the arena.

To Sels's right, Seuan stood and approached the railing. The crowd fell silent, awaiting her announcement. Her amplified voice echoed around the arena.

"Kerka has passed the first Trial. We have received word from the Healers that he will make a full recovery. The second Trial will be begin shortly."

When she returned to her seat, Seuan turned to Sels. "I'd like to hear your thoughts about Kerka's performance."

Sels looked over in surprise. "Shouldn't we wait until all three of them have finished?"

"Of course we'll compare them at the end, but it's important to evaluate each candidate on their own merits as well, and it's best to do that as soon as possible so you don't forget important details."

Sels nodded. His mother was right, she was always right.

*****

Nathira entered the arena below them, the crowd roaring in anticipation. Her ears drooped down to the sides and her tail curled up under her. She made her way to the center and took up a fighting stance.

Sels focused on the far side, where the chameleons had entered. A small hukra lumbered from the trees, led by a team of Jegera handlers. Its clubbed tail whipped around; the beast had already been riled up.

As soon as they released it, the shimmering barrier snapped back into place.

Nathira backed up, head swiveling, eyes huge and wild looking. Across the arena the hukra bellowed and charged forward. Nathira screamed, spun around and dashed away on all fours.

Sels sat forward in his chair, eyes wide. Why did she run away? He cast his mind back, wracking his brain trying to remember her village's hunt. The familiar scream triggered the memory. He could picture her now, screaming and running from the amphibious gator's toothy grin. It had taken the entire pack to convince her to come back and finish the hunt. He should never have let Sesay pick Nathira.

Without realizing it, he'd stood and moved to the balcony. The enraged hukra chased Nathira around in a circle. The hukra gained ground with every pound of its hooves. Nathira slowed down, sliding to a stop in a cloud of dust and flipping herself around. She crouched, coiling her back legs underneath her like springs.

The hukra lowered its head and charged. Right before the horns reached her she leapt straight up, flipped and landed on the hukra's back. She dug claws in between the gaps in the beast's armor and then bit into the joint at the base of its neck. The beast bellowed in pain and stopped, bucking its hind-quarters up into the air.

As it crashed down, it shook its head back and forth. Dust flew everywhere, making it hard for Sels to see. He squinted his eyes and leaned forward over the railing. The hukra reared back now, front legs and head visible above the cloud. He could barely make out Nathira, muzzle buried in the beast's neck, claws scrabbling for purchase on the hard armored plates.

The ground seemed to tremble when the hukra landed, and Nathira screamed for help, loud and high. The hukra bellowed and stomped the ground. There was a sickening crack, and Nathira's scream cut off. Sels gasped in shock with the crowd.

The Menagerie Masters ran forward, opening a hole in the barrier. A squad of Jegera guards and Kin healers ducked through the opening.

Two Jegera broke away from the group, waving orange blankets behind them as they ran. The hukra bellowed and charged after them. The healers descended on a small form laying prone in the dirt. Even from here Sels could see the healing magic's bright glow.

Strong paws grabbed his arms from behind, dragging him away from the rail. Sels struggled, keeping his eyes on Nathira, though dust still obscured his view. Moisture ran down his face and he realized at some point that he'd started crying.

He smelled his mother come up behind him. She pulled an embroidered hand cloth from out of her sleeve and patted Sels's face dry. The cloth stuck to his tears as mother cleaned his face. When she finished she tucked the cloth into his hand.

"There we go. I hate to see you so upset." The Queen smiled and took Sels's hands. "They were able to get to her in time. She'll be a few days recovering. The next few Trials are not as physical as today's."

His mother's calm demeanor surprised him. He gulped and nodded his head to indicate he'd heard, still shaken up from what he'd seen and unable to form the words to answer. She seemed to know what he meant, because she smiled and slipped her arm around his.

"She called to the guards for help right before the beast crushed her. A little late, but she still passed." She paused, and looked him over. "Would you like to go visit her in the infirmary?"

Although he did want to see Nathira, he pulled back. He struggled to form words around the lump lodged in his throat.

"Wait...what about Arara? Doesn't she have her fight next? I can't miss it."

"Of course." His mother looked at him and frowned. "After. Now, let's announce Nathira's successful first Trial."

*****

Arara awoke to loud voices having what sounded like an argument. Every part of her ached and glue held her eyes shut. A sour taste filled her mouth.

"..Eellp." Arara barked.

Someone gasped. "She's awake!"

"Arara," Kerka licked her face. "Thank the Moon!"

With a great effort she managed to pry her eyelids apart and turn her head. Kerka's face swam into view.

"I was so worried!" Kerka touched his nose to hers and licked her muzzle again.

"What happened?" She slurred.

"You were poisoned." A musical Kin voice answered. A green sleeve brushed into her view and cool Kin hands ran along her face. "Without the quick thinking of your heroic suitor here you might have never woken up."

"Suitor?" Arara blinked, wrinkling her nose. "Kerka, get away from me!" She lifted her leaden front paws and pressed against Kerka's chest without effect.

Kerka ignored her, instead gripping her elbow and helping her to sit up. Her hind legs dangled off the soft plant-bed, and her head swam for a moment, but Kerka's paw on her back kept her upright. Her paws shook, and her legs trembled. But even as she sat there she felt her strength returning.

A green-robed healing Kin stood before her. She leaned forward and examined Arara's eyes one by one.

"Your improvement is nothing short of miraculous." The healer said, stepping back with a frown. "I can't clear you to participate in the Trial today. But, since I know you'll ignore any advice I give you, I can only say be careful."

"The Trial?" Arara stammered. "Oh, no! Did I miss it?"

"Don't worry," Kerka said, tail wagging. He struck a pose, flexing his muscles. "I passed."

"They are preparing the arena for you now." The healer glanced at Kerka. "But if you'd slept any longer you would have missed it." She went to the entrance and parted the vines.

"I'm ready!" Arara clenched her paws together and gritted her teeth. She would win this, she would save her life. She would save the whole kingdom.

A black and silver garbed Alpha-Guard stepped through and gestured to her. Arara hopped down. Her legs collapsed under her weight and she fell to the floor. Kerka snorted while the healer helped her up.

*****

Thousands chanted her name, exactly as she'd dreamed in her youthful fantasies of being a famous singer. But now the sound scared her. Her fate and her life rested on this moment. She straightened, standing tall, trying to be strong. The hot sun beat down. Flies buzzed in her ear, and the tang of blood made her nose twitch.

They exited the covered walkway, and the volume intensified for a moment. As they caught sight of her, the crowd fell silent. The shocked thoughts of the crowd pounded at her mental shields. *This is the Prince's secret candidate? A little joke of a puppy?* She shook her head, trying to block the unwanted intrusion. But a part of her wondered if they were right.

Past a sparkling barrier she could see the arena's floor. Dark brown hills dotted the space. A hole opened before her. The guards ushered her through, taking up positions on either side.

Warm mud squished between her toes. A whole cloud of flies circled around her head, irritating her ears. She waved her arms around and splashed forward, trying to escape them. The magic hummed as the opening closed behind her, cutting off the sounds of the crowd.

The ground fell away underneath her, and she sunk into the muck up to her knees. She waded forward, the mud sucking at her legs. Mud mounds blocked her sight lines. Hidden somewhere in this mess was a monster or monsters, intent on tearing her apart. She leaned over and sniffed the ground, but all she could smell was stagnant water.

She headed towards the closest dirt mound and scrambled up its side. The top would give her a view of the area, with the added benefit of getting her up out of the muck. Although she could still sense the crowd around her, the barrier was opaque and sound-proof from this side. Once she reached the top, she looked around. Brown dirt and muddy pools greeted her in every direction. There was no sign of any creature.

<Arara.> Sels felt worried. *<They are hiding in the mud. Ambush predators. I don't know how many.>*

<Thanks.> She replied, eyes scanning the ground.

<And, be careful. I'm rooting for you.> She sensed him hesitate. He debated telling her something else, but she ignored him, trying to think.

If she opened her shields to look for the creature's minds, she would get the whole crowd. That would be worse than trying to spot them in the mud. But with her shields closed she wouldn't sense them until right before she stumbled over them.

All she needed to do was to get them to show themselves, then they would be easy pickings for her mental powers. Her new trick would be perfect. She could use mudballs to lure them out.

She crouched down and scooped up a pawful of mud. She tossed it in the air, intending to send it skimming along just above the ground. The ball wobbled in the air and jerked back and forth before falling to the ground with a wet plop.

She cocked one ear back and stared at the mudball's remains. She'd done everything right, hadn't she? Another ball flew away. It went farther this time before crashing, but she still didn't have the control she should have had after this morning's lesson.

Arara thought back to Darach's memory. Although she could remember watching the memory, the details were faded, hazy, just out of her grasp. Like a dream, half-remembered. She whimpered and fell to all fours. She must have done something wrong this morning.

Darach had assured her this would work. She tried again and again, but the balls never did what she wanted them to.

She gave up and made her way down the mound. She'd just have to flush these creatures out the hard way. The mud sucked at her paws, sapping her strength with each step. She ascended another mound, hoping perhaps that she could see more from the top of this one. The soft mud slid out from beneath her paws and she tumbled down, head over feet. Dirt slid down the hill after her. She landed on her back in the pool at the bottom with a splash.

This pool turned out to be much deeper than the ones she'd waded through previously, and she sank below the surface. Muddy water filled her mouth and she panicked, waving her arms and pumping her legs. After a moment one hind-paw hit solid ground. She pushed off and surfaced, gasping and choking. She coughed, spitting up muddy water. While stroking the water to keep herself afloat, she brushed mud from her eyes.

The water split before her in an odd serpentine pattern. Two round eyes slid from the water. Arara stared into those unblinking, reptilian eyes while she extended her claws. The eyes blinked closed and slid back beneath the water.

Without warning, sharp teeth closed around her leg, and a sudden tug dragged her under. She gasped in shock, and water rushed into her mouth. Teeth ground against bone in her leg as the monster bit down.

She twisted, trying in vain to see anything in the murky water. Her lungs screamed for air. She slashed at the water around her leg. Her claws bounced off a thick scaly hide.

Thick air bubbles escaped her mouth, and her vision dimmed. The beast twisted, and she spun through the water. Her arms flew wide, sliding off. She panicked and struggled to gain control, to think logically.

<Arara, call for help!> Sels mind-voice cut through her panic.

<*No!*> Arara struggled to stay conscious as the beast flipped her around and around. *<I won't lose. I won't be killed by beasts! I won't let down the kingdom.>*

To prove her point, she thrust out with her mind at the beast's life-spark. Pain stabbed her head, and the creature recoiled, jaws opening. She kicked herself free and windmilled her arms. Her head broke the surface, and she gulped down precious air. She needed to get to the shore and get solid ground under her feet in order to fight this thing.

Her injured leg screamed, but she ignored the pain. A barrier, she needed something to stop it from dragging her under again. Before she could finish the thought, she felt the beast approaching from her left. She flipped herself to the side, and teeth snapped closed in the water where she had just been.

Arara swam for shore and pushed out with her mind against the beast. The gator thrashed as it flew away, its massive tail throwing up waves in the water. The effort cost her, and she almost blacked out. Her head pounded, and her foot dragged behind her.

The shore loomed before her, a tail length away. She was going to make it. A head popped out the water between her and shore, the mouth opening wide. She glanced behind to see the one she pushed still moving away from her. Two of them.

The one in front slid forward, sleek and silent. Its snout cracked her in the head. It continued to swim by her, hitting her again with its tail, knocking her under the water and breaking her concentration. The first beast dropped back into the water with a splash.

Water filled her lungs again, and she panicked, flailing her arms around and kicking as hard as she could. She couldn't see any light underwater, and she had no idea if she was headed for the surface or not. Teeth clamped onto her arm, and she screamed, losing what little air she had left. The beast pulled her through the water for a moment before the pain hit her, and she passed out.

*****

Sels leaned over the balcony, scanning the pool for any sign of Arara. His leg throbbed, and he cradled one arm to his chest. The muddy water below frothed and bubbled as Arara battled the two gators. Sharp pain stabbed his other leg, and a moment later the water tinged red with blood.

The guards gave a cry. They couldn't wait any longer for her to ask for help. The barrier fell, and they splashed towards the fight. Several healers rushed after them, heedless of the mud splattering their robes.

The pain became too much, and Sels collapsed, sobbing for help. He'd told Arara to call for help, knowing even then that she wouldn't listen to him. He felt her distrust of others and her pride at being seen as self-sufficient. Again the pain vanished. Sels crawled back to the railing and watched between the branches.

His mother dropped down next to him and wrapped him in a hug. "Sels, don't worry. The healers will get to her in time."

The guards stabbed long spears at the gators, driving them away as they pulled Arara's lifeless, broken form from the water.

"Arara!" Sels gasped in shock and pushed his mother away. She stroked his back, pulling his head to her chest so he couldn't watch. But he heard the commotion as they loaded her onto a stretcher. Healing magic tugged at his senses.

"I'm sorry, Sels," The Queen said into his vines, her voice low. "I know she was your favorite. But she failed."

"Give her another chance!" Sels pushed back and sat up on his knees. "Please, mother!"

"We cannot grant favors, Sels." The Queen shook her head. Her lips pursed tight, eyes hard. Her vines rustled as her flowers twisted closed. "Nor can we circumvent our own laws, no matter how it pains us. She seriously injured a member of the Royal Family and conspired with terrorists."

Around them, the nobles murmured, whispering to each other about his unseemly behavior. He struggled to his feet, keeping his tears at bay through force of will. As soon as he cried mother would dismiss him, and he needed her to listen.

"Mother, please, at least..." He struggled around the lump in his throat. "At least give me a day to say goodbye." Jeron would help him. Together they could sneak Arara out of prison, give her a chance to get away.

The Queen sighed, and her expression softened. "Very well. I will instruct the infirmary to completely heal her injuries and place her in the palace dungeon. You may visit with her there. Guards will be present at all times. Her sentence will be carried out a week after your *sedyu*-bond ceremony."

CHAPTER FIFTEEN

NATHIRA

His mother tugged his arm, pulling him along. The suspended walkway swayed slightly as they moved. Throngs of Kin and a few Jegera made their way from the arena on the paths through the maze below them. The Alpha-Guard hurried forward to push open the vines covering the walkway's entrance into the medical ward tree.

Before they could enter, Tukura reached forward and placed her paw on Seuan's shoulder. Seuan turned and gave Tukura a hard look before Tukura let go.

"Go on ahead. Something important just came up that I need to take care of." The Queen and Tukura turned and headed back the way they had come, followed by three Alpha-Guard. Only Jeron remained with him, holding open the vines and motioning for Sels to enter.

As he pushed through the vine coverings, Sels could hear someone talking nearby. "...it all seems to be purged from her system, but I'm still a bit worried."

“Considering her tiny size, it was a huge dose.”

"Not just that, the poison is very rare. Even the Queen’s personal healer had a hard time identifying it."

Sels strained to hear more, furrowing his brow, but the two speakers moved and their voices faded away. It sounded like there had been another assassination attempt, but on whom? The statement about size brought Arara to mind, but if she had been poisoned he would have been informed.

Or, maybe he had. He remembered the Trial and how his arm and leg had started hurting when Arara fought the gators. Earlier, when he'd had the mysterious stomach pains that couldn't be healed, it had to have been when Arara got poisoned. Jeron had to have been informed about it by gefir. Why hadn't Jeron told him?

They were on the way to see Nathira. His mother had made it clear that he couldn't see Arara until tomorrow, but he had to see her now. Nathira could wait. He wished he could trust Jeron with this, but the fact that he hadn't told Sels about Arara's poisoning bothered him. He had to move fast since he could hear Jeron coming through the doorway behind him.

The hallway curved away from him on either side, and curtained doorways lined the inside wall. Focusing on Arara, he let his instincts guide him to the left, and he ducked through the second curtained entrance moments before Jeron entered the hallway. Jeron had an excellent sense of smell, so he had to move fast.

An empty Jegeran bed and a small dresser decorated an otherwise bare room. A second doorway exited the room on the other side. Sels ran through the room towards it and stepped through the thick curtains.

The place reeked of wet fur and fecal matter. Sels pinched his nose closed as he ran through the communal bathroom. At least it would cover his scent. A wet towel lay across a bench nearby. Sels snatched it up and rubbed it all over him, then ducked into another room at random. The random Jegera's smell would help to cover his own scent.

This room was not empty. A lone Jegera occupant lay curled up on the bed snoring. Sels dropped the wet towel in the corner and ran through the curtain at the exit. Luckily, this hallway was deserted. Sels could feel Arara nearby. He didn't know how, but he knew she was close. She was somewhere above him.

Sels ran down the hall and exited the tree. He ran up the spiral walkway set into the tree bark until he felt even with Arara. This level was laid out the same as the one below, except the walls were painted light pink. The wall colors indicated which patients were treated there, but Sels couldn't remember what the pink meant.

So far he'd been lucky not to run into any healers as they made their rounds, but he could hear soft footsteps coming towards him from the hall to his right. Of course, they were coming from the direction he needed to go. His heart pounded from excitement and fear of getting caught. He was sure his mother had ordered everyone to keep him away from Arara. On the other hand, he needed to be more assertive. He straightened up and jerked his robes into place. The wet fur smell persisted, but he just tried to ignore it. The healer wouldn't dare question him about it.

He walked purposefully down the hallway, straight towards where he felt Arara. The healer looked down at his papers as he walked. They passed each other, and Sels thought he'd gotten away with it.

"Prince Sels!" The healer's papers fluttered to the ground. He left the papers where they fell and turned, scrambling to catch up with Sels, walking next to him. "We weren't expecting you."

"I came to check on Arara. Go back to your duties, I can find the way myself."

"Sire," The healer paused. He stuttered and kept reaching his hand towards Sels arms then hesitating, clearly loath to physically restrain the Prince. "She is well, but she needs rest. She was badly injured by the gators, and the poison still hasn't completely worked out of her system."

"Continue with your duties. I'll only be a moment." Sels passed two doorways and stopped at the third. Voices murmured behind the vines. Sels pushed aside the vines and entered.

Inside, a soft bed-plant held Arara's unconscious body, half hidden behind some gauzy curtains. Two Kin stood over her, and they both turned towards the door at his entrance. Sels recognized the older Kin, her yellow petal hair darkened with age to a dull gold, as Lupa, the Royal Family's personal healer. Her assistant, a younger Vine Kin with white flowers, gave him a nod and a small smile.

"Your Highness," Lupa said, before turning back to tend to Arara.

The assistant, Sels couldn't remember her name, stopped her healing spell and walked over to him. She raised her arms in greeting just as the healer from the hallway came through the vines behind him.

"I came to check on Arara." Sels composed his face into his mother's favorite expression, one that commanded her respect where ever she went. "I heard she was poisoned." Sels gave the healer from the hallway a hard stare, and he apologized then backed from the room.

"Yes." Lupa said without looking back. "But her recovery from that was, well, remarkable."

"You were able to get her the antidote on time?"

"No." Lupa shook her head. "By the time we figured out what she'd been poisoned with, she'd already recovered."

The assistant sighed. "We're more worried about the injuries from the gators. They practically tore off her left leg before the guards got to her. And her right arm is badly damaged."

"May I," Sels tried to see past Lupa to see Arara. "May I hold her paw for a while?"

"Not a good idea, sire." The assistant said. "This is not something you want to see."

"I want to." Sels said, moving past the assistant and craning his neck to see Arara. "I...need to."

Lupa straightened and turned towards him for the first time. "Actually, that might be just what we need." She gestured for him to come forward.

He could see Arara's body past the curtains on the bed. She was in bad shape, even after the healing she had already received.

"Now sit here," Lupa patted the bed on the left side next to Arara's head.

"Why do you need me?" Sels sat down and took Arara's uninjured paw in his. Lupa's hands glowed as she went back to fixing Arara's leg.

"The healing magic isn't working as well as it should." The assistant said. "It's like she's given up."

"Talk to her." Lupa instructed.

"Arara, I need you." Sels pleaded, petting her arm with his other hand. He kept his eyes on her face, trying not to see the gruesome injuries. "Please, stay with me."

Sels watched Arara's face, squeezing her paw while he pleaded with her to come back to him. She lay still as a statue. Then, her eyelids fluttered and she squeezed his hand. Sels grinned, and turned to tell Lupa when Jeron burst through the doorway trailing vines.

*****

Jeron dragged him from Arara's side. He protested the whole way, but he couldn't escape Jeron's strong grasp. Jeron dragged up the stairs to the rooms set aside for nobles and important political figures. Once there, the healers shooed them out and said that Nathira still needed more healing before he could see her.

The waiting room was plush. He settled into a chair to wait. But a few moments later he jumped up and paced, restless. He watched the sun move through the sky through the massive windows set into the opulent lobby's outer wall. Jeron sat by the door, silent and watching.

Inside he fumed. Anger at Jeron and his mother for withholding information about Arara. Anger at Sesay. Anger at himself most of all, for choosing Nathira on a whim. For not standing up for himself. Guilt twisted at him over Arara's and especially Nathira's injuries. He knew Arara could take care of herself before he gave her a token, but he hadn't even cared to remember who Nathira was. He had been selfish, only thinking about himself and the humiliation waiting for him at home if he returned with Arara as his only choice.

Every few turns he tried to send to Arara, and he grew disappointed when she didn't respond.

An attendant bearing platters of succulent food rustled through the vines. The attendant placed the platters on a side table and left. The aroma of roast nuts and vegetables wafted over to him, and his stomach growled with hunger, but guilt robbed him of his appetite.

A bit later a young Kin page entered and greeted Sels with wide arms.

“Sire, she is ready for visitors now.” The page gestured.

Sels and Jeron followed her down the hall to Nathira's room.

The evening sun lit up the room in crimson ribbons. Jeron took up position outside the doorway and pulled the vines closed to give Sels and Nathira at least the illusion of privacy.

This room had flowering vines growing along the walls that gave the whole room a cheery atmosphere, unlike the bare walls in Arara's room below.

Nathira lay propped up on a bed-plant in the room's center. Her face was drawn in pain, although Sels couldn't see any obvious injuries remaining. Now she just needed food and rest.

"Nathira, I'm glad to see you are doing well." He approached and gave her a genuine smile. "I was afraid you were .. that you wouldn't make it when..." He cringed at the memory, and he couldn't bring himself to finish the sentence.

“Thanks to the quick response of the healers.” Nathira smiled wanly up at him. Her voice was so weak that Sels had to strain to hear her.

As it was, he wasn't sure how she would finish the Trials. It was for the best, since Sels knew she didn't feel her Potential. He swallowed hard. He had to tell her now, before some else hurt her.

“Nathira,” Sels knelt down next to the bed and looked her in the eye. “I... feel responsible for this. I'd like to apologize, and-”

"Sire," Nathira cut him off. "I'm happy to have had this chance. But," Her ears pulled down and she looked away from him. "I'm going to resign and return my token to you."

"I, what?" Sels jumped. "Oh, really?" For a moment relief overwhelmed him, he didn't have to confess to her. "I'm sorry to hear that."

"I've never, I mean..." She huffed. "I mean, you felt my Potential, so how could I have failed so miserably?"

"Actually," Now Sels felt even more terrible. "I have a confession to make." He sighed and took her paw. "I didn't feel any Potential in you. I, picked you because, well, I didn't even have a reason. I thought, well, that people would look down on me for not having any candidates."

"But you're, you're a prince."

"Yes, and it was selfish of me to put you in that position." Sels sighed again. He opened his mouth to say something else when the vines rustled, and his mother swept in with Tukura at her side.

The Queen frowned slightly at Sels, still kneeling by Nathira's side. However, the expression was so subtle he doubted Nathira noticed it. Sels jumped to his feet and smoothed out his robes, then stood stiffly and greeted his mother.

"Sels, glad to see you made it." The Queen turned to Nathira and graced her with a dazzling smile. "Lady Nathira, my heart blooms at seeing you alive and well. Don't worry dear, the healers have assured me you'll be on your paws by tomorrow for the second Trial."

"Your Majesty," Nathira sat up, wincing, and tried to open her arms in greeting. She fell back into the bed with a whimper. "I don't want to continue."

"Yes, mother." Sels cut in. "I was just... discussing it with her."

"I see." Mother pursed her lips and regarded Nathira. "Has she returned your token?"

In response Nathira opened her paw, revealing the token. She reached her paw up and dropped it in Sels's hand.

"I must say, I'm disappointed, Lady Nathira, but I understand how hard of a decision this must have been for you." The Queen smiled at Nathira. "I was impressed with your performance, how collected you were despite your obvious fears. We would like to offer you a position as ambassador between the Council and the coastal tribe's Chieftains."

Nathira perked up, her ears standing straight up and rotating forward. She smiled. "I...don't know what to say. Thank you, My Queen."

"Of course. As soon as you've recovered we can discuss the specifics. May the sun shine brightly upon you." The Queen turned and walked towards the room's exit, Tukura silently falling in by her side. Without looking back she called out, "Sels, attend to me."

Sels closed his eyes and sighed. "Of course, mother." To Nathira, "Swift recovery. I'm sure I shall see you again soon." He followed his mother through the vines and away.

"Sels, come walk next to me." His mother called back to him.

Sels picked up his pace, drawing even with his mother, opposite Tukura. The wide hallway accommodated the three of them walking abreast with plenty of room left on either side. Sels thought back to his brief lessons at the Infirmary.

His mother reached over and took his arm, steering him through a vined doorway into an unused room. Tukura did not follow them in, instead taking up position outside the door blocking access to anyone else.

She released his arm, and took his hands pulling him around until they faced each other. His mother looked down at Sels, her expression serene, which Sels knew meant she was secretly happy about something. "Sels, I know the loss of two candidates on the first day must be hard for you."

Sels pulled his hands abruptly out of his mother's grip and gave her a hard look. "Mother, I just found out Arara was poisoned before the Trial. Surely under such circumstances we can give her another chance to prove herself." Although he suspected she knew before Arara entered the arena, he didn't dare accuse his mother of anything.

"Sels," the Queen sighed and folded her hands in front of her. "Today's Trial was not about strength. It was about recognizing and acknowledging one's weaknesses. If she was too weak or hurt to participate, a simple request for a delay would have been perfectly acceptable. But she did not. She entered the arena of her own volition."

Sels opened his mouth to protest, but his mother held up her hand for silence.

"As I said, we cannot make exceptions. Think about it this way. The *sedyu*-bonded will be your final line of defense, your protector. In an emergency, a *sedyu*-bonded's pride will get you killed.

"And in the Council room. Your *Sedyu*-bonded is your adviser on Jegera matters. A *Sedyu*-bonded needs to be willing to ask questions, to listen. A prideful *Sedyu*-bonded who thinks they do not need the help of others is only a liability."

Her facade slipped away, her beautiful features pulled down in an angry frown. "Arara was not, and never will be, a suitable candidate."

"Arara is the only true Potential among them. She is the *only* one I've felt a connection to, the only one I feel I have a chance of successfully bonding with. I only picked Kerka and Nathira to make you happy." There, the truth was out.

His mother reared back as if she had been slapped.

At the same time Sels felt the peculiar, yet now oddly familiar sensation of Arara speaking in his head. *<Sels, I'm sorry! I deserve to be locked up.>* Sels knees buckled under him and he fell to the floor, shaking. Arara's presence left him, but he could still feel her pain shooting through his legs and arm. She must have woken up before the healers had a chance to finish.

By the time the sensation faded and he came to his senses, Tukura and a healer knelt next to him. His head lay in Jeron's lap and his mother stood over him looking worried. The healer had her hands on his head and her eyes were closed.

"What happened?" Sels asked, pushing himself up to sitting. The healer jumped in surprise and opened her eyes.

"You fainted." The healer answered, glaring at him. "Or at least, you tried to fake it." She turned and looked up at the Queen. "I could find nothing wrong with him, Your Majesty."

"Not with me, Mother." Sels stood up with Jeron's assistance and faced his mother, back straight and head held high. "With Arara. I've been feeling her pain, and her emotions. She is very upset, and combined with the pain from her injuries, I must have blacked out."

"Don't lie to me, Sels," Queen Seuan narrowed her eyes and clenched her hands together in front of her. "You pretended the same thing earlier. Only *sedyu*-bonded feel each other's pain, and only *sedyu*-bonded Kin can mind-speak. I'm appalled you would fake something like this, just to try to get your little toy back."

"What? Mother, I'm not pretending-" Seuan cut him off.

"Jeron, take him away. He is confined to his quarters for the remainder of the evening."

The Queen turned, her robes flaring out at the bottom as she stalked from the room.

CHAPTER SIXTEEN

ON THE RUN

Arara came to her senses again in a different room. Instead of the soft plant bed from the infirmary, she found herself in an unfamiliar room wrapped in a warm blanket on a familiar Jegeran bed. The smell of her mother's home-cooked hukra meat wafted in from the kitchen.

"Mother," Arara rolled over and burrowed deeper in the blankets. "Five more scratch-marks."

When her mother failed to answer her, she yawned and poked her nose out of the blankets. The strong hukra scent and the blankets had drowned out the other smells, but with her nose free she could smell that she wasn't at home. A dream.

Her stomach growled again. The hukra meat was real enough. She pulled her head out the rest of the way and looked around the strange room.

Living wood walls curved around her and over in a dome. Clear tiles set in the dome's center let in the moonlight, which bathed the patch of Kin sleeping soil underneath it in stripes of blue. A wooden stool next to the bed held a large chunk of cooling seared hukra meat.

Arara freed her front paws from the blanket and quickly devoured the meat. Still hungry, she licked the last few drops of juice off the plate with a swipe of her tongue. She gnawed on the bone as she took a closer look around the room.

The only pieces of furniture were the bed and the stool. A small window, covered in a latticed iron-wood bars, was set into one wall. A doorway sat in the wall opposite the window, but instead of vines or curtains, iron-wood bars covered this opening as well.

As hot as it had been during the day, the night had a cold nip to it. The wind whistled through the bars and cut right through her short fur. Arara snuggled back under the blanket, still gnawing the bone. Frustration coursed through her, and she resisted the urge to howl out her anger. The Elders said she was the only one that could save everyone, but how could she do that when she couldn't even save herself?

She could use her powers to contact someone for help, but who could she trust? Yegra, spying for Sesay, certainly wouldn't help her. Kerka had tried to poison her. Sels, she trusted. He'd tried to warn her about the Trials, and she'd been too proud to stop and listen to him.

She focused on Sels's mind-patterns and homed in on his location. He was close, in his palace suite and, surprisingly, still awake. Now that she concentrated she could feel the fury radiating off of him. The anger tugged at her concentration, threatening to distract her.

<*Sels! What's wrong?*> She pulled back her ears and involuntarily curled up her muzzle in a snarl, ready to tear apart the one who put him into such a state. The intensity of the feelings surprised her.

<*Arara! You're awake! I was so worried, and no one would tell me anything.*> His relief hit her like a bucket of water, calming her protective instincts. She grinned around the bone.

<*I'm better now. But that hukra-dung Kerka is dead the next time I see him.*> She burrowed deeper into the blankets as she related to him the story how she was poisoned.

<*Your account of the symptoms sounds familiar, but I can't remember where I read about it before...*> His mental voice faded out as he tried to pull up the memory.

<*It doesn't matter right now. At the moment I'm locked in a wooden room, please come get me out!*> She Sent an image of the

room's layout and the strange wooden grate over the windows and door.

<*You are in the palace dungeon.*> She felt him pull his feet out of the soil and begin pacing. <*Arara, I trust you, but I can't get you out. My mother has me confined to my room. I have a plan to get you out later. We have some ti-*<

His mind-voice cut off mid-thought, and pain coursed through the back of Arara's head. The bone dropped from her numb jaws, and she reached back with one paw. Her head was tender where she prodded it, as if she'd just been struck. She leapt out of the bed, falling to the floor in a tangle of blankets, only to be greeted by an empty cell.

<*Sels? Answer me!*> The pain faded away, and Arara cursed. Of course, Sels had been the one hit, not her.

<*I'm coming, Sels, don't panic.*> She ran over to the barred doorway. She grabbed the bars and pulled without any effect. Likewise her claws bounced right off the iron-wood without even scoring it.

"HELP!" She howled into the night air. She pressed her muzzle through the space in the bars and looked out the grate with one eye. A cobbled path led between what looked to be rows and rows of cells. She couldn't feel anyone nearby, and no one responded to her howls for help.

She scanned the room again, looking for inspiration. A cloud passed briefly in front of the moon, casting the room into darkness. It passed, and a bright shaft of moonlight speared the center of the room.

She looked up and grinned. The sunroof. It wasn't barred like the door and windows. The architects had mistakenly guessed that, being over eighteen tails up, it wasn't a security risk. She carefully positioned herself directly under the hole. Clear tiles covered the hole, but they didn't look thick.

Her leg muscles coiled as she crouched and sprang, straight up. At the peak of her jump, she mentally pushed under her feet, closed her eyes, and raised her fists. The push threw her the rest of the way. She hit the clear barrier with her fists, and it shattered around her, the sharp edges cutting into her skin and lodging in her fur.

She'd put too much power into the push, and it launched her high into the air above the roof. She hit hard when she landed at the edge of the hole, her breath whooshed out of her and she fell onto her rump, landing awkwardly on her tail with a yelp. Immediately, she began sliding down the slick polished wood of the dome. She extended her claws and she dug into the wood of the roof, trying to slow her descent. Fragments of glass slid down around her with a musical tinkle. Just before the edge she jerked to a stop, her claws finally finding purchase in the hard wood.

Already panting hard with the exertion, she turned and lowered herself gently down into the grass. Her head blossomed with a massive headache, and pieces of glass jutted out of cuts covering her front paws and arms. But she didn't have time to deal with that right now. She dropped to all fours and ran into the maze. When Sels had told her about being confined to his quarters, he'd unconsciously pulled up a map of the palace in his head which had filtered through with the gefir. She followed that now, using her mental-senses to avoid the guards that had finally come running at the sound of her escape.

Although the blow had rendered Sels unconscious, she could still feel the connection in her mind tugging her towards him.

She ran as fast as she could through the maze in the dark, taking the corners dangerously close. The moonlight lit up the night in shades of blue, bright enough to read by. The deadly points of the maze walls brushed her fur on every turn as she hurtled towards Sels. The shouts of the Alpha-Guards faded away behind her.

The layout of the maze itself slowed her down. She could feel Sels directly ahead, three tree lengths away, she estimated. He was on the move to her right, but the corridor she ran down ended in a left turn a tree length in front of her. She growled in frustration, and ran faster. They were just bushes, after all, even if they were poisonous and spiky.

She ran straight at the hedge, and right before she would have hit it, she used her mind-push to blow a hole through the center. Again and again she punched through the walls of the hedge maze, heedless of the consequences, making a beeline straight for Sels.

Arara smashed through the final hedge in a spray of wood and spiked leaves almost directly in the path of two Jegera. They carried Sels's limp form suspended between them. Sels's arms and legs were bound together behind him, and a thick cloth bag covered his head.

By now Arara's head hurt so badly she could barely see, but she let her anger fuel her. She leapt at the closest Jegera's throat with a savage snarl. He threw his free arm up just before Arara's jaws snapped closed. Arara hung off his arm by her mouth, clawing at his unprotected face and belly.

He cried out and dropped Sels, then used his now free arm to fight back against Arara's berserker attack. Arara's vision clouded to red, and she heard herself roar. She let go of his arm and clawed her way upwards.

Warm blood gushed into her mouth as she tore out his throat with a savage jerk. She jumped back, landing on all fours and shaking wildly to get the blood out of her eyes.

The remaining Jegera had scooped Sels up and run off while Arara tore about his companion. Arara howled and took off after them. She could feel Sels ahead of her, driving herself on through the savage pain in her head. The coppery blood in her mouth tasted sweet.

Her emotions warred as she ran, an equal mix of exhilaration and fury. Her four paws pounded on the cobbled path after her prey. The remaining Jegera ran ahead of her, but Sels's weight slowed him down, and running on two legs slowed him down even further. Ahead of them, the path turned to the right, and the Jegera slowed further to make the turn without brushing against the deadly leaves.

Arara lunged and caught the tip of his tail in her teeth. She hauled back, jerking the Jegera back towards her. She used the last of her mental strength to push Sels's limp body forward, away from the bushes. He fell, hitting the cobblestones with a dull thud. The Jegera fell sideways into the hedge with a howl of agony.

Arara sprinted around the corner, ignoring the Jegera struggling to extract himself from the hedge. Hundreds of pointy leaves had punctured and scratched his skin. She didn't know how long the poison would take, but it couldn't be long. Sels sprawled motionless nearby.

Arara skidded to a stop next to him and used her teeth to pull the bag off his head.

"Wake up!" Arara lay down, paws on either side of his head and licked his face. He stirred slightly, his eyes lids fluttering. Now that she was laying down, her exhaustion and headache caught up with her. Her eyes drifted shut and she rested her chin on Sels forehead. Sels's cool skin felt nice. She could have sworn just the touch of it made her headache recede, and she felt consciousness fading.

Rough paws grabbed her neck and hauled her up. Arara's eyes flew open to find herself face to face with the Jegera from the bush. White foam dripped from his open muzzle, and his blood-shot red eyes bugged out from his face. Arara screamed and swiped at him with her claws, but he held her outstretched away from him and Arara's arms flailed at air.

The Jegera mumbled and staggered back. His eyes rolled back in his head, and he collapsed to the cobblestones, dropping Arara onto his chest. Arara struggled back, but his dead paws held her tight. She finally pried his fingers loose and scrabbled back over to Sels.

Sels stared up at her, eyes frantic. A rough cloth gag encircled his head. Arara cut off the gag and the bonds, her heart still pounding from her near miss.

"Get up, we need to find Jeron!" Arara whimpered.

Sels only groaned in response, but he rolled over to his knees and sat up. With her encouragement, he managed to stagger to his feet.

"Arara, no." He slurred when Arara started pulling him back the way they'd come. "Stop. Look at that one." Sels pointed a trembling hand at the dead Jegera lying at their feet.

Arara peered down, the moonlight was bright, but the dark clothing he wore blended into the shadows. The collars and shoulders of his tunic glinted silver. Silver, like the Alpha-Guard uniform trim. Arara bent over and touched the breast of the tunic and felt the embroidered flower of the Royal Seal.

"What? Alpha-Guards did this?" Arara spun on Sels, her eyes wide.

"I don't know who I can trust, Arara." Sels looked close to tears, hugging himself and trembling. "Except you."

"Even Jeron?" Arara said, giving Sels a quick hug. She realized her mistake when he wrinkled his nose and pulled away. She gasped, looking down at the red smear she'd left on his pajamas.

"Even him." Sels looked away. "He, I mean, I think it was him who hit me over the back of the head. He was the only one in my quarters with me."

"So then, what do we do?" Arara whispered. "Even if we find real Alpha-Guards, they'll put me back in prison where I can't protect you. And if they're kidnappers, I'm not in any shape to fight them off." She held up her arms to show Sels the hundreds of cuts and the pieces of glass still embedded in them. "I got lucky, catching them by surprise."

"Then," Sels straightened his back and gestured for her to follow him. He took a deep breath. "We go with a third option. Avoid all the guards. There are emergency escape tunnels running through the maze, leading outside the palace." He led her along through the winding hedges.

A few scratch-marks later, frantic howling started somewhere behind them. They'd found the bodies and were in pursuit.

"We need to hurry," Arara tugged on Sels sleeve. "They'll easily be able to pick up our scent."

"I know. We're almost there. The entrances to the tunnels are hidden by magic. Once we get inside they won't be able to follow us." Sels walked faster, wincing and holding the back of his head.

"Magic? Then how will... I mean, what if..." She trailed off, not wanting to hurt Sels feelings.

"Don't worry about insulting me." Sels sighed. "The spell is keyed to the Royal Family, so anyone with Royal sap can open them, even me."

Suddenly, Sels stopped, causing Arara to pull up short so she wouldn't hit him. "Right here."

Arara looked around. The hedge ran along both sides, unbroken, and the cobblestone path continued on, curving around ahead. "What? Where?"

Sels knelt down and rapped out a pattern on one of the cobblestones. The stones split apart to reveal a staircase descending down into the ground. "Don't worry, only the highest ranking guards know where the tunnels exit."

"Let me go first." Arara crept down the stairs, her nose held high as she sniffed the air. Stale, and smelling only of dust, dirt and mildew. She gestured for Sels to follow as she descended to the bottom.

The tunnel ran on straight from the stairs. Smooth stone, punctuated seemingly at random, by arched doorways. The floor was rough marble, dusty from years of neglect. In the dim moonlight, Arara's paws left dust-free prints behind. Obviously no one had been in here for a long time.

A moment later, Sels reached the bottom of the stairs. Stones ground together as the stairway pulled into the wall, cutting off the blue glow of moonlight from outside, leaving them blind.

"Don't be scared." Sels whispered, slipping his hand into her paw. "We can't get lost. Just follow the wall."

Arara reached out her other paw until it rested on the cool stone of the wall. She ran her paw along it as they ran down the tunnel to freedom.

*****

Sels lost track of how long they were in the dark, but eventually the tunnel came out in the basement of a Jegera den. The hole in the wall closed up, invisible, Sels supposed, to Arara's eyes. To him lines of light outlined the escape tunnel entrance.

Piles of garbage lined the walls and were scattered around the basement. The smell was appalling, rotten food mixed with the stench of moldy fabric. Abandoned. Even with the smell, Sels was so exhausted that he just wanted to rest there. The guards had no way to follow them, after all. Until Arara pointed out that they would only be safe until another member of the Royal Family showed up and opened the tunnel.

They crawled upstairs over the garbage that almost blocked the tunnel. The upper level of den looked and smelled even worse than the basement. Garbage, and worse, completely blocked the bedrooms. Arara gestured for him to wait and crept forward to the dead vines still hanging over the doorway.

The gesture touched him. Already Arara acted like his *sedyu*-bonded, watching out for his safety. Even hurt, she thought of him first. Sels head still ached. Arara's arms still had glass embedded in them. They looked painful. And the way she winced whenever the light hit her face, she still obviously had a headache.

After a few moments, Arara waved him forward and slid out the door, the dead leaves barely rustling at her passing. Sels followed her out. The pre-dawn air chilled him through his thin pajamas. No one else was out at this hour. Even the moon-loving Jegera had already gone to bed, but it was still too early for most Kin to be up and about. It was the perfect time to move about the city.

By unspoken agreement they headed away from the palace, which they could see in the distance. Its tall tree towered over the smaller buildings of the rest of the city.

The street they walked down was narrow, smaller than any of the streets he'd seen around the palace. The dens were narrow and tall, and they cast most of the street into deep shadow. Even out here, trash littered the street.

"Sels, can you do a spell to cover up our smell?" Arara whispered to him as she walked.

"Don't you remember what happened in my pod?"

"Oh, good point." Arara tipped her head, one ear cocked back. "I have another idea." She pulled him off the main street down a side alley.

Arara pulled over the second trash bin they came to, spilling the contents over the street behind them. By now Sels had almost grown used to the smell, but the rancid stench of a dead raop at the bottom of the bin made him throw up on the side of the road. Arara gave him a dirty look and covered his mess up with the contents of another bin.

"How is this helping?" Sels said, still leaning against the wall of the alley between dry heaving.

"Trust me. They can't track us through the stink I'm leaving behind."

Sels just shook his head and followed after as Arara limped away. They wove their way randomly through the district, and Arara pulled trash bins over as they went. She kept every piece of clothing she found. Sels stumbled along behind her, legs trembling from exhaustion and head starting to hurt from being awake too long without sunlight.

Each alley and street seemed to be dirtier than the last, and they all blurred together in Sels's exhausted mind. By the time Arara pulled him through the door vines into a mud-brick den, the first glimmers of sunlight lit up the eastern sky.

They staggered together to the back room. Another abandoned den, but thankfully this one was cleaner than the last. Arara collapsed only a couple of steps into the room, curling up into a ball on the floor. Sels, too tired to even search for a root spot, curled up on the floor next to her and closed his eyes, just for a moment.

Sels woke up to the sun caressing his face. He tasted late summer morning sunlight filtered through a light covering of clouds. He groaned and opened his eyes. His leg and arm ached where they pressed into the cold dirt. Something warm pressed against his back. He pushed up onto his elbow and looked over to see Arara pressed up against him, still fast asleep. Sels stood up slowly, making sure not to jostle her.

Only a small sliver of sunlight came in through the dirty window set high on the wall. He stumbled around the piles of debris to the window. He rubbed at the brown grime with his sleeve, trying to let in more light, but he only succeeded in smearing the dirt around. In the trash next to him he noticed an old rag. He wrapped it around his fist and smashed out the thin glass. Glass tinkled on the street outside, and he winced, hoping no one came to investigate.

He stepped back and stripped off his dirty pajama top, dropping it on top of the piles of junk. He closed his eyes and basked in the sweet sunlight. Awake now, and feeling slightly refreshed from the jolt of sun on skin, he made his way back over to Arara.

The cold dirt on the soles of his feet made him shiver, and for the first time he noticed that the day's heat didn't seem to penetrate the thick mud walls. Dust motes danced around his face, revealed by the bars of sunlight streaming in through the broken window. Sels stopped and looked around, shocked at the sheer amount of garbage. In the dark the night before he hadn't quite realized how dirty this hovel really was. Although he'd grown used to it during the night, the stench still made his eyes water.

This was unacceptable. He tip-toed and hopped over the garbage, trying to touch as little of it as possible. Once across the room he crouched down next to Arara and brushed on old broken toy out of the way so he could kneel down.

Arara whimpered in her sleep and put her front paw over her ear. A large piece of glass stuck out of the back of her paw. Dried blood covered the end of it and trailed down to her fingers. Sels reached over and gently slipped his palm under her paw. The pads of her paw felt hot to his touch, burning the palm of his hand. Arara whimpered again and tried to jerk her arm back. Sels tightened his grip and took hold of the end of the glass shard with his fingers. He took a deep breath, bracing himself from the pain he knew would follow and eased the shard of glass out. Arara screamed, and pain stabbed his hand in the same place he'd just pulled the shard out.

Arara jerked hard away from him and rolled to all fours, growling, with her ears flat back.

"Arara, it's me." Sels held up his hands, showing her the glass. "I was just taking this out of your paw."

"Sorry," Arara lay down on her belly and rolled her head over to look up at him. "That hurt."

"I know, I'm sorry. I should have woken you." Sels sighed and crawled over to her. "But we need to get that glass out and get you healed. Your arms are hot. I think they're infected."

Arara sat up and held out her arms towards him. He squinted, trying to examine them carefully for more glass, but in the dim light he couldn't see anything past the dried blood, dust and fur.

"It's no use. Even if I could heal it, which I can't," he said, frowning at Arara. She looked up at him, her eyes wide, tail wagging. "These need to be cleaned, and we both need baths. I mean, look at me." He gestured down at his shirtless state and stained, dirty pants. A large stain marred one leg of his pants, and grime covered the legs from the knees down.

"I think the bath can wait. I'm hungry." Arara said, sticking out her tongue at him.

Sels's stomach growled, and Arara giggled.

"Alright, maybe we do need food." Sels admitted.

"So what's the plan?" Arara sat up, front paws dangling in front of her, and cocked her head at him. "You must know someone we can go to for help."

"No." Sels settled back and wrapped his arms around his knees. "Everyone I know either lives at the palace or works there. I don't know who I could trust not to tell the guards where I am."

"Are you sure we can't trust any of the Alpha-Guards?" Arara's cold nose pressed against his hand.

The memory of the night before pulled him away. He had pulled out of his rooting soil and touched a sun-flower to light up the room. Jeron lay curled up in his bed, blocking the door. He turned and walked to his closet, pulled out a robe, started pulling it on. A familiar chuckle came from right behind him, something hard hit the back of his head. He knew that laugh, that voice. Jeron.

"Positive." Sels whispered, holding back tears. He buried his face into his pants, unable to stop the tears.

"Do you, um, want to talk about it?" Arara's warm body pressed up against his side and she licked the side of his face.

"Why?" He said, low. "I know you overhear everything I think about. You already know why I'm upset." He was irrationally angry with her, although he knew she couldn't help it. That memory was personal, his private pain.

"I'm sorry. I hate it, always feeling like a voyeur. I...just, want to make you feel better." Her voice trembled.

"Oh." Sels looked up and rubbed at his tears with his arm. Arara curled up on the floor next to him, her ears drooping low. It suddenly occurred to him how horrible it must be for her, having voices in her head that she couldn't control. Feeling others' emotions as if they were her own.

"It is pretty horrible." Arara said, without looking at him. "But, it has its good points."

"Like what?"

She shrugged and fiddled with her tail.

"My mother," Sels hugged his legs tighter. "We need to get back to the palace and warn her, without the guards seeing us."

"What about Darach?"

Sels shook his head. "No, he trains the guard. We don't know if he's involved. In fact, any of the Elders might be corrupted. Until we figure out how deep this goes, we need someone totally unconnected to the palace or to politics in general."

"You know I've only been here for two days now." Arara cocked her head. "Don't you know *anyone* else?"

"I did make a few friends, sometimes my mother let Jeron take me to the library at Sunspire University." He pounded his legs in frustration. "But no one I know well enough to trust."

"We don't have any other options."

"I know." Sels sighed, and considered the few students and employees he knew. A few he discounted immediately as attention-seekers who didn't seem to enjoy his company. He'd heard them bragging to other students about their relationship with the Prince. In fact, he remembered once when he'd been reading alone in the corner, trying to hide from the other students. A very bright Kin girl he'd chatted with several times sat at a table nearby, gossiping with a few of her friends. He overheard as she told them about how she'd flirted shamelessly with the little Prince, and how he'd been so overcome by her beauty that he'd done nothing but mumble hopelessly. The girls all laughed at that.

While Sels had sunk down into his chair, flush with embarrassment, Mura, the head librarian's Jegeran research assistant, marched out from the stacks of books right up to the girl's table. Sels had met her several times before, but hadn't really paid her any mind at the time. Even with the way he'd treated her, she lectured them about their behavior before kicking them out. After that he'd made sure to spend time with her whenever he talked his mother into letting him leave the palace.

"I agree. Mura is probably our best choice." Arara said, starting Sels from his reverie. "Where does she live?"

"Um..." Sels stuttered. "I've only ever met with her at the University's library."

"Well, then let's start looking for her there."

"Except the University is on the opposite side of the city from where we are now, and half the population is probably out looking for us." Sels tugged on his pants. "All I have to wear is a pair of dirty pajamas." He paused. "And you're hurt."

"You grew up in this city. I bet you know lots of back ways to go to avoid the guards." Arara wagged her tail, throwing up a cloud of dust.

"Arara," Sels coughed and waved his hands around. "I've only ever traveled around the city inside a carriage. I don't even know how to get there on the main roads."

"What?" She sounded shocked, although he didn't know why. "Didn't you ever sneak out without your parents knowing?"

"I tried a few times, but Jeron always caught me." Sels shrugged. "It's not a big deal. We'll just ask for directions."

"Sels, you made a good point earlier. We're not going to blend in here."

"It'll be fine. We got all those clothes. We'll just put on some disguises. No one will recognize me without all my court robes and vine-style."

"That's probably true. But what about me?" Arara pointed to her tail. "We can't hide that, or how short I am, even if we had any fur-dye."

"Have you seen yourself lately? All the dust from that tunnel and sleeping on the floor... your fur is so coated with dirt and grime it looks gray."

"Hey! You don't look so hot yourself, *Your Highness,*" Arara humphed.

"And your height, we can easily pass you off as a puppy." Sels could only laugh as Arara stuck her tongue out at him. He stood up and retrieved the sack of clothing they'd gathered on the way there.

"Still, my tail? It's pretty distinctive." Arara jumped to her feet and examined the items as Sels pulled them out.

"I don't know yet." He admitted. "Perhaps something in here can help?"

CHAPTER SEVENTEEN

OFF TO MARKET

Arara draped the cleanest pieces of clothing out on the piles of garbage, trying to judge fit. While sorting, she half listened to Sels's thoughts. He knelt behind her, trying to remember the locations of the major roads by sketching out a rough map of the city in the dirt. Her arms hurt, and Sels's thoughts helped to distract her from the pain.

From outside she also occasionally picked up the thoughts of passersby going about their day. A few sniffed at the door, noting their intrusion, but no one came inside to investigate.

The majority of the clothing turned out to be much too large for her, but she was able to assemble an almost clean outfit that would fit Sels's taller frame. The outfit consisted of rough wool tunic, unraveling at the cuffs and seams, and soft leather pants, worn thin from use and complete with a Jegeran tail-hole in the seat. A wide leather belt with only a few stains completed the outfit. Sels would have to go barefoot, since Jegera didn't generally wear shoes.

She was curious to see if he'd really go through with wearing this disguise. After all, his normal clothing consisted of soft silks and woven plant fibers tailored to fit him perfectly. Even his pajamas were nicer than her best outfit. Did he even know how itchy wool could get, especially in the heat?

She folded the clothing up into neat little squares and piled them next to him. He looked over and wrinkled his nose, then looked down at himself. He debated internally about staying in his stained and soiled pajama bottoms for their trek across the city as he unfolded the outfit.

Arara clamped her paws around her muzzle, but a muffled howl of laughter still escaped at the thought of him strolling around the city clad in nothing but half a pair of stained silk bedclothes.

"Arara," Sels said, turning around and frowning at her. "Can you at least pretend to not hear my every thought?"

Arara nodded to him. She tried to look solemn as he shook out the shirt and gagged at the thought of it touching his delicate skin. Only the thought of his mother in grave danger from the fake guards prompted him to consider pulling the disgusting thing over his head.

Before Arara realized what he'd done, Sels had pulled his pants down to his ankles.

"What are you doing?" Arara yipped and spun her back to him.

"Changing, of course." The wool shirt muffled his voice as he pulled it over his head. The hasp of leather on skin followed shortly afterwards as he struggled with the pants. "As my *sedyu*-bonded, part of your duties are to help me dress."

To distract herself, Arara used her claws to rip the legs off the smallest pair of pants for herself. Paired with a long shirt, it would cover her tail well enough.

"What do you think?" Sels cleared his throat. "I think I make a pretty dashing poor person."

Arara rolled her eyes before turning around. Sels stood with his hands on hips, striking a pose amid all the garbage. The shirt sagged, and the neck opened so wide it practically fell off his shoulders. The short sleeves hung down past his elbows. He'd wrapped the belt over the top of the shirt, and an alarming amount of material puffed out above the waist. The pants hung low, but they fit him well enough that they didn't slide off. When he turned around for her inspection the tail-hole in the back gaped open.

"Stay right there." Arara said, fishing the portable sewing kit she'd gotten from Darach out of her pockets. "Hold the back of the shirt up a bit. I need to sew that closed."

"Couldn't you have done that before I put them on?" He said, trying to twist his head around to watch.

"Didn't want to waste the time if they didn't fit you." Arara said. She could feel his embarrassment as she used her fingers to pinch the fabric together. "Besides, a moment ago you stripped down to the nude right in front of me."

"Yeah, but your face wasn't a finger's length away from my butt when I did that."

Arara shook her head as she sewed up the hole. She wouldn't ever understand Kin. The soft leather was easy to work with, and soon enough she was finished. It was rough, but it only had to hold together for a few hours.

Sels beamed down at her and posed again. "This is perfect. Absolutely no one will recognize me."

"Probably won't recognize your smell either," Arara pretended to wave his stench away from her nose. She joked, but really, Kin's flower perfume was strong and distinctive. Any Jegera who knew the Prince's smell would know him instantly. The average townsfolk, however, would just smell another Kin. But, the odds were high that even now palace guards were combing this very neighborhood. The faster they got out of here the better.

"Your turn."

"Um, a few things might work...if they didn't smell so bad." The only small pair of pants, the ones she'd ripped the legs off of, had come from the first trash bin. The one that held the rotting roap corpse, and the fluids had soaked one side of the garment.

He brightened. "No, that's perfect. It will disguise your scent from their trackers."

In response she snorted and glared at him. “I know I have to wear them, but don’t sound so happy about it. After all, you’ll be walking next to me.”

“Oh, they can’t be that bad.” He put his hands on her shoulders and pushed her towards the pile of clothing. “Put them on, and let’s go.” He was anxious to get going, worried that even now his mom was already in trouble.

She sighed and picked up the shorts. Rather than having the disgusting things touch her skin, she pulled them over the top of her court clothing. The shirt followed. She pulled it around until she couldn’t see the court silks underneath. The shirt billowed around her thin frame, and the extra fabric did an effective job of hiding her tail.

While she changed, Sels had paced restlessly over to the window to peer up at the sun.

“Ready.” She called.

“Let’s get going.” Sels trotted back over to her, careful to avoid stepping on anything with his bare feet.

When he got close Arara reached up to take his hand. Her arms throbbed, and she wanted Sels's healing touch. Sels sniffed, then gagged, stumbling backwards away from her. He tripped on the hem of the long pants and fell back into a pile of refuse with a crash.

He lay there for a minute gasping for air before staggering back to his feet. “Ok, I get it. They stink, but we don’t have any other options.”

Arara hated to admit it, but he had a point. Her arms felt like they were on fire, and every little movement hurt. With Sels missing, the fake guards would have to strike soon.

Sels crouched down and rolled up the hem of his pants, laughing in his head. He thought Arara looked like a child dressing up in her parents clothing. Although she knew he badly wanted to laugh, his expression stayed impassive the whole time.

Arara put her paws on her hips to glare at him properly, but her claws got caught in the excess fabric. She hopped around, flailing, to get them loose. Sels struggled not to laugh out loud, but finally his face cracked and he let out a loud guffaw. The move hurt her already throbbing arms, but Sels's smiling face made it worthwhile.

While Sels tried to stop laughing, she gathered up his discarded pajamas and stuffed them into a sack she found in the rubble. She found a broom with the handle broken off and used it to sweep out the cooking pit. Sels came up behind her, curious about her actions.

"Set it on fire." She commanded, placing the sack with the pajamas in the pit. "We need to remove all trace of our being here."

"Arara, you keep asking me to do spells. You know I can't." Sels said with a shake of his head.

"You just don't give yourself enough credit." Arara humphed. "At least try."

Sels frowned, looking back and forth between Arara and the fire pit, debating with himself. He was afraid the spell would end with a boom, like what happened against the kwaso, or in his pod against the kidnappers.

"Sels, there isn't anything here you need to worry about destroying." Arara said, waving at the room. "If it makes you feel better, I'll stand back away, near the door."

Sels waited to begin his spell until Arara had picked her way across the garbage to the den's exit. She could hear him mumbling under his breath, trying to remember the incantation his magic teacher had taught him.

Shafts of light pierced the gloom around the door, as the shriveled remains of the door vines shifted in the breeze. Arara peered into the interior gloom, trying to watch as Sels waved his arms around and chanted, occasionally pointing in the direction of the firepit. She could feel his growing frustration at being unable to connect to the magic like before.

<Sels, we need to get going.> Arara sent him, not wanting to be overheard by the pedestrians passing by in the street just a few tails away. *<Just bring it along. We'll find another way to dispose of it.>*

<*I told you.*> Sels threw up his hands, then reached over and grabbed the sack. He slowly eased through the mess towards her, carrying the sack pinched between two fingers, held out as far as possible. <*This sack is absolutely disgusting. I cannot believe you asked me to touch it.*> He dropped it at her feet with a sour expression. <*You carry it if you insist on taking it with us.*>

Arara bared her teeth at him and picked up the sack in her less injured paw. Of course the sack stunk, she was trying to hide his scent!

<*Arara, something just occurred to me.*> Sels said. Arara paused, paw in the air ready to brush away the vines at the door. Arara already knew what he would say next, but she paused politely, waiting for him to gather his thoughts, rather than upset him again. <*By royal decree, all Jegera in the city must live in this district. We don't have to travel all the way to the University! Mura must live around here somewhere. We just need to ask around!*>

Arara just nodded at Sels, head cocked as she pulled an image of Mura from Sels memory. Mura was a common name, but her fur was a distinctive tri-color combination of black with brown and white highlights.

<*We'll start at the butcher.*> Arara gefired to Sels

<Really? Why?>

<*Everyone's friends with the butcher. That way you get the freshest, best cuts of meat.*> Sels could be so clueless. Of course everyone is friends with the person who provides the food.

Arara led Sels out onto the street, squinting in the bright sunlight after the gloom of the den. The few pedestrians, all Jegera, paused as Sels emerged from the doorway behind her. Arara growled a warning at them. Most huffed and turned away, dismissing her, but one caught her attention. That pedestrian, a nondescript medium sized brown Jegera, gave them a long look, then slunk off down a nearby alley. Arara tried to read his thoughts, but he moved off too fast, and the crowd of nearby people made her hesitate to drop her shields.

Although only a few pedestrians moved down this small side street, more Jegera occupied the dens around them.

Arara trotted off on two legs, Sels close on her heels. She would have preferred to run on all fours, as walking on two legs for too long hurt her back, but her arms felt stiff and hot, too hurt to use. Arara stuffed the stinky sack into the first garbage bin she saw, freeing her paws. Sels could have burned it, why wouldn't he have just tried? Now she had to leave it out where anyone could find it.

She sighed and shook her head. Sels just needed something to boost his confidence. Now that her paws were free, she tucked her arms into the large shirt sleeves, letting the fabric cradle them.

The narrow lane emptied out onto a much larger street, this one wide enough for pedestrians to travel along both sides and vehicles to travel one way down the center.

A dead-wood cart trundled down the center of the thoroughfare, pulled by a thick-bodied hairless domesticated elephant. Arara had only ever seem pictures of them before, as Last Home got too cold for them. They did best in the dry heat of the area around the capital. Its long trunk curled under its head as it walked, and its short tail swatted at the flies that buzzed around it. Arara hadn't realized she'd stopped to stare until Sels prodded her forward again.

Jegera pedestrians shoved past them, and Arara fell in line behind them. The buzz of so many thoughts around her battered at her shields, and Arara winced. The crowd grew in size for several blocks before spilling out into a busy marketplace. The amount of noise shocked Arara, reminding her of the noise at the arena. She moved out of the crowd into the shadows of a nearby doorway, trying to escape the din.

The sheer amount of chaos fascinated her. All around her Jegera were calling out about their wares, and others were haggling, practically shouting at each other to be heard in the din. Colorful signs and banners hung everywhere, advertising everything from combs, knives, and fur treatments, to wholly unfamiliar Kin plant-tech. An automatic fur groomer? That sounded nice. She hadn't had a good brushing since she left home. She turned to ask Sels about it, but he was no longer by her side.

Although Sels green skin would stand out against the muted tones of Jegera fur, Arara couldn’t see anything past the taller Jegera surrounding her. She almost called out his name, wishing they’d thought to come up with aliases to use in the city.

<*Sels, I lost you! Where are you?!*> Arara gefired, whimpering out loud as she scanned the crowds. She stood as tall as she could, craning her neck to see through breaks in the crowd for any sign of a Kin. She ducked and weaved under baskets and between people, sniffing the air for his scent.

A soft paw tapped her shoulder from behind.

"What’s wrong, little pup?" A small female Jegera knelt down to look her in the eyes with a motherly smile. Three pups peeked out from behind her. Barely three summers old, each had one paw wrapped tightly around their mother’s tail so as not to get lost. While normally Arara hated getting mistaken for a younger pup, today she seized the opportunity.

“I’ve lost my daddy.” Arara widened her eyes, lowered her muzzle, and looked up at the mother from under her brows while whining pitifully. In Last Home a Kin would never have adopted a Jegeran child, but Arara hoped the situation wasn’t so unusual in Sebaine.

“Can you describe him, little one?”

“He’s tall as you, with green skin and purple petals.” Arara yipped. “And he smells like flowers.”

The mother grimaced and pulled back her ears. <*What is the city coming to? Now the Kin are even taking our children. And look at what she’s wearing, too. Disgraceful. A Kin would be able to afford better than that.*>

“A Kin? In the bazaar?” The mother said, battling to look cheerful. “Shouldn’t be too hard to find. I’ll help you find him.”

The mother reached out for Arara's paw. Arara ducked back, not wanting the over-protective mother to see the state of her arms. She hit the knees of a Jegera walking past behind her, almost knocking over the massive basket he carried.

"Shhhh...calm down little one. I won't hurt you." She humphed and snorted, crouching lower down to meet Arara's eyes. *<That's what happens with little ones raised by a Kin. Afraid of their own kind.>*

Arara nodded and ducked her head. Her empty stomach betrayed her and growled loudly.

"Now, where were you going? Perhaps we can find him there."

"The butcher's." Arara said. In her head, Sels called out to her, having finally realized she wasn't with him.

<Arara, meet me at the butcher's. I'll ask around about Mura while I wait for you.>

"The butcher's?" The mother said, interrupting Arara's conversation with Sels. "Do you know which one?"

"There's more than one?" Arara's eyes got big and she whimpered. Once she considered the fact that in the last few scratch-marks she'd seen more Jegera than lived in the whole of Last Home, she supposed it made sense. She tried to ask Sels, but he was concentrating on moving through the large crowd and didn't hear her.

The mother took in Arara's expression and nodded. "That's what I thought. Why don't you come with me and we'll look for him?"

Arara nodded and followed after the friendly mother. She didn't see the harm, since the mother only wanted to help her.

*****

The kindly mother led Arara around the corner to a Jegeran eatery. The door to the eatery was made up of two wooden planks set on hinges rather than door-vines. They squeaked loudly when the mother pushed them open on the way in.

The mother took one of the empty tables, placing each of her three children on the bench seats beside her. The little puppies' eyes barely peeked over the top of the table. Arara took the empty bench on the other side of the table, being careful not to bump her arms against the table's edge.

"My name's Krasi, little one." The mother smiled across at Arara and tilted her head. "What's yours?"

Arara just stared at her, unsure what to say. She didn't want to use her own name, by now half the city were out looking for her and Sels. The three puppies peeked across the table at Arara.

"She has funny ears mama." One of the pups said, then ducked his head down.

"Shush." Krasi reached down and bobbed the pup on the nose with one finger. "What is your...daddy's name, then?" Krasi cringed.

"Um..." A server bearing a tray of roasted meat scurried past behind Arara. Arara stomach growled, loudly, and Arara turned around to watch it go.

"When was the last time you ate, little one?" Krasi gave Arara a hard look from across the table.

Arara shrugged and tucked her arms deeper in her shirt. "I don't know. We need to find my daddy. Why are we here?"

"I brought you here because you looked hungry, little one. Don't worry. I gefired the proprietor when we came in. My friends are searching the bazaar for your, um, father, as we speak." Krasi gave her a reassuring smile from across the table. "Now, can you tell me your name?"

Arara needed to tell Krasi something, before she began to get suspicious. She decided to use her mother's name, since it was familiar to her and she could easily remember it. "Athura," she said softly.

Krasi relaxed and sat back. "That's a pretty name." She barked, startling Arara. A server appeared at Krasi's side.

"We'd like three servings of hukra stew, an ale for me, and four waters for the little ones." She looked at Arara before adding, "Also, we're looking for the Kin that is visiting the market today."

The server nodded and disappeared back into the milling crowd. Arara got a sinking feeling in her stomach. Hearing Krasi say it so casually, she realized that here Sels stuck out like a shaved Jegera. This was a bad idea.

<*Sels, leave the market now. Be careful. We'll meet up as soon as I can get out of here without attracting attention.*>

<*I agree. I didn't realize how conspicuous we'd be. But I've had someone tailing me since we got here. I don't know if I can lose them.*> Sels sounded worried. That decided it for her. They'd already attracted attention. Arara started scooting down to the end of the bench. She couldn't do much in her current condition, but she couldn't let those thugs get him. They might not recognize Sels and try to rob him, not realizing he had no money or valuables on him.

<*Where do you think you're going?*> Krasi scolded her. <*Sit down, eat. I know you're hungry.*>

<*I am hungry,*> Arara thought fast, knowing Krasi expected a gefir back. <*But I, my,*> Crap, she'd called him her daddy, but she couldn't lie in a gefir. <*It's taking too long.*>

<*No, Athura.*> Krasi jumped up and led Arara back to her seat, pushing her back down. Arara fell forward and knocked her arms on the edge of the table. A whimper escaped as the hard table edge scraped along the cuts on her arms. Her arms burned and throbbed. Krasi let go in surprise, and Arara curled up into a ball on the bench, her arms pulled tightly to her chest sobbing in pain.

Krasi left her puppies and made her way around the table. She crouched down beside Arara. With a gentle touch, she used her claws to cut away the sleeves of Arara's floppy shirt. Fresh blood oozed down Arara's arm where the table had scraped off the scab.

"Oh, red moon!" Krasi's eyes grew wide. "I thought I smelled blood under that stench." Krasi turned and gefired to someone across the bar. <*Bring me some hot water and bandages. We've got an injured puppy here.*>

She gently pulled Arara's arms out to rest on the table and tore the remainder of the sleeves off Arara's shirt. The occupants of nearby tables craned their heads to watch and gasped when Krasi revealed Arara's mangled arms.

"That Kin and I are going to have a long talk when he gets here." Krasi growled under her breath.

"A Kin did this?!" The occupant of the table behind theirs jumped to his feet with a growl.

"No!" Arara glared at him. "He didn't do this. I jumped through a window. He was going to take me to the healers after we got something to eat."

Krasi shook her head. "Little one, every Kin can do a little bit of healing magic. Your daddy," Krasi's lips pulled back from her teeth in disgust, "could have healed you anytime he wanted."

"Oh." Arara just blinked up at Krasi in surprise. Now she understood a little bit more why Sels felt so inadequate, if he couldn't do something that even the most inept Kin should be able to do with ease.

A server hurried up, carrying a bowl of water with some rags soaking in it. The girl placed the bowl on the table and hurried away, casting a sympathetic look back at Arara as she scurried off. Arara narrowed her eyes, but in this crowd she didn't dare drop her shields to try to figure out why the girl was worried.

Krasi dipped the rag in the water and started cleaning Arara's arms and pulling slivers of glass out of the wounds. The puppies watched, quiet and solemn, as their mother worked.

"Probably your Kin didn't think you were worth the magic." The gawker said with a snort. Arara didn't reply, but the growing crowd around their table growled in agreement.

"Damn Kin," Another said. "Think they're better than us." The crowd barked in agreement, and someone howled for blood. Arara looked around, growing more worried by the moment. With all these people watching, and Krasi's grip on her arms, she wasn't going to get out of here anytime soon.

The crowd grew more agitated as they watched Krasi clean Arara's arms. A small glittering pile of bloody glass shards grew on the bench next to Arara.

The crowd parted to reveal a different server, this one bearing a tray filled with drinks and soup. He slid the tray on to the table behind Arara, then turned to the boisterous group of Jegera around them.

"Settle down, everyone sit back down. The Kin is being brought here as we speak." The server turned in a slow circle to meet everyone's eyes, no, not the server, the house proprietor, Arara realized. The proprietor grinned, flashing his fangs. "When he gets here we'll giving him a warm welcome, eh?" The crowd howled, barked, and yelled at that, breaking off to settle restlessly back into their seats.

Krasi's biggest puppy, ignoring the near riot going on around him, dived into their bowl of soup, spilling half of it onto the table for the other two to lap up. Arara frantically listened for Sels. If he was in trouble, and being brought here, why hadn't he contacted her?

<Sels, where are you?>

<Running from the pack hunting me!> She could feel Sels panic as he dashed behind stalls and down back alleys. *<They're cutting me off at every turn! Can't talk, can't concentrate enough to talk to you and run!>*

The gawker at the next table had continued to talk to Krasi while Arara spoke to Sels, although Arara hadn't really been listing.

"A Kin won't even help a little pup, clearly in need of a healer." The gawker harrumphed, and his table mates banged their wooden tankards on the table in agreement.

"Even worse," Krasi said without looking up. "He's adopted her. She called him her father."

The gawker growled and cursed, incoherent in his rage. Arara watched him with wide eyes, unsure of what to do.

"Don't worry," Krasi continued. "I intend to adopt this little one myself after we take care of that Kin."

The gawker grinned at Arara over Krasi's shoulder. Arara had her shields up, but his angry thoughts punched right through them. *<The Prince escaped us last night, bet they'd love having an abusive Kin to beat up on today.>*

Arara jerked, leaning around Krasi to look at the gawker. That big Jegera was part of the group that was trying to hurt Sels! Her protective instinct kicked into overdrive, and with a growl she stood and launched herself off the chair towards the gawker. Krasi grabbed her midair.

"Athura, I know it hurts, but you need to sit still." Krasi sat her back down firmly, then turned to the gawker.

"Can you help me hold down this little one while I finish?"

The big gray gawker grinned down at Arara, his grin reminding her of Kerka. He reached over and pushed down on her shoulders, pinning her to the bench. Her tail curled around, trying to tuck itself between her legs and her ears drooped as she had flashbacks to being forcibly shaved. She whimpered and squirmed, trying to get away.

Arara cried as Krasi's claws dug deep into her arm for the last few shards, but the big gray held Arara still. Arara could feel Sels getting closer, the thugs herding him relentlessly towards their trap. Arara's mind flashed back to the meadow, paws gripping her tight while the clippers stung her arms. She closed her eyes, trying to stop trembling.

"All done, little one," Krasi jerked her head and the big gray released Arara's shoulders.

<Sels, run, it's a trap!> Freed, Arara dived under the table and huddled up in a little ball, trembling uncontrollably. Krasi crouched down and peered under the table at her.

<I AM running!> Sels huffed, stumbling through the muck of the alley behind the tavern.

"Athura, aren't you hungry?" Krasi waved a bowl of soup under the table. "We're done, come eat."

The swinging door squealed and the bar fell silent. Arara peeked out from her arms, but someone's feet blocked her view of the door. However, it didn't matter. She could feel Sels, and knew it was him.

"Daddy!" Arara burst out from under the table, bounded through the sea of legs, and wrapped herself around Sels middle.

<Sels, run!> Arara pushed Sels back towards the door. *<They'll recognize you! They're part of the group that tried to kidnap you last night<*

The swinging doors hit Sels in the back as three massive Jegera came in behind him. The crossed their arms and stood across the doorway in a line, growling down at Sels and Arara.

"Those are the Jegera that have been chasing me." Sels pulled Arara away from the door.

"Sit down." Krasi growled, pointing to the bench seat across from her.

Sels pushed Arara off of him and took her hand. She led him across the room, swiveling her head around to find another way out. The thoughts of the crowd had turned ugly, and she knew they had to get out of there soon.

The whole room sat silent, watching them. A low growl followed them to their seats. Despite the tension, the smell of the soup wafting up her nose made her stomach growl. She grabbed the bowl and lapped at the lukewarm broth. It actually wasn't very good, but Arara was so hungry she didn't care.

"You obviously can't take care of this pup," Krasi said, glaring at Sels. "I'm adopting her. Everyone here," Krasi gestured around the room, "saw the state she was in - hungry, hurt, dirty, wearing clothes much too big for her. It won't go well for you if you refuse."

"Are you threatening me?" Sels straightened and glared back at Krasi. Arara perked up, but continued lapping at the hukra broth.

"Yes," Krasi growled. At the same time the big gray Jegera came up behind Sels and slammed his paw on the table to either side of him, rattling the dishes. Krasi's three puppies jumped and clustered up to their mother.

<*I recognize that scent, that's the Prince! I can't let this crowd find out, or they'll tear him apart before I can get him out of here and the boss wanted him alive.*>

"She said," the gray growled as Sels twisted around to face him. "A sun-cursed Kin shouldn't be raising a little Jegera." The gray leaned closer, showing Sels his teeth. "We're going to teach you a little lesson today."

<*'Rara, what do I do?*> Sels wrinkled his nose at the gray's breath, but otherwise held his ground.

<*He recognizes you, Sels, but he's right about one thing. If this crowd finds out you're the Prince you'll never make it out of this tavern alive. Play along with him until we can get out of here.*>

<*That's a terrible plan.*>

<*Then you think of a better one.*> Arara poked him in the side. <*It'll be easier to rescue you from a few Jegera outside than from an entire tavern full of angry drunks.*>

"I've done nothing wrong. It's perfectly legal for a Kin to adopt a Jegera." Sels said, turning his back to the gray. He reached around the gray furry arms to grab Arara's mug of water. Sels gratefully began gulping water from the mug.

"Is that so?" The gray Jegera snarled and pushed off the table, smacking the end of the mug with his paw as he did so. The mug upended over Sels head before spinning off to shatter all over the floor. Arara gasped and covered her mouth.

Sels jumped to his feet and stared down. Water ran down his head, dripping off his vines and soaking his clothing. She could feel Sels disbelief over what the gray had just done to his royal person.

"How dare you?!" Sels said, his voice low and tight with anger. He looked up at the big gray with fury in his eyes.

<Sels, remember you are pretending to be just a regular person.> Arara reminded him. *<Say, I got a poor orphan off the streets. And there is nothing you or your friends can do about it.>*

"I got a poor orphan off the streets." Sels breathed deep, in and out for a moment as he shook water out of his vines. "There is nothing you," Sels straightened and scanned the tavern with a smug expression. He raised his voice, it wasn't a yell but loud enough to be heard by everyone. "Or your friends can do about it. It's perfectly legal."

Arara followed his gaze around, satisfied to see every last eye in the place focused on them. Even the servers had stopped to watch, trays balanced on tables or chair backs.

<Perfect. I didn't realize you could be so high and mighty like that.>

<I'm picturing the royal court.> Sels said with a mental shrug.

Arara, still pretending to lick up the last of the soup out of her bowl, focused on the big gray. He did a private gefir to a young Jegera at the back of the room, an order to get the headquarters ready for a guest.

"Would have been better to leave her on the streets," the gray growled. He grabbed Arara's arm and tugged her off the bench. Sels grabbed her other arm and pulled back, causing Arara to drop her empty bowl on the floor with a crash. The remains mixed with the blood and water swirled around on the floor.

"Just having bad luck this week." Sels growled back at him. The gray tugged, his grip painful on Arara's arm. She felt Sels's weaker grip slide off as the gray pulled her away.

"Oh, you have no idea." The gray barked and backhanded Sels with his free paw. Sels fell backwards off the bench, hitting the hard dirt floor sideways with a thud. Pain flared up Arara's shoulder and the back of her head, mirroring Sels's pain. Arara's head swam as the gray Jegera hoisted her up and away. Two of the gray Jegera's friends rushed over and hauled Sels back to his feet. They twisted his arms behind his back and dragged him away towards the kitchen.

Arara howled and fought against the gray's grip, unwilling to use her mental powers and give herself away. She had to remind herself this was part of the plan and that she needed to wait a moment and follow unseen.

"Take care of her." The gray dumped Arara into Krasi's arms, then followed his buddies to the kitchen.

<Arara, help!> Sels cried to her. Arara could feel them in the kitchen binding his hands behind his back and gagging him.

Krasi petted Arara's head, murmuring something in her ear, but Arara ignored her. She focused on Sels and waited. As soon as they exited the building, Arara jumped out of Krasi's lap. Krasi grabbed the back of her shirt, but Arara wriggled out of the oversized garment and dashed after Sels.

"Athura, come back!" Krasi cried after her, struggling with her three little puppies and unable to come after her.

Arara dashed through the kitchen and wrenched the door open with her mind, not wanting to risk slowing down and losing them in the maze of alleys.

CHAPTER EIGHTEEN

THE CONSPIRACY

For the second time in less than a single sun cycle, Sels found himself taken captive. His head pounded where it'd hit the hard packed dirt of the tavern floor. The Jegera carrying him dug their claws painfully into his arms.

They dragged him through the alleys, seemingly at random. Arara gefired to let him know that she followed along behind.

Eventually they pulled him through an unremarkable door down the dirtiest alley they'd been through yet. The door led into a dank hallway reeking of wet fur and mold. Grime-covered skylights let in only a small trickle of light. They pulled him down the hall and shoved him into a pitch dark room, slamming the door behind him. Sels stumbled forward, and without his hands for balance he fell to his knees on the hard rock floor. The wooden rasp of a bolt sliding into place was followed by barking laughter.

Sels struggled to his feet, gagging on the stench of urine that pervaded the fetid air. He bumped around the walls of the room with his shoulders. His prison turned out to be a couple of tail-lengths deep and wide. He tried to cast a light spell, but with his hands bound behind him he couldn't even get a flicker. After the third failed attempt he gave up, realizing that even unbound he would still be stuck in the dark.

Sels curled up in the least smelly corner and tried not to cry while he waited for Arara.

<Arara, where are you?> Sels shuddered at the feel of tiny feet running over his bare flesh. *<I'm really scared. They took me in a building and locked me in a closet of some sort.>*

<I'm here, but I'm going to hang back for now. We have a chance to find out who the leaders of this group are.>

<And you really think they'll come HERE?> He was skeptical that the powerful Jegera in charge of what seemed to be a major organization would consent to come to the slums.

<I eavesdropped on your captors, they recognized you as the Prince. They went to get the leaders. If we can stop them, we can save your mom.>

<Arara, I don't think this is a good idea.> His arms ached and the tight bonds were cutting off circulation to his hands. He was so scared. He trusted Arara, but did she think the two of them were any match for a whole organization of criminals?

He wasn't sure how long he was in the little room before exhaustion and injury caught up to him and he fell asleep.

A Jegera shook him awake before jerking him to his feet. The light of a torch, held by a second Jegera, hurt Sels's eyes. They kicked his feet out from under him and dragged him by his throbbing arms out of the room and down the hall. A loud argument echoed through the building, and deep Jegeran voices growled and snarled back and forth. The walls muffled the words, but something about the voices sounded familiar.

<Arara, I hope you're still close by. Sounds like someone's here.> Sels strained to hear Arara's reply but was met with silence. He could feel her nearby, and her silence worried him.

By now Sels's eyes had adjusted to the light. He twisted and squinted up at his captors. The flickering torchlight revealed the big gray Jegera from the tavern and his friend. They bared their teeth down at Sels and chuckled.

"...the palace didn't announce he was missing. How can you be so sure?"

"I'm sure. They're trying to cover it up until he can be recovered. It's the perfect opportunity." The familiar voice came through clearly as his captors dragged him closer to the speakers. Sels lowered his head, trying to place why that voice seemed so familiar.

"I still think-" One of his captors stopped and knocked on the door, cutting off the speaker.

"Enter." A bolt rasped and the door swung open. The Jegera dragged Sels inside and dropped him. The stone floor cracked his forehead as he fell face-first onto the ground. Sels moaned, his head still hurt from his fall earlier. Now he watched stars swirl in his vision and felt himself blacking out. He could feel Arara, so close she had to be in the room with them. Hidden, waiting to save him. He struggled to stay conscious and aware.

Something sharp touched his arm, and Sels jerked his eyes open, struggling to get away.

"Hold still." The familiar voice said into his ear. The bonds holding his arms behind him fell away. Sels pulled his arms around and pushed himself to a sitting position. A warm cloth pressed against his forehead. Sels reached up and held it there.

"Thank you." Sels whispered, licking his dry lips. "Do you have any water?"

"You don't deserve water." The voice snarled from above him.

Sels snapped his eyes open and lowered his hand. His gaze traveled up, up, to see Darach towering over him. Darach leaned over and ripped the cloth from Sels hand and tossed it away across the room. It landed with a wet splat in front of Lolop, who leaned heavily on his wooden cane. Lolop's aged features had pulled back into a snarl.

Only a few candles lit the cavernous room. Behind Lolop and Darach, in the shadows, Sels could make out more furry shapes.

"You were correct, Darach." Lolop chuffed. "The Prince wasn't in the palace after all."

Sels whimpered and scooted backwards away from the Elders. His back hit something hard and furry. The big gray Jegera grinned at Sels before kicking him. Sels sprawled foreword onto his stomach again.

<Arara, help!> Sels hands trembled so bad he could barely push himself up to sitting.

Lolop hobbled around Sels. Sels pulled his knees to his chest, turning his head to keep Lolop in his view as the old Jegera hobbled around him.

"I can't believe it." Lolop said with a shake of his head, his loose skin flapping about his jowls. "How did Arara talk you into such a disguise?"

Sels stayed silent and tried to keep his fear from showing on his face. Lolop hobbled closer. Sels flinched away as the cane came closer. Lolop reached out with his paw and grabbed a chunk of Sels's vines. He wrapped them painfully tight in his paw, then jerked back Sels's head.

"You really thought you could escape us?" Lolop snarled into Sels's face.

"No," Sels's voice trembled despite his best effort.

Lolop twisted his paw, and Sels screamed. He could feel his vines tearing out by their roots, could feel the warm sap running down his head. He beat at Lolop's paw with his fists, but Lolop didn't even seem to feel his weak blows. Where was Arara?

"What, you just happened to stumble into that tavern?" Lolop pulled harder, and Sels screamed again as a big chunk of his vines ripped free.

"Yes..." Sels sobbed. How could he have known? He'd never even been out of the palace alone before, and he'd certainly never been to the Jegeran slums.

Lolop gave one last twist and released Sels's vines with a snort. Sels sagged in relief. Warm sap trickled down his face, and Sels wiped at it with his shirt sleeve. Bluish green ichor mixed with his sticky tears, staining his already filthy clothing. Sels knew he must look a mess, but he couldn't bring himself to care.

The gray Jegera grabbed Sels's arm and dragged him further into the room. The other guard reappeared with a lantern. The light revealed a rickety table and four chairs. Jegera occupied three of the chairs. An abandoned game of Claws and Bones covered the table.

The wavering light also revealed a small form laying prone on the floor. Her white fur shone in the light and bone charms glinted on her wrist.

"Arara!" Sels pulled his feet under him, turning and punching the gray with his free hand. The gray's grip loosed slightly. Sels continued to pull away and punch at his captor, and the gray's claws ripped deep furrows down his arm.

"Let him go." Darach sneered. The gray released Sels, who promptly ran over to Arara, heedless of the snickering group of Jegera gathered around the table.

He dropped to her side, and gathered her to his chest, heedless of the bleeding wounds on his arm. Her heart beat strong beneath his palms, her breathing deep and even, but as much as he shook her and cried she didn't stir. He tried to cast a healing spell, but he couldn't calm himself enough to even start the incantation.

"Enough." Darach kicked Sels in the head with a clawed hind paw hard enough to blur his vision and knock him over, although he kept a tight grip on Arara.

"Rupha, take this thing back to his cell. With him as a captive, the Queen will roll over and do anything we tell her. After we have the kingdom," Darach chuckled. "A public execution for the entire Royal Family will be a fitting tribute to the end of the enslavement of the Jegeran people."

"Enslavement?!" Sels managed to choke out, his throat tight with fear. "The Kin-Jegera Empire is a partnership between two equal races!"

“Equal?” Darach snorted. “Is that why the Council has three times as many Kin as Jegera, despite the fact that we outnumber Kin two to one? Or why there is a Kin Royal Family but not a Jegeran one?”

“The Royals take a Jegeran *Sedyu*-bonded. The *Sedyu*-bonded rules alongside the King or Queen.” Sels knew Darach couldn’t be reasoned with, but he couldn’t stand by and be quiet while Darach spouted such lies.

“That was the original purpose, yes.” Darach snarled, pacing back and forth in front of Sels. “But now they are no more than guards. The Kin sit high in their pretty gardens, attended by Jegeran slaves.”

“He can’t be reasoned with, Darach.” Lolop humphed. “Take him back to his cell, Rupha.”

The big gray, Rupha, grabbed Sels by his freshly injured arm and dragged him away. Sels winced at the pain, but kept a tight grip on Arara.

“Drop her.” Rupha growled down at him.

Sels shook his head, wrapping his legs around Arara’s middle for good measure. Rupha crouched down and pried Sels legs off of her. Sels used the opportunity to throw his arms around Arara’s shoulders.

"Don't worry Sels, we won't hurt her." Darach said, and reached over to assist Rupha.

"Then why won't she wake up?" Sels still refused to let go, locking his arms around her and gritting his teeth at the pain from his mangled arm.

“Through some misplaced loyalty to you, she fought us.” Darach growled, prying at Sels's arms while Rupha clawed at Sels legs. “Once we can convince her of the error of her ways, she'll be free to leave here unharmed."

"No, I don't believe you." He clung even tighter to Arara, ignoring the pain of the Jegera’s claws.

"Fine, you two deserve each other." Darach waved, and Rupha dragged the two of them away. “Lock her in with Sels.”

Darach picked up a metal collar off the table. He fitted it around Sels neck. Sels shivered at the cool touch of the metal collar. It seemed to suck the warmth out of him. He tried not to cry as Darach secured it with a small metal lock.

Rupha dragged Sels, who kept his death grip on Arara, back down the hall and shoved him roughly into the tiny room. The door closed behind him with a bang and the sound of a heavy bolt sliding into place.

*****

Arara watched them drag Sels into a large warehouse deep in the slums. She hid nearby, watching the entrance, waiting to see who showed up. The sun hung low in the sky by the time she spotted Darach and Johka limping down the street. Arara jumped out of hiding, sure the Elders searched for the missing Prince.

Arara wrapped her arms around Darach. He smiled at her, then everything went black. The pitch blackness of the room confused her for a moment, and she blinked several times to assure herself her eyes were in fact open. Her head swam, and it felt like something plugged her nose, because she couldn't seem to smell anything. After a moment everything steadied, and a foul stench assaulted her senses. She lay on something soft and warm. She struggled to sit up before releasing an arm wrapped around her, pinning her down. She blindly struck out with her fists and someone cried out with pain. The person released her and she tumbled back onto the cold floor with a thud.

"Arara, calm down. It's me, Sels." A familiar voice, tight with pain, called out from the darkness.

"Sels?" Arara whispered, barely able to form his name through her dry mouth. She tried to swallow, but her throat was too dry to even do that. *<Sels! Darach and Johka, they're the leaders!>*

<I know, Arara. I...he's going to hurt my mom! They're both crazy.> His fear and pain came through. He was worried about himself, but he was more worried about his mother.

<*Are you hurt?*> Arara crawled back into his lap.

<*Yes. Rupha clawed my arm up pretty good, and Lolop ripped out some of my vines and clawed my face.*> Sels trembled under her. <*Why didn't you warn me that you'd been captured?*>

<*I don't remember what happened.*> Arara said. Truly she couldn't. One moment she'd been following Sels's scent trails through the back alleys, and next thing she knew she'd woken up here.

<*Here, let me bandage up your arm, at least.*> She ripped the sleeves off Sels's shirt and wrapped his arm as best she could in the dark. <*Can you make a light?*>

<*Not like this. I can barely make light under the best of circumstances.*> Sels whimpered in pain as tightened the makeshift bandage and pulled it tight. <*It's dark in here, there isn't any magic here. And, Arara,*> Sels grabbed her paw and held it up to his neck. A cold alien thing wrapped around it. <*It's a metal collar. Even if we had some sunlight, the iron will repel the magic.*>

<*Please try. We need to get you out of here.*> His skin felt sticky and hot under her paws. <*When was the last time you had any food or water?*>

<*I had a little bit of water at the tavern. But what I really need is some sunlight. My head is pounding and I'm feeling weak.*> Sels moved under her and placed his hands together. She could hear him through their link, trying to concentrate through the pain.

Arara watched through the link as he concentrated. Sels's chanting echoed off the stone walls. He began moving his hands and arms around, hitting Arara in the forehead with his elbow. She slid off his lap and backed up, giving him space to move. The magic danced around, just out of his reach. Like trying to grab mist. Arara could feel it now, too, swirling around her head in little clouds.

The more he chanted and moved his hands, the farther away the magic felt. After a while, Sels fell silent. Arara could feel his frustration over not being able to do a simple light spell.

<*How did you do the spell on the pod? And in the forest?*> Arara asked, sending along with it an image of his spell casting ability.

<*I, um,*> Sels trailed off, thinking. <*I'm not sure.*>

<*Well, let's examine your memories of what happened.*> Arara smiled. Darach's teachings would come in useful after all. <*Think about the first time, when you helped me with the kwaso.*>

Sels sighed. "Alright."

Arara concentrated on Sels, like Darach taught her, and dropped her shields. She opened her eyes to find herself as Sels, running away in terror, the kwaso chasing her through the trees. A horrible shriek brought Sels to his knees. The kwaso leapt, Sels thought he was done for, but Arara knocked it away into a tree and fought with it.

Sels wanted to help, so he began casting a spell. The spell was meant to affect the air around the kwaso's head, to suck the air right out of his lungs. Sels, panicked, used whatever magic he found from around him. That magic felt different than the magic he'd tried to use today.

Arara shook herself out of Sels memory and opened her eyes to the black shadows of the prison.

<*The magic, when you cast that spell against the kwaso,*> Arara gefired Sels. <*It felt different than what you are using today.*>

<*Different how?*>

<*The magic you used against the kwaso felt more...wild, dark.*> Arara stopped and debated how to describe it. <*Out of control, almost.*> She sent Sels the memory, about the way the magic had sung and danced through his blood.

<*Arara, that's impossible.*> Sels sighed and she heard him shift in the darkness, trying to get comfortable on the hard stone floor. <*All magic is the same.*>

<*But, I thought there were different types: life, wind, water, earth.*>

<*Everyone uses the same magical energy.*> Sels replied. <*The elemental effect is determined by the Kin's special talents.*>

<But you have trouble gathering and using it.> Arara's ears pricked up.

<Well, yes.>

<So use the other magic. The stuff you used against the kwaso, and on the pod.>

<Arara, I can't...I don't even know how. Before, I was panicked. I don't know what I did.> Arara heard Sels hit the wood walls in frustration. *<I just used whatever I found around me.>*

<So do that again.> Arara's tail wagged unconsciously.

<Look, you remember what happened. Every time I do that, I lose control of the spell and it explodes.>

<So? It'll explode and blow a hole in the wall so we can escape!>

<Fine, I'll try if it will make you happy.> Sels grumbled, but began chanting again. Arara could feel it along with Sels as the strange magic washed over him, strong and wild. Moments later, Sels had a sizable glowing ball cupped in his hands. Arara blinked, the light blinding in the total darkness of the room.

"Down!" Sels gasped and dived to the side while throwing the ball. It sped away from him in a bright blaze of light.

Arara cowered next to him, paws pushing her ears to her head. The ball hit the wall with a roar and exploded outward. The entire building shook, and dust filled the room. Pieces of wood, clay, and stone rained down on Arara's back. Rays of light illuminated the dusty haze around them. Arara raised her head and turned, squinting. A jagged hole was all that remained of their cell's back wall.

<Let's go!> Arara tugged Sels arm. He coughed violently for a moment, before sitting up. Debris tumbled off of him as he stood. He leaned over and shook his head, and a cloud of dust puffed up off his swinging vines. He straightened, waving the dust from his face, then grabbed Arara's paw. Together they stumbled over the rubble and out into the open air. The sharp stones and splinters of wood pierced the delicate pads of her back paws and Sels bare feet.

The dust wasn't as thick out here, but Arara still needed to feel her way along the alley wall until they reached the street. In the distance she could hear shouts of surprise and cries of panic. Arara peeked around the corner. She could mentally hear several Jegera running towards them, but she couldn't see them through the haze. Hoping that meant they couldn't see them either, she squeezed Sels hand and tugged him out into the street.

They stumbled along for about a block, then crossed the street and ducked down another narrow alley.

"Arara, stop!" Sels panted behind her. "I need to rest."

Arara slowed to a stop and turned, intending to berate Sels. Instead she gasped and swallowed her words.

The left side of Sels's face had four long gashes down it, one of them barely missing his eye. Several of the vines on his head were hanging lose and bleeding sap. Deep brown bruises covered one side of his face, overlaid by a layer of dried sap that had run down from his torn vines. His right arm, which Arara had been using to tug him along, had already bled through the clumsily wrapped bandage she'd applied in the dark. His skin was an unhealthy shade of light brown, and most his blossoms were dry and dead.

<*Sels! I didn't realize...*> Arara moved next to him and wrapped his good arm around her shoulder. <*We need to keep moving. The Elders and their goons will be looking for us. I'll help you.*>

They exited the far end of the alley and ran across the street. Arara had hoped to avoid the Jegera she could hear in the area, but her attention was divided and she didn't feel the one approaching them. He came out of an alley further down the main thoroughfare they were crossing and spotted them immediately.

"Hey, are you hurt?" The Jegera called out to them as his path deviated to intercept them.

<*Stay away!*> Arara pushed Sels behind her. She growled as best she could through her parched throat.

"What's going on?" The brown Jegera replied, one ear cocked back and he slowed down, but didn't stop.

Arara backed up, still growling, only to fall backwards over Sels, who had collapsed behind her. As Arara flipped over to all fours, Sels sat up, his hands raised in front of him.

"St..stay away from her." He slurred. His hands trembled, and Arara could feel his fear.

"Hey, I only want to help you." The Jegera stopped and held his front paws up, pads out and claws sheathed. "Were you caught in that explosion?"

"G-g-g-go away!" Sels stuttered. A glowing ball formed before his outstretched hands. The red light lit up his face from below, setting off his high cheeks and sunken eyes. The passing Jegera's eyes widened and he stepped back, but before he could react further Sels threw the glowing ball at him.

The ball streaked forward, flames dancing behind it. The brown Jegera twisted away from the ball, landing on all fours then raced away down the street. The ball continued on its path, hitting the clay building across the street with a boom that knocked Arara off her feet.

Sels pulled himself up using the alley wall as Arara scrambled up to all fours. Arara could hear cries of alarm, and Jegera began pouring out of the buildings around them.

<*Arara, we need to help my mom before they do whatever they have planned!*> He was so upset, but Arara didn't know what to do to help him. She pressed up against Sels legs, which were trembling with exertion. She didn't have any idea where they could go. Sels needed a healer and she needed to get this muzzle off.

<*We'll think of something. But first we need to help ourselves!*> Arara led him away down a deserted side alley. The Jegera on the street focused on the explosion across the street and didn't see the two of them hidden in the shadows of the alley. Arara waited until the majority of the crowd had run by the alley, then she and Sels ran away.

They didn't stop moving until the sounds of panic faded behind them to nothing. The district was almost empty, it seemed that almost every available Jegera had headed towards the sounds of the two explosions.

Arara was unsure of what to do next, but as they walked down yet another dirty alley, Sels pulled away from her and dipped his good arm into a trash bin nearby. When his hand emerged it was gripping the bad end of a vegetable stalk.

He turned to her, and his eyes lit up with excitement. <*You know what this means?*>

She cocked her head to the side and shook her head.

<*It means that a Kin lives nearby! We can get food and help! Can you track which door this bin came from?*>

She grimaced but came closer and fell to all fours, then sniffed around on the ground. It was hard to smell anything over her own stink, but luckily the scent was fresh. She followed it back to a door they'd already passed. Sels waited by the trash bin, picking through it for something edible. He didn't look up until Arara growled at him. <*This one.*>

He hobbled over, holding his right arm tight against his chest, and knocked on the door with the knuckles of his left hand. Arara turned and kept an eye on either end of the alley, turning her head back and forth while they waited. A few scratch-marks later she could hear movement on the other side of the door.

"I'm sorry," A musical Kin voice floated through the wood. "We don't allow visitors to enter through the back. Please come around to the front of the clinic."

"Please," Sels managed to choke out, "help." He door again.

"I said, please go around to the front." The voice hardened this time.

<*Arara, I can't make it any farther.*> Sels wrapped his arms around himself and fell into the door with a thump, sliding down it to sit in the door frame. He curled up into a fetal position in the doorway.

<*I'm tired, and I hurt all over, and I want to go home!*> He dropped his head into his arms with a sob.

CHAPTER NINETEEN

THE PLAN

Arara lay for a long while cuddled up against Sels's back. The rough squeal of a bolt sliding back woke her up right before the door swung open. Sels, who had been leaning against the door, fell inside with a squeak of surprise. He landed at the feet of an equally surprised white Petal Kin lady holding a small bag of trash. The trash fell to the ground with a thud, the bag spilling open onto the floor, staining the hem of her deep green robes.

"Poy, fetch your brother and bring a stretcher to the back door." The lady yelled back into the shop as she knelt next to Sels.

Arara jumped to her feet, growling and baring her fangs. The Kin lady's eyes went wide and she raised her hands. Arara stalked forward on all fours until she stood over Sels, who had curled up on the floor crying in pain.

"Calm down, little one. I just want to help him." When Arara stepped back, the Kin slowly lowered her hands over Sels's neck and felt his pulse. "He's in bad shape. We'll get you both inside and fixed up. "Then maybe you can tell me what happened to the two of you, alright?"

"My name's Roel." The female Kin smiled down at her and placed her hand on Arara's front paw. Arara nodded in relief, Roel told the truth. Roel turned her attention to Sels and placed a hand on his forehead. "Can you tell me your names?"

Arara shook her head, and Sels just moaned. Arara could feel the cold pain constricting his head and winced, hoping Roel would hurry. Arara pricked up her ears and looked past the kneeling Roel to see the inside of the building. The open back door led into a straight hallway, with curtained doorways evenly spaced down each side. The whole building smelled of blood and pain, overlaid with the sharp tang of disinfectants. A healing clinic.

A moment later two young Jerlings, one gray and one brown, came around the corner at the end of the hall with a stretcher. Arara moved to the side, allowing the two to lift Sels onto the stretcher.

Arara trotted on all fours under the stretcher as Roel led the two Jegera through the closest curtain into a tiny room, sparsely furnished with just a bed and a single stool.

They carefully moved Sels from the stretcher into the bed, but even that caused him to cry out in pain. One of the claw marks on his arm pulled open, spilling fresh brown sap onto the clean white sheets. Arara jumped up onto the bed, wincing at the pain in her own arms, and curled up at Sels's side.

“Poy,” Roel placed her hand on the brown Jegera's arm as he went to leave the room. "Please bring one of the supply carts."

Poy nodded and ducked out, leaving the gray one staring down at Arara.

"Niq,” Roel walked over to the gray Jegera and pulled him away. “Do we have anything that can remove that collar?”

“No, ma’am.” Niq said. He faced Roel, but his eyes kept flicking Arara’s direction. “We should call the city guards. They’re probably dangerous criminals. Why else would they have metal?”

“Do they really look dangerous to you?” Roel glared at Niq and pointed to the bed. Arara wagged her tail and gave Niq a big toothless smile. “That pup can't be more than ten summers old. And the Kin, he's badly hurt. The Alpha-Guard wouldn't have done that to him, and they would have called for a healer if they brought in a suspect in such bad shape, I'm the only healer in this district and you know I haven't been summoned anywhere. Those wounds are recent, within the last day."

"But ma'am, she smells funny. And what if they try to hurt you?" Niq wrung his paws together and looked at Roel with wide eyes.

"If it makes you feel better, Niq, stay in here with me while I treat him." Roel turned away to greet Poy returning with a rolling wooden cart. Various tools, bandages, bowls of steaming hot water, and other supplies packed the cart to overflowing. Poy bared his neck to Roel, then slipped back out the door.

Roel sat down on the stool, turning her back to the door. She grabbed the first bowl of water and started sponging grime off Sels.

Niq glared at Arara and crouched down in the far corner of the room. He growled softly, almost to himself. Arara ignored him and reached over, taking the cloth out of Roel's hands.

"I'm glad you want to help. This will go faster. You keep cleaning the cuts on his face and head while I take a look at his arm."

Arara nodded and got to work as Roel unwrapped Arara's bandages from his arm. Roel hissed and dropped the filthy bandages to the floor.

"A Jegera did this?" She exclaimed as she took a closer look at the deep gouges.

Arara nodded and pointed to his face and vines.

"A Jegera did ALL of this to him?!" She sat back with a stunned expression when Arara nodded again. "I wish you could tell me who it was. Was it the same person who put that metal collar on him?"

Arara nodded again and looked down at Sels's face with a whimper.

"Don't worry, you got him here on time." She looked down at Sels again with a frown. "I seem to recall hearing that there was a Vine Kin in the market yesterday. Was that him?"

Arara nodded her head, her ears dropping. She honestly hadn't realized how much they would stick out by taking Sels to the market in the Jegera district.

Roel continued to examine Sels, occasionally giving Arara a strange look. A moment later, she sat up straight, a blank expression on her face.

"This Kin, I kept thinking he looks familiar, but I don't know any Vine Kin." She paused and Arara cocked her head to the side and her ears forward. Roel was close to figuring it out, but would she help Sels or give him to the Alpha-Guard? Before Arara had a chance to debate what to do, Roel jumped to her feet and backed away.

“Wait, you... Prince Sels?!” She gasped, hands clasping over mouth. In the corner Niq jumped up, eyes wide, then ran out of the room. Arara dropped her shields and focused on Niq, but he was already gone. Arara tried to bark, but it came out as a hack, scraping her already raw throat. Roel was staring at Sels and didn’t seem to hear or see Arara’s frantic gestures.

<Sels, she figured it out. What do we do?> Arara growled and narrowed her eyes at Roel.

Sels opened his eyes, they were glassy with pain. He didn’t respond other than to squeeze her hand before his eyes fluttered shut again. Arara whimpered. She didn’t want this responsibility. But she gulped and steeled her nerves.

“Yes.” Arara looked up and nodded. Roel gasped again and fell to the floor, landing on her butt with a thump.

"What happened to him? I didn't hear anything about him disappearing. They said the rest of the Trials were canceled, and that the *sedyu*-bond Ceremony would be delayed until the end of the week..." She stood up and shook her head in denial.

Roel’s hands fluttered over Sels's neck. “With this, this, thing on him, I don’t know how much healing I can give him. But I’ll try.”

Roel held her hands over Sels's arm and pale white light blazed from her palm. It lit up Sels's skin for a moment and the cuts on his arm began pulling closed when the collar around Sels's neck seemed to pulse.

The light died and Roel cried out, falling backwards onto the floor. Sels's cuts sprang back open, the movement tore the scabs off, and fresh sap oozed from the wounds.

Sels's eyes fluttered and he moaned, making his lips crack and bleed. Roel righted herself with a sigh and a frown.

"I'll just bandage him until we can get that off." Roel said, biting her lip in thought. "In the meantime, we can take care of the dehydration and sun-sickness." She turned and looked around the room, then walked over to the doorway and pulled aside the curtain. "Niq? Poy? Bring food, water, and a sun-flower to room three."

Roel left the doorway and began re-cleaning Sels wounds. When she finished, she wrapped fresh cloth bandages around his arm, then laid a round, flat leaf on the scratches on his face. She gently pressed around the edges of the leaf, sticking it firmly in place. Around the torn vines on his head she packed a greenish paste. She washed her hands in another basin and dried them with a towel. Finished, she looked over to the curtain and frowned.

"What is taking those boys?" Roel stood and headed to the door. "I'll just fetch it myself. Wait here."

Arara nodded and Roel ducked out of the room. She returned a few scratch-marks later with a tray bearing a pitcher of water as well as a plate of vegetables and roots. The vegetables were wilted on the edges, and the roots were almost old enough to be inedible.

Arara shook Sels's shoulder until he opened his eyes, then helped him sit up. Sels pulled his legs up and rested his forehead on his knees.

<*Everything hurts.*> Even Sels's mind-speak sounded tired.

"Your Highness." Roel ducked into a curtsy and the tray wobbled for a moment before she righted it. "Sorry about the food, this is the best I have."

"Oh," Sels sat up and cross his legs in front of him. He opened his mouth, then closed it and looked to Arara.

<*Um, she recognized you. Sorry.*> Arara told him, sheepishly.

“No, thank you.” Sels said softly, looking at his legs and wringing his hands together. “This is wonderful.” Arara could feel how embarrassed he was at looking like this, especially in front of a beautiful young lady. He lifted his hands so Roel could place the tray on his lap, balanced across his knees.

Sels picked the mug of water, but his hands shook, splashing the water all over the tray. Arara reached over and steadied his hands, then helped him lift the cup to take a long drink. Arara set the cup down for him, but instead of eating Sels clasped his hands together and stared down at the tray. She could feel his frustration about how badly his hands shook.

<*You need to eat.*> Arara picked up a long stalk of celery and held it out to him.

Sels pushed her paw away, thinking how he couldn’t stop to eat when his mother was in danger. Arara growled and pushed back, shoving the end of the stalk into his mouth. Roel giggled, then widened her eyes and her hands flew up to her mouth. Sels reached up and bit off a piece, glaring at Arara while he chewed.

“I’m sorry Your Highness,” Roel clasped her hands in front of her and bowed. “I shouldn’t have laughed. But I agree with your friend. You need to eat something.”

Sels finished chewing and swallowed, then licked his lips. "No, I don’t have time for this. I need to save my mom!" His voice dropped and he trembled. “We need to get to the palace before tonight! Some of the Alpha-Guard are traitors, she isn’t safe!” Arara took his hand in her paw and nuzzled his neck with her muzzle.

Sels reached up with a trembling hand and fingered his collar, then touched Arara’s muzzle. “We need to get this off you, but my collar can wait.”

“Poy said we don’t have anything here that will get those off.” Roel shook her head.

"Poy?" Sels asked, looking up from his examination of the muzzle. Arara pointed out the door. She was afraid Niq had run off to tell the guard where they were, but now that Sels was awake, he could talk to Roel.

"Poy and Niq, they live around here. They help me around the clinic in exchange for free healer's assistant training."

<Sels, tell her Niq ran out of here in a hurry when she said who you were. We need to get out of here before the Elders' goons show up!> Arara tugged on Sels hand and pulled. *<She'll listen to you!>*

Sels looked up at Roel. "Niq disappeared right after you mentioned my name. We need to get out of here, before he brings someone. Every Jegera in this district is suspect. I don't know who is in on the Elders' plot." As he spoke Arara pulled his hands, trying to get him to move. She was getting a bad feeling in her stomach and didn't want to stay any longer.

He slowly stood with her help, and Roel shook her head. "No, you're too weak. I'm sure he just went to find the guards for help. I'm sure they're all worried about you."

"No, you don't understand," he pleaded as Arara helped him towards the door. "The Alpha-Guards are the ones that kidnapped me!"

"What?!" She jumped up and in her haste knocked the platter of food everywhere.

Sels winced and Arara could feel through the link how hungry he was, despite his protests. She left him leaning in the doorframe and went around gathering up as much as she could carry from the floor. She stuffed a bunch of it in his pockets carried the rest, letting Sels lean on her shoulder. They moved out into the hallway, and Arara led him back towards the rear entrance. Roel followed them down the hallway.

"Are you sure? I mean, um, hold on, let me grab my bag and come with you. You should be in the care of a healer." She dashed the other way down the hallway. Sels moved slowly, so they'd barely opened the back door when she reappeared, running down the hallway towards them with a bag.

Before she could say anything, there was a crash from the direction of the front door, and the sounds of a fight. At the back door a Jegeran shape appeared in the doorway, back lit by the sun. Arara growled, but she didn't want to move and cause Sels to fall. She could hear Roel start to chant behind her, and a strong blast of air pushed the Jegera out of the doorway into the opposite wall of the alley with a crash.

"Run!" Roel pushed on Sels from behind, and they all stumbled into the bright light of the alley.

*****

Sels stumbled through the streets after Arara and Roel. He was so tired, but he couldn't stop now. His mother was in trouble. They'd left the Jegera Roel had taken out lying in the alley.

"Before I met you in the tavern," Sels panted. "I remembered something. Mura did mention where she lived to me once."

"Who's Mura?" Roel slowed down until she walked next to Sels.

"A friend. She won't turn us in. She lives on the outskirts of the district, near the border to the University district.

They stuck to back alleys, but they couldn't avoid everyone. A few of the Jegera they passed gave them strange looks, and Sels knew it was only a matter of time before the palace would be forced to announce him officially missing. Despite his fears, they made it to their destination unmolested.

Mura's home was a simple mud and wood hut. By the time they arrived, Sels leaned heavily on Arara. He was barely able to walk on his own.

As soon as Sels cleared the doorway he fell to the floor, pulling Arara down with him.

"Sels," Roel said. "I'm going to go find your friend Mura and let her know we're here." She gave him a worried look before disappearing further into the den.

His stomach growled, the sound echoing in the small space.

Arara giggled and handed him a stalk of celery from her vest. He took it gratefully and bit off a big piece. As he finished the last of it Roel came back, accompanied by a little gray Jegera.

"Prince Sels! It's really you!" Mura wagged her tail and crouched down next to them.

"Yes, I'm so glad to see you!" Sels gave her a weary smile.

"A collar, huh?" Mura cocked her head as she examined it. "I have just the thing."

Mura jumped up and bounded back out of the room, returning momentarily with a strange looking tool.

It looked heavy and had two thick handles. The other end had two wickedly sharp blades, mounted so that the sharp ends faced each other.

"Is that made out of metal?" Sels wrinkled his nose and pulled Arara back as Mura approached them.

"I think so." Mura stopped and held up the tool for Sels's inspection. "I found it on a dig up north and cleaned it up. It's really useful."

"No. I'm not letting you touch me." Sels glared at Mura from his seat on the floor.

Mura stopped and looked back at Roel, uncertain.

"That is contraband. If the city guards found that you would be sentenced to death."

"I've been very careful." Mura set the tool down and joined the circle on the floor. "It's not like we ever see Kin magic in the slums anyway."

Mura took Sels's hand in her paw and looked up into his eyes. "Roel told me about the threat to the Queen. If you want to save her we need to get you both healed. And Roel can't do that with that thing on you."

Sels shifted uncomfortably. Mura had a point. Although the metal didn't seem to prevent his unique magic, he knew the effect it would have on any other Kin.

"So it's un-natural," Mura continued. "I can use it to get those things off of you. Without a key, do you know any other way? We do this, then we go save your mother."

"Ok, bring it over." He shook his hands free of Mura's paws, hoping he wouldn't regret this.

"Don't worry," Mura jumped up, tail wagging and ears perked.

"They put a lock or something on the back to hold it on." Sels turned around and pulled up his long vines, to show Mura the back of his neck.

"Much better." Mura yipped. A snip, and Sels felt something in the collar loosen. Arara reached up and helped Sels pull it loose. He massaged his neck, grateful to be free of its cold touch.

Sels pulled Arara up next to him and gripped her paw in his hand. She flinched as Mura brought the tool up to her face, where the bars wrapped around her head to keep the muzzle in place.

"Now, hold still." Mura's tongue stuck out the side of her mouth as she concentrated. She carefully put the sharp edges up against the muzzle and pulled the handles together. The ironwood snapped like a twig. Another snap and Sels pulled the muzzle off of Arara.

"Thanks Mura!" Arara wagged her tail and lolled out her tongue.

Mura gathered up the discarded collar, muzzle, and cutters, disappearing with them into the rear of the den. Roel scooted forward and bathed both Arara and Sels in healing magics.

Already hungry, the healing left Sels ravenous. He munched on the food Arara had thoughtfully saved for him while Arara explained the situation to Mura and Roel.

"The Elders," Arara sighed, clasping her paws. "Along with an unknown number of Alpha-Guard and an underground support network, are trying to over-throw the Royal Family."

"Darach said," Sels shivered and put down his celery to hug himself. "They planned to execute me and my entire family publicly, 'As glorious tribute to the end of the Kin's enslavement of the Jegera.'"

Mura yelped and jumped.

"How did you hear this?" Roel frowned, obviously struggling to picture the old Jegera as a threat.

"They kidnapped me," Sels looked at Arara. "They were gloating over me. We were locked in a dark room for a long time. We only managed to escape early this morning."

"How?" Mura canted her ears. "A dark room, with metal on, so you couldn't have used magic. And you both were in bad shape..."

Sels hesitated, not sure what to tell them. Mura wouldn't understand what he'd done, but Roel would.

"I used my magic." Sels blurted.

"No offense, Your Highness." Roel furrowed her brow. "I'd heard you couldn't do magic." Then her eyes widened. "But, I'd heard rumors that the Queen thought that with a *sedyu*-bond, you might." She looked back and forth between Sels and Arara. "That's it! You used a *sedyu*-bonded's powers to escape."

"No," Sels shook his head. "I discovered my own unique magic. I used it to blow a hole in the wall."

"What do you mean 'blow a hole in the wall?'" Roel stuttered. "Magic can't do anything like that."

"YOU caused those explosions this morning?" Mura barked in surprise.

Sels shrugged, nodded, and took another bite of celery.

Roel frowned at him, but stayed silent.

Mura started pacing back and forth. "So, basically, we need a way into the palace in order to warn your mother, since we can't trust any of the Palace Guards."

Sels nodded.

Roel sat down next to him and Arara. "How did the kidnappers get both of you out of the palace? Maybe we go back in the same way?"

Arara puffed up her chest proudly and spoke up before Sels could say anything. "The kidnappers didn't. I saved Sels from them, and then we escaped from the Palace." She hung her head down. "But they caught us in the Marketplace when we were looking for you, Mura."

Mura stopped pacing and looked down at them in surprise. "For me? Why?"

"I knew you were trustworthy." Sels smiled at her.

Roel smiled. "That still didn't answer my question. How do we get back into the palace? Can we go in the same way?"

“No, I’m sure it’s guarded now.” Sels shook his head, thinking. “But there are other tunnels. My mother made me memorize all the escape routes when I was a little seedling. It’s just been a long time and I don't remember where they all exit to."

“Sels,” Arara tugged on his hand. “I can help you remember. Mura, do you have a map of the city?"

Mura bounded away and returned with a tattered map. “Here. I'm so excited. What are you going to do?"

“Sels, look at this map to jog your memory. Think back to your lessons.” Arara instructed him.

Sels nodded and closed his eyes, picturing mother showing him the map of the city, then her drawing the escape routes in the dirt, following along on the map with one finger so there was no written records of the routes. A moment later, he was back in time, sitting at his desk with his mother and Tukura. This was back when he wasn't a disappointment to his mother and she was smiling and laughing with him.

There was the palace in the center of the city. His eyes roved to the Jegeran District where he and Arara had come out.

Next he remembered she'd pointed out the tunnel that led out from the audience hall. Her long finger traced up through the city, past the Garden District, where it came out to the west.

"Perfect Sels!" Arara let go of his hand and grabbed the map. "Mura, do you have a writing quill?"

Mura retrieved one from the back of the den and handed it to Arara.

"So," Arara said, circling places on the map. "This one leads to the Audience Chamber, but it lets out near the University, which is too far away." She drew a dotted line indicating its position.

"This one," she drew a thick line on the paper from the palace infirmary to the far end of the Garden District, "is also too far away from where we are now."

"How long would it take us to get here?" Sels tapped the University, the tunnel that led to the Throne room. Most likely his mother was there meeting with the Council members about his disappearance.

"If we could start now, it would take half the day to walk there." Roel shook her head. "If they'll even let us into the district with two Jegera and you dressed like that." She swept her hand at Sels.

"Yeah," Mura said. "What happened to your clothes, Your Highness?"

"I was in my pajamas when we escaped... so we found these in an alley. I thought they would help me blend in better in this district." He hated to admit it after seeing the squalor in the Jegeran district, but he missed his nice clothing. This Jegeran wool was hot and itchy. He looked with envy at Roel's silk green healer's robes. That gave him an idea. Roel wasn't that much taller than him.

"What if I borrowed one of your robes, Roel?"

She blinked at him in surprise. "What? Oh, I see! We go into the Garden District as healers with our Jegeran assistants. But that still doesn't help with the timing problem. By the time we reach the tunnel entrance it will be almost dark, and then we will have to follow the tunnel all the way back."

"Maybe it would be better to try to sneak into the palace directly?" Sels said, pondering the map. His eyes kept returning to the tunnel he and Arara had used. It would be guarded, but with his unique magic Sels could easily take care of that.

"Sels, they would recognize your scent right away." Arara cocked her head.

Before he could answer, Arara and Mura both turned their heads towards the doorway. Arara held up her paw for silence.

"They just announced the Prince as officially missing." Mura informed Sels and Roel. "A crier is going through the district announcing the news in public gefir."

"They're saying *I'm* responsible." Arara's ears flattened and she snarled. "Dangerous, kill on sight? And they gave a good description of me."

"We're out of time." Sels sighed. That was something they didn't need, although he had expected it. He was sure several of the Jegera they passed on the way here had recognized him. "We'll have to use the Jegeran district tunnel and avoid the guards."

Sels turned to Roel. "I'd still like to borrow some clothing from you, if I could."

"Of course, Sels." Roel opened her bag and drew out a light yellow robe, trimmed in green and blue. "Luckily I have extra, in case I get blood or sap on them during the day."

Sels blinked. "That's not a healer's robe."

Roel blushed. "No, I don't wear healer green when I go into the Garden District. I flunked out of the Healer's college. That's why I set up shop here instead of one of the Kin districts. The Jegera are grateful for any healing at all."

"Is there somewhere I can change?" Sels nodded and took the robe. That was something he intended to change. He'd never seen this part of town before, and it sickened him how the poor Jegera here lived in such poverty.

Mura gestured to where she'd just come from. "Yes, Your Highness. Any of the rooms at the back of the den are yours."

Sels headed deeper into the house and into the first room he found. It looked like a bedroom from what he could see in the dim light. However, it was hard to tell since it was sparsely furnished. He'd thought that Arara's family den had been austere, but it was cluttered compared to Mura's home. The more he saw of the Jegeran district and its people, the more he wondered if perhaps the Elders were indeed correct.

He pulled off his soiled Jegeran clothes and slipped into the robe. The rough trader's silk felt like heaven as it slid across his skin. He closed his eyes, wishing he had kept his own soft silk pajama bottoms to wear underneath them. He supposed it was better than nothing. They were a little loose on him but better than what he'd been wearing.

When he returned to the living room, Arara, Mura, and Roel were deep in conversation, but they all stopped talking as he walked in. Arara wore a different outfit as well, a brown and white vest and shorts combo.

Arara opened her mouth in a grin. "Much better looking, Sels. I didn't want to say anything before, but you looked really silly in those other clothes."

Roel blushed and smacked Arara on the side of the head. "Arara, you don't say things like that to the Prince!"

“Your Highness,” Roel handed Sels a patterned scarf. “I hate to cover your beautiful flowers, but you'll need to wear this over your head.”

“If anyone asks, we'll say you have petal rot and need to keep the sun off of them." Rocl instructed as Sels folded the scarf and tied it in place.

They headed out the door, Arara happily padding next to Sels. They were going to save the Queen and save the Empire. Just like the prophecy foretold.

CHAPTER TWENTY

LONG LIVE THE QUEEN

Arara skipped along ahead of the group, her tail wagging. She was so excited to have that muzzle off. She'd felt so helpless and frustrated when that Jegera had come running towards them. Arara felt ashamed that Roel had been the one to save Sels instead of her.

Sels and Roel walked with their heads leaned together, whispering low to each other as they followed her. Through their connection she could feel Sels's attraction to Roel, and she had to squash down a spike of jealousy.

Every few scratch-marks Arara and Mura heard public gefir announcements about the missing Prince. On top of that, Alpha-Guards were combing the district. It was hard to remain unspotted even in the back alleys.

They'd been forced to duck through dens to avoid being spotted. Roel used her magic to mask the group's scent from the patrolling guards. By the time they were climbing over the debris blocking the tunnel's den entrance, the sky lit up with the rosy pink of the setting sun.

The group made their way down to the basement. As soon as she set foot in the room, Arara could feel the presence of a fifth mind nearby, a Jegera male, although she couldn't smell anything through Roel's masking spell.

"There's someone here." Arara whispered over her shoulder.

Roel murmured something into the dark, and a ball of light lit the small room.

"Wow, bright!" Arara shaded her eyes with her paw and squinted around the basement. The piles of garbage cast strange shadows on the walls. Arara crept forward, peered around and tried to spot the intruder.

"The tunnel entrance is right here," Sels strolled past her and tapped on the rear wall. It slid open with a groan, revealing a massive Jegera.

Everyone froze. The Jegera looked just as surprised to see them as they were to see him. Arara dropped to all fours and charged forward howling.

The massive Jegera reached behind him, pulling out a small ball. From the Jegera's thoughts, Arara knew the gas inside would knock all of them out for quite some time.

<Sels, duck!>

Sels shot Arara a startled look, then dropped down and covered his head. The male smiled and threw the ball, then hit his paw against the side wall of the tunnel. The door began sliding closed as the gas bomb bounced off the floor in front of Roel. It cracked and a white, sickly sweet smelling smoke poured out of it.

"No!" Arara snarled, slapping the smoking ball with her mind. It flew back through the crack in the wall, trailing a smoky haze, just before the wall rumbled closed.

Still charging forward, Arara scrambled on the loose dirt floor but couldn't stop her forward momentum. She slid into the rock wall next to Sels, and her breath whooshed out of her.

"Arara, are you alright?" Sels crawled over to her.

"I'm fine," She wheezed as Sels helped her to stand. She felt light-headed just from that little bit of smoke. "Roel, can you clear the air?"

"I'll try." Roel coughed, then chanted. A light breeze swirled around them, ruffling Arara's fur as it passed. It pushed the white smoke up the basement steps, then died away.

"That's good." Arara could barely smell the smoke anymore. She probed the intruder's mind. He was already unconscious, but she wanted to wait and let him breathe more of it in before they reopened the tunnel.

"I'm sorry, Arara." Sels said, hugging himself. "I should have waited for you before opening it up."

"No, it's my fault. I should have made you wait upstairs while I scouted ahead."

"What are we going to do now?" Mura said. "That Jegera is still on the other side. And what was that smoke?"

"The smoke was sleeping gas." Roel piped up before Arara could respond. "I recognized the scent. We use it on patients in the clinic sometimes."

"She's right." Arara nodded to the wall. "We don't have to worry about him anymore. He won't wake up for a while. Roel, can you make it windy again?"

"Yes, but after that I can't do anymore until we get out of the tunnel." Roel held up her hands and closed her eyes. "I'm ready."

Sels looked down at Arara.

<*It's safe.*> Arara said. No one else had come. Apparently they hadn't actually thought that Sels would come back this way and had left only the one guard.

Sels tapped on the wall again and stepped aside, holding his shirt sleeve over his mouth. Arara backed up with him, using his other sleeve over her nose. A thick ooze of white fog seeped through the widening crack in the wall.

Roel's breeze whisked it away, and by the time the wall shuddered to a stop only a faint hint perfumed the air. The big Jegera lay snoring face down on the bricks a couple dozen tail lengths down the tunnel. The group shuffled around him, Mura in the lead.

"Wait." Arara said, looking at the Jegera. Something under his paw glinted in the light. Arara crouched down and tugged out a round wooden disc attached to a rawhide cord. She stood and held it up to Roel's magic light bobbing above their heads. Lacquered to a shiny finish, the disc was smooth on both sides. The wood grain was formed into the shape of the Royal Seal.

Arara trotted forward, holding it up for Sels to see.

"Where did you get that?" Sels said, staring at Arara's paws.

"From him." She pointed at the big Jegera behind her.

"Ah," Sels grinned and crossed his arms. "I'd wondered how he closed the tunnel door. You should keep it Arara."

"Thank you." Arara slipped the rawhide strap over her head then tucked the dangling amulet into her vest.

"So without that he can't follow us if we drag him out of the tunnel?" Mura said.

"Yes." Sels nodded. "Good idea."

Working together the four of them managed to drag the Jegera's big form out into the basement. Sels closed the door behind them, then they hurried away down the tunnel. Roel's light dimmed as they walked, and her petals began drooping down. By the time they reached the exit she could barely keep her eyes open, and the light was only a tiny pinprick in the darkness.

<*Sels, wait.*> Arara held her paw in front of his chest. She concentrated. Two Alpha-Guards stood in the path above them, and two more patrolled nearby.

"Two above us, and two nearby." Arara said, her voice low.

"Roel, what elements can you use besides Wind and Healing?" Sels whispered.

Arara heard petals rustling as Roel felt her way to them. "That's it."

"Once you get in the sunlight can you do what you did at the clinic?"

"Yes, but it will take me a few moments before I can do anything."

"My magic is too..." Sels trailed off.

"It will give away that we are here." Arara finished for him. "I'll take out the two above it. If I pull it off the other two won't even know we're here."

Arara closed her eyes and found the minds of the guards. She mentally stabbed out, trying to hit both of them at once. She felt their surprise and their resistance. She redoubled her efforts. Their minds gave way, and she lost her connection to them as they fell unconscious.

Shaken, she opened her eyes. She felt sick about doing that to Jegera. Her head throbbed, and her vision dimmed as a vice squeezed her skull. She welcomed the pain, trying to keep from crying.

"Done." Her voice cracked, and she had to gulp before continuing. "You can open it now Sels."

Sels reached overhead and tapped on the ceiling. The walls trembled, shaking dirt onto their heads. The ceiling descended into a staircase, spilling bright sunlight into the tunnel. Roel perked up immediately and pushed past Sels to run out into the fresh air. Mura followed her.

"Arara." Sels squeezed Arara's paws in his hands before she could move. "I could feel how much that hurt and upset you. Thank you for doing that for me."

At his touch Arara's headache receded until was just a dull ache. She felt Sels surprise and realized he'd felt it too.

"What was that? What happened to your headache?" Sels blinked down at her.

"You healed it for me. Just like before." Arara tugged him up the stairs.

"You're right. We don't have time right now." Sels followed her.

At the top they turned around so Sels could close the tunnel behind them. The staircase folded up and merged seamlessly into the path.

Mura crouched over one of the unconscious guards and rifled through his uniform. Roel stood still, eyes closed, her arms and face lifted towards the setting sun.

<*Nothing.*> Mura shrugged and stood up.

Arara scanned the area. The patrol had moved off, continuing their route. They hadn't heard anything.

<It's almost dark.> Arara turned to Sels. *<We need to find your mom, and quickly. Where would she be?>*

<With all this chaos? The Throne room. The Council is going to want to know why they were not notified of my absence for several days. Especially since I disappeared in the middle of Sedyu Trials.>

"Everyone, we're headed to the Throne room." Arara whispered, confident in Sels's analysis. "Sels, lead the way."

Sels led them through the maze while Arara did her best to steer them around the patrolling Alpha-Guards. After a while, they came to a T Junction. Sels headed down the leftmost path, but Arara could feel guards up ahead. She pulled Sels back and pointed to the rightmost path.

<Arara, that way leads to a dead end. We need to go left.>

<There are Guards stationed at the end.>

<Well, can you do what you did before?>

Arara hung her head.

Roel and Mura were watching their silent exchange with puzzled looks on their faces.

"What's wrong?" Roel asked in a whisper.

"We need to go left to get to the Hall, but Arara says there are guards that way." Sels whispered back. "Arara, take care of them. We need to hurry." He pointed up at the sun, only the top sliver visible above the horizon.

Arara grabbed Sels hand with her paw. *<I can do it, but this time I want you to concentrate on seeing and feeling what I feel.>*

Sels nodded, a puzzled look in his eyes. *<Alright...>*

She waited until she could feel Sels in her head watching. Her eyes closed in concentration. She threw her mind darts at the two guards. The slimy feeling was back, worse this time, although she didn't get more than a small twinge of a headache.

Sels gasped and pulled away from her, almost falling into the spiky hedge wall. <*What was that?!*>

<*We can talk about it later. Now let's go.*> She grabbed Sels's hand and tugged him down the path, gesturing for Roel and Mura to follow. They ran down the path and leapt over the two unconscious Alpha-Guards.

Several steps beyond the Alpha-Guards the hedges ended, and the path led down the center of a curved depression in the earth. Tiers lined either side of the curve all facing in towards a stage at the very bottom. With a start Arara realized this was where her trial had been held, only the seats had all been empty.

Today almost every seat was filled with Kin. A handful of Jegera sat segregated on the very top two tiers. On the stage, Queen Seuan sat in her throne. Tukura stood to one side, her eyes roving the Council Hall. Sesay sat in a smaller throne on the other side, Recka behind her.

"Mother!" Sels pulled his hand out of hers and ran down the path before she could stop him.

All eyes in the Hall turned to towards him, and several let out gasps of surprise. They all started talking at once. The sky dimmed as the sun disappeared entirely.

<*Sels, no, wait!*> Arara ran after him, leaving Mura and Roel standing on the path behind her.

By the time she caught up, Sels stood on the stage next to his mother. The Queen held his hands, a small smile pulling up the corners of her lips. However, as soon as she saw Arara climbing the steps onto the stage her expression turned angry.

"Guards, arrest that girl!" Queen Seuan pointed at Arara.

"No, mother!" Sels moved between them. "Arara saved me. The Elders-"

A piercing shriek rent the air and something heavy hit the stage behind them. A familiar stench hit Arara's nose. She and Sels turned at the same time to see a kwaso leaping into the air, its sharp clawed feet pointed straight at the Queen.

*****

Sels screamed and jumped between his mother and the bird. A tail length from his face the kwaso squawked as it bounced off an invisible wall.

"What?" The Queen gasped behind him. "Tukura!"

Sels spun to see Tukura wrestling with a second bird. His mother stood up, hands pressed to her mouth. Recka and Sesay fled towards the back of the stage, towards the secret passage hidden there. He could feel Arara behind him, fighting with the first kwaso.

"Mother, let's go!" He grabbed her hand and led her after Sesay. She followed, but kept her eyes on Tukura. Ahead of them Sesay and Recka had just reached the rear corner of the stage. Before Sesay could reach up to open the secret door, the wall slid away.

A short Jegera stepped out of the opening. He wore a stiff gray suit made of interlocking metal circles that shimmered in the dim light and held a rope leash. The leash attached to the collar around a kwaso standing behind him.

Sesay shrieked as Recka pushed her out of the way. Recka tackled the much smaller Jegera, and the two fell together back into the tunnel with a crash. The leash fell free.

He felt Arara use her powers to take out the first two kwaso then collapse to the stage with a migraine. He had expected it, but Sels still gasped as the pain hit him. He fell to his knees next to his mother.

Tukura, her opponent vanquished by Arara, joined him and the Queen. Sesay scrabbled back away from the leashed kwaso. It hadn't yet realized that nothing held it back, and it stood still, its bobbing head following Sesay's movements. Tukura snarled and leapt for its collar. The bird allowed Tukura to lead it away, and she tied the leash to the throne before slitting its throat with her claws.

Another four small armored Jegera, all leading collared kwaso, spilled out of the tunnel.

"Run!" Recka lifted Sesay up into his arms.

Tukura did the same with the Queen. Sels pushed aside the pain, pulling himself to his feet. He ran after his mother, away from the danger behind him. He stopped briefly to help Arara up.

Tukura and Recka had stopped at the front of the stage. The entire Hall was in chaos. The sun had set entirely now, and the light came from the large sun-flower growing down from the ceiling of the stage.

At least a dozen kwaso leapt among the seats, indiscriminately attacking the helpless Kin. Even from here Sels could see the bodies littering the Council floor.

A few Jegera and Kin had banded together to fight the kwaso. The Jegera circled, protecting an ever-growing group of Kin in the middle. Fewer and fewer spells split the air as the last of the sun's light faded away into night.

Tukura and Recka, still carrying their respective *Sedyu*-bonded, leapt off the stage and together ran up the path towards the Throne room's rear exit. Sels looked over his shoulder and saw the small Jegera mounted atop their kwaso. The giant birds charged towards them. Sels took Arara's paw, and they leapt off the stage, landing hard on the path. Sels knees throbbed, but he forced himself up into a run.

A few steps later a weight slammed into his back, throwing him face-first into the bricks and knocking his breath out. He couldn't even cry out as sharp claws dug into his back.

"Sels!" Arara screamed. He could feel her hit the bird with her mental powers, ripping it from him. The bird and its rider crashed into the seats next to them.

Arara pulled Sels up and pushed him along in front of her. Sels hobbled forward, crying in pain.

A screaming Kin ran in front of them, pursued by a large kwaso. Sels stopped mid-step, and Arara stumbled forward. He concentrated on the magical energy in the air around him, drawing it out into his palms. For some reason it was much easier now than it had been earlier that day, in the street.

A flaming ball flew at the kwaso from his outstretched hand. The ball hit the bird on the side and exploded. Flames ran down the bird's feathers, and the smell of roasted meat filled the air. The bird collapsed, still smoldering. The Kin continued running without a backwards glance.

Next to him, he could feel Arara's stomach rumble and she licked her lips, imagining what its meat might taste like. Sels tried to push the image out of his mind and looked up. Tukura and Recka were gone.

Sels limped forward to look for them when a piercing shriek brought him to his knees. Sels covered his ears, but the sound seemed to spike into his thoughts. He couldn't do anything but lay there screaming in pain. His head felt like it was splitting in half from the kwaso's yell. He could feel Arara in his head trying to tell him something, but the pain drowned out her words.

Suddenly, the pain was gone. His back didn't hurt, although he could still feel the wounds. He pulled himself upright and looked around. Arara lay curled up in a fetal position next to him, and she didn't respond to his probing. The air smelled of burning feathers and the sickly sweet aroma of Kin sap.

From where he stood he could see the bodies of several Council members. To his left several kwaso surrounded a group of Kin. The Kin huddled on the ground, helpless, as one of the kwaso shrieked. As much as he disliked most of the Council members, he couldn't leave them like that.

This time the magic came even easier, and he threw an entire barrage of fireballs at the birds. Three of the balls hit their targets and exploded in flames. The rest hit the wooden chairs around them. The living wood sizzled and crackled as the flames ate wet wood.

The three remaining birds turned their beady black eyes in his direction. One let out a piercing shriek, its head frills vibrating wildly. Sels winced, expecting pain, but he didn't feel a thing. Arara moaned.

While the one bird screamed at him, the other two charged. Their long legs took them easily over the wooden benches.

Sels held up his hands and this time released the magic slowly. A wave of flame rolled out in front of him, completely engulfing the surprised birds. The last bird stopped its cry and ran away.

As soon as Sels saw that the Council members were safe, he leaned over and shook Arara. Her eyes were glassy, but he helped her to her feet. They needed to find his mother.

Groups of Kin were overpowering the last few remaining kwaso in the Throne room. A few healers were tending to the injured. Sels could hear the frightened Kin questioning where the Alpha-Guard Jegera had gone and why they'd disappeared right as they were needed.

Sels put his arm under her shoulder and helped Arara along the path. He ignored the Kin calling his name asking for answers, instead trying to think of where his mother and Tukura would have gone. They left the Throne room and entered the hedge maze. Mura and Roel were gone, but strangely he could smell that they hadn't been gone long. He hoped they had gone with his mother to help protect her.

Sels had the strangest sensation of being able to feel the presence of three creatures behind him. It felt like they were gaining on him, but when he looked back all he could see was the curve of the hedge leading back to the Throne room.

From behind them came the screech of a kwaso. Arara convulsed and collapsed, pulling Sels down with her. He struggled to lift her back up to her feet when she flailed her paws. She struck him in the chin, leaving a deep gash on his neck.

Sels fell back. Arara's front and back legs continued flailing around. Afraid she would hurt herself, he crawled on top of her and straddled her chest, holding her arms and legs down.

"Arara, stop!" He pleaded. He could feel tears rolling down his face. They'd messed up, hadn't been able to get here on time, and now his mother was missing and Arara was hurt.

He licked his lips and closed his eyes. With the kwaso around, it was dangerous to leave himself vulnerable, but he had to try healing her. He didn't dare use the other magical energies he'd found until he could control them better.

For several tense moments he chanted the basic healing spell. He held his hands above her head without success. He stopped and opened his eyes. He'd just have to bind her wounds. Except when he examined her he couldn't see anything physically wrong.

He could feel his connection to her in the back of his mind. She didn't answer him, but maybe she didn't need to. He just needed to know what hurt her. Time seemed to slow as he mentally followed that connection back.

Pain radiated out from his back, and Sels collapsed on top of her. This was his pain. She had kept it from him so he could save people. Sels tried to pull the pain back to himself, but Arara resisted.

Arara twisted away from him, and they were both screaming, her howl merging with his scream until he couldn't tell which one was which.

Suddenly, it was gone. Even without opening his eyes he could tell that all three kwaso would be here in less than a heartbeat. A small tug on his mind showed him Arara throwing up a dome shaped mind-wall around the birds, trapping them inside. He felt a jolt when the first one hit the side of the barrier, then another.

<Sels, I'll open a hole so you can throw some fire in with them.> Arara's plan unfolded in front of him, making her words superfluous.

She didn't even have to tell him where the hole was placed, he could feel the force she was exerting with her mind and knew exactly where to aim the ball. As soon as it passed through he felt the hole close. He wasn't sure how he did it, but he reached out with his mind and helped to hold the wall in place as the energy exploded.

The fire vaporized the three kwaso inside and then hammered into the wall. It was like someone had hit him between the eyes with a pick, but after the pain he'd felt a few moments prior, it was like a gentle tap, and he was easily able to ignore it.

"That was so strange. It was like you were sharing my head when you did your magic." She flicked her ears as she looked down at him. "Um, by the way, thanks for stopping the pain. How did you do that?"

"I don't know. I was just trying to find out what was wrong with you. You shouldn't have taken my pain like that. You could have hurt yourself." He'd been so worried about her that he'd forgotten about his mother.

"Mother!" Sels sat up. Tukura alone wouldn't be able to help her, not against kwaso. These creatures were part of the reason the Kin had started working with the Jegera for protection. Kin magic was a magic of healing and creation, not of destruction. His magic was an exception. His mother wouldn't be able to fight them off if Tukura was injured.

"We have to find her, Arara! What if there are more of those things?" He gestured to the charred remains of the birds. "Or the Jegeran guards. Did you notice they all disappeared right before the attack?"

He could feel Arara's agreement in his head before she even answered. She dropped to all fours and sniffed around. An awful charred scent hit him, and he covered his nose. The stink almost covered up the crisp, minty smell of the hedge.

Arara sneezed, and the scent was gone. "Too stinky," she said and waved a paw in front of her nose. "Let's try farther up the path."

Sels followed her, wondering why he'd never noticed the minty scent of the hedge before.

At the next junction Arara put her nose to the ground and walked around in circles. Now he could smell the hedge, overlaid with the scents of hundreds of different Kin and Jegera. Sels could tell how old each scent was and pick out the distinct scents of individual people from the mess.

Since when did Jegera have a distinct smell? He'd always enjoyed how each Kin's petals had a slightly different scent, but before now all Jegera had just smelled like musty fur.

<*Everyone has a distinct scent. You just probably never noticed before now, because your nose isn't as sensitive as mine.*> Arara answered his confusion. <*Tukura has been through this intersection a lot, so it's hard to find the most recent trail, but I think they went this way.*>

Sels nodded and they tore off after Tukura and Recka's scent. Sels pushed the strange happenings out of his mind. Saving his mother was what was important.

CHAPTER TWENTY ONE

BLOOD AND LIES

Arara followed Tukura's and Recka's scent out of the garden maze to an archway covered in a curtain of vines.

"You must be following an old trail, Arara." Sels said from behind her. "We're heading towards the Royal Suites."

"No, this trail is very fresh." Arara ducked through the vines, Sels on her heels.

She stepped out into another world. A living wood path meandered away from the archway through a riot of plants. Flowers of every color and shape lined the walkway. One flower, a large lily, had rainbow petals. The purple at the center morphed through the entire spectrum until it ended at blood red.

At intervals smaller paths branched off, leading to small benches set under flowering trees. Behind it all, with the moon rising behind it, was the largest tree Arara had ever seen. The base of the trunk had to be bigger around than her entire village. The bark ran smooth and straight up to the top, where the tree ended in a tangle of branches topped with brilliant emerald leaves that sparkled in the moonlight.

<The Royal Residence. You think they're hiding there?> Sels told her, although she'd already gotten that from his mind.

Arara skipped off the path. Its twists and turns would take too long, and they were in a hurry. Sels followed her, but she could feel his dismay as they crushed the delicate flowers and snapped the limbs off small bushes as they ran. The dark made it hard to avoid them, especially around the trees.

A familiar scent hit Arara's nose moments before a kwaso leapt out from behind a large tree and landed in front of them. For some reason, she hadn't been able to sense its presence.

This kwaso wore a bridle, and overlapping pieces of beaten metal ran down its neck, covering its backside. A metal helmet covered its head, and a small form perched on its back.

"Pra athla miturt xiuw!" The figure yelled, pointing his knife at them.

When they didn't respond, the figure growled, and Arara felt a strange force trying to push itself into her head. She could feel Sels under the same attack. Arara pushed back, strengthening her mental shields and pushing them out to cover Sels.

The figure... it spoke the strange language from Darach's memory and it used mind-powers. It was a Yaka! Just like her!

The Yaka's lifted his muzzle to the sky and howled.

Arara couldn't understand the Yaka's speech, but she knew that howl was a call for reinforcements. Arara mentally shoved the Yaka's side, sending him tumbling off the kwaso. The Yaka kept hold of the reins as he fell.

The bird stumbled to the side with a squawk, so the fireball Sels threw over her head missed, flying over the bird's back to strike a blue cherry tree. Arara felt Sels's dismay as the rare tree burst into flames.

The firelight lit up the area, and Arara could finally see the Yaka clearly. He wore a beaten metal outfit, like the bird, with a helmet that covered his head and ears, leaving only his eyes and muzzle uncovered. In one hand he gripped the reins. The other held a metal knife like the one from her bag, only much larger.

"You," The Yaka jumped to his feet with a snarl. "Your Prisoner control better. And uniform where, soldier?" The Yaka's thick accent and strange phrasing made Arara cock her head.

Arara blinked, unsure of what to do, and felt Sels confusion as well.

<*Under all that metal he looks just like you!*> Sels thoughts gave Arara an idea. <*Answer him.*>

"Blending in, throw uniform away." Arara said, trying to imitate the Yaka's accent. Then she grabbed Sels's arm and wrenched it behind his back. Sels read her thoughts and moved with her, so she didn't hurt him.

"Ah, told about spy," The Yaka marched towards them, pulling his mount behind him by the reins. His metal suit clanked as he walked, and Arara couldn't help but think how impractical it was for hunting.

Arara struggled to keep her ears and tail straight to hide her confusion. Instead she kept one paw on Sels and bared her neck to the armored Yaka.

"So, this Prince." The Yaka stopped and his gaze roved over the Prince, from the scarf still tied over his head to the yellow women's robes. Sels flushed and the Yaka laughed, red tongue lolling out the side of his mouth.

"Queen captured too?" Arara's hackles rose at this insult, but she swallowed it down. The Yaka shielded his thoughts and she needed to know if this Yaka had seen the Queen.

"Weak Queen helpless without Jegera protectors." The Yaka laughed harder now. "Crying for life, by time was done."

Under Arara's paws, Sels stiffened. She could feel him drawing magic out of the air around them.

<*Sels, stop! He can take us to her!*> Arara pleaded with him, and grabbed his other arm. His anger became her anger, and she struggled to remain calm while keeping Sels pinned.

<*Arara, he hurt my mom!*> Sels cried. His imagination showed them images of the Queen, hurt and alone. It was too much for her. Arara let him go and staggered back, whining for mother.

Sels brought his palms up, and a blast of fire rolled out in front of him toward the Yaka. The Yaka shot him a look of contempt and held up his hand.

The fire parted around the Yaka and his kwaso, alighting the flowers and bushes in a circle around him. Then the Yaka pushed his hand forward.

A wave of force hit her and Sels, throwing them backwards into the bushes. Burning leaves and charred petals fluttered down around them. Thick black smoke from the burning plants obscured her vision, and the acrid smell burned her nose and mouth.

<*Run!*> Sels grabbed Arara's paw and led her through the haze. Arara resisted the urge to cough and give away their position. Sels navigated through the garden by memory, leading them away from the deadly warrior.

<*Where are we going?*> Arara wheezed as they ran, glad she didn't have to try and speak out loud to Sels.

<*Away from here.*> Sels sped up, and Arara followed his thoughts as he tried to think where in the palace they might have imprisoned his mother. She had to still be here. They hadn't had time to move her anywhere else.

*****

Arara's nose and throat felt like they had been scraped raw. She wished she had a waterskin with her. Her tongue lolled as she panted heavily, trying to cool herself down.

After what seemed like ages, but was probably only a few scratch-marks, they emerged from the smoke to find themselves right in front of the palace.

The wood had been artfully grown and shaped, and it seemed to merge with the garden around them. Raised murals covered the surface of the wood, and Arara realized at a distance that she had mistaken it for bark. The murals showed Kin of all ages frolicking in luxurious gardens with a variety of tame exotic animals. Arara stared at the pictures in awe until Sels poked her sharply in the side.

<*I think we're in trouble.*> Sels pointed.

Arara followed Sels's gaze. Six metal-encased Yaka riding kwaso stood between them and the entrance. Arara whirled around in time to watch three more stumble out of the smoke behind them.

<Arara, we can't fight all of them. We couldn't even beat one.> Sels trembled and huddled down behind her.

Arara gulped. Sels was right, but she could feel the presence of the Queen and Sesay inside the hall. They needed to get inside. That first armored Yaka they'd encountered thought she was one of them. Maybe these would too?

<Sels, no matter what I do, don't get upset. Just play along.> Arara told him. She felt his acceptance and knew he could feel them too.

A group of three Yaka from the entrance had started towards them while she and Sels conversed. The two lesser ranked Yaka flanked the obvious leader. Unlike the rest, sharp spikes adorned the fists and shoulders of the lead Yaka’s armor. His helmet had a beaked visor and looked like a stylized kwaso head, complete with a feathered crest that ran along the top and down the back. The helmet’s beak covered his face and muzzle.

“You are late.” The leader growled, the helmet muffling his words.

“Sorry, sir.” Arara straightened and offered him her neck.

"Kragu rekai e' gra, QWERADRU!" The leader leaned forward. The visor's beak was now barely a pawspan from her nose.

When Arara didn't respond, he picked up his spear and pounded it into the ground, and she flinched.

"Kragu rekai e' gra!" He repeated at her. "Qweradru! Qweradru!" He pounded his spear at each word, as if to emphasize it.

Arara swallowed a growl. She didn't want to antagonize him further. "I don't know what you are saying." She spoke slowly, enunciating each word carefully.

He snorted, the sound echoing oddly out of his visor. "Of course not." He pounded the spear again for good measure. "Follow me and bring your prisoner."

<*This isn't a good idea.*> Sels thought as Arara took hold of his arm and pulled him after the marching Yaka.

From behind, the Yaka leader's white curly tail stuck out of his armor at an odd angle, and the top of the curl was bent backwards. Obviously it had been broken several times. The other Yaka only had short stubs of their tails remaining.

The three Yaka led them over to the entrance and pushed aside the vines. They ushered Arara and Sels in ahead of them and then followed behind. The two underlings took up positions on either side of the door.

Bright sun-flowers growing from the walls lit up as they entered, momentarily blinding Arara after the darkness outside. When her eyes adjusted Arara gasped in delight.

The inside was just as beautifully decorated as the outside. A curved ramp had been grown out of the wood to their left, and it circled the hall to disappear into the darkness above. The floor had been polished so finely that Arara could see her reflection, although now it was marred in places from the armored Yaka's metal boots.

The leader was already halfway across the room when the Yaka who had followed them in poked her in the back. He growled and pointed towards the red and black armored figure of the Yaka leader. She sighed, vowing to have Sels bring her back here later so she could see the gorgeous paintings. She and Sels made their way across the floor until they joined the leader in the middle of the room.

Arara could feel the Queen and the others nearby, but when she swiveled her head around she couldn't see them. In addition, she sensed the four Elders' presences close and getting closer.

<*Tukura, where are you and the Queen being held?*> But her gefir went unanswered.

A bark of laughter from the shadows drew her attention to the hallway on the far side of the foyer. The four Elders emerged, Johka in the lead leaning heavily on his cane. Darach strode next to him, a smug expression on his face. Pira and the giant Lolop followed behind them.

<Arara, we're right back where we were, as their prisoners again.> Sels trembled in her grip.

<Don't worry, I'll protect you.> She squeezed his hand, trying to project confidence.

“Arara,” Darach chuffed. “I'm blocking all gefir to and from you, so don't even try.”

One of her ears went back in puzzlement. What was he talking about? She and Sels were still communicating just fine. She glanced up at Sels, and he looked as puzzled as her.

"Look what escaping got you." Darach shook his head and paced around them, oblivious to their exchange. "But no matter. We'd already gotten what we needed from you.” He held up a round wood talisman, identical to the one Arara had taken off the Jegera in the tunnel. Darach manipulated it with his paw and the wood split open, revealing a chunk of vine embedded inside.

Sels gasped and reached his free hand up to feel his vines under the scarf. He remembered Lolop twisting his vines, and he'd felt them tearing. And the secret passages only opened up for members of the Royal Family. They'd used his torn off vines to open the way straight into the heart of the palace.

Darach laughed again and snapped the amulet closed. He turned to the Yaka leader, who stood at attention next to Arara.

“Kragu o' zedru denyo.” Darach barked at him. The Leader inclined his head and responded with more gibberish.

Arara focused on Darach and dropped her shields, trying to mentally hear what they were talking about. Darach shot her a look, and suddenly it felt like someone was squeezing her head in a vise. She whimpered and pulled back, and the pain stopped as soon as she did so.

The leader turned to look at the Yaka that had followed them into the hall and bobbed his head. One of them clanked forward, grabbed Sels's other arm, and pulled him away. Arara growled and pulled back.

"Arara," Darach growled at her. "Let him go. You will stay and give your report, Qweradru."

<Arara, it's alright. Stay, see what you can find out. I'll keep in contact with you.> Sels soothing mind-voice calmed her enough that she was able to let go, but her protective instinct screamed at her as the Yaka dragged him away.

The Yaka led him up the spiral ramp. Arara watched until Sels's feet disappeared from view. She craned her neck, trying to keep him in view, until Darach's fist hit the side of her muzzle. She fell with a cry, blood dripping from her bloody nose.

"I said, give your report, Qweradru!" He snarled down at her. "Not pine over a defective Royal Seedling."

"I, um, report on what sir?" Arara stared up at him, trying not to flinch.

Darach stepped back a step, looking surprised, and exchanged glances with the other three Elders.

"Yorik, didn't you say the phrase to her?" Lolop growled to the Leader Yaka.

"I say, sir." Yorik barked back, pulling up the visor on his helmet.

Arara peeked over so she could see what he looked like. His muzzle was wide and tapered like hers, with white fur and blue eyes.

Darach's ears went back and he snarled. He stepped forward and grabbed Arara's vest in one paw, then lifted her straight up off the ground until she was face to face with him.

"Kragu rekai e' gra! Qweradru." He yelled right into her face.

She whimpered and put her paws over her nose. His breath stunk of old meat. Darach seemed to be expecting more of a reaction because he shook her and repeated the nonsense words over and over until she was whimpering from the pain. He snarled one last time and threw her backwards to the floor. She recovered enough to use a mind-push to slow her fall right before she would have landed on her tail, then stood trembling before Darach, her tail tucked between her legs.

"Well?" He yelled down at her. "Report."

"What are you talking about?" She was so terrified her legs shook and she felt herself pee, involuntarily. She wished Sels were here. He would know what to do.

Darach ignored her and turned to Pira. Pira must have Sent him some information because Darach responded by bobbing his head and cocking one ear. It was frustrating not being able to listen in on everything.

"But it worked perfectly well before." Darach growled, apparently in response to a question. What was he talking about? She hadn't ever heard that strange language before.

Yorik growled. "Perhaps because she cannot understand words? Maybe in Kin-Jegera Common she obey?"

Arara felt sick. Obey? She started to panic until Sels calm mind-voice called out to her. *<Arara, they're just trying to scare you. I trust you.>*

Darach's foot tapped on the polished wood floor, considering. "Can't hurt, I suppose."

He looked down at Arara. "Code Prince trap. Over-ride. Now report."

*****

The Yaka pulled Sels's arms up behind his back, claws digging into his freshly healed arm. They marched through the Royal Suite. The familiar hallways looked abandoned and empty without the usual activity of the servants. They passed by Sels's own suite of rooms, as well as Sesay's.

They passed Sels's favorite balcony. Today smoke marred the spectacular view of the Royal Gardens, and unfamiliar forms moved about below, trampling the flowers underneath their feet. He felt sick.

They wound their way back down the tree via a servant's staircase to the live-in servant's dens in the basement. Sels hadn't ventured down here since he was a seedling, and he didn't know which room he was in. The Yaka dragged him down the hall towards a second Yaka standing guard. The second Yaka stepped aside and opened the door behind him, revealing a dark storage closet. The light outlined wooden shelves filled with cured meat lining the rock walls.

At the very back, hidden in the shadows and covered by a tarp, was a massive box. Metal wheels poked out beneath the bottom. The Yaka pulled the covering up to reveal bars. The Yaka leaned over and slid a key into the lock. The door opened with a high-pitched squeal that hurt Sels ears.

The Yaka shoved Sels forward into the cage. He landed awkwardly on his knees on a hard surface. An armored foot slammed into his back, sending him sprawling forward onto his stomach.

The clang of a door slamming behind him was followed a moment later by the screech of a bolt. What little bit of light filtered in from the sun-flowers in the hall cut off suddenly as the Yaka dropped the tarp back over the bars. Footsteps clomped away, and a wooden door slammed.

The cold metal of the floor froze his fingers. Shivering, Sels sat up and felt his way back to the door. He wrapped his fingers around the bars and rattled them, but the Yaka had secured them tight. Sels sat, propping his back against the door, and pulled his knees to his chest, trying to think. Now that he was looking for it, he could still feel an abundance of the strange magical energy in the air around.

However, the only spell he'd been able to cast with it had been a very destructive fire spell. Trapped in this metal cage, he'd only hurt himself.

"Who goes there?" A familiar voice called from darkness in front of him.

"Mother!" Sels sat up and swiveled his head, trying to locate her. "It's me, Sels."

Cloth rustled in the darkness, and a moment later his mother's familiar scent enveloped him as she wrapped him in a hug.

"Oh, Sels, you're alright!" Queen Seuan released him and sat back. Sels took her hand, trying to reassure himself she was really there.

"I didn't get there in time, Mother." Sels's eyes filled with tears. "And, and, it's all my fault!"

"Sels, you knew about this?" He could hear the disappointment in her voice.

"No, not until last night." Sels shivered again and wrapped the robe around him more snugly. Roel's borrowed robes were thin, and the basement was very cold. The metal floor seemed to be sucking all the heat out of him. "Arara and I tried to get here in time to warn you, but we didn't make it."

"And now? What are they planning?" Sesay asked, her voice low and angry. He hadn't heard her moving, but he could smell her perfume now, on his other side.

"They said," Sels swallowed and had to force himself to speak past the lump in his throat. "They plan to execute us publicly, to legitimize their occupation. Arara is downstairs with them now, trying to find out more."

"How will that help us?" Sesay sniffed. Was she crying? "I can't feel Recka anymore, Sels! They fastened some kind of strange metal collar around his neck, and that was the last I felt from him."

"Same with my Tukura," Queen Seuan said sadly. "We're deaf and blind here, Sels. Arara has no way to contact us."

Sels could still feel Arara at the back of his mind. If he concentrated on her, he could hear her conversation and see out of her eyes. Reassured, he tried to contact her.

<Arara, are you there? My mother and Sesay are here with me. Try to find Tukura and Recka. They're missing.>

"Sels," A hand shook his shoulder, breaking his concentration, and Sels opened his eyes. Not that it made a difference.

"Mother, stop." Sels took her hand again and held it between his. "I'm trying to talk to Arara. I'm not used to this and I need to concentrate."

"What? The only way you could do that..." The Queen raised her voice, then trailed off into silence.

"Mother, I didn't form a *sedyu*-bond with her, if that's what you think. I've been able to hear her in my head since I met her in Last Home." He whispered. "Now quiet. I think they left a guard in the hallway."

"Sels, why didn't you tell me?" The Queen sounded shocked and sad as she squeezed her hand around his. "Can you feel when she is sad, or angry, or upset? Can you feel when she is hurt?"

"Of course, mother." Sels snapped, impatient with her questioning. "But that doesn't mean we've bonded. We didn't do the ceremony."

"The ceremony is just a formality, Sels." Sesay sighed, and moved about, her silk robes rustling together.

"You and Arara are *sedyu*-bonded." The Queen said with a sigh.

CHAPTER TWENTY TWO

THE SERPANT'S HEAD

Arara stared up at Darach, her mouth hanging open. Prince-trap? What did that mean?

A hush fell over the group. Five pairs of eyes stared down at her.

“Well?” Darach growled, leaning closer. “I’m waiting.”

"Uh,” Arara shuffled backwards a few steps. "I, uh, brought the Prince here, just like you ordered.” Arara lied, unsure what Darach expected her to say.

Darach stepped back, a stunned expression on his face. Arara scanned the group, all of whom looked at her with a mixture of awe and disbelief. She’d obviously said the wrong thing.

“Hold still.” Yorik reached over and grabbed her arm before she could shuffle farther back. He closed his eyes, and she felt a powerful force trying to climb inside her head. It blasted right past her shields.

<*Sels, help!*> She instinctively reached across the connection to him and pulled some of his energy into her. The wave of energy pushed the strange force out of her head, and her ears popped. Yorik's head flew back, and he collapsed onto the floor with a crash. The spikes on his armor tore free a massive splinter of wood from the center of the gorgeous floor.

"Stay out of my head!" Arara yelled at his prone form. Before the surprised Elders could react she spun about, dropped to all fours, and sprinted for the ramp leading upwards. After Sels.

Darach let out a roar and chased after her, his long legs gaining on her every stride. She had almost made it to the ramp when he pounced on her from behind, pinned her to the floor and punched her in the back of the head. Her vision spun. There was a clanking sound, and one of the Yaka soldiers rushed forward with a strange metal collar that glowed a sickly green in the light of the sun-flowers.

As soon as they snapped the collar closed around her neck, she fell deaf. No, not deaf. She could still hear everyone talking, but she could no longer hear the gefirs that a moment before had been filtering through the back of her head. Sels's thoughts, which a moment before had been a steady hum in the back of her mind, vanished.

While Arara reeled from the sudden loss of her sixth sense, Darach attached a chain to the collar and dragged her across the floor. Arara scrabbled for purchase on the slick surface, scratching the polished wood.

"That Prince, he must have done something to her! Broken the conditioning." Johka snarled as Darach dragged her back. Johka and Pira crouched by Yorik, trying unsuccessfully to wake him up.

"Doesn't matter. The plan is still the same." Darach leered down at Arara. "She kills the Prince. It's perfect. The *sedyu*-bond candidate - once an equal of the Royal they bonded with - now nothing more than a glorified guard. Symbolic of the enslavement of the Jegera."

"I won't do it!" Arara growled up at him.

Darach punched the side of Arara's muzzle and then wrapped his paws around it, holding her mouth shut. "Shut up!"

Arara gulped but managed to keep quiet. Darach hauled Arara up by the chain until she balanced on the tips of her back toes.

"So here is the plan. Tomorrow morning we announce our takeover of the city. Then tomorrow night we publicly execute the entire Royal Family, starting with your beloved Prince Sels."

The collar was slowly strangling Arara, and she thought she misheard. "Wha?" was all she managed to get out.

“When we give the word, you will approach the Prince with this." From his belt he pulled out a small metal dagger. He showed it to Arara then strapped it back on his belt, "and then you will slit his throat."

Arara growled up at Darach, clutching at the collar to try and relieve the pressure. “And why would I do that?”

Darach chuffed with laughter and tugged her higher, until her hind legs kicked at empty air. He snapped his fingers, and four of the Yaka soldiers clanked in from the back of the hall dragging two familiar figures. “Because if you don’t, I kill your parents.”

*****

These Yaka didn't seem to speak Kin-Jegera Common, or at least they hadn't responded to any of Arara’s questions when they'd dragged her outside and staked her chain in the gardens. They'd set up a camp of sorts on top of the flower beds, with portable dens made out of hides. She'd been given food, water, a brush, a blanket, and clean clothing, although the clothing was of a strange make and cut that she'd never seen before.

Arara didn’t sleep well, despite the fact that for the first time in several days she was clean and well fed. Her stomach kept tying herself in knots about what she was going to do.

His plan still echoed in her head. He’d taken her parents with him. He hadn’t even let her speak to them before he’d dragged them away.

After tossing and turning for what felt like half the night, Arara decided to sit and watch the moon set. The Yaka had all bedded down for the night. A lone guard sat in front of a campfire nearby, idly flicking flower petals into the flames.

Unable to sleep, Arara watched the stars wheel overhead when a form blacked out the night sky. She started up and scrabbled backwards. In the dim light of the fire she couldn't see his face, but she recognized his scent. Kerka.

"What do you want?" Arara hissed softly. She glanced over at her guard and was relieved to see he apparently hadn't noticed Kerka. Much as she hated Kerka, she didn't want him to get caught by the Yaka guard.

"Don't worry about him." Kerka nodded his head towards the guard behind him. "I convinced the Elders that I'm on their side. But..." Kerka squatted down next to her.

Arara snorted and scooted away until she hit the end of her chain. Kerka remained where he was. It was hard to tell in the moonlight, and the fire behind him cast his face into shadows, but she thought he looked sad.

"I know what Darach can do." Arara growled. "You couldn't have passed his test if you didn't agree with them."

"Arara, I *do* agree with the Elders that the Jegera need more respect from the Kin." Kerka growled back at her, his ears flattening to his head. "I even saw their point about abolishing the Royal Family. Sels is a nice guy, but he is weak. They're all weak. But, then I overheard their plans for you." He sighed. "Look, Arara. I know I've been...less than kind to you in the past."

"Get to the point." Arara crouched on all fours, hackles raised and teeth bared at Kerka.

"What they are making you do, it's wrong." Kerka sat down on his butt and hung his head. "I know you probably don't like me, but I..." Kerka hesitated. "I want to help you."

Arara hesitated, unsure. He sounded so sincere. But then again, he had before too. She felt so blind without her telepathy. How could she trust him if she didn't know his true thoughts?

"I don't need your help again, Kerka." Arara huffed.

"I'll rescue your parents." Kerka dropped to his belly and wiggled towards her, tail wagging.

Arara froze, her stomach twisted into knots. Mother, Father. He could save them. Darach had said he'd let her and her parents go after she killed Sels, but she trusted him less than Kerka. Why did he insist that she kill Sels? She suspected he wanted a scape-goat, that he didn't want royal blood on his own paws. He would have her, Recka, and Tukura do his dirty work, then kill the three of them to appease the furious Kin.

Kerka had no reason to wish her parents harm. She had to take a chance on him again.

"Alright, Kerka." Arara whispered, laying down onto her belly in the dirt. The chain stretched taut, and she was as far back as she could get from Kerka, now less than a tail's length in front of her. "But, how do you think you can you defeat the Yaka guarding them all alone?"

"Who said I was alone?" Kerka wriggled the rest of the way up to her and licked the side of her face. Arara flinched back and whacked him on the nose with the claws of her front paw. Kerka didn't seem to notice, instead leaping to his four legs and dancing around behind her.

"Yegra is with me, along with two others who say they are your friends." Kerka pranced a few more steps sideways. "Mura and Roel."

Arara perked up. "They made it out of the palace safe then?"

"Yeah, Yegra and a bunch of loyal Alpha-Guards saved them and a whole group of Kin." Kerka now stood directly in front of her again. Even in the dark she couldn't miss the smug grin on his face. "They're already in town gathering those Kin and Jegera loyal to the Sebaine family, getting ready for tomorrow night."

Arara cocked her head. "What good will the Kin's help be? The execution is scheduled after sunset and their magic is useless at night."

"I don't know." Kerka shrugged. "But I already know the Elders have insisted most of the audience be the Kin nobles. They've already started lining the arena with sun-flowers to make sure they stay awake for the show. Roel said that since the rebel Jegera won't count on the Kin being able to put up resistance, it will be easier to catch them by surprise."

"Should you really be discussing this with him," Arara tilted her head towards the Yaka guard, who now had turned and was watching their exchange. "So close by? I know he doesn't speak Common, but he can still hear your thoughts."

"Naw, it's safe." Kerka tapped his shadowed forehead with a front claw, and something gave a little metallic ding. "They gave me this thing to keep those mist ghosts out of my head."

Arara frowned. Just like the assassins on the Poku. So they had been sent by the Elders.

"Don't worry, your parents are safe with me." Kerka danced forward and patted her on the head with a front paw. He raced away into the darkness before Arara could react.

*****

Something connected hard with Arara's ribcage, jolting her out of her fitful sleep. Arara grabbed her chest, gasping, and opened her eyes to see a white curly tail of a Yaka retreating away from her. A biscuit and a full waterskin soaked in the mud by her feet.

Arara snatched up the food, gnawing on the hard biscuit as she watched the activity going on around her.

Armored forms rode kwaso back and forth in formation, trampling what remained of the flowers and bushes of the Royal Garden. Unarmored Yaka ran back and forth with armfuls of equipment, panting in the rising heat.

Arara blinked in confusion. It was like seeing hundreds of herself running around. She craned her neck about looking without success for familiar brown, gray, or black fur. How had the Elders been able to sneak so many Yaka and kwasos into Sebaine without attracting any attention?

Even though the sun had barely peeked above the horizon, Arara could already feel the heat of it beating down through her fur. Under her short fur coat, her skin burned a painful red. She pulled to the end of her chain and ran in a circle, but she couldn't reach the shade of any of the nearby trees.

She lay in the grass on her side, panting, and dumped the remains of the waterskin over herself in an attempt to cool off. The sun continued to rise, and the shadows moved slowly across the ground. The flurry of activity continued around her. The top of her head, muzzle, and ears hurt, and when she touched the tip of one ear it came away bloody.

Noon came and went. Another Yaka, this one wearing only a thin pair of shorts, came up to her. He was panting hard, clearly overheating with his long fur. Arara considered the short fur on her arms, shorn close by Kerka. The skin underneath was now bright red and throbbing hot.

The young Yaka dropped another biscuit and waterskin by her chain without a word before scurrying off to another task.

The shadows were long, and the sun rode low in the sky by the time Darach, Jeron, and Yorik marched towards her across the lawn. Yorik wore his armor and carried his helmet under one arm. Darach and Jeron wore gold braided shorts and vests in a dark blue.

Darach came close, and pulled her upright with the chain. "Good, good. That clothing fits you perfectly." He pulled out a key and with a quick twist, unattached the chain.

In the fading light the green glow from the collar lit up the underside of Darach's scarred face into a twisted leer.

"Now, don't get any ideas. I'll be watching you closely. Do anything or say anything suspicious and I'll give the order to have your parents killed." Darach huffed and stepped back.

"Now, follow me." Darach turned and marched off with Yorik, leaving Arara to hurry in their wake.

Jeron walked at her side as they wound their way through the camp. Darach and Yorik stopped occasionally to yell out orders in that strange language.

Now that she was up and moving, Arara realized there were not quite as many Yaka here as she'd initially thought. She counted twenty tents, and the tents were small enough that at most she figured only three Yaka could comfortably bunk down in each one.

Arara's curiosity finally overcame her after the third stop and she addressed Darach when he turned in her direction. "Is that the Yaka language?"

Darach ignored her and marched away with a huff. Yorik seemed to take pity on her, and dropped back to take her arm. "Yes, little one. I teach it to you soon, after we rule city."

Arara flattened her ears and snarled, then pulled her arm away from him. "I don't want to learn it. I'm a Jegera."

Yorik shook his head then hurried to catch up to Darach. Jeron grabbed her upper arm and Arara yelped as his paw touched the sun-reddened skin. He barked a quick laugh and squeezed tighter, until Arara sobbed for him to stop.

"Jeron, leave alone." Yorik turned to growl at him. "You have revenge soon enough." Jeron dropped her with a huff, his lips curling up in disdain.

"What did Sels ever do to you?" Arara sniffed, moving away from him. "He loved you like family." She'd felt the hurt and betrayal in his memory at Jeron's actions.

"That spoiled brat." Jeron snarled. "He insists I be at his side day and night. I never get to even see my own pups. Last time I went home they didn't even recognize me. And then when I got back to the palace, the Prince was furious at my absence. The Queen docked my pay for not attending to him when I should have. I could barely afford to feed my family as it was, and now they're starving on the streets."

"I'm sure Sels didn't know." Arara whispered. "He-"

"He knew, all right." Jeron leaned over towards her. Froth dripped from the corners of his mouth. "That little brat was the one who insisted on it. Said it would teach me a lesson."

Arara fell silent. Sels hadn't known, not really. She remembered him offering her the bag of money on the stage in Last Home, what seemed like ages ago. He didn't understand what would happen if you didn't have it, he only saw it as a tool to get what he wanted. The Jegeran slums had been a shock to him. He hadn't any idea that anyone had to live like that. But she could tell there was no reasoning with Jeron.

The last of twilight bled away as they exited the gardens and entered the hedge maze. Yorik unhooked a strange metal and glass contraption from his belt and twisted a knob on its front. A small fire started inside of it, and then light flooded the path around them.

Yorik handed the metal lantern to Darach, who lifted it high to light their way. The hedge maze was just as beautiful as the last time she'd seen it. It seemed the Yaka had confined their destruction to the Throne room and the Royal Gardens and Residence.

Too soon, they emerged from the maze. The tall trees of the arena soared high overhead. Cheerful baskets of sun-flowers, their bright lights bobbing in the wind, sat nestled in the crooks of the trees and hung from the branches overhead, filling the arena with light.

Row after row of silent Kin filled the boxes above their heads. Their terrified faces were fixed forward at the arena's floor. Jegera, some still wearing the black and silver of the Alpha-Guards, and Yaka wearing chainmail shirts lined the arena's edges. More Yaka guarded the suspended walkways above. Five more armored Yaka mounted on kwaso circled the outside of the arena.

The Jegera joked around, pointing and laughing.

Arara could see Queen Seuan, Sels, and Sesay. They knelt in the center of the arena on a wooden stage, hands behind their backs and heads bowed. The other three Elders stood behind them. Johka, leaning heavily on his cane, looked down on the Queen. The massive Lolop towered over Sels, and Pira's small form stood behind Sesay.

Recka and Tukura stood nearby. The collars around their necks glowed with the same eerie green light as hers. Three Yaka wearing full plate armor stood around them.

Darach and Yorik passed through an opening in the ring of Jegera and Yaka. The Yaka saluted as they marched by, and Yorik returned the gesture.

Arara stopped a few steps before she reached the guards. What if Kerka went back on his word? What if he hadn't been able to save them?

A rough paw hit her back, sending her stumbling forward. Jeron kept prodding her forward, across the dirt. They passed the kwaso, their beady eyes focused on her face, their sharp beaks glinting in the bobbing light of the sun-flowers.

Darach and Yorik reached the center and marched up the stairs onto the stage. They came to a stop directly in front of the Queen. Yorik lifted one leg and pivoted on his heel, then slammed down his foot, causing his armor to crash and squeal together. The Queen started, then curled her back and lowered her head until it touched the ground.

Arara reached the stairs. She put her back paw on the lowest step, and it groaned as she placed her weight on it. Sels was on the side of the stage closest to her, and he turned his head at the sound. His tear-filled eyes met hers.

Arara slowed, her breaths coming in short, quick gasps. A flood of scents filled her nose, the perfume of thousands of terrified Kin.

Jeron cuffed the back of her head, then pushed her up the rest of the steps.

"Everything is ready." Pira warbled.

"Excellent. Arara, wait here." Jeron shoved Arara to the back corner of the stage. She stood trembling as Jeron joined Darach and Yorik at the front of the stage.

Yorik lifted his head until the beak of his helm pointed straight up, and then he howled. The crowd fell silent, and Arara could hear the rustle of the leaves and the whisper of the breeze ruffling her fur.

Darach stepped forward and lifted his arms.

"Honored Kin," Darach's voice boomed, and he slowly turned in a circle as he spoke. "Your Royal Family has been manipulating you."

A hushed murmur began spreading through the audience.

"The Greeting Magic may seem to only make harmless rainbows." Darach spun and pointed to the Queen kneeling and trembling at his feet. "It is actually a brainwashing spell that commands the devotion of those that witness it."

The Kin in the audience gasped, and the murmurs grew louder. Arara covered her mouth in shock. No wonder the Elders had been so worried about her having seen the Greeting magic in Last Home.

"It can't be." A familiar voice whispered, so low Arara barely hear it over the sounds of the audience. She glanced over at Sels. He stared at the planks under him, his eyes wide and disbelieving. "Mother was so insistent-" Sels mouthed under his breath.

"We, the Elders," Darach's booming voice drowned out whatever else Sels said. He waved his hand over the assembled Jegera on the stage, "discovered this many years ago, and went to the former Queen Se'lvn, begging her and her family to stop using this horrifying magic on her own people."

"And do you know what she said?" Darach growled. "She said that the ignorant masses needed someone to look up to, to give them purpose in their lives."

"Because of this spell, the Jegeran citizens of this empire have been systematically lowered and beaten down without complaint for generation upon generation. While the Kin have reaped the benefits of their labors."

The Jegera and Yaka in the audience booed and hissed.

“We scoured the land for a way to counteract this vile magic, when we discovered our new Northern Allies.” Darach turned to Yorik, who bowed.

Arara tuned out as Darach extolled the virtuous Yaka, promised an era of peace and prosperity for those that supported the new government, and vowed swift punishment on those that would go against it.

Arara only half listened as she scanned the audience for any sign of a familiar face. Yegra, Mura, Roel, even Kerka. She needed to know her parents were safe.

“But before we can celebrate the freedoms of our new kingdom, we must clear out the last vestige of the old Empire.” Darach droned on, and Arara’s stomach dropped.

Darach stepped back to Yorik and gestured. Jeron stepped forward and placed one knee on Sels bent back. He wrapped a paw around Sels vines and pulled back, exposing Sels neck and forcing his head back at a painful looking angle. The crowd gasped in horror.

“No!” The Queen screamed, crawling forward on her knees until Johka hauled her back. She collapsed, sobbing, to the stage.

“And what better purveyor of justice,” Darach boomed over her sobs, holding up the metal knife he’d shown her the night before. “Than one of the poor candidates whom would have been bound in servitude to the Prince on this very day if these benevolent Yaka had not intervened?”

Darach gestured grandly to Yorik, who bowed again. A couple of brave Kin in the crowd booed.

“Arara, step forward.”

Arara gulped, forcing her trembling legs forward. Darach pressed the dagger into her trembling paws and stepped back.

The knife gripped tight, she turned to face Sels. Sels wide eyes looked up into hers, and his lower lip trembled.

"Now witness the death of the old Empire and the birth of the new." Darach turned to address the crowd again as Arara stepped forward.

Arara lifted the heavy knife and stepped forward, her eyes on the boards in front of her.

CHAPTER TWENTY THREE

FINAL HOUR

Sels stared up at the knife Arara had pointed at him. Iron bonds secured his hands behind him. His back ached where Jeron's knee dug painfully into his spine beneath his bound hands, and his neck was bent back so far he could hardly breathe.

Sels raised his eyes to the tapestry of stars wheeling above Arara's head. He heard his mother scream again as Arara raised the knife. Sels wasn't worried about Arara; he'd seen inside her head. She wouldn't hurt him. He was more worried about Jeron behind him and the Yaka around him.

Between the darkness and the iron bonds they thought him helpless, but Sels knew better. He could feel the magic, now that he looked for it, in the darkness around him.

Sels gathered the magic inside his fists and lowered his gaze to meet Arara's. Her eyes looked sad and resigned. Sels winked at her and opened his hands.

The fireballs hit Jeron with a crack. Jeron screamed and fell back, and his hands released Sels's vines. The sudden loss of pressure caused Sels's head to whip forward, and his forehead hit the planks in front of him.

Smoke and the stench of burning fur filled the air. He heard a Kin yell, then another. A Jegera howled, and Yaka growled something in their strange language. Pawed feet ran by him.

Dazed and coughing, Sels crawled forward on his knees. Behind him, Jeron's screams cut off abruptly amid the panicked shouting.

Still coughing, Sels sat up to see Arara on the ground wrestling with Johka. Arara's ceremonial dagger was buried up to the hilt in his side. Johka's cane lay on the stage a few tail lengths away.

The Yaka from the night before, with the big spikes on his armor, stood over them. He attempted to grab Arara, but she moved too quickly for him.

Sels pulled his arms to the side and twisted his back until he managed to get one of his hands pointed towards them. Fire streaked from his fingers and engulfed the armored Yaka. He shrieked and dove away, tearing at his armor as he went.

Arara used the distraction to pull free the dagger. She plunged it in again and again until Johka shuddered and went limp.

Sels struggled to his feet and looked around. The Kin in the audience were fighting against the Jegera and Yaka guards with what looked to be gardening tools.

Nearby, Recka and Tukura fought with the Yaka guards. Although their teeth and claws did little damage against the Yaka's armor, their superior size and the sheer savagery of their attacks drove the Yaka back towards the edge of the stage.

"Sels, Tukura, Recka - kneel down and surrender." Darach growled behind him.

Sels spun around. Darach held the Queen in front of him, a paw around her throat. He caressed the front of her neck with one claw. Lolop and Pira stood at his sides. A Yaka soldier had Sesay pinned to the stage and dangled a metal spear over the back of her neck.

"Mother!" Sels cried out, taking a step forward and jerking his arms against his bonds. But there was no way to hit Darach without also hitting his mother.

Sels choked down another sob and knelt down. Out of the corner of his eye he saw Tukura and Recka place their paws on the back of their heads and crouch down to the stage.

“I knew you’d see it my way.” Darach chuckled.

A presence bloomed in the back of his mind. A metal collar rolled past him and tipped over with a clink.

<*Sels! Don’t worry, I’ll save her.*> Sels gasped with relief at feeling Arara in his head again.

Arara snarled, concentrating. Sels could feel the trembling in her limbs, knew she was exhausted and suffering from heat stroke. He opened his mind, and poured his own energy towards Arara. He swayed and fell sideways. The world slid away into a gray haze.

*****

Arara straightened. It felt as if she’d just gotten the best night of sleep in her life. All her aches and pains faded away. Her skin tingled and she felt as if she were going to burst from all the power coursing through her.

Arara mentally punched at Darach, while at the same time she pulled the Queen. The Queen stumbled forward and Darach blew backwards off the stage, past a shocked Pira and Lolop. He hit the ground almost thirty tail lengths away with a crunch and lay still.

Arara pivoted, intending to hit the Yaka soldier over Sesay, when a blast of force hit her side. She stumbled sideways but with some quick steps managed to stay upright.

Another blast hit her front, and she slid backwards, her back claws pulling up furrows in the wood. She pushed herself from behind and slowed to a stop just a claw’s length from the edge of the stage.

Yorik clanked towards her, spinning a long metal tipped spear.

“Why?” He growled at her as he approached. “You would be a Yaka hero, your name living through the ages. Instead you side with those, those,” he struggled for a word, “plants.” He finally spit out.

Arara gripped Darach’s dagger tighter in her paw and circled away, keeping him at a distance. In her peripheral vision she could see Lolop and Pira herding the Queen and Sesay away from her. Sels lay passed out on the stage behind her.

Yorik got closer and stabbed out one-pawed with the spear at Arara. She dodged to the side and skipped back, then hit the side of the spear with a force push.

The spear pulled out of his loose grip and spun away, off the side of the stage.

Yorik snarled and lunged across the space at her. She waved her dagger wildly at him, forcing him back.

He growled at her and pulled down the visor of his bird helmet, then pointed at her. She felt a stabbing pain in her head and fell to the floor.

Arara tried to fight back, but the pain consumed her ability to think.

White pawed feet entered her vision, and she snarled as one of them lifted then came down on her head. Her face bounced off the hard wood, and she could feel her nose start to bleed.

The pressure increased as Yorik rested all his weight on his leg then leaned over to snarl into Arara's face. "Give up, little girl. Your plant Prince is as good as dead."

Arara's vision shifted, and she saw herself from behind with Yorik standing over her. She sat up and struggled to move a hand forward. Magical energy sang through her blood, and she spun red fire out of her fingers.

The fire rope twisted through the air and stabbed down through Yorik's visor.

The pain in her head snapped away as Yorik yelped and jumped back, pulling off his helm. The fur on his head smoldered, and smoke and flame licked the back of his neck until he patted and smacked it out.

Arara scrambled backwards, the smoke burned at her nose and she coughed. Had she done that or had Sels?

She didn't have time to wonder as an armored Yaka tackled her from the side, driving her to the planks. She landed on her side and rolled onto her back, the Yaka on top.

The Yaka snapped at her throat. Arara threw her arm up in the way. His teeth closed on her arm, and he shook his head, ripping and tearing at her flesh.

She punched at his muzzle with her good arm as he growled and gnawed on her, but he refused to let go.

The Yaka continued to chew on her arm and clawed at her unprotected stomach. She couldn't concentrate enough through the pain to hit him with a force burst.

Suddenly the Yaka's eyes rolled back in his head and he collapsed on top of her, his jaws still locked around her arm. Arara struggled to push him off and get up, but with the armor he was too heavy for her to move one handed. She panicked, crying and howling.

<*Hold still.*> Sels face appeared above her. He grasped the Yaka's armor and tried to pull him off. She whimpered.

"His jaw," she slurred in pain.

He reached over and pried at the Yaka's mouth, trying to free her, but the dead Yaka's jaw was locked shut. He narrowed his eyes in concentration and Arara felt a tug on her mind.

Arara widened her eyes. Sels was using her powers! Just like she'd done with his.

Sels pried at the Yaka's mouth, using a force push to force it open. Arara pulled herself free as Sels pulled the Yaka off.

<*Hurry, we're still fighting. Tukura and my mother are rallying the Kin in a defense against the Yaka. A lot of the Jegera turned against the Yaka, too.*> He grinned down at her.

<*How did you get free?*> Arara stepped back, cradling her injured arm against her chest.

Sels gestured, and Kerka shuffled forward. "Hi Arara." Kerka said softly. He kept his gaze low, glancing up at her from under lowered brows.

"Yegra is here, too, along with Nathira. They went with Sesay and Recka to free a bunch of Kin being held captive in the garden." Sels grinned and patted Kerka's arm. "I heard from Yegra that Kerka here spent all night and day rallying crown loyalists to our aid."

<I understand if, when you do your Bonding Ceremony, you pick Kerka.> She sniffled and looked away.

Sels crouched and took her paws in his hands. *<It's a bit too late for that.>*

<Huh? What do you mean?> She cocked her head up at him and smiled. Sels wanted her to be his *sedyu*-bonded. Arara had never felt happier.

<I'll tell you later. Right now, we need to find Yorik, the Yaka general. He escaped in the confusion.>

Sels grabbed her paw, pulling her towards the edge of the stage. Arara trotted along next to him, tail wagging at the thought of being Sels's *sedyu.*

Kerka trotted after them. Smoke filled the air, and she coughed and covered her mouth. Several Yaka bodies lay around, smoke curling up from their still smoldering fur.

As they reached the bottom of the stairs, Arara could see Pira and Lolop lying prone on the ground. A group of Kin wielding wooden shovels and vine clippers stood guard over them. They saluted Sels as they passed. Sels smiled and waved at them.

"Kerka, you are my legs." Sels said, pointing to the arena's back exit, the one Arara had been brought in by during the first Trial. "Sorry, Arara." Sels shrugged as Kerka allowed Sels to climb onto his back. "We need to move fast, and you're too small to carry me."

Arara swallowed a growl when Sels touched Kerka. She didn't like it, but he was right. They needed to move fast.

Kerka sprinted away. Arara dropped to all fours and ran after, struggling to match Kerka's pace with her short legs.

<Sels, where's Darach?> Arara panted hard, thankful for the cool night breeze. The dirt below still burned the pads of her paws as it released the day's heat. *<I know my throw didn't kill him, but I didn't*

see him with the others. He's the ringleader behind this attack, not Yorik.>

They passed a group of Kin and Jegera fighting against a troop of Yaka mounted on kwaso. Sels opened his hand and tossed fire at the Yaka, and several of the birds toppled over, their riders leaping for safety. The Kin cheered and whistled, and a couple of the Jegera waved at Sels as they rode by.

<*What happened? I thought the Jegera had all joined the Yaka.*> She was trying to figure out what had happened while she had been on stage.

<*Not all of them. Many Kin-sympathizers still remained among the Jegera, and they managed to get many of them in with the Yaka's volunteers. Their signal to move was you saving me.*>

Arara would have pulled up short, but Sels tugged her arm and kept her running. They'd reached the stands and were weaving between the trees.

<*But, how did you know I would save you?*> She asked, puzzled. She herself hadn't been sure what she was going to do until the time came.

<*I saw your true self, Arara. I knew my sedyu-bonded could never do such a thing, no matter what was at stake.*>

They entered the hedge maze, Kerka and Arara stopping to sniff at the intersections, searching for Yorik's or Darach's scent. No sunflowers bloomed in the maze, forcing Arara to rely on her scent to keep from running into the hedge walls.

<*Darach!*> Kerka blasted Arara with a powerful gefir. <*I found his scent! Follow me!*>

He was right. She could smell Darach's scent. He'd passed this way not a scratch-mark before them.

They ran off, Kerka in the lead, following Darach's scent deeper into the maze. Kerka had his Jegeran dark-sight, but Arara couldn't see anything. She moved closer to Kerka, following his wagging tail through the darkness.

Arara could feel Darach just ahead of them, around the corner.

<*Look out!*> She warned Kerka as he slid around the turn.

Her warning came just in time. Darach had been crouched around the blind corner, and he threw a spear right as he saw them appear. Kerka dropped down and rolled, throwing Sels free.

Sels tumbled sideways, towards the poisonous spikes of the hedge. Arara lowered her head and concentrated, putting a force barrier up right before Sels hit. Sels impacted the barrier just a hair's breadth from the spiky points of the leaves. His breath whooshed out of him, and he fell to the path winded but otherwise unharmed.

Kerka was not so lucky. His roll saved Sels, but it put him right in the spear's path. It hit the side of Kerka's chest and drove in deep. The shaft quivered, and Kerka collapsed. Arara could still feel his presence, but he was fading fast.

Darach barked out a quick laugh. "Traitor. Serves him right. Who would have ever thought he was smart enough to fool me?"

"You're the traitor." Arara rounded the corner and planted herself between Sels and Darach. Her sides heaved and she panted heavily, barely able to stand upright. She could feel Sels pulling himself to his feet behind her, but he too was tired. He'd shared most of his energy with her earlier and had used a lot of magic tonight. However, he stood tall, staring down the path at Darach.

"You're the biggest traitor of all, Arara." Darach laughed again, backing away. "Who brought the Prince to where we had the kwaso waiting in the woods in Last Home? And who led the little Prince right to us in the city, when he escaped our kidnapping attempt?"

"I did no such thing," Arara growled back.

"But you did." Darach grinned and tapped his nose. "You are the key to the prophecy, the doomsbell of the Empire."

"You said I was prophesied to save the Empire, not to destroy it!" Arara snarled, to keep from whimpering. She had just wanted to help.

"Well, yes." Darach frowned and chuffed. "We needed you eager and willing to help. But Yaka mind control is so limited, in its way."

"Mind control?" Sels glared at Darach. Arara had almost forgotten he was there. "Not a claw mark ago you declared the Royal Greeting Magic evil for inspiring devotion."

"You left us no choice." Darach wrinkled his nose. "We needed a Yaka to be invited into the Palace willingly for the prophecy to work. On her own, Arara never would have had a chance. Even with her saving you," Darach laughed. "Saving you. Ha. All a setup, all of it. Anyway, even with her saving you twice, Jeron still had to prod you to give her a token."

"And you," Darach pointed at Arara. "Useless. Never seen such a hopeless, stubborn pup. How you survived the first Trial I'll never know."

Arara growled and pushed at him with her mind, trying to push him into the hedge. Nothing happened except Darach laughed again.

"Little pup, you caught me by surprise before." Darach chuffed and walked away, waving at her over his shoulder. "I know more tricks than you could dream of."

Arara tried to charge after him, but her legs refused to obey her.

"Arara, what's going on?" Sels, too, struggled in vain to move. Darach had almost reached the turn in the path. Arara pulled a map of the maze from Sels's head and realized that intersection led straight out of the palace. Once he reached the streets, they would never find him.

Behind them, Kerka's presence faded further. Arara could barely feel him now.

<*Sels, use your magic!*> Arara couldn't bear the thought of Darach going free after what he'd done to them.

Darach's mind pressed down on hers, threatening to crush her. In desperation she mentally pushed out for Sels's mind. Their consciousness met, intertwined like it had the day before.

They saw as one out of two sets of eyes, and thought as one with eight limbs. Now that they thought in harmony, Arara could feel the dark threads of Darach's will twisting through their shared mind like a worm.

They plucked it free with a thought. They moved in harmony, drawing the singing power of the magic out of the darkness around them, winding it through and from both of themselves.

Fire sprung from around them, dancing along the hedges and wrapping around Darach. The fire flared, brighter and brighter, until Darach writhed in a white blaze tinged at the corners with yellow and orange.

As sudden as it began, the fire faded away. A wisp of smoke against the stars was the only evidence of its passing. Where Darach had been standing, nothing remained but a black circle melted into the stones.

CHAPTER TWENTY FOUR

TEA AND CAKE

Sels knelt in front of Kerka. The shaft sticking out of him quivered as he struggled for breath.

"Sels," Arara had ripped off her vest and pressed it around the shaft, trying to stem the flow of blood. "You have to try healing him."

"You know I can't," Sels struggled to keep from throwing up at the sight of so much blood. "He needs a real healer."

"It's dark, Sels." Arara whimpered, and Sels could feel her distress through their bond. "He won't last until morning light."

"He saved your parents." Sels didn't know how he knew that, but he knew it was true. "But after what he did to you..." Sels trailed off. He knew Arara hadn't told him everything, but he knew enough.

"Sels," Arara glared at him. "I don't forgive him, but after what he did for my parents... you have to try."

Sels sighed and scooted closer, trying not to kneel in the blood pooling around him. He did have the magic, but he didn't know how to control it. It always seemed to want to burn. He reached out his hands and held them over the wound.

He thought back to the few healing lessons he'd received before his mother had given up. First, assess the damage. Spear through the lung. He'd see the air bubbles frothing up from the blood, heard the whistle as Kerka struggled to breathe.

Next, send the magic inside. The step that had always stymied him in his lessons. Closing his eyes, he drew the darkness magic to him. This time, instead of it allowing it to fly free, he directed it to go inside Kerka. He visualized the spear being pushed out, the lungs sealing, the wound cauterizing closed. Then he let it trickle out, a little at a time.

Under his hands, Kerka gasped, then screamed. Sels's eyes flew open, and he scrambled back as Kerka convulsed. Arara tried to hold Kerka down, but he outweighed her by so much she ended up just riding on his chest, still pressing down on her makeshift bandage.

The shaft flew free, flying straight up past Arara into the darkness. Arara tumbled free, landing next to Sels on the cobblestones. Kerka screamed again and again, convulsing and writhing on the ground. Fresh blood streamed out from the hole in Kerka's chest, and the stench of burning meat seared Sels's nostrils.

Gradually Kerka's limbs slowed, then stopped moving altogether, as if his strings had been cut.

"What happened?" Sels whispered, shaken.

Arara crawled forward and put a paw on Kerka's neck. Sels could feel Kerka's coarse fur through their link, but the distinctive thump of the Jegera's heart was missing.

"I think he's dead." Arara whispered, closing her eyes and pressing her nose to Kerka's. "He saved us. And my parents."

"I know. He died a hero's death." Sels said, flopping onto his back in the path. He wiped at his eyes. They'd won, but laying here next to Kerka's corpse, the victory felt hollow. The rebels had been telling the truth about the Greeting Magic. He had seen it in his mother's eyes.

*****

"Your Majesty, we found them!" A Kin voice woke Sels up. He opened his eyes to the sun shining brightly overhead. He must have fallen asleep where he lay.

Arara! Kerka! Sels jumped up, blinking. Arara lay curled up next to him. Kerka lay where he'd been last night, but now two Kin healers hovered over him, performing the sun rituals to guide his soul up to the heavens above to take his place as a light in the night sky.

"Sels!" Queen Seuan rushed up from behind him and wrapped him in a hug. "After you disappeared last night, we were so worried!"

"Mother," Sels hugged her back, then stepped out of her embrace. "We took care of Darach, but we didn't see any sign of Yorik."

"I'm just glad to see you safe," His mother wiped something from her face. Had she been crying?

Sels leaned over and shook Arara awake. She blinked up at him for a moment before noticing the Queen and Tukura.

"Your Majesty!" Arara scrabbled to her feet and presented her throat.

"No need for that, Arara." The Queen smiled down at her. "As my son's *sedyu*-bonded you are a member of the Royal Family now."

"His *sedyu*-bonded?" Arara looked at Sels.

"I didn't get a chance to tell you last night." Sels blushed. "We, well, that connection we have. That is the *sedyu*-bond." Sels glanced at his mother. "Apparently the Ceremony is just a formality."

"Yes." Tukura said, her rough voice the only thing that betrayed her emotion. "We have much to talk about. We should go somewhere more comfortable."

*****

Smoke still lingered in the air over the gardens. The view from the balcony wasn't as spectacular as usual, with many of the flowers trampled, but Sels's heart lifted to see it all the same.

He sat with his family on the balcony. Their favorite round dining table had survived the destruction inside, and the servants had found ten undamaged chairs to go around it. A feast for both Kin and Jegera covered the table.

Arara's parents stared around themselves in open-mouthed awe at their surroundings. Arara sat in between them, a big smile on her face.

Sesay seemed to find the whole thing amusing, although she had made Recka sit between her and Arara's father.

Yegra, by way of apology, had tracked down Mura and Roel. She'd apologized profusely to Arara for spying on her, explaining that she hadn't wanted to, but as a brand new Alpha-Guard she couldn't say no to the future Queen.

Roel sat next to Sels, with Mura on her other side next to Arara's mother. Roel's stained and faded healer's robes clashed with the finery around her. She kept her eyes downcast, fiddling with the torn hem of her sleeve.

"I want to thank you again for your help." Sels smiled at her, trying to put her at ease, and took her hand. "If it weren't for you and Mura..."

"Of course, Your Highness." Roel blushed emerald, and pulled her hand back.

"If there is anything I can do for either of you..." Sels looked back and forth between Roel and Mura. But they both just shook their heads.

Roel's white petals seemed to glow in the sun. Sels barely contained himself from leaning over to inhale their scent, contenting himself with the watching the way the light sparkled on them. White petals were considered the least desirable color, most considering them plain. Sels used to think so too, but now watching Roel he couldn't imagine why.

"Sels," his mother's words broke the silence and Sels blushed, realizing he'd been staring. He coughed and picked up a piece of tandy root.

As they ate, Sels told his mother and Sesay everything that had happened, starting with Arara saving him from the kwaso attack in Last Home, to the strange events of the last few days. When he got to the part about breaking out of the warehouse, Seuan gasped.

"I know I saw you doing offensive magic, but I still can't believe such a thing exists." The Queen murmured, setting down her tea.

"You really can do magic in the dark." Sesay shook her head. "I wouldn't have believed it if I hadn't seen it."

He looked down in embarrassment. "Yes, it seems so, although I still don't have much control over it."

"That will come in time." The Queen reached over and squeezed his hand. "Why I remember the first time I cast a raincloud spell. I nearly drowned the entire garden just trying to water the petunias."

Sels smiled over at her. "I hope so. Although it was odd. It was so easy to use my magic at night, but when we escaped from the warehouse... when I threw that spell during the day. I had to struggle to get enough magic to even make that small spark."

Sesay nodded. "That's how it is for me, trying to cast spells in the evening."

"Yes, that explains why you were never able to learn from the tutors." The Queen tapped a finger on the table.

Sels continued with his story. He told her of the help they received from Roel and then Mura. He was still too shaken to mention the devastation they'd seen in the Council Hall after his Mother had escaped, so he skipped forward to when he and Arara had fought over the pain the kwaso had caused him. He described how it had felt like they had merged into one and how since then his senses had increased.

"Yes," Recka said with a snort. "The *sedyu*-bond being formed."

"I don't understand, mother." Sels said, finished with the revelations that Darach had taunted them with. "Why didn't you ever mention this prophecy before?"

Seuan exchanged a long look with Tukura, then sighed. "It's an old, old prophecy. My mother, Se'lvn, told me of it, before her death, but I dismissed it. After all, the Yaka were long gone."

"The archives." Arara piped up, remembering what the Elders had said to her that first day in Sebaine. "The Elders said there was a copy there."

“I had people check first thing this morning,” The Queen sighed. “All the copies are missing or destroyed.”

Sels fiddled with his napkin. There was something else he wanted to ask, but he didn’t know if he wanted to know the answer. Arara encouraged him across their bond.

“Mother, what Darach said,” Sels sat up and turned, looking her in the eyes. “The Royal Magic? It’s true, isn’t it?”

“Yes, it is.” The Queen met his gaze, her mouth turned down at the edges. “But it is not evil. It only encourages and enhances the feelings that are already there.”

Sels shifted. “But, still. It doesn’t seem right to manipulate people's emotions like that.”

“I understand.” The Queen said, her voice low. “But it is necessary.”

“There must be a better way.” Sels said, frustrated.

“Then you should find it.” His mother smiled, breaking the tension. “After all, your birthday is tomorrow. You’ll be an adult, and you and your *sedyu*-bonded will both be granted seats on the Council.”

THE END

<<<<<<<<<<<<<<<<<<<>>>>>>>>>>>>>>>>>>>>>>>

Thank you for reading the adventures of Sels and Arara. Look for their continuing adventures in *Flower's Curse*!

Afterword

If you want to be notified when Madison Keller's next book will come out, sign up for the mailing list at http://eepurl.com/3eO3r

Reviews are vital to an author! Please consider leaving a review wherever you purchased it. Even just a few lines sharing your thoughts on this story would be helpful to other readers. Thank you!

Other Works by Madison Keller

Snow Flower: Arara's Tale - Young Arara must learn to face her fears and stand up to the pack bully

Lady Numbers vs the Lawn - D&D and lawn maintenance collide in this hilarious short story

Flower Buds - Five short stories set in the world of Flower's Fang

Flower's Curse - The Next book in the Flower's Fang series

ABOUT THE AUTHOR

Madison Keller lives in the Pacific Northwest. When not writing she can be found bicycling around the woods of Oregon or at the dog park with her adorable Chihuahua.

http://www.flowersfang.com